DATE DUE

NOV 1 5 2005			
NOV 2 9 2005			
DEC 2 3 2005			

OUT OF SEASON

OUT OF SEASON

Robert Bausch

HARCOURT, INC.

Orlando   Austin   New York   San Diego   Toronto   London

Requests for permission to make copies of any part of
the work should be mailed to the following address:
Permissions Department, Harcourt, Inc.,
6277 Sea Harbor Drive, Orlando, Florida 32887-6777.

www.HarcourtBooks.com

Library of Congress Cataloging-in-Publication Data
Bausch, Robert.
Out of season/Robert Bausch.
p.   cm.
1. Children—Death—Fiction. 2. Loss (Psychology)—Fiction.
3. Fathers and sons—Fiction. 4. Ferris wheels—Fiction.
5. Ex-convicts—Fiction. 6. Sheriffs—Fiction. I. Title.
PS3552.A847O88   2005
813'.54—dc22   2005002393
ISBN-13: 978-0151-01014-1
ISBN-10: 0-15-101014-5

Text set in Minion
Designed by Cathy Riggs

Printed in the United States of America

First edition
A B C D E F G H I J K

This is for Tim and Steve—

brothers and friends, tried and true

In memory of the twins:

Lauren Claire and Kate Elizabeth Bushee.

In fall, all the colors . . .

OUT OF SEASON

i

Because it was the off season, the clerk (and owner) of the Clary Hotel was surprised to hear that a lone man, about forty or so, with only one suitcase, wished to know the weekly rates. It was early Thursday morning in mid October. The front lobby was still bathed in bright sunlight.

The clerk's name was Jack Clary. He had worked at the Clary Hotel all his life. He had run around in this very building as a little boy. His father and mother ran the hotel when it was called the Hotel Columbia, and after he and his wife inherited it, he re-named it the Clary Hotel. He maintained it mostly by himself—painting, woodworking, window washing, plumbing, repairing the heating and air conditioning, and installing a new floor in the lobby—and although he almost never rented more than a few rooms on weekends in the off season, there were always plenty of tourists in the summer, even with the decline of the town's fortunes. He worked very hard in the summer, and so did his wife—the hotel's only chef and maid—but during the winter months, when the tourist season was officially over, he always felt quite successfully retired, even though he was not yet fifty years old. He stood behind the counter in his hotel and stared into the face of this man who wanted to know the weekly rates.

"What you want to know that for?"

"I'll be staying for a while." The man put down the suitcase, put his hands on the counter. Clary noticed they were clean, the fingernails neatly trimmed.

"Have you been here before?" He turned the book around, so the man could sign it.

"Used to bring my family here every year."

"A long time ago?"

"You might say," the stranger said. He signed the book with a steady hand. His face was thin and long. His hair was thick and came to a perfect widow's peak in the middle of his forehead. It was cut close, but not so close that it wouldn't drape over his brow if he let it. He wore a long gray coat, too heavy for the weather, open down the front. A black scarf draped around his neck.

The name he wrote in the register was David Caldwell.

"It's a different place now," Clary said, studying the name.

"Yes, I guess it is."

"Well, Mr. Caldwell," Clary said. "I certainly hope you weren't expecting . . ." He didn't finish the sentence.

"Expecting what?"

"Nothing. You can see it ain't too lively now."

Caldwell turned the book around again. "A key?" he said.

"Sure." Clary got the key off the wall behind the office door.

As he was handing the key to him, Caldwell said, "And those rates?"

"Well, I don't know. Long as I've been here, nobody stayed over a couple weeks."

"I don't really know how long I'm going to be here. I'm looking for a place. But the county keeps you on a pretty restricted expense account. I can't afford to pay you daily rates." He held the key up, read the number on it.

"Let's see. If you did that it'd be . . ."

"I can't do that. It would be too much. But perhaps . . ."

"At the daily rate that'd be close to four hundred a week."

"I'll give you two hundred."

"A week?"

"You wouldn't have anybody here, it looks like. For sure nobody else'll be here come winter."

"That's right."

"I'm offering two hundred you wouldn't have, then."

"I'm not arguing," Clary said. "It sounds fine to me."

Caldwell almost smiled, picked up his bag and turned for the stairs across the lobby.

"You say the county's paying for it?"

"That's right."

"You some sort of inspector or something?"

"No. I'm visiting on behalf of the county."

"Really?"

The stranger put both bags down at his feet. "And I'm meeting someone, too."

"What's the county got to do with . . ."

"You got a problem here, right?"

"What kind of problem?"

"Law enforcement."

"There ain't none."

"Well, that's why I'm here. I'm the sheriff of Dahlgren County. I came down here to see about setting up an office for a deputy or two."

"You don't say."

"That's right." He leaned down and picked up the bags. "I may be moving down here myself," he groaned with the weight. "Who knows?"

"What we need is a whole police force."

"What I'm going to set up will be better than that. Trust me."

"Oh, I trust you. But you never had to deal with Cecil Edwards."

"Who?"

"Cecil Edwards. He's the problem you mentioned."

Caldwell was silent, but he didn't look away.

"Just the other day he pulled a gun on the fellow that runs the gas station out at the highway."

"Really?" Caldwell was still holding the bags.

"Fellow named McDole runs that place."

Caldwell hefted the bags to get a better grip and started moving toward the elevators across the lobby. Clary came around the counter and took one of the bags, a heavy garment case with a long strap. He draped the bag over his arm.

"I don't suppose you heard that name?"

"What name," Caldwell said, a little winded.

"McDole?"

"Can't say I have."

"I thought maybe he went ahead and lodged a complaint. He was mad enough, I thought he might go ahead and do it." Clary put the strap over his shoulder and hoisted the bag as they walked along. "We got a jail, you know."

"I know."

"Nobody's used it in years. Not since they outlawed gambling," Clary huffed.

"I went by it," Caldwell said. "It's still standing." When they were a short distance from the elevator, Clary stopped and set his bag down, leaning over to let the strap fall off his shoulder.

"Want me to get that?" said Caldwell.

"No. I got it." He put the strap over his other shoulder and lifted the bag again. "Did you say you were meeting someone here?"

"My son," Caldwell said. He was already in front of the elevator when Clary put his bag down next to the door.

"That thing's a bit heavy."

"It's got clothes, boots, some books, a gun and lots of ammo in it," Caldwell said, smiling. "I can take it from here."

They both stood there, watching the door. The stranger pushed the button again.

"It's a wonder that folks do that," Clary said. "Ain't it?"

"What?"

"I do the same thing. I push the button, it lights and then I wait a little while and if the thing doesn't come I push it again."

"Oh," Caldwell said, still smiling. "Yes. I do that, too."

"You just did it," Clary laughed, and then he was conscious of how loud he had been, and was suddenly embarrassed. He felt awkward and too friendly and as though he had been fawning over this man who hadn't even really told him his name.

The elevator door opened and he helped Caldwell put his bags in, then he stepped back and watched as the door closed. Caldwell didn't look at him, and neither of them said anything. He went back to the counter and studied the name written neatly on the white page of the hotel register. "David Caldwell," he said out loud. "Well. This is just the right time and place for you, Mr. Sheriff Caldwell." He closed the book, went back into his office and got a bottle out of the lower right hand drawer of his desk.

"Chivas," he said. "God bless you."

• • •

The first thing David Caldwell did when he got into his hotel room was call his wife, Laura.

"Guess what," he said.

"Have you seen Todd yet?"

"No, he's not here. I'm a day early, though."

"I thought he might already be there."

"I'm staying at a place called the Clary Hotel. Remember the big yellow building with the white shutters that looked out over the water? Well that's where I am."

"I hope it's not too trashy."

"No, it isn't bad. I'm in a room on the fourth floor. I don't know why this particular room or floor. The place is mostly empty."

"It's out of season, isn't it?"

"A lot of the windows are boarded up, I guess for the winter. But my window isn't, so I can see the water. Maybe that's why I was given this room."

"I wish I was with you."

"Me, too."

She was quiet for a moment.

"I almost said the word 'ocean' instead of 'water,'" Caldwell went on. "But of course you know it's just the river. It looks like ocean sometimes, though, when the haze across the river in Maryland masks that shore."

"Call me as soon as he gets there," she said.

"I will."

It was quiet for a beat, then Laura said, "What did you want me to guess about?"

"What?"

"You said 'guess what' when I answered the phone."

"Oh. The old hotel—the one we always looked forward to coming to? It's gone. There's nothing there but a pile of sand with a little grass in it. I was amazed when I first got here."

He stopped talking and gazed out the window. He came here to meet Todd, his twenty-year-old son, who had been released from Rockingham Juvenile Detention Center, in Petersburg, Virginia, two years ago. He had been there for almost seven years. He did not want them to come get him when he was released. He insisted on stepping out of the detention center alone, without anyone to welcome him. "I want to be on my own for a while," he'd said. "I hope you can understand." Todd had not been home yet, nor had he spent much time on the phone talking to his parents. He told them he wanted to find work and get on with his life; he wanted to forget the past. He said he'd get in touch, and then he just sort of disappeared. No calls, no cards or letters, or even e-mails.

Laura wrote several e-mails to him, but got no response and had no way of knowing if he'd gotten them.

"We have to go on with our lives," she said one day.

"Oh, I intend to," Caldwell said.

But she continued to send her son weekly e-mails, believing that he must be reading her words; that they perhaps sustained him in ways she would never know. She filled each e-mail with news about the family, busy talk about the new television shows, and the enthralling chokehold computers had gotten on the world. She wrote him about the turn of the century, the panic about the year 2000. What she did not ever write about was the crime that put him in the detention center: he had killed his little brother, Bobby. It had been an accident—that is what Caldwell and his wife believed as firmly as suspicion and fear would let them. But the state didn't believe it. They found Todd guilty of involuntary manslaughter and sentenced him to the youth facility until he was eighteen years old. He was just eleven years old at the time.

For two years after Todd's release, the lack of response seemed almost natural, although it still was a source of hurt for Laura. To Caldwell, it was a constant spring of troubled memory. Then after Laura had written in an e-mail to Todd that his father was going to be staying in Columbia Beach for most of the fall and even perhaps into the winter, and that the family might actually be moving down there, Todd called her. He asked for this meeting, and these were his requirements: that father and son meet at the Voyager Beach Hotel—the same hotel they always stayed in when the family vacationed there—and that Caldwell come alone.

"I guess," Caldwell said now, "he'll know to come here when he sees the Voyager Beach is gone. Except for an old motel out on the highway, this is the only hotel in town."

"I hope he gets there soon."

"I have to admit, I'm nervous, honey."

"Nervous?"

"I'm afraid of what we might say to each other."

"Of what *you* might say."

"It's been more than two years since I've seen him."

"I know." They had both visited the detention center as frequently as possible in the beginning, and they spent a good portion of their income on lawyers, trying to get him released into their custody. But then, as the years passed, and it drew closer to the time when he would be released, they stopped trying. The visits, too, began to space out more. As Todd matured, he grew quiet, almost sullen. He always had a look in his eyes as if he were waiting for somebody to say something to hurt him; as if he were expecting to be rebuked. Something about the high windows and the gray walls seemed to eat at him—even though he had been free to roam the grounds and he was never actually incarcerated in a traditional jail cell. When the time for his release arrived, it was kind of a shock to hear that he did not want them to come to the place and pick him up.

"Maybe he wants to come home finally," Laura said.

"I don't know if I can look in his eyes and not wonder what they saw, what he was up to when the little one was lost to us."

"Don't," she said. "Please don't now."

"I know I shouldn't be bringing it up again—what was it Dr. Dunne called it? Rehashing? Somehow the word does not quite describe what it does to me when I think of what may have happened between Todd and little Bobby."

"If you talk like this when you see him, you'll . . ." She paused. "You said you would just listen."

"I will. I will."

"You promised."

"Christ," he said. "It's still a battle, you know. Even here. And even now."

"I know. But you can't give into it. We can't give into it."

It was quiet for a while, and he thought of his daughter, Terry—the middle, and now the last child.

"I miss Terry," he said. "Tell her that for me."

"I will."

"And honey," he whispered. "I still miss the little one so much it hurts me to think of him. And yet, I think of him all the time, as if he were alive."

"I miss Todd," Laura said.

"I do, too. I do," he said.

"Think what he has been through."

"I know."

"You think we feel guilty for leaving them by themselves—for not being . . ."

"I know."

"Think how he feels."

Caldwell ran his hand over his mouth and chin, staring out the window. It was quiet again, and he moved over toward the bed and sat down in a chair by the desk. The silence in the phone seemed to sap his energy.

"Well," he sighed. "I should get unpacked."

"Are you all right, dear?"

"I think this town really wants some representative of the law," he said. "But the jail is in a mess. I may have to bring in contractors and get estimates. But it's not going to be a long process."

"I hope you don't have to spend too much time down there."

"I wonder how these folks will feel with a sheriff always in their midst?"

"I thought that was what they were clamoring for."

"I guess."

"Be careful, honey."

"Maybe I will take a weekend here soon, if things go well, and I can drive up for a visit. Maybe I'll have Todd with me. Or you could come down here and we'd all be back in this place one more time." The thought came to him at first like a pleasant breeze, and seemed peaceful; a brief, sweet excursion into innocent summer. Then he remembered that in all their previous visits, Bobby had been with them. "Perhaps that would be too painful."

"I'd love to come down there," Laura said.

"I want to tell Todd I forgive him."

"Good."

"I do forgive him."

"Say it to him."

"If I could just be sure that what he told us about it was true."

"Honey . . ." Her voice was plaintive, sadly frustrated.

"It would be nothing to forgive him if I knew what he told us was true."

"I forgive him, even if it isn't true. It was so long ago, and he's grown now and a different . . ."

"You can't mean that."

"I have to mean it. So do you."

"I wish I could find some place in my heart where there is no grief or anger and see clearly how I feel. That's what hurts. I don't really know if I forgive him."

"You have to."

"Yeah, well . . ." He stopped. It was quiet for a long time, and then he said, "Tell Terry I really do miss her."

"I will."

"I miss you, too."

"I know you do."

LATER THAT morning he lay down on the bed and stared at the ceiling. He thought he heard someone in the hall, and for a second his heart increased and he almost leapt from the bed to open the door, but it was nothing. It was quiet again, and he watched the sun climbing up beyond the top of the window. His stomach growled. He had not slept well the night before, but he could not relax enough to fall asleep now. Something solid in him seemed to dissolve, and a hollow sensation overcame him—as if the memory of all joy slipped out of some chamber in his heart and only death and numb sadness rushed to fill it. This is horrible, he thought. Something doesn't spin right anymore. Here he was: David Caldwell, husband and father. He had work to do. The county supervisor had said, "It's not like they're rioting down there. But maybe you'll be a quieting influence. Do what you think is best. It's county money, but I trust you to know the best way to spend it."

His work would keep him busy and happy. Truly happy. He would be thoroughly engaged with getting things done and working toward something of which he would almost certainly be proud. And yet he was without joy. When he was a young man, if someone had told him he'd one day work a job that kept him enthralled and challenged, and that he'd have the sort of income where he would be able to buy pretty much all he ever wanted to buy, he'd have believed in his own happiness as if it were the revealed word. He would not ever have accepted the notion such a future would be bereft of simple joy.

He got up and went to the window, looked out at the pale, bluish sky across the water, and beyond that, the green, distant shore of Maryland. It had been a clear, white day and when he first arrived, the hotel looked almost new in the bright light of the morning sun. From a distance it appeared to have been freshly painted. But now, all along the north wing that jutted out away from his window, he was close enough to see thousands of cracks and bubbles in the yellow paint; places where the seasons had buckled the wood and weather crinkled and rumpled the paint as if it had been linen. All the windows in his sight were covered with plywood. He could see far down the boardwalk toward the old jail. Beyond it, he saw the huge Ferris wheel rising up out of the dune grass and scrub pines like a great spider's web—thin, black vines clinging to the outer wheel and the spokes as if it really was part of an intricate, gene-driven design.

And then he remembered a summer night long ago, his daughter, Terry, laughing next to him, Laura cracking her gum, and Todd sitting in one of those cars on the Ferris wheel, holding Bobby close, both of them soaring high over the lights, curving down, down in front of them, their waving arms brushing the starless night.

"Look at me, Daddy," Bobby called. "Look at me." His first ride on "the grownup's wheel," as he called it, his first movement away from earth: Bobby, high up on that old Ferris wheel. It was a vision Caldwell could not give up. Could it have been so long ago? The old wheel seemed abandoned now. When did it go to ruin? Bobby was six then—he died that winter. Terry was seven. Was it so long ago? Ten years? Todd's been out of the detention center for two years and he went there just after his twelfth birth-day. He was there for six years. So it was more than ten years ago. Ten summers. He realized he was doing the math in his head, counting the years to get the puzzle stated, not to solve it. How did the place go to such ruin in only ten years?

He remembered laughter, exhilaration, after a three mile run in the drizzling rain; and then, how it felt to lie next to his wife, breathing the last excitement of their lovemaking, discovering, once again, innocent, childlike sleep.

YOU BECOME someone, he remembered saying to the parish priest. When you lose a child, you become someone you don't want to be, and you have to be that person for the rest of your life.

"I know," Father McManus had whispered.

"No," he said. "You don't know. Nobody who hasn't lived it knows."

The priest said nothing.

"You understand what I'm saying to you?" Caldwell asked. He was surprised at the force in his voice, at the anger he suddenly felt. "You know it?"

"I'm sorry, my son," Father McManus said.

"Christ," Caldwell said. "I'm probably ten years older than you. I'm not your son."

"Christ is the redeemer," the priest said. "Think of him that way instead of with a curse." His voice was gentle, but it struck Caldwell exactly as it was apparently intended. The priest seemed helpless. He looked longingly away. Sweat dripped down the side of his face. It was unbelievably hot. They were standing on the front steps of the church, and Bobby's funeral had just ended. The pallbearers had taken the small white casket down the steps and were heading for the hearse with it. Laura followed behind, weeping silently. Terry walked on one side and Todd on the other, each holding her hand. A blazing sun seemed to hammer down from above them.

"I am a person I never wanted to be," Caldwell said. "A person who has lost a child."

The priest nodded again. Caldwell was still fighting tears though they ran down his face. He took out a handkerchief and wiped under his eyes. He was ashamed and he did not know what to do with his anger. He had said nothing to Todd. And here was this young priest talking of redemption.

"I wish there was something I could do," Father McManus said.

"You know that church where the statue of the Virgin Mary started crying?" Caldwell asked.

"What?"

"It was in all the papers."

"I think . . ."

"In Woodbridge or someplace like that. Right here in Virginia. A priest would just enter the church and whenever he did, the statue of the Virgin Mary would seem to start crying. You remember that?"

"Yes, I do."

"What do you think of that?"

Father McManus seemed confused.

Caldwell said, "Don't you think it was kind of strange that everybody interpreted those tears to mean that the priest was somehow blessed?"

"I don't know if people looked at it quite like that."

"No, that's what the papers said. It was a miracle and this priest was blessed. Like the Virgin Mary was happy with him."

The priest nodded, his eyes shifting a little. He was clearly uncomfortable and as he met Caldwell's gaze, raising his hand as though to speak in secret, only to Caldwell, he said, "Not so loud."

"Why couldn't it be that the Virgin Mary was unhappy with the priest? You see what I'm getting at? Maybe he was one of those child-molesting parasites who hides in the church like a rat in a cupboard. Maybe the Virgin Mary was crying because this lowlife scum of a priest had the temerity to enter her church."

"Please," Father McManus said. "Try to calm down."

Caldwell said, "It's grief." He felt tears still, in the back of his throat. He turned and looked at his son's coffin, then looked back at the priest. A long time seemed to pass while they simply looked at each other. Then Caldwell said, "I'm sorry," as he broke into tears again. "I'm sorry, Father."

"It's all right, Mr. Caldwell," Father McManus said.

• • •

Northern Neck is a stretch of green land between the Rappahannock and Potomac rivers in northern Virginia. Along some of the beaches of the Potomac, on the Virginia side, one can stand ankle deep in the water and look out over the blue river as though it is an ocean. Maryland, on the other shore, is not visible unless the weather is very clear. Here, the river is saltwater, washed back from the Chesapeake Bay where both the Potomac and the Rappahannock empty.

Everything that inhabits the Chesapeake Bay—hard-shell crabs, jellyfish, striped bass, spot, blue fish, weakfish and hardhead—also resides in the Potomac along Northern Neck, at least as far as the naval station at Crown Point, which is well over sixty miles from the bay. So there was always some doubt in the minds of the few remaining natives whether the water that rippled outside their windows was river at all; some thought it might be bay water, and that the river ended somewhere further north and west, toward Washington, D.C.

The beaches are really beaches—with natural sand and even a few small but regular waves on windy days—and until the Virginia State Legislature took the slot machines away, the beaches flourished each summer as such places do that offer the hope of easy money and a classic battle between man and machine to get it. Most summers, especially after the Vietnam war, Columbia Beach and all the other beaches on Northern Neck were as crowded as any beach in Maryland or New Jersey. People began arriving in late March, and by May not a single hotel or rental house or motel had a vacancy of any significant duration until early in October. The income derived from the summer season was usually just enough for the permanent residents to live quite comfortably during the short winter months. Indeed, for some, off season was their vacation.

From November to December they worked hard making repairs and painting, dismantling boardwalk displays, and boarding up windows. When everything was closed up, they'd settle in for the winter, living a life of leisure—visiting each other occasionally for cards or just to sit and talk. In late March, they'd start tearing down the boards, sweeping and cleaning, and washing windows for the new season. In spite of its decline, Columbia Beach was pleasant enough for family vacations. The water was always slightly warm, never deep enough to be dangerous. At that part of Northern Neck, the river's current was lazy and hardly noticeable. More to the point, Northern Neck was not usually so vulnerable to the kind of late summer storms that pounded Hatteras, Ocean City, and other resorts out on the ocean.

There were even places on the shore at Columbia Beach where you could stand on your back porch and watch the sun setting over water in the evening. This little miracle of California sunsets on the East Coast was a product of the way the river bends there; only Cape Point in Buxton, North Carolina, and Brooms Island, on the Patuxent River in Maryland, present the same western sunset over blue water.

Once the slot machines were made unlawful, it was as if the beaches, too, were outlawed. Within the first five years, the beaches were abandoned—first by the people who owned the machines, and then by the people who owned the buildings where everyone who ran the machines or came to play them slept and ate. Columbia Beach was left with a modest boardwalk—the fresh new boards installed near the Ferris wheel and amusement park right after World War II were now rotting in the hot sun and salt air—and a few traditional carnival games like Toss the Ring and

Shoot the Pigeon. There was also a pool hall—Mauldin's Billiard Room and Shooting Gallery—and, of course, the old amusement park itself, which was completely overrun by shifting dunes and beach grass. Most of the other beaches along Northern Neck didn't survive the exodus of patrons and business concerns, and so they died completely, victims of time, growing vines, and the impatient weather.

Of what was left, most of the resort hotels, restaurants, and game halls of Columbia Beach were frequently empty. Even the deputy sheriff's station and the small jail were abandoned because of budget cuts. The people who remained did so out of a peculiar sort of stubbornness—a belief in the idea that what had happened to the crowds, the loud music, and bright, popping flashbulbs of summer's late-night madness was not only a good thing, but an absolutely desirable and worthwhile occurrence. "All this is ours, and it's private, and we can have our choice of where we swim, or fish, or eat, or even sleep if we want," one of them might say. Tourists were, in fact, a confounded nuisance, and the retired natives were glad the numbers of them had diminished to a trickle, if only a trickle by comparison. To be sure, the beaches were no longer crowded, but most summers were still well populated with loud teens and small families, all eager to swim in the calm water and lie on the beach under the naked sun.

"Who needs the big crowds?" Vince McDole often said. He sold gasoline and his station was near the main highway that led out of Northern Neck to Route 95 and points north and south, so clearly he didn't need them.

During the off season, Columbia Beach looked like something out of a haunted and disastrous future: an emblem of the world in some millennium hence when all life on earth has vanished and nothing remains but our own sad, nonorganic monument to plastic and steel, brick and mortar.

Cecil Edwards ran the Ferris wheel at the amusement park in Columbia Beach. He, too, had grown up in the town during its better days—back when it was loud and prosperous—and he had witnessed its slow descent, so he felt as if he owned it, even though it wasn't really worth owning. Along with the other beaches in Northern Neck—Dewey, Dahlgren, Arlo and Hawthorne—Columbia Beach had settled into a sort of permanent paralysis. What had once been a thriving and affluent resort area had, by the time Cecil had reached his fourth decade, devolved into an abandoned stretch of barren beaches and decaying boardwalks.

ii

Two days before David Caldwell checked into the Clary Hotel, Cecil Edwards drove his black Chevy pickup into McDole's gas station. McDole stepped out of his office and approached Cecil's truck as if it might suddenly explode. Cecil had parked directly behind the hydraulic lift in the first bay, so it was clear that he didn't need any gas or mechanical work. This made McDole nervous. He had already spent several hours the week before working on Cecil's truck and he never did find what was wrong with it. Cecil had dropped it off one morning early, complaining that the engine would stall for no apparent reason, and it didn't seem to matter how fast he was going. "The damn thing just quits," he said. "No sign or warning, it just stops, like the gas gets choked off or something."

"Sounds like water in the gas or some kind of fuel line problem," McDole had said.

"Yeah, well. Figure it out and fix it. It's damned dangerous to be chugging up the highway at high speed and have the thing just shut down like that."

"I'll have a look at it." McDole had been reluctant to do anything for a man like Cecil Edwards—who was nothing but a dangerous sort of nuisance to everyone in Columbia Beach—but he didn't really want to turn him down, either. The truth was, he thought it might be more trouble than it was worth to say no to him. So he agreed to see what he could do, and he had spent a lot of time on it, draining the tank and cleaning the fuel line. Nothing seemed to work. Finally he told Cecil he couldn't figure it out, and Cecil said, "Forget it then. I'll come by and pick it up." The next day, when McDole came to open the garage, the truck was gone and Cecil had not yet paid for all those hours of work.

McDole brooded about it a few days. Then he sent a bill through the mail, with a notation that he would take legal action if he weren't paid within thirty days. He had just about made up his mind he was going to have to go to Cecil's trailer and ask him for the money, but now here was Cecil, waiting in his truck. He seemed to be sitting up in the seat, his head cocked a little to the side, as if he had summoned McDole to approach his window.

"You come to settle up?" McDole said.

"I'm waiting for somebody to deny that I owe you money," Cecil said. He sat behind the wheel like a malevolent Buddha, his round, fat fingers crossed in his lap, his head so close to his shoulders it seemed as if he didn't have a neck. He had black hair graying around the edges and growing sparse at the forehead and back toward the center of his head. He never combed the hair on top, so it just seemed piled there—thin, tangled, and wiry looking. His eyebrows were dense and thick, without a trace of gray at all, and they crowded around each eye like they might uncoil and strike anything that got close to them. Beneath the brows, his blue, lightless eyes stared straight ahead, as though searching for prey.

"What are you talking about?" McDole asked.

"Somebody deny that I owe you money." It was a command. Cecil still wasn't looking at him. His eyes seemed fixed on something beyond the front windshield.

"What?"

"I want somebody to deny that I owe you a red cent."

"You do owe me money. A hundred sixty-three dollars."

"A hundred sixty-three?"

"And change."

"You emptied my gas tank."

"Right."

"Removed all that excess water that was keeping my truck from running."

"You don't have to talk like that," McDole said. "It was acting just like it had water in it."

"It was the electronic ignition." Now Cecil looked at him. With his great pink arm resting on the door of the truck, he seemed to study McDole's face, then glanced briefly at his arm— as if he were looking for some reaction from McDole to the sheer size of his bicep. Blinking slowly, looking almost bored, he turned back to the windshield, seemingly waiting for a response from the glass or from someone standing in front of the truck. His arm was heavily tattooed at the shoulder, a series of purple swirls and spiked circles confusingly overlapped, and below that, a series of small faces, lined up like some sort of vertical Mt. Rushmore along his bicep and forearm.

"I thought it was water in your tank," McDole said.

"Truck still stops. Sixty miles an hour. Makes no difference. It just quits."

"I'm sorry to hear it."

"Fellow up at the Chevy store in Romney—he says it's the electronic ignition."

"I wouldn't know about that," McDole said.

"A dealer," Cecil said.

"Well, that's good. I'm glad you found out what was wrong with it."

"I'll pay him."

"You still owe me. I did honest—"

"Somebody deny that."

"I worked a solid seven hours on this here truck," McDole said. "I emptied the gas out of the tank and purged the fuel line.

I ran tests on it. I checked the spark plugs, and did other things as well. Those things cost money. I could've charged you a lot more, if you want to know the truth."

"I want somebody to deny that."

McDole watched the side of the other man's face. He didn't know what to say to him. It was quiet for a short time, and then McDole heard the engine increase a bit on the truck and he realized that Cecil was not going to say anything more.

"Ain't nobody else here," McDole said. "And I sure as hell ain't gonna deny it." He felt his skin tighten when Edwards turned his head slowly around and looked at him. McDole was almost sixty, lean for his age, bald and gray around the ears. His face was long, and deeply lined, with bright black eyes and a nose and mouth that, from certain angles, made him look a little bit like Lincoln. He always wore an Atlanta Braves baseball cap and gray coveralls with the name of his garage printed on the back.

"You scared?" Cecil said.

"No."

"Well, goddamn." He moved his head slightly, took his arm off the door and rested both hands on the wheel. "I'm waiting for somebody to deny I owe you money," he said. Then he smiled as though he was proud of his phrasing.

"I ain't going to do it." McDole turned and walked back toward his office where there was a telephone and where he had a gun in the desk drawer under the cash machine. As he walked, he heard the engine shut down on the truck and the door open and close, so he walked faster—although he didn't want anyone to think he was running. He'd fought in the Vietnam war, and he truly was not afraid of anyone—not even Cecil Edwards. He knew Edwards was coming toward him, but he did not pick up his pace. He walked steadily, saw the door of his office, and knew he would make it. He would defend himself, if he had to. Just as he put his hand on the knob of the door, he felt Cecil's hand on his shoulder. He didn't even look. He opened the door and gently pulled away. Inside he went to the desk and opened the top side drawer. "I'm not going to take any shit," he said, and just as he saw the gray pistol resting on a stack of checks and receipts, right there in front of him, he felt something hard touch against the back of his head, and he did not move.

"What's that you said?" Cecil asked. His voice was almost tender. McDole felt his heart beating in the balls of his feet. "Go on," Cecil said. "You after this?" He reached around McDole and took the gun out of the desk. "What we got here?" McDole said nothing. "You planning on something here?"

"No."

Cecil put McDole's gun down next to the cash machine. "That's a little bitty old thing," he said.

"What are you going to do?" McDole's mouth was dry.

"I don't rightly know what I'm gonna do. Do you know?"

McDole closed his eyes. He was thinking, *I'll be damned. I'll be goddamned. The son of a bitch*

"This here's a big gun. Much bigger than that little puny thing of yours." Cecil talked lovingly, almost in the voice of a minister in quiet prayer.

"You're going to shoot a man over a hundred sixty-three dollars?" McDole stammered.

"A man. I don't see no man."

"Christ," McDole said.

"Don't see Christ, neither."

"For chrissake," McDole said. He leaned forward, toward the cash machine, his neck straining away from the hard barrel of the gun against the back of his head.

"You shouldn't take the Lord's name in vain," Cecil said.

"Over a lousy hundred sixty-three dollars?"

"You willing to die for a hundred sixty-three bucks?"

McDole looked at his reflection in the glass, and Cecil behind him, a huge black revolver in his hand. "You ain't gonna shoot me, Cecil. Goddamn it. Goddamn it."

"You think I won't shoot you?"

"You know you won't, and I know you won't. Now quit this shit for chrissake."

Cecil pulled the trigger. The gun made a pure and clean-sounding metallic click. "Whoops. A empty chamber."

"Goddamn it." McDole felt feverish.

Click. "Another one," Cecil said.

"One hundred sixty-three," McDole said. He was almost whispering. He closed his eyes again. He was telling himself that Cecil would never really shoot him. This was a game. A voice in the center of his brain kept saying, *It's a game, it's a game, it's a goddamned game*

Then Cecil said, "Let's try this one here," and picked up McDole's pistol.

"Goddamn it," McDole said, a little louder. He thought it was the last sound he would ever make.

"You're a stubborn son of a bitch," Cecil said. "I think your gun's definitely got a bullet in it." He placed it against the back of McDole's head. It almost felt hot.

"Wait." McDole had no idea he would say that, and when he heard the word escape from his lips, he was momentarily shocked. He opened his eyes and stared at himself in the glass.

"Well?" Cecil said.

"Okay. You don't owe me any money."

"I don't know where those rumors get started, do you?" Cecil put the pistol back in the drawer and closed it, then he walked around the counter and over to the door. "I know. Why don't you let me have a look at those bills hanging on the wall there?" He reached up on the wall and withdrew a handful of work orders, flipped through them and found the one he wanted. "Here it is. And lookee here, my spare key's here too." He put the other bills back up on the nail in the wall. McDole said nothing. "This is how rumors like that get started. See here?"

"I see it."

"Where you 'spose a thing like that came from?" McDole looked down, shaking his head. "I swear it sure is a mystery."

"You just think you can do anything you want, don't you?" McDole said, staring straight at him now. Cecil slowly tore up the bill. "You don't get to break just any law you want."

"What law?"

"This is a goddamned robbery."

"It ain't no robbery. You denied that I owe you the money."

"You can't just do anything you've a mind to."

"Who's going to stop me?"

"You don't own this town."

"I never said I did." Cecil had the bill in little folded pieces, between his thumb and forefinger.

"Goddamn it. I did honest work for you. Hard work. I removed the gas tank and . . ."

Cecil let the small pieces of paper flutter to the floor. "No you didn't," he said. "There ain't no record of it." He smiled.

"One of these days . . ."

"What?" Cecil said. "Tell me, what?"

"You're going to bark up the wrong tree."

"Well, I'm pissing on this here tree, ain't I?" McDole said nothing. "Just a pissing away. What you gonna do about it?"

"Fuck you."

"You want to discuss this with me outside? I don't need a gun," he said.

"What'd you bring one for, then?"

"I thought you might have one." McDole looked at the drawer where Cecil had replaced the pistol. "I was right, too. Wudn't I?"

"Fuck you."

"You want to come over here and say that to me?"

"Fuck you."

"Maybe you'd like me to come over there." McDole looked down at the floor. It was quiet for a long time. "Well," Cecil said. "You have a nice day." He tucked his own gun in the front of his pants. "Or I guess I should say evening, shouldn't I?"

McDole watched Cecil's wide back and bulky arms as he squeezed through the door frame and strolled over to his truck.

He felt his heart beginning to return to normal, his limbs getting heavy. He suddenly felt very tired, almost sleepy. In spite of what felt now like a kind of exhaustion, he was still shaken and he could feel his hands trembling. "Goddamn his soul," he said out loud, still watching Cecil Edwards as he put his truck in gear and slowly drove by the front window.

Cecil waved, a wide smile on his face, and McDole gave him the finger, leaning into the frame of the window so he could definitely be seen. Cecil only turned away, still smiling as he pulled out and drove on up the street.

· · ·

Cecil's troubles began, some said, when his father left. They said that when there is no authority in a child's life, he has no one to look up to, so he learns how to behave watching TV, and everyone knows that's no place to get breeding.

But the truth was that when Mr. Edwards packed his bags, patted his wife on the shoulder and said, "I'll be back very soon," then disappeared forever, Cecil was not even slightly moved by it. He did not even feel sadness. He was fifteen years old, and he believed a father was a person who drank too much in the afternoon and slept on the couch all evening. Cecil got nothing from his father—neither a cross word nor a kind one. He felt the same way when his father was no longer there as other children do when their parents throw out an old couch.

No. It was not his father leaving. It was not the two year tour of duty in the Marines, which only seemed to silence him further, nor was it the fact that two years after they outlawed the slot machines, his mother died and left him a piece of corner property with a Ferris wheel sitting on it. The death of his mother only seemed to make him stronger. He never did talk to anyone in the town except to conduct business, and he had no friends anyone could remember, either. But he wasn't unfriendly. He was just a big, awkward, shy man who kept to himself and didn't bother very much with the people in the town. For a long time, when he ran the Ferris wheel, his only problem seemed to be that he had become slightly overweight, and he was painfully isolated by the great disparity of his size and weight around normal people. He towered over most of them. He was strong enough to lift children up all day and set them gently into the cars, and sometimes, when a belt broke or the engine acted up, he actually turned the wheel himself. He'd do that and the kids would howl at him: "faster, faster." Sweat would drip off him, but he'd smile, spinning the wheel, trying desperately to imitate the speed of the motor. Once he got it going, the momentum of the full cars as they cascaded down seemed to feed his strength, and then he could actually match the work of the machine. He sometimes surpassed it. It was a display of human power everyone loved to watch.

Everyone in the town would say he was a reasonably good man until after his mother died and he was alone. But the trouble started a little over seven years ago when he got involved with the county court over property taxes—an episode that made the *Richmond Times Dispatch*—and he was never really the same after that.

It started innocently enough. One Thursday not long after his mother died, Cecil opened the door of his trailer and found Jack Clary standing on the bottom stoop looking up at him, his eyes squinting in the sun.

"What's the matter?" asked Cecil.

"I spotted a bit of news in the morning paper."

"What paper?"

"The county newspaper." He held up a copy of the *Sentinel News*.

"I don't read that one," Cecil said.

Most people were nervous back then—watching the tourists diminish week after week, month after month, wondering which shops and amusements would close and which would survive. Clary couldn't believe his eyes that morning when Judy, his wife, put the newspaper in his lap and pointed to a legal notice in the lower right-hand corner of the "News from your Neighbors" section of the paper. It read:

TAX SALE

Lot 16A Cora Edwards, et al.
to be auctioned
for nonpayment of delinquent taxes
and sold to the highest bidder.

Friday, August 14th, 1992

"What do you think of that?" Judy said. He was sitting in his favorite chair, watching the morning news, sipping a cup of coffee.

"What is it?"

"That's the Ferris wheel. That whole piece of property at the end of the boardwalk."

"No kidding."

"You can buy it."

"I can?"

"A tax sale, hon. Don't you see? All you do is pay the taxes on it and it's yours."

"That can't be."

"I'm telling you." Judy wore an apron that hung loosely from her neck. Her hair was piled high on her head and tied in a tight bun with a yellow bandana. She was beginning to puff and sag in all the wrong places, and it embarrassed him sometimes when she would slip on a tight-fitting shirt and red shorts and walk around the hotel in her bare feet with no makeup on, cleaning the stairs and the lobby floor. She worked hard, and she could make herself look very good when she wanted to, but when it was just the two of them she'd let herself go. Sometimes Clary would look at her with sadness in his heart for what was happening to both of them. They were only in their mid-forties, and he did love her, after all. He was certain of that. And he would never think of demanding that she get dressed or spend time making herself presentable each day. He told himself that most of the time he wasn't much to look at, either. But every morning when he got out of bed, he made sure to wash his face and comb his hair before he went downstairs.

Clary wasn't interested in Cecil Edwards because the big man had no family, although he certainly felt sorry for him. Clary wanted the property. Judy wanted him to see about getting it. Still, he had liked Cora, and he didn't want to simply buy her place out from under her son. He was a fair-minded man, and he knew such a thing was not fair and he said so.

Judy said, "Who cares if it's fair? It's the law."

"The law ain't always fair."

"So why do you have to be?"

"Because I'm a fair man." Judy sat on the arm of the chair. "Careful, you'll spill my coffee," Clary said.

She put her arm across his shoulder. "My fair man. That's why I love you so much." He smiled up at her. "But see about it," she said. "We can own that property, if you want it."

"I'll look into it."

"Today?"

"If you want. I'll find out if Cecil's going to abandon the place and leave it for the auctioneer's gavel or not."

"You going over there?"

"I expect so."

At that time Cecil was just a big, strong, poor man whose mother had died, leaving him the property and the Ferris wheel that rested on it. He never had anything to say to anyone and he minded his own business. Since the wheel had started to flag a little—in the height of the summer season, even with all of its sparkling lights and loud music, it frequently sat empty, without a single rider—it seemed reasonable to assume Cecil had decided to let it go.

So Clary figured it was not insensitive to consider taking advantage of the tax sale; as a matter of fact, he believed he was being charitable by telling Cecil about it first. But that Thursday morning when he did tell him about it, Cecil didn't know what he was talking about.

"A tax sale?" he said. He was standing on the top step of his trailer, and Clary tried to stay in his shadow so he'd block the sun. The trailer leaned toward Clary when Cecil opened the door. "I don't know what a tax sale is."

"Just what it says."

"I don't understand."

"Nonpayment of taxes," Clary said. "If you don't pay taxes on the property, they put it up for sale in order to collect."

"How can they sell something that belongs to me?"

"It's the state," Clary shook his head. This was the first real conversation he'd had with Cecil Edwards, and he was beginning to understand why he seemed so alone all the time.

"I don't know anything about taxes," Cecil said.

"Didn't your mama pay taxes on the land?"

"I don't know." Cecil rubbed his chin. It was broad and round and looked as though it was punctured by little black needles. Clary could see a thin ring of sweat in the creases of skin above Cecil's collar.

"Well, tomorrow's the sixteenth. You better call the county."

"What's the number?"

"How should I know?" Clary turned to leave. Then he remembered why he'd come. "You want to get rid of the land, don't let them auction it off. Sell it to me."

"I want to keep it."

"What for?"

Cecil stepped back into the trailer, watching Clary as if he expected him to rush up the steps and try to force his way in.

THAT WAS the beginning of it. Cecil called the county and talked to the clerk in charge of property taxes. There was nothing she could do. "I'm sorry, sir," she said. "Once it's in tax sale, we can't do anything unless you come down here and pay the tax."

"How much is it?"

She told him to hold the phone and he waited. A long time passed. When she came back on, she said, "It's a lot of back taxes—close to sixteen hundred dollars."

"I don't have the cash," Cecil said.

"If you could get a certified check."

"I don't have that kind of money now."

"I'm sorry, sir."

Cecil opened his checkbook and looked at the balance. He had eight hundred thirty-eight dollars and nineteen cents. That was all he had in the world. "Look," he said. "My mother just died. I never saw a notice to pay taxes."

"You get one every year."

"I never saw one."

"Perhaps your mother got it?"

"But she's dead. You understand."

"I'm sorry, sir."

"I never saw the notice. I didn't know I owed the tax."

"Perhaps you'd like to talk to my supervisor?" the woman said.

"Okay." He waited, listening to static in the line, and then a busy, recorded voice telling him that his call was important and to please stay on the line. It was easy to hold his temper because he knew somebody would understand what had happened to him and give him more time. His mother's death would eventually pay him twenty thousand dollars in life insurance. He knew he could find someone in the tax office who would listen and be willing to make an exception in his case, since he *was* an exception.

"Yes?" A male voice came on the line.

"This is Cecil Edwards."

"Who?"

"Cecil Edwards."

"C-C?"

"Cecil. Cecil."

"What can I do for you?"

"It's about my taxes. Didn't the clerk explain it to you?"

"No, she didn't."

"I have to start over?"

"What can I do for you, Mr. Edwards?"

"You're going to sell my property at auction tomorrow."

Impatiently the man said, "What property, sir?"

Cecil looked at the ad. "Lot 16A, Cora Edwards."

"Just a minute."

After a long pause, the man came back. "Yes sir, it's going on auction tomorrow."

"I didn't know about the tax," Cecil said.

"I see."

Cecil told him the story. When he was finished, he said, "My mother may have gotten the tax bill, but I never saw it. She died. I've got twenty thousand dollars coming to me soon. From her insurance. Four thousand of it goes for her funeral. The undertaker was willing to wait for payment, so . . ."

"But Mr. Edwards, this bill is delinquent."

"I never saw it."

"Well—that's what you say. I don't have any way of verifying that you're . . ."

"I'm telling the truth. Check the obituaries, for chrissake." Now Cecil was getting angry.

"There really isn't anything I can do," the man said. "We have a policy here . . ."

"Let me talk to your boss," Cecil said. He knew there had to be somebody who would listen. He waited on the line again, this time tapping the table with his fingers, switching the phone from ear to ear. The cheerful, buoyant voice on the recording now talked about the various services provided from state real estate taxes, then it again said that his call was important. He believed he would remain calm.

"Assessments, Mrs. Harrison," the voice on the phone said.

"This is Cecil Edwards. Have you heard of me?"

"Sir?"

"Are you aware of my problem?"

"No sir. I'm not."

"I . . ."

"What did you say your name was?"

"Edwards!" he yelled. Then he took a deep breath. "I'm sorry. I've got a problem with my property," he said more calmly. He went over it again, this time gulping for air a little when he talked of his mother. "She died," he said. "She died. Without telling me about the taxes. She was pretty sick for a long time at the end there and probably didn't think of it."

"I'm sorry," Mrs. Harrison said.

"I know I owe the money. When the insurance comes, I'll pay it. Right away."

"What do you want me to do?"

At last, he thought. "I just want you to take the property out of the tax sale."

"What's the property you're referring to?"

He told her. She went away for a few minutes, then came back to the phone. "Mr. Edwards, I can't do that."

"Why?"

"We have a policy here. Once a house is in tax sale, only a cash payment can be made to fulfill the tax obligation."

"What am I supposed to do?" he asked. He really wanted to know.

"I don't know, sir. Can you pay the tax?"

"Haven't you been listening to me?"

"It really won't help matters if you start yelling at people." Mrs. Harrison sounded like a teacher.

"Who can I talk to that will understand?"

"You could call the commissioner of revenue in Warsaw."

"What about there, in that office?"

"Sir, I supervise this office. I'm as high as you can go here."

"And you won't help me."

"I can't. We have a policy . . ."

"Fuck you and your policy," Cecil said.

"I don't have to listen to this," Mrs. Harrison said, and she hung up the phone.

Cecil dialed the number again and got the first clerk he'd talked to. "Mrs. Harrison, please," he said.

"I'm sorry, she's stepped out of the office. Can I help you?"

"What's your name?"

"I'm Mrs. Sellers."

"I just want to get it right."

"Pardon?"

"I'll see you in just a few minutes, Mrs. Sellers."

THAT AFTERNOON Cecil came very fast through the front door of the tax assessment office. He was carrying a twenty-gauge shotgun. He moved swiftly around the front counter and to the desk of a woman who stared blankly at him, as if she could not fathom what she saw. He placed the cold, hard black barrel of the shotgun under her chin. She opened her mouth but no sound escaped.

"Mrs. Sellers?"

She blinked.

"I'm Cecil Edwards, remember me?"

She closed her eyes and nodded slightly.

"Get up," Cecil said.

He raised her out of the chair with the barrel of the gun, pushed the cold metal against her throat, and guided her toward the back offices.

"Mr. Comstock?" she gasped when they reached the first office.

Comstock came out, a short, wiry man with horn-rimmed glasses and thick bushy hair. He was dressed in a black suit, a neatly turned collar, and red tie. He could not take his eyes off the gun.

"My god," he said.

"Tell him who I am," Cecil said to Mrs. Sellers.

"What?"

"Tell him who the fuck I am," Cecil shouted.

She jumped at the sound of his voice, then she spoke very fast. "This is—," she stopped, trying to gain control of herself. Her chin trembled. "I can't remember your name."

"I just said it."

"I'm sorry." She had tears in her eyes.

"Cecil Edwards."

"Mr. Edwards," she gasped. "He wants to talk to you. He wants to talk to you about—," she stopped. Her voice grew a little stronger as she went on, perhaps because Cecil had pulled the barrel of the gun back slightly. "He is very unhappy about a tax sale."

"Now," Cecil said, "take some time and tell this man what my problem is and all. You know, so I won't have to keep repeating it."

Mrs. Sellers explained the problem well, speaking about it quickly and evenly, as if she were reading it out loud from a book. When she was finished, Cecil said, "Very good." Then he put the gun to Comstock's throat. "Let's go talk to Mrs. Harrison."

As they moved down the hall, Mrs. Sellers let out a lungful of air and trembled back to her desk. Cecil didn't care what she might do there, or if she left the office. Mrs. Harrison had apparently heard the commotion because she was down on all fours underneath her desk, whispering into a telephone, when Cecil and Comstock came in.

"Get up," Cecil said.

Comstock was crying, sobbing so fitfully it was hard for Cecil to keep the barrel of the gun on his neck. "Mrs. Harrison," Comstock said. "Oh, my dear lord. Mrs. Harrison."

"Shut up," Cecil said. Comstock closed his mouth, and breathed loudly through his nose. He closed his eyes and stood there, shaking. "Get up," Cecil said again.

Mrs. Harrison rose from behind the desk as if she were arousing herself from a comfortable seat in a restaurant. She was a tall, thin, regal woman, with gray hair, black pointed glasses and a long sharp nose. She said, "I've called the police."

"Good for you," Cecil said. He nudged the barrel of the gun against Comstock to push him back out of the way. Mrs. Harrison brushed the front of her dress, which was black too, like Comstock's suit, and said, "What is the meaning of this?"

"Now," Cecil said to Comstock, "you tell her what my situation is, like Mrs. Sellers told you."

Comstock couldn't talk. He kept stammering "M-M-Mr., M-M-Mr., M-M-Mr." Tears ran down his face. Cecil put the gun hard against his neck again. Comstock spoke slowly and deliberately. "Mr. Edwards wants his mother to be taken out of tax sale."

"My mother died," Cecil said.

"Yes. That's it. His mother died."

"I know the story," said Mrs. Harrison. Behind her two great windows looked out over the town. The office walls were all brown wood, with orange carpets and white lampshades. A couch rested in the far corner by the entrance and huge green plants filtered the bright sunlight through the windows. Cecil could hear the slight whisper of the air conditioner, a telephone ringing in some other office. He did not yet hear a siren.

"Why don't you put the gun down," Mrs. Harrison murmured.

Cecil pushed Comstock to the floor, guiding him there by pressing the gun against the back of his neck. Then he moved around the desk and placed the barrel under Mrs. Harrison's right ear.

"The police will be here," she said. Her voice was still strong, calm. He was amazed at her courage.

"Sit down," he said.

She pulled an orange chair around, and sat down at the desk. Cecil picked a pen out of a blue cup on the corner of the desk and handed it to her. Then he picked up a memo pad, slapping it in front of her as if he were finally showing everyone his hand in a poker game.

Mrs. Harrison turned, looking up at him. "Well?"

"Write what I tell you."

She took the pen and placed it on the paper.

"Dear Mr. Edwards," Cecil dictated. He watched her write it. Comstock whimpered on the floor in front of him.

"For God's sake, Larry," Mrs. Harrison said.

"Dear Mr. Edwards," Cecil said.

"I've got that . . ."

"I'm sorry to hear about the tragic loss of your mother." She repeated it as she wrote it. "In view of your tragic circumstances . . ." She wrote furiously, trying to get it all so he wouldn't have to repeat it. ". . . we are giving you an extra sixty days to pay the taxes on the property she left you in her will." Cecil's voice was almost gentle. When she was finished, he smiled. "Sign it."

She wrote her signature and gently placed the pen next to the pad of paper. Cecil ripped the paper off the pad and stepped back, still pointing the shotgun at her. "Are you satisfied?" she said.

"Get an envelope and a stamp."

"Look, Mr. Edwards . . ." He cocked the hammer back on the shotgun. "Okay, okay." She opened the left-hand drawer and removed a roll of stamps and an envelope. The drawer squeaked when she closed it.

"You ought to oil that," Cecil said.

She picked up the pen again. "What's the address?"

"P.O. Box 1216, Columbia Beach, Virginia."

She addressed the envelope with a steady hand. Cecil took one of the stamps, walked around the desk and leaned down in front of Comstock. "Lick this," he said.

Comstock stuck out his tongue, tears still running down his cheeks. "It's too dry," Cecil said. He put the stamp against the skin under Comstock's eyes. "It's pretty wet here, ain't it."

"Are you quite through?" Mrs. Harrison said. She rose from the desk in front of her as if something were lifting her out of the chair.

"Almost, thank you," Cecil said. "If you'll walk with me to a mailbox."

"There's probably police out there by now," she said. Her voice trembled slightly, and he knew she was as frightened as Comstock. He admired her for not showing it.

"You remind me of my mother," he said. She looked at the desk as if she might find something to say written on the blond surface. "Shall we go?" he asked.

"What about the police?"

He leaned over the desk, letting the barrel of the gun rest against the bright wood. "Mrs. Harrison?" he said. "I don't give a damn about the fucking police."

She came around the desk, and the two of them walked out of her office. Comstock was still crouching down on the orange carpet.

OF COURSE as soon as the letter was mailed, Cecil was arrested. He didn't resist at all. In fact he sat down just outside the office and waited for the police to arrive. It was David Caldwell, in his first year as a sheriff's deputy, who came to get him. He had to come from Dahlgren, which was a fairly long drive. Cecil handed over his shotgun and put his hands behind his back so Caldwell could put handcuffs on him. When Mrs. Harrison came out to witness his arrest, he turned to her and said, "Thank you for your time."

"You know, Mr. Edwards," she said, "after your property is sold at auction, you have a year and a day to pay the tax." Cecil laughed out loud and couldn't contain himself enough to get in Caldwell's cruiser. "If you pay the tax within that year, your property is returned to you," Mrs. Harrison went on, her voice getting louder so she could be heard over his laughter.

"Nobody told me that," Cecil said. "I talked to all of you and nobody mentioned anything but a policy." He was still laughing. Mrs. Harrison looked at him with a kind of stern sadness, then smiled briefly under the frown on her face. She shook her head, still gazing at him. "I guess we were all just too frightened," she said. "And it is our job to get the money if we can . . ."

Comstock pressed charges and went into a Warsaw courtroom to testify against Cecil Edwards. Cecil pleaded guilty. But once he told his story, the judge—a man near seventy, with hollow eyes and gold glasses—told the court that the law was not so cut and dried as to be removed completely from the human heart. He said he understood Cecil's frustration and didn't think it would serve justice to put him in jail. So at the request of Cecil's attorney, he granted first offender status, put him on probation for one year, and fined him two hundred dollars. Cecil walked out of the courtroom as if he'd just gotten some sort of award. He waited on the front steps until Comstock emerged. The little taxman's lips looked small and white, and his tremulous hands were clasped in front of him as though they were cuffed. He looked like a prisoner himself, and he held his head down like a man trying to avoid the broad light of news cameras. Cecil smiled. "Leave me alone," Comstock said.

"I think I'd like to test your reflexes sometime," Cecil said.

"You don't dare come near me," Comstock said.

Cecil smiled. "Hide and watch, muthafucka."

SINCE THAT time Cecil was looked upon as a violent and dangerous man. He never killed anyone, as far as those who cared about such things knew, but he was usually in the center of violence when it erupted in the bars and clubs near the naval station. One day, the summer before David Caldwell returned to Columbia Beach to meet Todd, Cecil took a sailor under the boardwalk, near Mauldin's Billiard Room and Shooting Gallery, and broke his breastbone. Some thought he must have hit the sailor with a piece of driftwood, but Mauldin said the sailor told the nurse that Cecil just butted him with his head. The sailor nearly died, and there was general fear in Columbia Beach that if he did, somebody would have to go up to Dahlgren to swear out a complaint.

OUT OF SEASON · 39

But the sailor got better, was released from the hospital, and disappeared back into the naval station. In any case he did not press charges, and most of the residents of the town knew why. The law along Northern Neck, as everywhere else in this republic, was very slow, and there was no one to guard the jail. David Caldwell, who was now the sheriff of Dahlgren County, had his offices in Warsaw, more than forty miles from Columbia Beach, and he couldn't spend any extra time away from the county seat. There was no money to man the jail, so it had fallen into disrepair. Anybody who pressed charges against Cecil Edwards had to live in the same town with him until the county or the state got around to taking care of the problem. As Stan Mauldin said one day to one of the gatherings in front of his shooting gallery, "Cecil goes his own way and makes his own trouble. When he dies a lot of folks will be willing to make formal complaints against him."

In truth there was also a certain loyalty involved in ignoring Cecil's sins against the sailors, and occasionally the people of the town enjoyed going over their "boy's" exploits. As long as he didn't commit a crime that got the police in Fredericksburg or Warsaw involved, it didn't seem to matter that Cecil "went his own way."

He lived alone, in the trailer behind the Ferris wheel, and he almost never had any company until Lindsey Hunter came to the town. She was seen very often near Cecil's trailer, and although no one ever saw her come out of there in the morning, it was pretty hard not to speculate that she must be giving him some kind of pleasure, if not service. She was plain looking from some angles, rather too heavy in the middle, but with long, well-formed legs that tanned beautifully in the summer. Her hair was a light blond—not to say white, but almost a translucent color of light brown—and it sometimes adorned her face in such a way that she looked almost beautiful. Besides, she carried herself with such self-assurance that most of the men believed she was really quite attractive in her own way. Stan Mauldin said she was "just plain sassy, and I like a woman with sass."

She had naturally dark brows, thick and well shaped, and a face that seemed molded from the most delicate fabric. She was from somewhere in northern Virginia—Fairfax or someplace like that—and folks in the town believed some terrible thing had happened to her there, though she never mentioned anything to those who talked to her. No one in the town knew anything of her history. Most were sure that her lover had been murdered, but some favored the notion that her mother had killed her father. They talked as though these were simply the unknown facts, but facts nonetheless.

Lindsey was twenty-three the year David Caldwell returned to Columbia Beach. She stayed with Mrs. McCutcheon, who rented to the young woman a room on the second floor of her eighteenth-century, two-story frame house, and who was primarily interested in her flower beds and pet cats. When Lindsey wasn't arousing curiosity by visiting Cecil Edwards that first summer, she'd go down to the beach and sun herself. She'd come down from the highway and walk to the creaking boardwalk in her blue bikini, her light hair rising and falling in the bright currents of air like a lace curtain. She had to know everybody watched her. She'd find a place near the water and sit there in the sun reading books all day—without once going in to get wet—and by the time summer ended, she looked like an Indian. Nearly all the males in Columbia Beach were disappointed when the weather cooled off and she stopped coming down to the beach, but it was only for a short time, and then the next summer came, and there she was, reading her books.

Because she frequently wore only her bathing suit, or shorts and a halter top, it was possible to notice a change in her appearance from the previous summer—a change nobody wanted to mention yet. But recently, big, unsightly bruises appeared on her left arm and the top of her left leg. When something has been perfect in your memory—even in the collective memory—you don't want to point out the flaws you notice in the real thing, so for a long time no one said anything.

"Cecil's tough on everybody," Jack Clary said that day David Caldwell came to his hotel. He watched Lindsey move along the boardwalk with a slight limp. She was heading out toward the old amusement park. Clary and McDole stood in front of Mauldin's Billiard Room and Shooting Gallery. Mauldin leaned on the door frame, eating a hot dog. He was one of the youngest businessmen in town, not yet forty-five. He was a lean, hawk-nosed man who always seemed to need a shave. His hair was as black as potting soil, and he had a tattoo on each red forearm which said, "No Way Hozay." He, too, was a lifetime citizen of Columbia Beach, but he didn't think he owned any part of it except his little shooting gallery, seven electric guns, hundreds of stuffed dolls, nine pool tables and all that went with them.

It was a very warm day for October, so they were glad to see Lindsey in her halter top and shorts. "You know," Clary said. "I like the way her belly sticks out a little in the middle. It's such a smooth place on her." He had a wide face, thick, bushy gray hair, and glasses that made his eyes look like marbles. "I bet when she's dressed up she's classy as hell."

"Maybe she sprained her ankle or something," Mauldin said.

"I swear to god," McDole said, "Cecil held that pistol to the back of my head. I could feel it. He was going to kill me." McDole's gas station was not only nearest the only major highway that led into Columbia Beach, it also occupied the only corner in the vicinity of the town that had four thriving businesses. The other three were also related to automobiles: a tire store, a used car lot, and an auto parts store. The owner of all three of those businesses, a man named Mitch Hamlin, strolled up the street and stood next to Mauldin puffing on a cigar. He was almost never seen in public without a cigar in his mouth, and all he ever wanted to do was tell jokes. The others found it impossible to believe that he could manage a single account, much less three fairly thriving businesses. On this day he was sweating a lot. When Hamlin heard McDole's story he said, "You know, being able to talk about the fact that Cecil held a gun on you the day after it happened is a pretty damn good thing." At this, Clary laughed. "Of course, it's probably just as bad on your nerves knowing he might do it again."

"It may as well have been a robbery," McDole said. He was more than a decade older than the other three, and he always carried himself around them as if he knew more, as if his venerable age commanded respect.

"Well, he didn't really take anything else, right?" Mauldin said. "I mean, he just took the bill. It wasn't really a robbery in the—"

"It was robbery. At gunpoint," McDole answered.

"He gets away with something like that," Hamlin said, "and the next thing you know, he's always got the gun with him."

"Right," McDole agreed.

"He'll carry that around instead of a checkbook," Hamlin said.

Clary laughed. He'd had a few swallows of Chivas, a sort of morning offering, and it didn't seem that what happened to McDole was anything to worry about. "Hell, he didn't shoot you."

"He didn't pay me, either."

Clary watched Lindsey getting further down the boardwalk. "Maybe Cecil put those bruises on her."

"She probably sprained her ankle or something," McDole said. "Look the way she's walking."

"It sure is a nice ankle, whoever did it," Mauldin said.

"Oh, I think her ankles are too fat," Clary said.

McDole whistled. She heard him. They watched her turn slowly and stare at them. "We was just deciding if we like your ankles," Mauldin hollered. She did not smile. "Go on, honey," McDole said. She gave them the finger and turned away, limping on down to the end of the boardwalk. They hooted and hollered at her, laughing and whistling.

"I like that girl," Hamlin said. "Even if she does hang out with Cecil Edwards."

"What the hell could she possibly see in him?" McDole said. "It sure makes you wonder, don't it?"

"You can tell she ain't had a easy life," Mauldin said.

"None of us has had an easy life," said Clary.

"Hell," Mauldin said, "what we got now? Would you say we got it hard right here? Right now?"

"You forget, Stan," McDole said, laughing, "you don't live with Jack's wife a hounding you." Mauldin and Hamlin laughed.

"She doesn't hound me," Clary said. He didn't like the joke.

"I was just kidding," McDole said. "Don't get your panties in a bunch."

It was quiet for a while, then Mauldin said, "Yeah. She's got nice ankles."

iii

It had been a long time since Caldwell had thought so much of his lost boy. He had even gotten to a place where laughter was again possible. He lived every day with the certainty of his loss, but over the years the memory of Bobby softened and broadened in his mind—so that it became something very much like a memory of his own boyhood, of himself as a boy, and his sorrow became tinged with affectionate longing and sadness over lost innocence.

He had struggled a long time before he could give up the pain of remembering. Apart from his overwhelming feelings of guilt and responsibility—his constant musings about what he could have done differently that day, about the horrible result of letting the boys stay alone for those few hours in the house—he could not escape the turning and turning of his own mind about what had really happened. He could not ever know what really happened. For months immediately after Bobby's death, sleep was an impossible flight, and when he lay in bed listening to the night and only a pale moon or distant stars lit the bedroom walls, he could see the boy's face in the lightless space behind his eyelids. He could conjure all of Bobby's voices during the busy living time they'd had together. All the things the boy said to him. Eventually, listening to his wife's breathing as she slept angered him. How could she sleep? How could she fall into quiet unconsciousness while the soul of her baby boy had slipped free? But gradually, as the days and weeks and then years went by, the pain became a feature of every night and every day. Any thought of Bobby made him sad, and almost fearful that the sadness would never stop. Then he'd make a conscious attempt to remember the joy, the exquisite happiness of being a young father—to recapture a fraction of it, without the pain. When he failed, as he often did in the beginning, he'd simply give in to the whole thing, like a man accepting a kind of punishment. Thinking of the days and hours with the living boy had become a form of prayer.

"Heydad," the boy would say. One word. "Heydad." And he knew that Bobby was going to say something that would make him laugh or give him the kind of pleasure he didn't think was possible from only a voice or an idea. "Heydad, don't you think trees are pretty comfortable?"

"I don't know. I never thought about it. Why do you think they are?"

"Because they never have to move. If they ever got achy they'd move, wouldn't they?"

Or, "Heydad. I notice that you treat Todd like he's a little older than I am."

"Well, he is older than you are."

"You think if I'm real good next year I can be older than him?" When he said this, he was only five years old. Caldwell had laughed until he couldn't see through his tears. He held Bobby against himself and rolled back and forth laughing, and Bobby laughed, too. Then when it had almost subsided, Bobby looked into his eyes, seemingly waiting for him to get control of himself, and when he had gotten his breath, the boy said, "Heydad."

"Yeah?" Caldwell was wiping his eyes with a corner of his shirt tail.

"What are we laughing at?"

There had been so many moments like that with his children. Todd, too, had made him laugh, had filled him with a kind of tearful joy. One fall he had taken Todd hunting with him. "I'm going with a few buddies to hunt deer," he said. "You want to go?"

"Yes, sir," Todd said. He couldn't wait.

They went out on a cold, snowy morning in late November. There was very little wind but the snow drifted down hard, as if it carried too much weight to simply float dreamily to the ground. It was almost rain the way it fell. They had walked a long distance into the woods, the two of them alone, away from the others, to a special place high on a ridge overlooking a deep ravine where a small stream meandered through the trees toward an overpass and the highway. This was where Caldwell had always come. He'd sit in the brush there, at the top of the ridge, and watch for deer walking along the creek. In the past he almost always got one. But this one time, Todd's first time, he hunched in the downward-driven snow trying to keep warm, Todd sitting next to him, proudly holding onto his twenty-gauge shotgun. Todd kept looking at him expectantly. He held the gun as if he would need it to defend himself, as if he were a soldier in a desperate army, waiting for the last assault of a powerful enemy.

Caldwell tried to imagine what must be going through the mind of his son, a boy in the company of his father. He wanted such experiences for his boys. He wanted them to remember him in ways he could not remember his own father: as a comrade, a genuine force in their lives, a teacher, and friend. He wanted to give them a life he had never had, so he would be what his own father had never been: a presence in his sons' lives.

The snow shifted a little when a breeze stirred in the pine branches, and he felt a cold blast of it on his face. Todd looked at him and seemed about to speak. Caldwell put his finger up over his mouth to shush him. "You have to be very quiet," he whispered, wanting to let the boy know that in his own way he was listening, or at least he was willing to listen. Todd turned and looked out at the deepening snow, seemed to be concentrating on something down the hill in the trees or thinking of some insoluble problem. The breeze died down, and once more the snow resumed its vertical velocity. Todd took a deep breath and shifted a bit, moving his legs so that they more comfortably supported him. Then he whispered, "Dad?"

Caldwell looked at him, mouthing the response, "What?"

Todd said, "When are we going to start hunting?"

His instant laughter echoed in the forest like a sudden cry for help. He couldn't stop laughing at first. He put his arm around the boy and said, "We're hunting now, you idiot." And then Todd was laughing, too.

Times like that did not seem real to him now. It was as if he read about them and didn't quite believe such things were possible. Still, thinking about them now, he almost laughed. The tears in his eyes seemed to forbid it, but he had long stopped weeping about it. His grief was now only a feature of life, like light, or air, or weather, a thing he woke to and lived with and went to sleep each night remembering. They had moved from the house where it all happened, and in their new house they gradually returned to the business of living. Nothing in the new house served to remind them of what their earlier life had come to. He made himself busy in life. During the long and fruitless fight to get Todd released, he resigned from the Fairfax County Police Department and took a job as a deputy sheriff in Dahlgren County—far south and east of Fairfax, a long way from the house where Bobby died. And at night, with the help of a few sips of whiskey, he usually fell asleep before too much of what happened came back to haunt him. In fine, the whole event had taken on the same character and emotional magnitude as the knowledge of his own mortality; it was a feature of his existence that he chose not to dwell on.

Now HE got out of bed and went to his suitcase, as if he were told to tend to it. He picked it up, put it on the bed, and in the yellow

light from the boardwalk below, he carefully opened it, laying all
the clothing out on the bed. He worked quietly, like a thief. There
was no bureau in the room, so he would have to stack all his underwear and T-shirts on the shelves in the closet. He draped two
suits over the chair.

From a small, black leather bag with a long strap, he retrieved
his gun—a .38 long-nosed revolver that he rarely loaded. He also
took out a glistening badge and a holster and belt that had a long
row of bullets on it. Under all that he found his sheriff's uniform—olive drab green, with a gold leaf cluster for one side of
his collar and an insignia that said "County Sheriff" in small gold
lettering, for the other. The belt was polished and perfect, as were
the shoes he wore. His slacks were dark brown, with a darker
brown stripe down the side of the leg.

When he was finished, he went to the little telephone stand,
turned the lamp on there, and sat down. He opened his laptop
and signed onto the Internet and saw that he'd already gotten an
e-mail from Laura.

> Dearest, I'm glad you're settled in. It's late and I didn't
> want to call in case I woke you up. But I want to say this
> to you. I wish you would just be ready to accept Todd with
> open arms. No matter what he has done, we love him and
> we know he must love us. You don't have to apologize to
> me about anything you say on the phone. I'm okay. I think
> we'll begin to miss each other again, and then the only
> thing that matters is bringing Todd back to me. That's
> what should matter to you. Even if he meant for it to hap-
> pen, we should still love him. Right? He says it was an ac-
> cident. I think it was. Imagine how he feels. Try to do that,
> dear. Imagine how Todd feels. Don't accuse him of any-
> thing. Just listen to him. See what he has to say.

That was it. No closing farewell or expression of love. No
postscript. He wrote back to her:

I'm going to listen to him. Of course. You don't have to keep repeating that to me. Everything we agreed on when I left is still

He stopped typing. Still what? It wasn't a contract. He couldn't say what they'd discussed was in force. He went on:

the same. I just hope he doesn't keep me waiting too long. I've got a job to do here, too. You know, it's very strange being back here. And I'm not talking about all the times we came down for vacation, either. I came down here on business once when I was in my first year as a deputy sheriff, shortly after we lost Bobby and they took Todd away from us. I had to arrest a big fellow for brandishing a firearm and threatening the lives of some folks in an office down here. Something over delinquent taxes. (You remember? I told you about it. The guy was a great big strong man, and I was so glad he was willing to go peacefully.) Anyway, I don't feel the same way now, seeing this place, our old vacation spot, as I did then. Back then it was so painful just being here again, I could hardly take in air. I think the big fellow I arrested thought I was about to cry because of his troubles. It doesn't bother me so much now, though. I'm going to be all right and I will get it right, dear. I promise. I'll try to call you tomorrow. I love you.

He went back to the suitcase, and withdrew from one of the pockets a brown envelope. He stood by the bed, holding the envelope as if he needed to figure out where to place it.

Outside, a car backfired. A young girl laughed, her voice echoing between the old wooden buildings along the street. He tried to think of youth and summer, of all the days he knew in his life without grief or pain. He could hear the wind blowing off the water.

He went over to the desk, placed the envelope there very gently, then turned off the light and found his way back to the bed. He didn't even push the suitcase off. He pulled the covers back and got in, sort of curled around the suitcase. He put his head under the pillow, closed his eyes, and without a drink or any other help, drifted into impatient sleep.

• • •

Todd arrived in Columbia Beach early the next morning. He was feeling apprehensive, as though he were advancing unarmed into some sort of hostile territory, but it was not harm he feared. It was being in his father's eyes before he was ready for it. He had been a free man for two years, and the way he felt, he had only been a man that long as well. For most of his childhood he had been locked up. That was how he tended to describe it. Locked up. During all that time, he had seen his mother and father only as well-dressed, polite visitors. They came to see him always as though they were dressed for church. They'd smile at everyone—even the other young inmates. In the summers, the three of them would walk out to the baseball field or stroll over the grounds toward the riding range. There were horses, stables, tennis courts. The Rockingham Juvenile Detention Center was intended to treat the whole individual—intellectually and physically. Each "resident" attended school six hours a day, exercised twice a day for thirty minutes, and was alotted two free hours each evening for recreation, and then one hour before bed for reflection and study. Caldwell once described it as "nothing more than a summer camp," and immediately apologized when he saw the look on Todd's face. "I sleep in a barracks with forty-four other guys," Todd said. "I can't leave or do anything on my own—I have to work all day in school and then . . . I can't leave the grounds. There are guards at every gate."

"I didn't mean it's easy being here," Caldwell said defensively.

A very tall fence surrounded the perimeter—even that part

of the complex that disappeared deeply into the trees. In the beginning of his sentence—for the first few months he was there—he could not see his parents, and all he did was dream of climbing over that fence. But once he was settled into a routine, he was allowed to have visitors on weekends. He rarely heard from his parents during the week. It was as if they could not store enough small talk for their visits if they called him or wrote to him. So he'd only dream of them, missing them, hoping they'd call. The following Sunday they'd arrive, quiet, respectful, smiling. They'd tell him briefly of their latest efforts in the legal process, of their hopes of getting him released into their custody. But the law was slow and costly. He had been tried and sentenced without a jury, a bench trial as it is called, at the family's own request. They had gotten the trial before the judge they had wanted, and at the advice of their lawyer they had requested first offender status for Todd. But the judge, Harvey H. Bass Jr., had decided, unreasonably according to their attorney, to go strictly according to state sentencing guidelines. Todd was sentenced to the youth facility until his eighteenth birthday—a period of almost seven years. The brief trial had been fair, so the attorney essentially attempted to get the court to reconsider such a harsh sentence. Judge Bass did not think the sentence was harsh. He thought it was just right and said so. "A boy's life was lost," he said. "I don't take that lightly."

On their weekly visits, sometimes Todd's parents would bring Terri, and she'd talk for a long time about things going on in school, about friends he might remember, and what they were up to. Eventually the room would fall awkwardly silent and they all avoided looking at each other. Todd would strive to get them started again by talking about what went on in his busy week of school work, chores, and the short periods of recreation time. He'd carry the conversations and sometimes they'd all get into it and then they'd relax a little, talking freely and openly with each other until the time came for them to leave. Then he would want to grab hold of his mother and never let go. He could sense their sadness, their awful hatred of the hurrying clock. No one ever said anything about what happened to Bobby. And eventually, when his parents hugged him and said goodbye—when finally his father took to shaking his hand and telling him to behave himself—he felt less and less abandoned. Over the years he gradually began to feel as if he had moved into an odd sort of adult life away from his family. But he loved them. That was the thing. And he knew he loved them. For a long time, whenever he thought of them he'd get this aching feeling in his throat and chest, and he'd have to sit down or find something to occupy his mind just to keep from breaking into tears.

But now Todd was free. That's what he told himself. And he could do or say or think almost anything he wanted. He could remember the littlest detail of almost every day, but he did not let himself think very often about what had happened when he was only eleven years old. That all seemed so long ago now. As the years went by, and as the visits from his parents became more and more difficult to look forward to, he realized that neither one of them knew anything at all about his life. He learned how to be away from home and didn't long for it so much anymore. As his release approached, he almost feared the outcome of returning home. When Caldwell called him to talk about what he was going to do and when they should come for him, he found himself telling his father that he didn't want them to pick him up.

"I want to be by myself for a while," he said. There was no response from the other end. "Are you still there?"

"I'm here."

"I'm going to need some time on my own, and I think I want to just take care of myself for a while."

"What will you do for money?"

"I get a hundred when I'm released, and I've saved a bit from the work here."

"Well, if you need anything . . . ," Caldwell's voice trailed off.

A part of Todd's soul seemed to sink. He did not want to hurt his father, but he could not face him—as a free man, outside, back in the world. He just knew he could not do that.

So he walked out of the detention center by himself. The day he was released seemed like a dream to him. He walked around the barracks, staring at the walls and the people—at the very tiles in the floor—and realized this was the end of something as well as a beginning. A part of him actually felt cast out—as if he would come to miss this place, come to regret leaving it. He stepped into the bright afternoon, a small duffel bag hoisted over his shoulder, and waited patiently for a bus that would take him to Richmond. It was May fourth, a Tuesday, one month after his eighteenth birthday. He took a deep breath and stared across the road to a white field that rose gradually away from him and high over a ridge in front of the prison. At the crest, in the distance, a stand of green trees, looking dark, almost black against the hay field, cast shadows and shifted slightly in the spring breezes. To his left the road dipped down out of sight then reappeared and wound away from him like curling smoke, around and behind a gray house—the home of the Youth Center Administrator—following along the edge of the field where a beaten fence appeared to stagger in the bright sun. It seemed to him that the road was his whole future, stretching out toward the blue rim of the sky and the ends of the earth. He felt propelled into this future—and not really free at all. He had been hurled into this day like an astronaut launched into space. Except he was not coming back. He would never come back.

He liked to believe that he was beginning to make a way for himself. Shortly after his release, he got a job working in the kitchen of a small French restaurant called Reneau's, in Richmond. Sometimes he prepared salads or peeled potatoes. The head chef liked him and began teaching him how to cook. Todd would not have said he was happy, but he was saving all the money he could so that he could quit his job and go to college. He didn't think of this as a vague, dreamy future idea. He put fully half his income away each month until he'd saved almost fifteen thousand dollars.

He finished high school in the detention center—"an outstanding student with a bright future," according to the program administrator who signed the graduate forms. He had grown tall and lean. He had short, very close-cut brown hair. He let a slight stubble grow under his chin—the beginning of a small beard. His arms were long and wiry, but he was very strong. In the detention center he had spent all of his recreation hours in the gym, trying to wear away time. He wore a tattoo of a rose on one forearm, and another of a shoehorn that gleamed like a blade on the other.

When he got to Richmond, that first day after he was released, he left the bus station and walked up the street a while until he saw a small diner. He went in, set his bag down next to a stool at the counter and ordered a cup of coffee—his first acquisition as a free man. When he paid the waitress and collected his change, he felt like he was in a movie. He sat on the stool and sipped his coffee, watching cars pass outside the window. He was doing things now he'd only seen in movies. He'd never purchased a cup of coffee in his life. Never paid for a meal in a restaurant. It was all new to him, and wondrous. When he was finished with the coffee, he went to a phone booth in the back corner, out of the light from the front windows, and called home.

"I just knew I'd hear from you today," his mother said.

"You did?"

"Your father and I were wondering what happened. We knew you must have been released after your birthday. I wish you would have let us come get you." He said nothing. "Where are you, son?"

"I'm in Richmond."

"Are you coming home?" Laura asked.

"No." His answer was quick and sure. It seemed to stun his mother into silence. "I'm going to get a job down here. I don't think I should come home, just yet."

"Why?"

"I've got to get used to being out . . ."

"You're free now, son. It's over."

"Yeah." But he didn't believe it.

"We can get past this."

"Mother," he said. "I'm already past it. I'm going on. I'll keep in touch." Again, silence on the other end. He couldn't tell if she was holding her breath in fearful apprehension that he might disappear out of her life forever, or if she was fighting tears, remembering all that had happened to them. "Tell Dad I said hey," he said.

How could he go home? He had done something to his family for which no one is ever forgiven, and he was certain he only served as a reminder of intolerable suffering and sorrow even in the face of willful attempts to deny it. "We can get past this," his mother had said. She had said it many times over the years, and he had no doubt she wanted to very much. He believed his mother loved him and worried over him, and he hated himself for knowing that and not being able to change it. He had heard from her many times in the two years since his release. She continued to send him occasional letters. The e-mails she sent to his Hotmail account had started to sound so similar he was tempted to stop reading them after a while. She always offered a kind of forgiveness in her notes, in her voice on the phone, but the act of forgiveness only brought it all back. They would never get past this thing that had happened, and he knew it.

DURING THE first months in juvenile detention, he almost always felt as though he was going to start crying. He resisted it all the time, as much as he could, but it was not easy. He would pretend to fall down, so he could claim an injury and then crying seemed at least understandable. He spent many hours alone, thinking about things and wishing he could have himself rescued, wishing his father would come and get him and take him to safety and back to the time before he had killed his younger brother. That's what he wanted more than anything, what he hoped for on many long, endless nights. He measured his life—the beginning of his manhood—based on the gradual decline of this hope, the gradual realization of his past as a thing he could never change; when you are eleven, then twelve, and after, you don't think like an adult. You don't appreciate the passage of time in the same way. He knew that now. He always thought he would wake up someday and the whole thing would go away, not be true.

But it was true. And it was permanent.

After a while during those early years in the Detention Center, he'd pray that his life was really only a test, something his mother and father and all the other adults in the world had cooked up to teach him a lesson. In his dreams he'd see them coming for him, his father with a stern smile and gentle hands, his mother looking at him with loving approval and understanding. "We just wanted to teach you a lesson about caring for and taking care of your younger brother," and then Bobby would be there, and Todd would say that he has learned his lesson and he won't ever let anything like that happen again. At first his young mind told him this was possible. He believed it with a kind of fury, but then belief dwindled with time and grew weaker and weaker until he gave it up entirely. He realized that when he did give it up, he had crossed a line; he had gone into something more like a kind of freedom—if only because he came to see he was becoming a man; he was growing into his crime and his guilt and this life he'd have to lead with his brother's blood on his hands.

THIS IS what Todd remembered most, and most often, about his father: long before Bobby's death, when Todd was only eight years old, he found the family dog—a yellow Lab named Buster—lying cold on a blue stone in the back yard. Todd had picked the name for the dog himself, and he had taken very good care of him, so he did not think he would ever get over finding him like that. This was his first experience of death and loss. Nobody knew what had happened, either. The dog was less than six years old, which is relatively young as Labrador retrievers go, and there he was, lying on the stone at the bottom of the back porch, his eyes staring blankly at the sky. Todd watched his father lift the dog up, carry him back to the end of the yard, and lay him down by the back fence. The dog's head dangled down over his father's arm and swayed as he walked. Todd stood by, sickened in his soul, tears running down his face, and watched his father climb over the fence and turn to look at him.

"Can you hand him to me?" Caldwell said.

"What?"

"Lift him up, son."

Todd stooped down and tried to get his hands under the dog. Buster was not dead for long so he was limp and heavy. It was almost impossible to pick him up—he felt like a sack full of water—and Todd couldn't get a grip on him. "Don't drop him," his Dad said. He leaned back over the fence, took the two front paws in both hands and hauled the dog up over the rail so he dangled there, one half on, the other off. "Push him over, son."

"It's hurting him," Todd said.

"He doesn't feel anything," Caldwell said, breathing heavy with the struggle of lifting the dog. "Come on, push him over." Todd grabbed the hind legs and heaved them up, and Caldwell got the whole thing in his arms. "Hand me that shovel," he said. Todd did so. "You stay here," Caldwell said, and then he carried the dog and the shovel back into the woods and out of sight. Todd waited by the fence. When his father came back, with dirt on his pants, he handed the boy the shovel and climbed back over the fence.

"Did you bury him?" Todd asked.

"Where's your little brother?" Caldwell said.

Later that night, talking about it, Todd felt himself getting ready to cry. "You think he got hit by a car?" he wondered.

"He probably got into some garbage that was bad," Caldwell said.

"I wish he was alive," Todd said. Bobby was crying too.

Caldwell knelt down and took both boys in his arms. "Listen, now," he said. "Listen to me." They quieted down. "This is something about life you have to learn, sooner or later." They said nothing. Bobby sniffed and wiped his nose with the sleeve of his jacket. "All things die eventually. That's part of life. So we will think of Buster from time to time, and maybe we'll get another Lab to replace him. But he's not suffering now."

"He's not?" Todd said.

"He feels nothing now. And he was lucky to have had you and your brother to keep and take care of him."

"I wish he wasn't dead," Todd said, fighting tears.

"He was a good dog, and he was happy here. Not much more you can ask out of life." Bobby was sniffling, his head leaning back on his father's arm. "I wish I could protect you from this kind of thing," Caldwell whispered. "But that's just not possible, and it probably wouldn't be right, either."

"It wouldn't be right?"

"It's the world, son. No use lying to you about it."

"I wish Buster wasn't dead," Todd cried. "Don't you?"

"I wish it too, son. I guess that's true enough. I wish it, too." He seemed to grow bigger, and he drew Todd and Bobby in against him. Todd was close enough to smell Bobby's hair, and the Old Spice cologne his father patted on his cheeks every morning after he shaved, and for a transient moment he almost grasped what this kind of thing meant to him: there was no place he would rather be than in the crook of his father's arm, watching his little brother gradually stop crying. That world, that remembered place, was his father's dominion, and Todd felt safe in it. Utterly safe. Many times over the lonesome years in the detention center, he would remember that time—fighting tears, his throat aching from the effort. It was all he had of his father before they lost Bobby and all he was ever going to get.

Now, if someone had asked him what he was doing here in Columbia Beach, his immediate answer would have been, "To see my father before he dies." That was really what moved him to tell his mother he wanted this meeting. When she told him his father was coming to Columbia Beach, and that they might eventually move down there, he felt something in his mind give way—as if a chord of harsh music had dropped out of his memory somehow and cleared space for a more lovely sound. He had been through two years of a gradually developing and capable routine—working in the hot kitchen at Reneau's and then going back to his attic apartment in a Richmond suburb and collapsing on the bed until the next morning, when he would get up, get dressed, and go through the same kind of day. He worked seven days a week. And he had finally saved enough to go to college. He told Mr. Reneau he was leaving at the end of the summer to begin school. He was not enrolled anywhere, but he felt sure he could be, when the time came.

And then, his mother e-mailed him about this town—the old place they all used to come to when he was a boy, and where he loved to swim until the moon rose. He called her right away, and when she had gotten over the shock of hearing his voice, when she had finished expressing her relief and gratitude for his call, he told her why he was calling. "I want to meet Dad at Columbia Beach." He blurted this out.

"What?"

"Tell Dad I want to meet him there. At the old hotel we always stayed at."

"Why don't you just come home?" Laura asked.

"Will he meet me?"

"Yes. I guess. I don't know. I'll have to ask him."

"I've saved a lot of money. I've got plans. But I want to talk to him."

"That's fine, but why do you have to talk to him down there?"

"Well he's going to be there, right? Maybe I can—," he stopped. "I just want to talk to him and tell him I'm sorry."

"He knows you're sorry, hon."

"Well. Maybe he'll forgive me this time," he said and immediately regretted it. "I didn't mean . . ."

"That's not fair."

"I know. I'm sorry."

"You know," she said, "you're the one who's dropped out of our lives."

He had no answer. He knew that it was always there, in plain sight for all of them, and he didn't want to talk about it.

"Honey?" she said. "You still there?"

"Yeah, I'm here."

"I'll tell your father."

"There's something I want to ask him."

"What?"

"I want to ask him in person." He realized as he spoke that this was true.

"What do you want to ask him?"

"I can't tell you that," he said. He thought maybe he could never tell her. He wanted to ask his father why he had not believed him.

So here he was, in the early morning mists near the river, looking for the old hotel in Columbia Beach. He had all the time in the world because he had quit his job at Reneau's early. His plan was to straighten things out with his father and then search out the best college in the state and apply for admission. He was a day late because it had taken all of his courage to finally get into his car and begin the drive that would take him here. That was how he did it. He got in the car and started driving and when he had driven long enough, far enough away from his apartment, he knew he would finally do this.

When he couldn't find the Hotel Grand, he had a moment of panic. But then he drove down to the end of the boardwalk and parked next to the Clary Hotel. It was easier for him to park his car and head for the lobby of the hotel because now the possibility existed that his father would not be there. The old hotel was gone, and there was no reason to expect that this place would be where he went. Todd could step up on the boardwalk and approach the front door of the hotel with quiet purpose, like any man looking for a place to rest.

iv

M cDole you got no reason to bitch," Mauldin said. "If you ask me, Cecil's got a point."

"What point?"

"If you knew what you was doing, you wouldn't have drained his gas tank, right?"

McDole looked insulted. "Why you taking Cecil's side?"

"I ain't taking anybody's side. I just said Cecil had a point."

"His truck had signs of water in the tank," McDole said. "How was I to know the electronic ignition behaves the same way when it goes bad? I've never seen the problem before."

"Folks been driving round with electronic ignitions for a long time. You never saw the problem?"

"No."

"Ain't it your job to know?"

"It's my job to know how to diagnose. You know what diagnostics is?" Mauldin just looked at him. It got quiet for a while, and they sipped their coffee. Mauldin took his glasses off and laid them on the table. He rubbed his face and eyes, not paying much attention to anyone. It was Friday morning, and they were sitting around a long oak table in the café that opened off the lobby of

Clary's hotel. They met there every morning to drink coffee and talk about the latest gossip in Columbia Beach, or Virginia politics, or car racing and various cars. Sometimes, in the right season, they talked about sports. "I would've gotten to the electronic ignition eventually," McDole said. "But since I've never seen one go bad, I figured it was smarter to start with water in the tank. That was my guess."

"Well," Mitch Hamlin said, apparently wanting to put an end to the conversation, "maybe Cecil figured he'd have to pay for something he didn't get."

"You're always defending him, Hamlin. Why is that?"

Clary said, "He sure doesn't need anybody to defend him." On this brightening October morning, the warm air reminded Clary of summer, and he did not want the conversation to get too deeply into McDole's problems with Cecil Edwards. There was a stranger sleeping upstairs who had rented his room, expecting to pay by the week.

Hamlin went on about how he was only being reasonable, and that he wasn't defending anyone. "I got a guest," Clary said.

"A guest," McDole said.

"That's right."

"So what?" said Mauldin. "There's always one or two families here this late in the season. And with this kind of weather, it'll probably be pretty crazy tonight."

"If this weather holds up we're gonna be pretty busy this whole weekend," Clary said. He leaned back in his chair and took a sip of his coffee. He had extremely high cheekbones—bulging, perfectly shaped spheres under each eye—so that if you didn't know him you would think he came from a long line of Indian stock. But his people were from Holland and had come to this country more than five generations ago—a fact Clary discovered when he lost himself for an entire winter studying his family's history. Genealogy had become an obsession with him for a while, and even Mauldin had to tell him that his family's history, though interesting to Clary himself, didn't necessarily translate into entertainment for everybody else.

"This new guest is alone," Clary went on. "And he's gonna be here a while. He asked for the weekly rates."

"He's by himself?" McDole said.

"So far. Says he's meeting his son here."

"What's he planning to do here in the cold weather?" asked Mauldin. "Did he tell you that?"

"He's going to be occupying an empty office in this town that we've always wished wasn't so empty."

"What do you mean?" McDole asked.

"I mean maybe your problems with Cecil Edwards are about to take a turn for the better."

McDole shook his head. "I swear, I wish you'd just come out and say it."

"We're going to have a new sheriff."

"You ever hear the joke about the sheriff that talked with a real southern accent?" Hamlin said. There was no response. "This sheriff comes into a bar where folks said somebody had fired a gun, and he says, 'All right. I wanna know who farred it. I know somebody farred it, I can smell it in heah.'" No one laughed. "Who farred it," Hamlin said. "Get it?"

McDole put both hands around his coffee cup and sighed. Mauldin gave a short laugh. "A sheriff in town. It's just what we need, ain't it?"

"He told you he was a sheriff?" Hamlin said. He was not as tall as the others, but he was not what you'd call short, either. His hair was wiry and red, and usually sat bunched up around where his hat band would be, if he wore a hat. He had a perfectly round bald spot in the middle of the top of his head—almost like a monk's cut, and as always he was puffing on a cigar. "A bona fide sheriff? How can he claim that? The only sheriff in this county is up in Dahlgren."

"He said he was here to set up an office for a couple of deputies. He's the Dahlgren County sheriff."

"Who is the county sheriff, anyway?" Mauldin asked.

"David Caldwell," Clary said.

"How do you know that?" McDole said. "I don't know who the damned sheriff is."

"He told me his name."

"Anybody ever hear of him?" Hamlin put in.

"Says he's gonna use the old sheriff's office. I guess that means he's going to be a kind of sheriff for a while, anyway. At least until he gets the deputies down here."

"Maybe one of us can be a deputy," Hamlin laughed.

"I don't think he's looking for a sidekick," Mauldin said. "He'll probably install a couple of police officers in here."

"Yeah," Clary said. "People with training."

"Ain't that much to do around here, even for a sheriff," Mauldin said.

"I told him that, and you know what he said?" The others waited for him to answer his own question. "He said, 'You got a problem here, right?'"

"He did?" McDole said.

"When he said that, I just thought of Cecil Edwards. I figured I knew exactly what he was talking about," Clary said.

Mauldin looked at McDole. "I never said nothing to anybody," McDole said.

"You didn't file a complaint up in Warsaw or Dahlgren?"

"No."

"Well maybe somebody else did," Hamlin said.

"I'm not the only one Cecil's pissed off over the years," McDole said. "Goddamn."

It was quiet for a long time. All of them seemed to be considering the possibilities. The sun began to leak over the windowsill, and the shadows in the room lengthened. Clary loved these gray, half-lit mornings, when his friends all gathered at the long table in the café for his coffee and a little conversation. Summer mornings were the best, but it was the same all year round. He loved going over his life in brief anecdotes and stories, laughing at

Hamlin's jokes, listening to petty grievances and small pains, the little humiliations that everyone found amusing. Finally McDole broke the silence, "Any coffee left in the pot?"

"No," Clary said. He got up and started for the kitchen behind the counter. He used the kitchen in there to do his cooking sometimes. Until recently Clary's wife, Judy, had been there, acting as a kind of reluctant waitress. She seemed to enjoy the banter between the four men, but lately she had not been attending. "You can get your own coffee," she said to Clary one morning.

He agreed that it was fair. "We none of us expected you to wait on us," he said.

"Well maybe you didn't, but some of them got to. And I don't feel like it."

"Fine."

The men missed her, and they told him to be sure to tell her that, but when he came back that night, she asked him if they had mentioned it and he said, "No, not a word."

"They didn't miss me?"

"They didn't say a thing."

So she stopped coming down in the mornings. She stayed in their permanent apartment on the top floor of the hotel and did a crossword or cleaned the linens or watched television while she manicured and painted her nails.

Now, before Clary got all the way back to the kitchen, McDole hollered, "Don't bother making any more coffee. I've got to get over and open the station."

"Maybe Cecil needs some more work done," Mauldin said.

Hamlin laughed. "Maybe he's over there now, just waiting for you to open up so he can make another purchase or two."

"You guys can laugh," McDole said. "Wait until he crosses one of you."

"I had a run-in with him once," Clary said.

"We've all heard about it." Mauldin put his cup on the table and pushed his chair back. He always wore blue work shirts and

Levi's, even in the heat of the summer. "I don't expect we need to hear about it again this morning," he said, getting to his feet. He lifted his jacket off the back of the chair and put it on. His tall, lean frame looked almost spiny in the shadowy morning sunlight.

"Maybe you'll believe it this time."

"I always believed it," McDole said.

"He didn't pull a gun or anything, but he turned over his breakfast plate right on top of a tourist's head." McDole got up, too. "That food was hot, I guarantee it," Clary continued. "Roast beef and potatoes."

"Nothing you ever cooked in here was hot," Mauldin said.

"Speaking of hot, did you hear the one about the doctor?"

"Not now, Hamlin," McDole said. Hamlin was clearly determined to do better than he had earlier with the one about the southern sheriff. It bothered McDole, though, that Hamlin seemed interested in joining the group only to tell jokes; he didn't seem able to carry on a normal conversation.

"Go ahead, if you have to," Mauldin told him.

Hamlin went on, without looking at him. "This doctor sits a guy down in his office and says, 'I've got good news and bad news, what do you want to hear first?'" Everyone watched him, waiting patiently. "The guy says, 'Hell, tell me the bad news first, Doc. I can take it.' So the Doc says, 'You got a bad aneurysm near your heart on your aorta and it could burst any minute. There's nothing medical science can do for you. It'll probably kill you within the week. I'm sorry.' And the guy starts crying and carrying on, and then he remembers that the Doc said he had good news, too, so he says, 'Wait Doc. Didn't you say you had some good news, too?' And the Doc says, 'Oh, yeah. Did you see that tall, blond, hot-looking nurse out in the reception room when you came in here?' and the guy says, 'Yeah, what about her?' The Doc nudges him and whispers, 'I'm dickin' her regular.'"

Everyone laughed. Even McDole.

"That's a good one," Clary said. McDole moved toward the door. "Where you going?" he asked.

"I got to open the station."

Mauldin shrugged. "I thought I'd open the gallery, sit around." In spite of his leanness, a small portion of his belly hung over his belt like a thick, melting thing. The black hair on the side of his head was bristled, and twisted from the hat he wore. Five years ago his wife died, and for a long time he did not think he would be able to go on living without her. He, too, had spent time trying to get Comstock to understand that he was bereaved and not able to think about his taxes. Mauldin approved of Cecil Edwards' little foray into the assessment office the minute McDole told him the story. It didn't matter that Cecil had gotten much worse since then.

"Nobody's even up yet, Mauldin," Clary said. "You won't have any customers."

"I know. I just don't feel like hanging around here this morning."

"Maybe I'll come over to the gallery," Clary said.

"Suit yourself." Mauldin went out the door behind Hamlin and McDole.

Clary sat at the table for a while, watching the sun creep into the front window. It would be an empty sky today, with a bare sun overhead refusing to admit the change in seasons. It would almost be hot outside, except the slightest breeze would bring a hint of cool air and blustery winds—the real October. He thought about the movement of the sun—a circle of time and change he almost never noticed until recently. He was not the kind of man to think very much about his life. He liked to say he just lived it; he went into each day as if it were a supermarket and he would know, as he passed down the aisles, what he wanted out of it. But lately he found himself thinking about his age. He would not have said he was bored—or perhaps he would not have admitted it. He did not want Hamlin, McDole, and Mauldin to leave the hotel this morning. He knew it was only the end of another coffee session with his friends, a way of marking the passage of another day. It would be the same tomorrow.

Still, when he could see the sun burning in the middle of the frame of the front window, he got up and cleared the table. Then he went to the counter, sat on a tall stool back there, and stared at the telephone. In front of him were pads of paper, some pencils, and the morning paper. He read the headline, "World Braces for Y2K."

November, he thought. It's already almost November.

He walked across the lobby and took the elevator to the top floor. His apartment smelled of tea. In the living room, sitting in front of the TV, the sound turned all the way down, was Judy, doing a crossword puzzle. "Finished with the morning coffee klatch?" she said.

He didn't answer her. He stood by the door for a moment, looking at her, then he went in and sat down in one of the soft chairs situated in front of a sliding-glass door and looked out over the water. He rested his arms on the sides of the chair and stretched his legs out.

"What's a four-letter word for witticism?" Judy said.

"Joke."

"Of course," she said. "Why couldn't I think of that?"

It was quiet for a long time. He looked at the clock on the wall above the TV and saw that it was exactly nine o'clock. "You know we got a guest?" he said.

She looked at him. "We do?"

"Checked in last night." She said nothing. "One guy, by himself. He asked me for the weekly rates."

"What'd you charge him?"

"Two hundred dollars."

"That's all?"

"It's better than not having anybody stay," he said. "He could go to a motel up on the highway. I was glad he took it."

She shook her head. "Still my fair-minded man."

He smiled. At one time, words like that from her made him feel like the most important person in the world, but lately something in her tone made him feel as if she was accusing him of some failure touching both of them. He never said anything to her about it because it was only how he felt, and he couldn't really trust that his feeling was accurate. But he inwardly squirmed when she praised him now. Sometimes he thought she might be having a joke at his expense, laughing at him because of inadequacies in himself he could not fathom.

"Anyway," he said. "If I charged him the going rate, he would have just gone up the street."

"Well," she sighed. "We'll never know, will we?" He stared out the window. The water looked flat and calm—almost like ice. "What's a seven letter word, beginning with *L* and ending with *WN*, that means disappointment?" she asked.

"I don't know."

"Come on. Seven letters."

"Are you trying to tell me something?"

"What?"

"You know."

"No. I don't. What on earth do you mean?" She put the paper down in her lap and looked at him. Her glasses, perched on the end of her nose, made it necessary for her to tilt her head back to see him. "What would I be trying to tell you?"

"Nothing," he said. He got up and went into the small kitchen on the other side of the room. "Is there any more coffee?"

"Didn't you just drink a gallon of it downstairs?"

"Yeah," he said. "You're right."

"Are you quite all right, dear?"

"I guess I'll go down and watch the front desk."

She pushed her glasses back on her nose and went back to her puzzle.

"The word you're looking for is 'letdown,'" he said.

"What room did you put our guest in?" She was still studying the folded paper in her lap.

"Four-fifteen."

"I'll be sure and take care of it today. Would you let me know when he goes out?"

"Sure." He drank a glass of cold water, left the apartment, and went back down to the lobby. At the front desk, he picked up the phone. He sat there for a moment, holding the receiver against his ear. For some reason, he felt a cold draft in his stomach—a vague, tremulous sensation almost like fear. Then he dialed the number 415.

"Hello," a voice said.

"Mr. Caldwell?" he said.

"Yes." Caldwell sounded groggy.

"I wondered if you left a wake-up call?"

"What?"

"Did you want me to wake you at any hour?"

"I'm awake now," he groaned.

"I see. I'm sorry."

"Yeah, well."

"I couldn't remember if you told me a time. That's all."

"I didn't tell you anything."

"Well, that's good, then."

"What time is it?"

"It's a bit after nine, sir."

"I didn't want to be wakened."

"Since you're awake, would you like me to make you some coffee, or maybe some breakfast?"

"I don't want anything."

"I was just trying to . . ."

"It was thoughtful of you," Caldwell said. Then he was gone.

Clary sat there looking at the phone for a moment. Then he put it back on the receiver and folded his arms in front of himself on the counter. "What kind of man sleeps the whole day?" he muttered. He picked up the newspaper and went back into the office. "Well," he said out loud. "Guess I better get going on this day." He sat down in a big stuffed office chair that squeaked whenever he turned himself in it and pulled himself up to the desk. He spread the newspaper out in front of him. He turned the pages until he found the crossword puzzle. He picked up a pencil and leaned forward in the light from his desk lamp. He looked like a man getting ready to do some very crucial work.

v

Lindsey chose the name Hunter because she was in search of something most people don't ever have to seek, and she believed she would have to look for a long time. Maybe the rest of her life.

She was not the sort of young woman who injudiciously expressed romantic notions about the world, but still, she wanted to approach life unswervingly, leaning forward in the currents as one leans into a strong wind—determined to weather the coming days of her long future with a strong sense of life's mystery and its possibilities. She was in love with books. She wrote the name Lindsey Hunter on the front flap of all her newest books, although she could not take the time to do that with the whole collection. She had more books than anyone she knew—history books, novels, story collections, plays, books about art and folklore, about famous people, and great wars. Each new book she got was like a small, discovered fortune, a sort of old trunk or treasure chest that she would open carefully, turning the cover back to see what secret correspondence might be hidden in its crisp new pages. But she almost never finished any of them. She carried books with her when she went to the beach and looked forward to getting back to them when she was busy doing something else. She would read three or four books at once, taking the time every day to read at least twenty pages in each one. But before she finished any of them, she'd see new books she wanted to read and she'd get one or two of those, and eventually the ones she had begun would end up on a shelf in her room, little pieces of paper still marking where she had stopped reading. She always made sure she was reading at least one novel, one book of poems, one history book, one book of short stories, and then what she called a "free subject" book—which might be anything: a true crime story, a biography, a study of the Supreme Court, or even a collection of the best essays of the twentieth century. She did not think about the fact that she rarely finished a book—each volume was a kind of relationship to her; you couldn't be done with it if you never finished it. She kept a bookmark in each one of them because she believed at some point in her long life she'd get back to them.

When she came to Columbia Beach two years ago, she was twenty-one years old and completely alone. She was finished with men. And she had a purpose.

She did not want to go back to school, or do any traditional thing until she looked into the eyes of her real mother. She had been adopted and she knew it, yet she loved her adoptive mother and called her Mom. But she wanted to see and talk to the woman who had borne her. The people of Columbia Beach wondered about her. It pleased her to think so. She did not seem to need money, but she did eventually go to work for the gas company.

If they had known—if Mauldin, or Clary, or McDole, or Hamlin, or any of the permanent residents of the town had known her real reason for being there—she would not have seemed so mysterious. She lived alone because she preferred it that way.

Lindsey's adoptive mother, Alicia, lost her husband three years after they adopted Lindsey, and she had raised the little girl all by herself and made no apologies to anyone about having given her a fatherless life in the suburbs. But once her daughter was full grown, once Lindsey made it clear she was moving out to "get started on life," as she put it, Alicia decided to move back to Cleveland, where her mother and father still lived. She would get a new start herself. This was at the beginning of the first summer that Lindsey came to Columbia Beach. The adoption agency that provided the real name of her biological mother had listed Columbia Beach as her last known address.

"I'm just staying the summer," Lindsey told her adoptive mother that first year. "I can take care of myself."

"I know you can," Alicia said. "I taught you to do it."

"Maybe eventually I'll find a job down there."

"If that's what you want." They were sitting in their small living room, brown boxes piled in all the corners, clothes lying like bodies on the top of them.

"And if you find your mother," Alicia said. "What then?"

"I just want to know her. She's not my mother. You are." Alicia was quiet, looking at the boxes. "I won't let her replace you," Lindsey said.

"I know you won't. Or you won't intend to."

"I won't."

"You've heard what they say about blood," Alicia said.

"Mom," Lindsey groaned, "I told you I just want to know her. I'm not looking for a mother. I have one." Alicia smiled, but her eyes were glistening and looked like they might any minute brim with tears. "You'd do the same thing if you were me," Lindsey said.

"Yes, I probably would."

It was quiet for a while, and they looked at each other. Then Alicia said, "You know, honey, when you're young it's easy to think you can manage everything—"

"I've heard this speech before," Lindsey broke in.

At the same time, Alicia said, "—but you really can't."

"I can manage my own affairs," Lindsey said. "I'm over twenty-one."

"And I wonder if you've thought about the ways you have let men—," she stopped.

"Go on, say it."

"You know."

"No. Say it."

"I just wonder sometimes if you haven't been—if you aren't easily manipulated by men."

"No. I'm not easily manipulated."

Alicia shook her head, slowly. "I'm sorry. I didn't mean that the way it sounded."

"How else can a person mean something like that?"

"Honey, I don't know. I just feel bad for you. For your . . ." Lindsey waited. "I know you've been hurt."

"I'm not lucky, Mom. That's all. It's not that I'm stupid."

"No. I didn't say you were."

"I'm finished with men for a long time, you'll be glad to know."

Her mother smiled. "Yes, so you've said." She was a thin, short, self-possessed woman with steel-gray hair and brown, tear-drop plastic glasses. She wore a business suit and high-heeled shoes. It was clear that at one time she had been very striking. Of course Lindsey did not resemble her at all. Her eyes were not dark brown and she was a full head taller. Her limbs were long and heavy boned, though she believed she was thin enough. Her skin was smooth and tan, even in the wintertime. During the summer she got very dark and mysterious looking. Her face was narrow, and from certain angles her nose looked to be a bit too pointed, perhaps a shade too long. She had small ears that she covered with her light brown, almost dirty blond hair. The dark shaded area under her jaw was especially alluring, particularly when she wore white pearl earrings or bright gold ones. She was aware of how it looked when the earrings dangled in that dark shadow, and she took advantage of it when she wanted to look her best.

"I know about permanence and change," Lindsey said. "I don't expect the world owes me a thing."

This had been one of her adoptive mother's favorite topics—the need to understand the world's indifference and how so many adults remained in a kind of adolescent trance because they never did. "So many adults believe the world is about their own happiness," her mother would say. "And when happiness is thwarted, it's always somebody else's fault. Such people think the world owes them a living." She was right, of course. Lindsey had her own tales to tell about the adolescent adults she had already known who blamed their failures on everything else in the world except themselves; and failure was what they seemed to covet and court every day of their lives. These people, mostly men, never had enough money, never had enough luck, never had enough of anything but smallness of spirit, envy, and a kind of artistic bitterness that passed for critical awareness.

In fact, both of the men on whom Lindsey had lavished her affections and her beliefs had turned out to be this sort—grown little boys who ranted at the world for its unfairness. The first, a sleek and rebellious motorcycle enthusiast named Brad, had taken to slapping her if she expressed the slightest disregard for anything he valued. She was only with him for a few months, and when she broke off the relationship, he blamed her mother. "Your mother doesn't like me," he said. "No," Lindsey said. "I don't like you. I don't."

The other adolescent man in her life was an older, seemingly more mature sophomore at the University of Maryland named Henry, who one day, quite without warning or notice, moved to Portland, Oregon. He did not say goodbye. He simply dropped out of college and vanished for a while, then he sent her a card from Portland. He wrote on the card that he needed to find his "primal self" and that he hoped she would discover what she wanted out of life. He signed the card, "Have peace. *H*." Lindsey immediately sent him a reply in which she said what she wanted out of life was not to ever see him again, if she could help it. She glued three baby green peas at the end of the note, and under them she wrote, "Have peas. *L*."

Alicia's own husband had some of the same adolescent characteristics. She was quite certain that he would have blamed his own death on the absurd requirement that to lower his cholesterol, it was necessary to stick rather assiduously to a strict diet and a firm regimen of exercise and medication. His attitude was, "No one I know has to do this. Why do I?" It wasn't fair to him, and he was childish enough to believe the world ought to be fair. Especially to him.

Of course he wasn't quite as bad as many of the other elder children Alicia had known, or the two men in Lindsey's life, but it hurt her sometimes to think of how much he needed to grow up when he died. She never talked to Lindsey about him, nor did she use him as an example of immaturity, but she frequently had him in mind when she broached the subject.

"I'm not going to lecture you about the world," she said to Lindsey that day she was packing to go to Columbia Beach for the first time.

"Just wish me luck. Why don't you do that?"

"You know I wish you the best of luck, dear."

Lindsey smiled. "And I'll be Lindsey Hunter."

"Yes. Hunter." Alicia took a long, deep breath.

"It's not that I don't like Jensen," Lindsey said. "Why can't you understand this?"

"I do." Alicia seemed unable to look directly at her. "We've been all over the name, dear. It's okay."

"If I met somebody and got married I'd lose the name anyway."

Alicia nodded, smiling. "We fought that battle. You won. Remember?"

Lindsey sighed. "It wasn't a battle."

"Whatever, dear," Alicia said. "Just remember to let me know when you change it again, so I can keep track of you." She snapped open her purse and withdrew a pack of cigarettes. When she had smoked for a while, both of them sitting in silence among the boxes, Lindsey said, "I will never be anything but your daughter."

"You were always a willful child." Alicia's voice had changed. She said it with true affection.

"I'm going to find my mother."

"I hope she's worth the effort, honey."

"I don't really have expectations, so I won't be thinking about what it's worth."

"She never cared about you. Never even saw you."

"Well now she's going to see me."

"Do you know where to look?"

"I don't know a lot," Lindsey said. She got up and went into the kitchen, came back out with an ashtray. "The folks at the adoption agency seemed to think it wouldn't be too hard. Columbia Beach isn't that big a place. She ought to be easy to find."

"And you won't call her first, or write to her?"

"Everybody keeps telling me that's what I should do."

"It's probably the right thing to do. That's why."

"I've dreamed about how I would do this," Lindsey said. "I want to just knock on her door."

"Well, be prepared for a shock."

"I will."

"Just because you've imagined it a particular way, doesn't mean it will turn out that way . . ."

"I know, Mother."

Alicia smiled. "Seems odd to hear you call me that now—when you consider what we're talking about."

"I'm prepared for her to deny she even knows who I am."

"But you'll convince her."

Lindsey shrugged. "I don't know. I haven't imagined much beyond when she opens the door and sees me standing on her doorstep."

So Lindsey came to Columbia Beach. It did not take her long to find her way to Cecil Edwards' trailer. She asked McDole, her first day in the town, if he knew of a woman named Cora Edwards.

"Sure do," McDole said. "Used to run the Ferris wheel."

"She doesn't run it now?"

"Nope," McDole said. "The thing hardly runs at all now except in the summer."

"Who runs it now?"

"You don't want to know that fellow."

"I don't suppose you know where Cora Edwards lives now, do you?"

"Only one family ever owned the wheel," McDole said. "Cora Edwards and her boy ran it."

"Are they still around?"

"Cora died a long time ago, but the boy's still here. Only he ain't no boy no more."

"She died?" Lindsey said.

McDole looked at her. "What's the matter?"

She didn't know what to say to him. She looked off into the high white clouds that hovered over the blue water.

"Are you all right, miss?" he asked.

She looked at him. "She died?"

"I'm sorry. You didn't know?"

She shook her head. Now she had the whole wide future in front of her and it was suddenly empty—she had no idea what she wanted to do, or even where she might suddenly decide to go. Her whole immediate future had been stolen before she could even begin to realize it.

"Cecil's still living in the trailer there," McDole said.

"Who?"

"Her son. Cecil."

"That's his name?"

"That's it." She said nothing. "What you want with Cora?"

"Nothing."

McDole said, "Look, miss. Cecil Edwards is the meanest cuss I've ever known. You don't want no part of him."

"Is that so?"

"I'm telling you, miss. You'd do better to stay away from him."

"Thanks for the advice."

"I mean it."

"Where'd you say he lives?"

"He's in the trailer." McDole was leaning down next to Lindsey's yellow Cavalier, looking through the half-open window. "Go to the Ferris wheel, make a left next to it. At the far corner of the property, there's a trailer."

"Okay," she said.

"You can't miss it."

"Thank you." Lindsey started to roll up her window.

"Need any gas?" McDole said.

"Not now. Thanks." She went out of McDole's station slowly, as if the fact that she was thinking, scheming what to do next, made her car seem to be thinking too, as if the two of them were concentrating too much to pay much attention to the road. She drifted out into the street, stopped momentarily, then turned toward the Ferris wheel. She decided she would go to Cecil Edwards' trailer and look upon her brother. It never occurred to her that he wouldn't believe she was any relation to him at all.

• • •

In fact, Cecil closed the door on her. She said, "I think I'm your little sister," and he made this sound in the back of his throat, almost a laugh, and simply closed the door. She waited on the small lower step of the trailer, her hands shaking so badly she thought she could see the trailer move. She didn't know what to do, so she stood there, staring at the small blue door. After a while, she knocked again.

The door opened, and Cecil stepped out. "What do you want?"

She could not believe how big he was. It was clear that he had begun to put on weight in all the wrong places, but even without the extra weight he was huge—the great stomach and chest, the arms bulging out of his short sleeves like heavy, naked animals—he looked almost like an oversized version of the human form. He had bristled black and silver hair loosely piled across the top. His brow looked like it was formed from some sort of heated rock. She noticed a thin, untrimmed beard, darker than his hair but still invaded by occasional gray strands. He loomed over her, blocking out the blue sky and the trees beyond the trailer.

"I don't want anything," she said. She was surprised by the resolve in her voice. "I only know what I don't want." Cecil laughed. It was not a real laugh, but a kind of response that excused him from speaking. Lindsey said, "Your mama was Cora Edwards?"

He looked at her. "She's been gone a long time."

"She's my mama, too."

"Really."

"She put me up for adoption twenty-one years ago."

"She's been dead for five."

"You don't remember her when she—you were here, weren't you? Twenty-one years ago?"

"I don't know what you're talking about." He started to open the door and go back in.

"Were you here?" Lindsey said.

"I was in the Marines. Two years."

"So I guess I happened when you were gone."

"I guess you did."

They stared at each other. Lindsey thought she saw his eyes soften momentarily, but then he seemed to remember something and his visage began to freeze against her. "How do I know anything you say is true?" he said.

"Why would I lie about it?" He shrugged. "It's not like I'm looking for any inheritance." Now he smiled. "I'm your sister," she said. "And now that I know that, maybe you can help me figure out who my father was."

"Get out," he said waving his arm. "Just get out of here."

"I don't have anyplace to go right now."

"Just go on," he said. "Get out."

"I'm not going anywhere," she said.

"Well I am." He hesitated briefly, then he opened the blue door on the trailer, stepped inside, and closed it. She was still standing on the bottom step, looking up.

OF COURSE Lindsey went back the next day. When she knocked on the door, Cecil opened it right away, almost as if he had been waiting inside listening for the sound of her knuckles on the cast aluminum surface. He leaned on the door handle, stared at her with a slight turn of his mouth that suggested he might actually let a smile cross his face. "Shit," he said. "Come on in."

She could not find a place to sit down in the clutter. The trailer was small and seemed smaller when Cecil moved around in it. Newspapers littered every surface, even the small white kitchen counter.

"You read a lot of newspapers," Lindsey said. She felt vaguely embarrassed; she did not know what she should say to him or what he may have planned to say to her. She was afraid if she said the wrong thing she would anger him and ruin everything, although if someone had asked her what might be ruined, she couldn't have said. She was glad Alicia wasn't there to ask her what she was expecting. She was glad she didn't have to explain to anyone what she was doing there.

Cecil stood next to a tall thin refrigerator that rested next to the counter. Near the sink—a miniature silver thing with a tiny drain—there was a wafer of a table, which folded up against the wall. He would have to let the table down soon if he was going to collect any more newspapers.

"I only read the legal notices," he said.

"Can I sit down?"

He moved some newspapers off a small chair that sat in front of a fairly large TV. A metal tray next to the chair leaned over slightly—as though it had been asked to bear too much weight. An empty cup with coffee stains all over it teetered on the edge of the tray, and under that, a stack of comics from the newspapers.

Lindsey tried to smile but her stomach seemed to tremble, and she realized she was nervous again—truly afraid. She remembered what McDole had said, but she did not really fear harm. She feared the silence, the absence of words in front of this man who was at least half brother to her.

"I guess I'm nervous," she said.

Cecil didn't move. He watched her as if he were waiting for some crucial mistake—a little fissure in her behavior that would destroy her apparent composure and reveal her true motives. She imagined that he had expected her to come back. She believed he must have discovered an interest in her that morning, and that he almost hoped she would return. And now, here she was.

"Are you nervous?" she asked. She seated herself in the chair. Across from her was a long, thin couch. Cecil shook his head, a slight, almost unconscious movement. "I could clean up this mess," she said.

"If I wanted it cleaned up, I'd do it."

She looked out the rectangular window next to where she was sitting. Dead flies lay in the thin track of the screen. Outside, she noticed a renegade breeze pushing the tops of the trees. "Maybe it'll cool off today," she said.

"What do you want?"

"I like it cool, don't you?"

"What do you want?"

"I guess I don't know what I want."

"I don't have any money."

"I got money."

"You do?" Cecil seemed to rouse himself from a kind of drowsiness. "How much money you got?"

"Enough to last me the summer." She had worked in Fairfax, at a private school, during the school year. It had been a temporary job, but she lived at home with Alicia, so she could save most of the money she earned.

He straightened, crossed his arms in front. "Where'd you get money?"

"I worked all winter for it."

He shook his head, still looking hard at her. Then he said, "Shit. I got that kind of money."

"What?"

"I got money like that."

"Like what?"

"It ain't rich money. It's just enough to get by. That's what you're talking about, right?" He still had not moved from where he stood by the refrigerator.

"I guess."

"When folks say they got money, they mean lots of it. More than they can spend."

"That's not what I mean when I say that."

"Well." He looked away now.

It was quiet for a long time. She watched him fumble a bit with the buttons on his shirt, then he moved to the couch, made room for himself, and sat down. When he looked at her she said, "I really could clean this place up pretty nice."

"You ain't living here," he said.

"I don't want to live here. I'm renting a room in town."

"Where?"

"Well, I'm at the motel now, but I've got an appointment this afternoon to see a room."

"Good for you."

"You know Mrs. McCutcheon?"

"Yeah, I know her. Clapboard house up the hill from here— a few blocks from the beach."

"She's got a room on the second floor of her house—it's got a kitchen and a bath and . . ." He stared at her, and it fell silent again. She reached into her purse, searching for a cigarette. "I mean if you have a brother, you can't just forget about it," she said. "So that's that."

"Why can't you?"

"It's family. Isn't family important to you?"

"We're both orphans." She looked at him. "Ain't that the end of it?" he said.

"I don't know what you mean."

"You married?"

"No. I'm only twenty-one. I'll be twenty-two this month."

"You got any other kin?"

"My mom—," she stopped. "I'm adopted. But my father died when I was very young. My mom lives in Cleveland. She just moved there, actually. She's not really a blood relative, but she's the only family I got besides you."

"You ain't got me."

"Well, you're kin," she insisted.

"That's what you say."

"It's true. If Cora was your mom, she was my mother too."

"Well, but what difference does it make?" He raised his arms slightly, as if to rest them on armrests, but there was nothing to hold them. He folded them across his belly and looked at her. "We're both grown now. I ain't got money. You ain't got money. There ain't nothing to divide. I ain't letting you have any part of this here wheel. And I don't have to, neither. It's rightfully mine."

"I don't want any part of the wheel."

"We don't need to be hounding each other about nothing. So what's the point?"

"We're brother and sister."

He nodded. Then he said, "So?"

She shrugged, but she looked at him as though this was something he should understand. All she could say was, "Family."

He shook his head, and let a smirk cross his face. "Family," he said.

"I'm supposed to care about you and you're supposed to care about me."

"And that's what this is?"

"Not yet."

"It ain't automatic."

"I know that."

"What if I told you I don't want to be nobody's brother?"

"I'm not just anybody."

"Whoever you are."

"Lindsey. I'm Lindsey, and I'm your sister."

"That don't make me a brother." He raised himself up with some difficulty and moved to the other side of the trailer by the door. She felt the whole room shift.

"I never really had a brother or a sister," she said. "So I don't know how to do it." She lit her cigarette, watched him swing the door open. She said, "You want me to leave now?"

"For the smoke," he said.

"I'm sorry." She looked for a place to put the cigarette out.

"Use the sink for your ashes," he said. "That's what I do."

"Does the smoke bother you?"

He put his foot on the top step of the trailer and sat in the sunlight of the doorway. He made a loud grunt when he sat down, and she noticed drops of sweat running down the side of his face. "I don't care if you smoke," he said. "I can't breathe in any kind of air."

They were silent for what seemed like a long time. Cecil stared out the door, his face as empty as a desert landscape, his eyes unblinking, apparently seeing nothing. Lindsey smoked her cigarette, feeling a little more at ease. She was almost glad that he had said that about his breathing; he did not seem the kind of man who told strangers about his private ills. She told herself it didn't matter that he was not at all what she expected. He was her brother, and no one ever really had a choice in such things. She watched him, studying the way his hair barely touched the top of his ears, the way his brows moved as he gazed out toward the water and the huge Ferris wheel in the distance. She tried to imagine him when he was just a boy, full of reckless purpose and proud of his strength, a wild youth, with black hair and light blue eyes, in the bright lights of this carnival town.

When she finished the cigarette, she got up, put it in the sink, and ran tap water over it to put it out. Cecil turned, looking at her as if he'd just asked her a question, then he got up and seemed to struggle to the sink. He was very near her when he reached in and picked up the cigarette butt. "I wasn't going to leave it there," she said.

"Look," he said. "I don't have nothing. I run that goddamned wheel all summer and I can barely keep up with the taxes on this property." He gestured with the cigarette butt as he talked. Then he opened a small door under the sink and threw it in a can under there. He almost slammed the door closed. He looked into her eyes and seemed disappointed that he could not read a response. She waited for him to finish. "I ain't got nothing else to say," he told her.

"I have a pretty good job during the school year," she said. "I work in a school. I mean, it's temporary and all, but they asked me back for next year."

"I haven't worked a steady job ever in my life."

"How old are you?"

This exasperated him. "What?"

"How old . . ."

"I heard you. What do you care?"

"I just want to know."

He shook his head. She liked his face. If she could have put into words the reason that she did not simply open the door and drop down out of that trailer and disappear from his life altogether, it was that she liked his face. She imagined that he must have noticed something that he always saw in his mother's gaze, or perhaps it was the way she looked directly at him, without averting her eyes, but something made his face soften whenever he looked at her. And his eyes were so blue they seemed to have the vast depth of a northern sky.

"You're big enough to just throw me out. You could have done that a long time ago," she said. "Why didn't you?" He looked away. She pressed on. "Really. Why didn't you just throw me out?"

"You want me to throw you out?" She said nothing. He shrugged, averting his eyes. "You look a little like my mother," he said.

"I'd like very much to see a picture of her." She smiled, but his expression didn't change, so she straightened herself a bit and sat back down. "Sometime. If you don't mind."

"I guess that's why I didn't just slam the door in your face yesterday."

"How old are you?" she asked again. "I told you how old I am."

"I'm forty-seven," he said. It was quiet for a moment, then he moved to the couch and sat down. "I work construction sometimes. I do odd jobs I'm not even trained for. I drink too much, I smoke too much, I've got asthma, and everyone in this town is afraid of me."

She looked at him, noticing the faint odor of hair oil mixed with sweat. She thought he would not like it if she said anything, so she crossed her arms in front of her and adjusted herself in the chair to let him see she was willing to listen.

"I take what I need, and nobody has the nerve to stop me. I don't let any bastard get the best of me." He leaned forward, staring directly into her eyes. "I come and go as I please, and I don't give a damn about nothing or nobody. You tell me what you want with somebody like that."

"I don't." He nodded, sat back. "I don't want—," she stopped. "I don't want anything at all."

"Heh." He almost smiled. "I just told you all there is to know ..."

"You don't want to know about me?"

Again, something in his face softened, but he said, "No, I don't want to know about you."

She looked away from him. "Well, I guess I'm not nervous anymore." She was just coming to realize that she was absolutely calm now, and this seemed to give her strength. She turned back to him. "Are you?"

"I ain't never nervous."

"You don't want a sister, I can see that." She was almost laughing with this. Her voice was bright with promise, but there was a kind of sadness in her heart as she spoke, and she thought perhaps he noticed it. Her voice echoed in her memory like a mournful song thrown to the wind. She just went on and on, afraid to fall silent. "I mean, if you don't want a sister, you don't have to have one I guess. But I am your sister. That's just biology and all. I am your sister. Or your half sister I guess. And you're my half brother, and don't two halves make a whole?" Now she felt foolish under the gaze of his serious eyes.

"Jesus," he said.

"I mean . . ." She could not think of another thing to say.

"What the fuck," he said. "What do you want?"

She was puzzled, but she shook her head briefly, looking in his eyes, and then she said, "Nothing."

"Nothing?"

"Maybe to visit once in a while."

He looked at her, sweat running down the side of his face. It was quiet again. She did not turn her gaze from his. "So that's what you want," he said.

"I guess so. Yes."

"You want to visit once in a while."

"I don't know what else I should want. I never had a brother or sister, either." Now he let himself back a little in the cushion of the couch, smiling. "Maybe we should have dinner some time. I'm a good cook."

"I like to eat."

She laughed, briefly—just three small notes.

He was still smiling. "Look, lady," he said, letting a frown come back to his face. "I never needed nobody. Not ever."

"I don't have to take care of you." He shook his head slowly as she spoke. "And you don't have to take care of me, either." Suddenly she felt strong, like she was speaking to her brother and no longer had to fear silence or the wrong word or even saying good night and leaving the trailer. "You know," she said. "All the years you've been here, and I lived only ninety miles away."

"Where's that?"

"Fairfax." She smiled. "Did you ever know about me?"

"No."

It was an admission of a kind, and she knew it. He believed her now, and this made her very nearly ecstatic. She rose to her feet and held out her hand. "Glad to meet you," she said. "I'm Lindsey Hunter."

He looked up at her, then got to his feet and took her hand. "Yeah, yeah." He was not smiling, except with his eyes. He looked as though he was perplexed by a problem that was nonetheless pleasing to him. She leaned toward him a bit, letting go of his hand. "I'm Cecil Edwards," he said. It was almost a whisper.

"We'll talk again soon," she said. Then she stepped down out of the trailer and walked to her car. She did not look back.

WHEN SHE returned the following afternoon, he told her he would be her brother—even though he couldn't be really sure of such a thing—but she was never to tell anyone about it.

"Why not?" she asked.

"It's none of their business."

"Why do you care so much?"

"I don't care. That's the point."

"And yet, you seem to care a whole lot."

"I don't care," he said with finality.

"What'd the folks in this town ever do to you?"

"I don't like a lot of questions. You want me to be your brother?"

"You are my brother."

He frowned, rubbed the sides of his face. "Damn."

"What?"

"I don't hate those folks. They got no use for me. I don't

want them to have some other way to hurt me." She looked at him. "If they don't know about you, they can't mess with you. You understand?"

"I guess."

"So keep your mouth shut about it."

"Okay."

"First time I hear it, first time anybody mentions it, and you can forget it."

"Okay."

"I mean that."

"All right," she said, frustrated herself now. "Can we talk about something else?"

"I do what I mean."

"Jesus Christ, okay," she said. She could not believe his vehemence or his persistence. They spent the rest of that afternoon not really speaking. She cleared the newspapers away and stacked them neatly on the floor of a barren closet. Then she cleaned the counters and the sink and washed the windows. Cecil washed and waxed his big Chevy pickup out front, coming in now and then for water. He grumbled to himself when he saw what she was doing, but he said nothing. Near the end of the day, when they were getting ready to discover if they could have a meal together, Lindsey said, "Do you want me to cook?"

"I don't have any cash right now."

"So you want me to cook." She was sitting on a small bench by the thin table, which she had folded down and set up so she could put plates and knives and forks there if he decided she should cook. Cecil sat on the couch.

"I don't care," he said. "If you want to cook, it's all right."

"Do you want to eat?"

"I could eat something. I'm not really hungry, though. Not now, anyway."

"Whatever I decide to cook will take a while. Does that stove work?"

He glared at her. "What do you think?"

"I could lend you some money, you know."

He put his head down and stared at the floor, slumping like a man losing his last hand in a poker game. "Just eat if you're hungry," he said.

"I'll eat when you do."

"If my mother was anything like you I would have run away from home."

She watched him for a moment, thought about what he said, then she laughed. It was a lonely sound, but she felt happy because he had actually relaxed enough to make a joke. "I'm sorry," she said.

He grumbled something, sat back, and put his arm up on the rim of the couch. She thought he acted as though he was pleased with himself, but he had nothing more to say.

"Do you think about her very much?" she asked.

"No." It was the truth. Later he would tell her that he had always strived never to think of his mother at all, and he didn't often fail until he looked into Lindsey's eyes.

"I wish I had met her," Lindsey said. "And I still want to see a picture of her."

"Yeah, well," he said. He tried to cross his legs, leaning into the effort until he noticed her looking at him. Then he planted both feet, put his hands on his knees, and got to his feet. He crossed the trailer and opened a drawer under one of the cabinets next to the window. Inside was a shoebox, and he lifted it out and set it on the table in front of her. He lifted a few of the papers in the box out of the way. There were several small blue spiral notebooks in the box, and under them, an assortment of loose photographs.

"What are those?" Lindsey asked, pointing at the notebooks.

"Nothing. Accounts and such." He picked them up and held them close. With his other hand he retrieved a five-by-nine color photograph of a woman sitting in a lawn chair in the hot sun, a beer in one hand and a cigarette in the other. It was an old photograph, slightly faded, but the woman's face was clear, the bright skin seeming to glisten in the sun. Her eyes were blue and appeared to collect the sunlight. She wore bright red lipstick, and her hair was clearly died red—pushed back off her forehead and bunched in a ponytail in the back. White earrings dangled under her ears. She was greeting someone, holding the beer aloft to say hello. Her face was plain, a little worn looking, but the lively smile seemed almost obstinate—as if this woman had made the conscious choice to have good fun in spite of all that is most obviously wrong with the world. Lindsey could hear Cecil's breathing as he leaned over her, holding the photograph before her eyes. He said, "She liked to watch me push the kids on the wheel." There was a sadness in his voice that touched her.

"She's very kind looking."

He stood back, raised the picture to the light through the window and looked at it for a moment, then placed it back in the box.

"So, do you think I look like her?" Lindsey said. She lit a cigarette, and he got up and moved to the door.

"She was carnival people, used to traveling all over," he said as he pushed the door open. "When she settled here, had me and all, it did something to her."

"Don't you miss her?"

He looked at her with eyes that seemed dead and cold. "Like I told you, I don't need nobody."

AND TRULY he didn't. As the weeks passed, and she came to know all that she would ever know of him, she realized that he went through all his days in a sort of self-imposed solitary confinement. His only contact with people was out of necessity and seemed an unbearable imposition—as if he waged a lonely war and only occasionally hollered to enemy troops in opposite trenches. She was his only respite from loneliness—if he ever felt lonely. She could not be sure he knew the feeling. More and more, when it became necessary to deal with folks in the town, he would rely on her, trying to get her to conduct his business so he wouldn't have to. Her feelings for him grew from intrigue, to vague concern, to something else altogether. She was certain she did not love him, but there was something in her heart that considered him. She could not have put into words how she felt about him—only that he was important to her—like a quality of nature or an attribute of the landscape that she must always contend with. He was not the same man in her presence. In his own way, he even demonstrated a sort of crude affection for her. He began to clean the trailer by himself, then when she came there he'd grumble about having to do it because she came into his life. "I'd of had a long nap this afternoon if it wasn't for you," he'd say.

She realized that in some ways she needed him. At least she needed to feel that her visits with him provided some time in his life when he wasn't angry. And each time he did some begrudging thing to show his affection, she felt a kind of pride she could not have described, a sense of importance and significance she could not get from any other thing. She had a friend once who was a skilled rider and who talked about dressage and getting a horse to behave in a particular way and how it felt when she finally got the animal to do what she wanted. Lindsey thought being with Cecil must be a little bit like that. Here was a man everyone said was mean, a man who no one in Columbia Beach was close to, and she could talk to him, even scold him, without fear. He was a satellite, a foreign thing on the outskirts of the town, and nearly every day during the summer, when she journeyed out to see him, she made voyages to one of the stars. It did not matter to her that everyone in the town, including Mrs. McCutcheon, believed she was Cecil's lover. Like her brother, Lindsey did not consider the perceptions of other people at all.

That summer she applied for a job at the gas company—a little white building at the far end of the main street that led away from the boardwalk and up the road to McDole's service station and the highway—and she was lucky enough (or good looking enough, Mauldin said) to start work there almost immediately as a receptionist and bookkeeper. She wrote a formal, courteous letter to the private school in Fairfax and then moved permanently to Columbia Beach. After that, she only sunbathed on weekends in the summer.

She began her regular sojourns to the beach that first summer. Before she got the job at the gas company, she went there every day that it didn't rain, carrying a few books and a towel. And she would emerge in the evening a little darker and, she hoped, a little more beautiful.

She told herself she did not need anything more than her books, her solitary trips to the beach during the summer days, and a few good evenings or afternoons with her brother. She did not care what the people of Columbia Beach knew or didn't know, or what any of them thought. In the fall of that next year, when she first met David Caldwell, she would have said her one true goal in life was to find out who her father was.

vi

Even though it was off season, when the October weather warmed up, young revelers still crowded the streets of the town. The traffic increased and young men from the naval station, local high school kids, and even some college students from Warsaw or Kilmarnock strolled up and down the boardwalks. Mauldin's place was usually noisy and well populated. With both street and riverside doors wide open, people wandered in from the boardwalk to get out of the bright sun on the beach, and they'd stand around in the cool dark around the pinball machines and then stroll out to the other side of the Shooting Gallery to the street. They stood on the sidewalk eating ice cream cones or sipping ice cold drinks. Every now and then a few of them would take a turn shooting at the targets in the gallery or playing a game or two of nine ball or eight ball at one of the tables. The Clary Hotel only had eleven or twelve vacant rooms most nights, and on the weekends the hotel was mostly full. It was not what you'd call a rush—and there was usually plenty of time to get things done in the mornings after coffee—towels in the rooms and beds made—but Judy always seemed to enjoy being busy again, and Clary didn't mind it, either. They were generally done before three, trading brief stints at the registration desk most of the afternoon and evening.

Even though the hotel was still mostly empty, the unseason-
ably warm weather attracted enough people wanting one last
day of summer, that on Caldwell's second night—a Friday—the
boardwalk looked and sounded more like an average night in
August. There was enough noise in the street that he was afraid
he would not be able to fall asleep. He had expected Todd and
waited for him all day in his room. Later in the evening, he got
in his car and drove up the highway a few miles from McDole's
place to a Burger King he'd seen on the way to the town that first
day.

Sitting in the Burger King eating a cheeseburger, he tried to
concentrate on a local newspaper he found on one of the tables.
He stopped at a headline that talked of the "passing" of a local
real estate developer. He thought about the word "passing" with
a sort of diffused bitterness, a mixture of emotions bordering on
wry humor and despair. He knew the idiocy of using such a verb
to describe death—as if a person passed from one situation to
another. He hated the idea that Bobby—a laughing, talking,
whining, playing, and crying little boy with windswept hair, large
glittering eyes, and miniature hands—was gone out of the world
forever. There was accuracy in the word "away." The inventors of
the euphemism knew at least a measure of the truth about death
and couldn't disguise it; they could not keep it from leaking into
their polite description of the end. Bobby had passed away. Away.

And yet the memory of him seemed so vital and real sometimes. The voice of the boy would come to him from a great distance—as though Bobby were on the other side of a mountain
and had called out.

"I can hear him sometimes," he had told Laura one night
during that first year of grieving, while they were lying in the
darkness before sleep.

"Really?"

"It's a real sound. It's not memory of him. It's really his voice.
Like an echo in my brain. *Heydad.* Like that. One word, the way
he used to . . ."

"That's memory," she said. "I hear it too."

"It doesn't feel like memory."

He turned, resting his head on his hand, and looked down at her face in the moonlight.

"Oh," she said.

"What?"

"Nothing."

He reached up and lightly moved the hair from her brow. He let his hand brush her face, but he did not caress her. She lay still. He put his arm down at his side, still looking at her. For months they could not find their way back to themselves, back to the intimacy, the familiar touches and loving caresses, the lovemaking. They lived together as though they had been assigned to the house they came back to every day, the room where they slept.

He lightly touched the skin at the base of her neck and felt her stiffen in the bed next to him. It was almost as if she registered an electric shock or a stab of pain. "I'm sorry I brought the whole thing up again," he said. She looked at him. The moonlight seemed to gleam from her eyes, and he thought again that she was beautiful even in her sorrow. "I wish—," he stopped. He had nothing to say, really.

She moved against him and put her arms around him. She held on, as if the bed might start to rise and turn. He smelled the hair by her ears, the perfume she wore, and lightly kissed her cheek. It was nothing but a kind of desperation, a desire for tenderness in the face of helplessness, as if this holding onto each other—this embrace—could somehow provide safety and permanence. He was not thinking anything. He closed his eyes and continued to caress the back of her head and the side of her face.

"It's never going to be enough, is it?" she said.

"What do you mean?"

"We're never going to get it back." She was crying.

"Don't. Don't cry."

"It's not grief anymore."

"I know."

"It's just sadness."

"Yes."

"We'll never have love again."

"Don't say that," he said. But he believed she was right. He didn't know how he would ever want to make love again. The death of his boy took all joy out of the world, and all loveliness. It was as though the event itself had murdered tenderness and lust, love and desire, had devoured ecstasy and turned it to something hostile and even painful. The slightest pleasure was tinged with an odd mixture of emptiness, sorrow, and terror—like a sudden premonition of his own looming death.

"It's hard enough just finding the will to eat," she said.

"Maybe that's what we need. A will to love." He felt her nod against his breast. He kissed her hair and moved gently to the other side of the bed.

But they did come back to love. In an odd way, they seemed to dissolve into it, as though they became a single entity, conquering space. Nothing ever attended their love as it used to, and their lovemaking, no matter how passionate, never produced the wonderful sensation of wellness it had always provided before, but it did return. They did become husband and wife again, but with a quiet distance between them, an unspoken riff they did not ever discuss. It was almost as if one of them secretly hated the idea of love and only pretended to it, and the other was aware of it and refused to admit it. Neither of them would have been able to say who was who in such a scenario; it just seemed that way to both of them, as if they were making love to each other to fulfill some biological need between them.

Now HE looked at one of the newspaper articles in front of him and mechanically finished his sandwich. The story was of a local boy who won the state wrestling championship. He thought of Bobby again—of that possible future lost forever. The depth and strength of the old sorrow always surprised him, always left him wondering at the power of this loss. It seared his heart, burning through muscle and sinew until he believed he would not survive it—would not recover the simple, effortless ability to breathe. He felt a tremor in the center of each bone and rose from the table as though he were realizing everything for the first time.

He did not want to go back to the hotel—could not make himself look upon the landscape of their last vacation together, a time framed and sturdy in his mind, when they were merely a family like any other—mother, father, two sons, and a daughter—and they celebrated the scarcity of other people, other loud vacationers disturbing the sand of Columbia Beach. He sat back down and stared at his empty hands. Then his cell phone rang and startled him. It was Terry, his daughter, and the connection was very bad.

"Hi Dad." She sounded bored. "Wondering . . . up . . . weekend."

"Speak up, honey," he said. "You're breaking up."

"Can you hear me now?"

"That's better."

"You seen him yet?"

"No, not yet."

A long silence ensued. He waited, thinking she might be talking. "I can't hear you, honey," he said loudly. Other people in the restaurant looked at him. "Honey?" Outside he could see the sun beginning to sink below the tops of the houses in the town. In the distance he saw the Ferris wheel beginning to move.

"Mom said I should call you," Terry said, finally.

"Okay."

"I have to ask you something." He said nothing. He watched the wheel as it began to turn, breaking vines and twisting long stalks of pampas grass. "Well, Mona and Larry are going up to Maine for the weekend and they wanted me to go with them."

"Mona and Larry. Just Mona and Larry?"

"Yes," she said, bitterly.

"For a weekend?"

"It's okay. Larry is a good driver, and his parents said he could go."

Caldwell hated Terry's small group of friends. He realized it was irrational hatred—he had no good reason to feel the way he did about them—but he could not bring himself to look upon any one of them with compassion or charity or warmth. They were drifters to him—aimless young kids with no resources, no intentions, no ambitions. They just seemed to want to play. It was a major achievement when one of them could sit still long enough to endure another body piercing—they talked about it as if they had scaled a challenging mountain, breaking some sort of longstanding athletic record. Terry had silver rings, six of them, that curled up her left ear. A silver ring with some sort of blue stone in it was attached to her right eyebrow. She had a pearl in her navel. She wore her hair in a variety of colors, including pink, blue, and green. And with each change in her "presentation" as she called it, he flew into a kind of private rage. He could not bring himself to rebuke her too strongly—the loss of Bobby made him incapable of letting any sort of open conflict erupt between them. He knew she had gotten away with things he would never have tolerated if he were not a man who had lost a child. But the tension between them was palpable, anyway. It was evident in the tone of her voice—the bitter sarcasm with which she greeted him whenever he even suggested that what she was up to might not be wise or worthwhile. She was ready for his disapproval—so ready that whenever he even hinted that he was not happy, she would fly into a rage and storm out of the house. She appeared to suffer unalterable wounds if he told her to turn her music down a little bit. Over the last few years, he was shocked to realize that he did not like her very much, and when he knew this, it did something to his will for guidance or setting limits.

Now he listened to Terry's whining voice on the phone. "It's just for the weekend."

"You're going to drive eight hundred miles for a weekend?" She said nothing. "I can't hear you," he said. "Are we breaking up again?"

"No. I'm here."

"What does your mother say?"

"She said I should ask you."

"Do Mona's parents know she's going up there with him?"

"Sure."

"They don't mind that their sixteen-year-old daughter is going on a road trip with a seventeen-year-old rookie driver?"

"I knew you'd just be shitty about this."

"Then why'd you call me?"

"Larry is a good driver."

With his free hand, he gathered the papers on the table in front of him. A young woman came through the door, and a breeze that rushed in with her smelled of water and sand. It was almost a hot breeze, a brief gust of summer. "Wow," he said. "It's almost summer down here. If you're talking, I can't hear you."

"Are you listening to me?" she demanded.

"I hate these fucking cell phones."

"Can you hear me now? I opened the window, I've got my head out the damned window."

"I'm sorry," he said. "Why don't you bring your friends down here? It's like a summer day out there."

"I don't want to . . ." It was silent for a moment. Then he heard her say, "What would we do . . . there with you, for . . . sake."

"Why do you want to go to Maine? It's so cold this time of year."

"Larry's got friends there and stuff. He used to live in Maine."

"That's a long drive for one weekend, honey."

"It is not."

"Of course it is."

"God, Dad. I mean, god." She was coming through loud and clear now, and he could not stand her tone. It was as though he owed her something exquisite and spectacular, and he was refusing to let her have it.

"Tell your mother I said you can't go," he said.

"I knew you'd say no. Thanks a lot." She hung up the phone.

He dialed his home number and Laura answered. "Let me talk to Terry again."

"She's not here."

"I just talked to her on her cell phone. Do you know where she is?"

"She isn't here."

He covered his eyes, rubbed the skin over his brow.

"Did she ask you if she could go to Maine?" Laura asked.

"I said no."

"Good."

"I wish you had just told her that."

"I've been telling her no. For a long time. It's your turn."

"Okay," he said, irritated. He wanted to hang up the phone.

Laura said, "She's got it in her head that if Larry's parents will let him drive up there, we're clearly wrong to tell her she can't."

"Does she even know what I'm up to down here?"

"You know she does."

"Is she interested in seeing Todd again?"

Laura said nothing. He listened to the static in the line for a time, and then he said, "I haven't heard anything from him yet. He's not here."

"You told me that in your e-mail."

"I thought you might be wondering." There was a long silence. "Laura?" Caldwell said.

"I'm here."

He had no words to describe how he was feeling. After all the days and nights, the months and long years of living with it, of going beyond it even, something in him wanted to resist the return of this mantle of grief. It was like a cloak that clung to him as closely as skin, and he could not free himself of it. "I feel like a thing with peeling paint," he said.

"What?"

"Like something old that's beginning to crack."

"You said you'd throw yourself into the work down there and get things straight with Todd."

"I know."

"You just have to bring him home," she muttered, and he knew she was fighting tears. In a stronger voice, she said, "You promised."

"I will."

"I know things will be better if you can do this."

"And the move down here?"

"That, too," she said. "After battling with Terry tonight, I actually thought I'd be glad to get out of this house forever."

"We will."

"Just bring Todd home."

"Make sure Terry doesn't try to sneak out of the house and go to Maine anyway."

"This isn't a jail," she said.

"Yes it is."

She laughed, momentarily. Four brief notes of music. He was gladdened by it, but then she said, "Well, it's a jail to us. It shouldn't be one to her."

The house was the temporary three-bedroom bungalow they had moved into right after Todd went on trial for manslaughter. He was tried as a juvenile, but it still made all the newspapers, and he was sentenced to the detention center until he turned eighteen years old. Caldwell did not want to stay in the house where everything had happened, the place where Bobby had died, and where Todd had tried to hide his body, had actually buried him in a green plastic bag.

When he left the Burger King that night, he decided to take a long drive down the road that led off the highway and down to Kilmarnock and beyond. It was still country, with trees covering the road like a long, green, darkening tunnel, and with very few houses casting light in the shadows.

• • •

In Columbia Beach the boardwalk was brightly lit again. It was as if all the permanent residents had invited distant family and friends for a brief visit, and they all arrived at once. Contrasted with the usual eerie silence and calm of a normal off-season, it seemed like a sudden retreat to summer and its constant public celebration.

What everybody always forgot during the long off-season was the noise after dark, in the street and on the boardwalk. One of the less endearing traits of the young is their infinite capacity to ignore the fact that there are human beings on earth—a great many human beings—who appreciate and even covet silence. Not quiet music, not old fashioned hymns and solemn concertos and quartets—you can play Beethoven's ninth symphony loud enough to shake the walls of any rock studio and bring it down as though it were constructed of cigar ash. But simple silence. No noise at all. The youth of the world always assume not only that the music they like is universally beautiful, but that other people really like to hear it, too. In fact, it is a prerequisite of youthful well-being and self-esteem that all other people in the vicinity should be allowed to listen to their music at the same time they do. It is a way of saying, "Look at me," which may be the first full sentence any child actually puts together in the process of acquiring language.

So at night the various music boxes and car stereos blared so loud up and down the boardwalk and Main Street that many people who stopped for gas at McDole's station out by the highway assumed the music was the brash, stentorian song of an amusement park. In fact, with the Ferris wheel spinning in its lighted nighttime glory, it was very easy to assume that Columbia Beach was some sort of traveling carnival, especially at this time of year.

Long after sundown a group of young people were standing in front of Mauldin's place, when an old taxi cab came slowly down the street from up by McDole's gas station. It was clearly not a working cab, but somebody hollered "Taxi"—just trying to be funny, one witness said later. The cab screeched to a stop in the middle of the road. One of the young men standing in the street, smoking a cigarette, leaned over and tried to see into the cab, and then the door opened and a man got out. He was fat—with a potbelly that hung down in front and broke through his shirt so that the bare skin and hair of his stomach bulged out of it. He wore a striped mechanic's jersey and dirty white pants. His reddish hair was long all around his head and he had a full beard. He stood at the door of the cab a moment, then he walked around to the trunk, opened it up, and withdrew a short rubber bungee cord with some sort of thick iron bar attached to the end of it. The bar was no longer than a cigar, but it had considerable weight, and when he swung the bungee cord over his head you could hear it whipping through the air.

"Come on," he said. "Come on, muthafuckas." He was not loud. It was almost a quiet request, except he was swinging the cord.

People backed away. The young man who had leaned over to look in said, "Nobody wants trouble here."

"Did you holler for a taxi, muthafucka?"

"We don't want any trouble."

The fat man, unsteady on his feet, approached the young man swinging the bungee by his side—low, like a cowboy with a rope. "Oh?" he said. He laughed, a guttural sound in the back of his throat. "You don' wan' no trouble," he said. He stood tottering a moment, still swinging the bungee cord. "Well, you got trouble." He swung the cord outward, hard, and the tip of it with the iron bar in it hit the young man in the face. The impact made a sound like a popped balloon. The young man fell instantly to the pavement and blood seemed to empty out of his head like something thrown forcefully from a bucket.

People scattered. Some ran towards the hotel, others scattered back through Mauldin's place and out onto the boardwalk. Mauldin saw them running and tried to stop somebody to ask what was happening. He looked out to the street at the car and the young man lying on the ground, and saw more people running. The thought ran through his mind that somebody had been hit by a car, but then he realized what had happened. The fat man was screaming now, "Go for it muthafuckas," as he swung the bungee over his head. Mauldin picked up his cell phone and called the Clary Hotel.

"That sheriff of yours in his room?" Mauldin said.

"Who?" Clary said.

"That sheriff you got staying there."

"No, he left just before dark. What's going on?"

"You ain't seen him?"

"No. He's not here."

Mauldin hung up the phone, though he heard Clary again ask what the problem was. Now he called the county sheriff's office in Dahlgren. A deputy answered the phone.

"Sheriff's office," he said. The deputy's name was Lewis. He was young, inexperienced, just out of the Marines. He'd learned all he knew about police work from his two years as a military policeman. Mauldin told him who he was and what was going on.

"I'm forty miles up the road," Lewis said.

"Well who should I call?"

"I think the sheriff is down there, isn't he?"

"Who?"

"Sheriff Caldwell."

"Hell, he's around here somewhere, I guess. How do I contact him?"

"I don't know. He checked in here already."

"You don't have a number for him?"

"Well, he's staying at the Clary Hotel."

"I already called the fucking hotel. He's not there."

"Sir, the state police might have a car in the area."

"The state police barracks is almost the same damn distance away, for chrissake."

Lewis said, "All right. I'll send somebody right away. Stay out of the street and keep everybody away from him."

"He's going to kill somebody."

"Call the state police. I'll try to get the sheriff on his cell phone."

"Hurry up," Mauldin said. "He may have already killed that fellow lying in the street."

"Can you get to him?"

"I'm not going near that maniac."

"I don't want you to go near him. Can you get to the fellow that's hurt?"

"Oh. I don't know."

"If you can get to him without endangering yourself, see if you can drag him out of there and tend to him."

"If I can, I will."

"I'll call the rescue squad in Dewey too," Lewis said. "And I'll see if the state has a car near there."

"I'd like to know what's the point of having a damn jail here if nobody's going to be here to run it," Mauldin said.

"Sir, keep folks away from the perpetrator if you can."

"Right."

"Just tell folks not to go near him. Help's on the way." He broke the connection.

It had gotten quiet outside. Mauldin walked carefully to the opening and looked out. The young man was still lying in the street, not moving, and the driver of the taxi stood over him, dangling the iron bar now, swinging it slightly in little circles by his leg. He did not seem to be aware of anything else around him. Even the bugs circling the lights overhead seemed to pause. The fat man bent way down, studying the damage he'd done. Then he straightened up and started swinging the bungee again.

Mauldin couldn't help himself. Without thinking, and immediately regretting it, he hollered, "Jesus Christ. Don't hit him again."

"Hey," the fat man said. "It's me. Christ amighty, it's me!" He seemed to leap up, throwing his heavy arm in the air, the iron bar whirling over his head. "I'm here and now going to kick somebody's ass. Here and now, by Christ amighty. Somebody's ass." He moved slightly toward the back of the car and almost lost his footing. He was clearly drunk or very high on something. His eyes looked small and red. "Whoo-hooo!" he hollered. "Kick some ass."

Mauldin saw some people approaching from down by the hotel and he waved them back. They stood, entranced by what they saw. Then, to his right, a slight movement caught his eye. He turned, and there, strolling down the middle of the street as though he were merely heading for the boardwalk or the hotel for a cold beer, was a lean, hard-looking young man with a cigarette dangling out of his mouth.

"Don't go near him," Mauldin shouted.

The fat man seemed confused, turning to look at Mauldin. "What'd you say muthafucka?"

"Stay away from me."

"Ahm gonna kick some ass. Whoo-hoo! Kick some old ass." He moved forward a bit, then staggered back again. "Goddamn the fuck. Kick some fuckin' ass."

For a fleeting second Mauldin felt a forlorn wish that Cecil was there—that the whole town could have the pleasure of watching Cecil handle this predicament. Where was Cecil when you really needed a henchman? How many children could be on that Ferris wheel at this hour? And this late in the year? The wheel turned now in the background, and Cecil was probably there, standing in the lights, watching the faces of his passengers. Cecil would not tolerate this drunken violence for a minute if he knew what was going on. Mauldin had the thought that he would call Cecil somehow—or walk up there to the wheel and tell him about this danger in the street.

The young man with the cigarette in his mouth was Todd. He had not registered at the Clary Hotel. He was staying up on the hill above the town near the overpass of the highway, at a cheap place called the L&M Ranch Motel. He had not prepared himself for the shock of seeing this town, the one place where he remembered his easy life—that time when he was a child and he had a mother and father and a brother and sister, and he had not yet killed his little brother. He had gotten to the front desk of the hotel, had asked a woman there if David Caldwell was registered, and when she said he was, Todd felt his heart stutter. So he fled. He actually found himself running to his car and leaving the hotel parking lot as if he'd robbed it.

He had stayed in his motel room all day and as the sun began to weaken, he realized he did not want to spend another minute lying on the bed staring at the ceiling and falling in and out of lethargic sleep. So he got up and lit a cigarette, then sat in a chair by the window of his room, staring down at the main street of the town. When he saw his father emerge from the hotel, get into his car, and drive up the road past McDole's place, he left his room and drove back down to the hotel. He cruised by a few empty parking spaces there but then drove up the street and parked in a public lot just east of the boardwalk and only half a block from Mauldin's place. He went down to the beach and walked up and down the boardwalk in a sweet, despairing daze, thinking of ghosts. He watched the sun sink below the distant trees and felt the increasing darkness in his heart. The air seemed to get warmer and promised more sun the following day, but the thought of seeing his father almost made him sick at heart. It wasn't panic, but it felt like it—like anticipation and fear together.

He walked down to the water's edge. In the waning light, everything seemed to glitter with sparks and points of reflected light. There was no moon. He smoked another cigarette, standing near the whispering water, then he walked back up to the boardwalk and out to the parking lot. He was just about to get in his car and drive back up the hill to the motel when he saw what was happening, and he did not hesitate. Perhaps, in some corner of his mind, he was thinking of what his father would do, or he was thinking of protecting him from something. But what he did seemed automatic, even to him. It was as if he'd planned it, but he wasn't really thinking at all. He stepped around behind his car, opened the trunk, took out a tire iron, and walked with a clear purpose, steadily and directly, toward the fat man who was staggering now, as though he might fall down any second.

When Mauldin first noticed him, Todd was a good distance away, coming down the street in the dark. Just as Mauldin started to shout another warning, he noticed the tire iron Todd carried in his left hand. When Todd was only a few yards from the fat man, Mauldin said, "Watch out, son. He's got some kind of weapon there, too."

Todd did not look at Mauldin. He did not lengthen his steps or shorten them; he did not increase his speed or slow down. Everything he did after he got to where the fat man stood in the street, waiting for him, he did without pause, in one motion. He made a short, swift swing of the tire iron and struck the fat man across the wrist on the arm that held the bungee. It dropped out of his puffy fingers almost at the second of the blow, as if the tire iron had knocked it out, and the man grabbed his arm and screamed. Todd picked up the bungee and threw it away, then he swung the iron again and hit the fat man in the back, just above the shoulder blade. The blow made a sound like a hardball thrown against a brick wall. With another pitiful scream, his eyes bulging out of his broad face, the fat man went down on his prosperous knees, his bare stomach quivering like a white sack full of water. Todd seemed in a hurry now. He walked around the man, watching him. He remembered briefly playing T-ball when he was a little boy, and how he'd step up to the rubber tee with the ball planted there for him and swing as hard as he could—a motion so perfect he barely felt the ball on the bat. He made the same motion with the tire iron, with both hands on it, like a baseball bat, and hit the fat man in the side of the neck, just under the jaw. This time the man went to the pavement without a sound. He lay on his side, his eyes closed, his foot twitching and jumping as if an electrical current surged through him. Todd went to the cab, still carrying the tire iron in his left hand, and turned off the engine. He slammed the door and walked back to the fat man's victim, who still lay bleeding in the street. Mauldin remained standing at the entrance of his place, watching in stunned silence. Todd knelt down and put his hand on the side of the young man's neck and held it there for a second. Then he looked up at Mauldin. "Call 911," he said. "This guy's still alive."

THE YOUNG man who had been hit in the head suffered a concussion and a bad cut, but no fracture. He'd lost a lot of blood, but by the time the rescue team got to him, he was starting to regain consciousness. The paramedics worked over him for a very short time, and when he sat up on his own, the crowd standing around cheered. The fat man was still unconscious when the rescue squad pulled away with him. He had come down off the highway for gas, and when he saw the bright lights and heard the music in the town, he decided to drive down Main Street and see what he could see. He'd been drinking all day, apparently, and had consumed at least a bottle and a half of whiskey. Somebody on the medical team said he'd bet a lot of money the guy was high on PCP as well. Everybody clapped for Todd when he walked away from the scene and headed back toward the boardwalk. No one knew who he was. It was the first time Mauldin had ever set eyes on him.

Very early the next morning, before sunrise, Lewis finally got Caldwell on the phone. "Sorry to wake you, sir," he said.

"You didn't wake me. I just got in."

"Where were you?"

"I went for a drive. What's the problem?"

"I tried your cell phone."

"What's the problem, Lewis?"

He told Caldwell what happened. He said the deputy reported the incident to the state police. He had stopped his cruiser in front of Mauldin's place, but the street was clear and no one was outside anymore. Mauldin had left the garage doors wide open, though, and he was sitting in his lawn chair by himself, watching the few people who were still playing pool at a back table. They'd been talking about all the excitement and many of them couldn't wait to tell the deputy all about it. He saw the streak of blood in the street when he got out of his car, so he knew it was bad. Up the road behind him, the Ferris wheel still lit up the night sky, but it wasn't turning anymore. A lot of the music had stopped.

"Everybody was pretty impressed by the kid with the tire iron," Lewis said.

"Nobody knew him?" Caldwell asked.

"No, sir. And he didn't hang around, neither. But he put an end to the trouble, that's for sure."

"What about the fat man with the bungee?"

"He's in the hospital up in Warsaw. Got a broken shoulder blade, a broken jaw, a bruised neck, and a bad concussion. I guess, he'll be pretty well hung over in the morning, too."

"Anybody want to swear out a complaint against him?"

"No, sir. They said he got what was coming to him."

"I guess he did."

"That kid was a hero."

"Or another criminal type, enjoying the fray."

"No, I don't think so, sir. The folks down there were very happy he showed up. He was a hero."

"Well, maybe."

"I'll make out a report and have it on your desk in the morning," Lewis said.

"Don't bother going to all that trouble. I won't be back up that way for at least a few weeks. Forget about it."

"Well, I dispatched a cruiser."

"Okay, but you don't have to finish it now. Hell, get some sleep."

"If you say so, sir."

"The morning will be fine. Go on home."

"I'm on duty another hour, sir."

"Did a state car show up?"

"No, sir. I called them. But the deputy said not a one showed up while he was there."

"Who'd you send?"

"Cobb." Cobb was the most experienced and the most reluctant of Caldwell's deputies. He had been hoping to run for sheriff, in fact, so he could not have been happy to get sent out on such an errand so late at night.

"Why didn't you call me?" Caldwell said.

"I did. I couldn't get you on the cell. It was so late, and I wasn't sure where you were. My main worry was to get somebody there right away. And Cobb was on duty."

Caldwell shook his head. "Good god, Lewis. I was right here."

"I called the state police and they said they had a trooper over in Dewey, and that he'd be right there." Caldwell said nothing. "Cobb didn't see a one, though," Lewis said.

"Well, tell Cobb I said thanks for coming all the way down here for me."

"I wish I'd a seen it," said Lewis.

When he hung up the phone, Caldwell poured himself a drink and wondered if the fat man had been the same fellow he'd taken into custody over the tax problems the last time he'd ventured down to Columbia Beach. It really was beginning to be a problem down here so far away from any sort of law enforcement. Still, it was his jurisdiction. And it might have been much worse. Somebody might have been killed. That would have been an awful mess.

He went to bed that morning, exhausted. He tossed and turned while the sun barely smoldered on the horizon. He finally fell asleep without the usual haunting thoughts of his lost boy or of what Todd might be up to. He was thinking of heroes.

vii

The next morning the sun rose in a cloudless blue sky and seemed to heat up as the day wore on. It was almost as if the seasons changed in an afternoon. By three it was almost seventy degrees, and resentful birds flew in odd circles above the trees, chattering as though they, too, were talking about the weather.

Mauldin sat outside the street entrance of his shooting gallery, fighting sleep. He watched a UPS truck wind its way down the road and stop in front of the bank down the street, just off the entrance to the boardwalk. A black car went past and turned up the main road that ran away from the beach. He noticed it was Mrs. McCutcheon with her head tilted back, as though she needed to look through bifocals at the obstacles in front of her.

Beyond where Mrs. McCutcheon turned, in the far distance out by the highway, he could see McDole's service station, with cars from the main road pulling in and out as they would all day. To his right, down near the end of the boardwalk, the Ferris wheel had finally stopped moving. Cecil was probably finished turning it, trying to keep the gears oiled and slick, ready for perhaps a few more nights of use. Eventually, weeds would climb so high on the wheel it would look like a great spider's web, but Cecil would turn it anyway, breaking the vegetable grip and clearing it of unwanted greenery. Within the month, if it the weather stayed warm enough, he'd have to do it again.

This day seemed like early summer to Mauldin, so he did not want to leave the gallery closed up. He raised the double-wide garage doors that faced the street, and then he opened the glass doors that looked out at the boardwalk and the river. He liked sitting in his lawn chair watching the street and waiting for an odd tourist or two, even though he knew most of the beach hotels and motels were empty and the season was well over. He enjoyed the breezes from the river, and he did not have to turn very far in his chair to look through the pool hall and see the sun sparkling on the water. The warmer weather was a nice trick on his imagination. It made him feel lazy and happy—as if the tender sun was a benediction, and it was his duty to rest in its light until the day was over.

He looked down the street and saw Jack Clary coming up from the end of the boardwalk. He sat up, rubbed his eyes, and tried to come more fully awake.

"I swear," Clary said, as he approached. "You'd think this was June."

"Warm, ain't it?"

"Got another one of those?" Clary pointed to Mauldin's lawn chair.

"Sure. In the back."

Clary disappeared in the gallery and came back out with a small foldable chair. He placed it next to Mauldin and sat down. "You'd think the place would be crawling with kids, as warm as it is."

"It was crawling with kids last night."

"How come you're sitting out here?"

Mauldin shrugged, not looking at him. Clary studied the inside of the shooting gallery for a while, then looked beyond, to the water. "Wouldn't you rather sit on the boardwalk?"

"Nah. More things going on out here."

"We missed you down at the hotel this morning."

"You should have been here last night."

"Really?"

Mauldin told him what happened.

"Who was the kid with the tire iron?"

"I don't know. Never saw him before. But you should have seen him. It was like in a movie or something. I mean, that kid just took him out."

"Damn."

"See that?" Mauldin pointed to a long brown stain in the street. "That's blood. I thought the kid that fat man hit would die right in front of me."

"Jesus. That looks like a lot of blood."

"Poured out of him like somebody poured from a pitcher." Clary stared at the stain in the street. "It was wild. And no sign of a cop until it was all over. Somebody from the sheriff's office drove all the way down here so he could keep me awake telling him about it."

"Where was Cecil?" Clary asked.

"He was up running his wheel. He didn't see any of it." It was quiet for a long time. Then Mauldin sighed, "I just been sittin' out here watching the traffic, thinking about it."

Behind them, not more than a hundred feet away, was the water—lapping the sand in small, steady gasps. The wind was calm, and it was quiet enough to hear the steady roar of traffic up on the highway behind McDole's place.

"I saw Lindsey go down to the beach with a book in her hand," Clary said. "That's better than watching traffic."

"That it is."

"She must've took the day off."

"Well, it's a hell of a nice day for this time of year."

"That bruise on her leg looks a mite bigger."

"You don't say."

"I wonder what's going on between her and Cecil."

"I was actually wishing Cecil was around last night, until that young fella showed up."

Clary shook his head, staring out at the road. It was quiet for a long time. Finally Mauldin said, "What a day." Clary looked at him. "Hard to put in a day's work when the weather's like this."

"Doesn't seem natural," Clary said. "I know I just didn't want to be sitting in the office another minute."

"What's Judy doing?" Clary gave a little smiling grimace. Mauldin thought he looked almost apprehensive—as if he was afraid the wrong question might spoil something he was trying to hide. "You fighting with her again?" Mauldin said.

"You know, I just don't think she's happy." Mauldin said nothing. "We're going up to Quantico later next month—you know, for the holidays, to visit her dad and all, and so I packed my suitcase for the trip . . ."

"You packing already?"

"Well, that's what she said." Clary seemed disgusted.

"So?"

"What's wrong with packing early?"

"Three weeks early?"

"Why not?"

"I don't know why not. But I can't figure out why, neither."

"It's done now. See?"

"Yeah."

"I don't have it hanging over my head."

"Packing hangs over your head?"

"Is there a set time a person has to wait before he packs a suitcase?"

Mauldin laughed. "I swear, Jack, you draw me into more stupid conversations than anybody I know."

"What's that supposed to mean?"

"You got me considering the most opportune and effective lead time for packing to go on a trip."

"Well, that's what I said to Judy. What the hell difference does it make if I pack my bag early?"

"Don't you need some of those clothes packed away in the bag? How about that?"

"If I needed them between now and the trip, I'd leave them out now, wouldn't I?"

"I guess."

"Anyway, I can always unpack an article if I need it, right?"

"I swear, you beat all," Mauldin said, laughing. "You really do beat all."

"It ain't easy being married. I can tell you that."

"I been married," Mauldin said, quietly. Clary looked at him. "It wasn't that bad."

"Oh, I didn't mean it like that," Clary said.

Mauldin sat forward a little and stretched his back. He didn't want to talk anymore, and he was aware that Clary was just now remembering that his wife had died, and that he had not been able to resign himself to it for a long time. It embarrassed him the way Clary looked at him, and he wanted to be out of his sight suddenly.

Clary said. "I know you were . . . I didn't mean that the way it sounded."

"Yes you did," Mauldin said, ruefully. "For you, marriage ain't easy. You forgot it was easy for me. Don't worry about it."

Clary shook his head. "I just don't think Judy is happy. That's all."

"Maybe you should ask her," Mauldin said. "What do you think?"

Clary started to speak, but his eyes seemed to freeze on something up the road. His face changed. "Look at that," he said.

Mauldin turned and saw a man stepping up onto the boardwalk and heading between the buildings toward the beach. "Who's that?"

"It's my new tenant."

Mauldin watched the man disappear from sight. Turning in his chair, he saw him emerge on the other side of the shooting gallery, cross the wide doors on the other side, and then turn parallel to the beach and start walking along next to the murmuring water. He had his head down and his hands in his pockets, and he seemed to be studying the small dips and rises in the sand that lay before him. When the man disappeared from view, Mauldin turned back to Clary. "That's gonna be our new sheriff?" he said.

"That's him. His name's Caldwell."

"Well, he was useless last night. His own office couldn't find him."

"I saw him this morning and he didn't say a thing about it."

"I'll be. He don't look like he could last more than a few seconds with Cecil Edwards. And I bet that kid with the tire iron would give him fits, too."

"I wonder where he's going?"

They were quiet for a while. Then Mauldin said, "Nope. He won't be no match for old Cecil."

"Maybe we should do something about Cecil."

"Like what?"

"I mean, he is our problem, right?"

Mauldin looked at him. "What are you suggesting?"

"Nothing in particular. Except it seems like if he can just do anything he wants, maybe we can, too."

Mauldin put his hands on the arms of his chair and leaned forward a bit. "You saying what I think you're saying?"

"Well, are you afraid of him?"

"No."

"I'm not."

"Go on."

"Well, Hamlin was saying yesterday that maybe we ought to get together and teach Cecil a lesson. You know, let him know a thing or two."

"Really."

"He'd be no match for all four of us. We could—we could make sure he leaves all of us alone for a long time, it seems to me."

"You talking about hurting him?"

Clary smiled. "Well, let him know he can't mess with us."

Mauldin shook his head. "Leave me out of it."

"So you *are* afraid of him."

"No. It ain't fear."

"What is it then?"

"Maybe it's respect."

"For Cecil?"

"No," Mauldin said. "The law. Respect for the law."

"What law? There's no law around here. That's the problem."

"There'll be plenty of law if we start ganging up on folks."

"If we put a hurt on him, he'll leave us alone," Clary said.

"Have you talked to McDole about this?"

"No, not yet. Why?"

"No reason."

"I'm not saying we got to do anything right away. We can wait and see what happens when Cecil gets his hands on my tenant—our new sheriff."

Mauldin pointed to the tattoo on his arm. "You see that? No way Hozay. Got it?"

Clary laughed. "Okay. Okay."

"I don't mind telling you—or the rest of them either—I ain't got nothing against Cecil. Okay? He ain't never done nothing to me, see."

"I see."

"If he did, I'd swear out a complaint and follow up on it."

"If he didn't break your legs or something."

"Oh," Mauldin waved his hand disgustedly. "He ain't broken any legs around here."

"What about that sailor that got his chest bone broken?"

"Maybe the sailor deserved it. I don't know. I do know I ain't going to be joining no lynch mob to go after Cecil."

"I'm not talking about any lynch mob. Jesus." They didn't say anything for a long time. Cars passed in front of them, gleaming in the sun. Clary saw Caldwell emerge at the end of the boardwalk and step into the sand up the beach. He watched him stroll up along the water to where Lindsey was sitting on a blanket reading. "Look," Clary said.

Mauldin turned in the chair, craning his neck to see them. Lindsey had gotten to her feet and they were standing there talking. Still straining to see, Mauldin said, "If he's going to be the sheriff around here, what's he doing walking on the beach?" Clary got up and stretched. Mauldin turned back to him. "You going already? You just got here."

"I have to go make sure Judy takes care of my tenant's room. He might want to come back there pretty quick, now that he's struck up a conversation with Lindsey, you know what I mean?" Mauldin stared at him. "Look at the way she's posing there in front of him," Clary said. "I swear that girl flirts with everybody." Mauldin shook his head, but he didn't look back toward the beach. He gazed blankly out at the road. Clary said, "The son of a bitch rang me up at two in the afternoon yesterday and told me to be sure and leave him clean towels today."

Mauldin turned back to him. "So? Ain't that what you're supposed to do for him?"

"He didn't have to call up and demand it like that. Like I'm some kind of servant."

"But you are his servant, ain't you?"

"Shit."

"Sometimes I think the only reason you like running that hotel is that almost nobody stays there no more."

"I'm plenty busy during the season."

"All the guy did was ask for clean towels."

Clary picked up the chair he'd been sitting in and folded it, then went back into the gallery to put it away. Mauldin didn't want to move yet. He leaned his head back and closed his eyes. He sat up again when Clary came back out. The two men looked at each other but neither said anything. Clary made a slight wave of his hand and Mauldin nodded at him, then Clary turned and walked back to the hotel.

• • •

Caldwell had not been walking along the beach for long when he ran into Lindsey. He was concentrating on keeping his mind empty, so he did not notice her at first. She was sitting by a thick clump of wild grass, staring out at the water. She held a book in her hands, marking the place with her thumb, and when Caldwell approached she folded the corner of the page she had been reading, set the book down on her blue blanket, and said, "Hello."

"I'm sorry," Caldwell said. "I didn't see you."

"I saw you coming a long way off." He started walking again, awkwardly, not knowing where to let his eyes fall, when he heard her say, "Where you going?"

He stopped. "Nowhere in particular." He turned back toward her. "I'm just walking."

"Nice day for that." He noticed the way light played in the strands of her hair, thinking about Laura, their early time together. Lindsey's brown legs were splayed out in front of her, and although she was leaning back on her hands, he noticed the extra weight around her stomach. She was, he could see, not self-conscious at all. She looked at him—at his eyes—as if she might remember his face from some earlier meeting. "I'd walk with you," she said. "But I fell off the top step of my brother's trailer and nearly broke my leg." She showed him the bruise. "And look at my arm." She turned her arm over and he saw a black and blue mark just above her elbow.

He didn't know what to say. She said she'd walk with him, and those words took a little time to register. But once they did, he felt discomfited by them. There was a small mark under her right eye, and she stared up at him, waiting. Behind him the water made soft falling slaps against the wet sand, and he was vaguely conscious of the swirling air—as if he were in a kind of slight motion against a tender breeze. The smell of the sand and water was mixed now with suntan oil.

"I almost never talk to tourists," Lindsey said.

"Really?"

"But you looked kind of lost. And sad." He didn't respond. She leaned further back, studying his face. The sun was rising behind him, and it made her squint when he moved his shadow away from her face. "Where are you from?" she asked.

"Up north a ways."

"Really? Where? I'm from Fairfax."

"I'm up in Warsaw now. I got elected sheriff of Dahlgren County about three years ago. But I used to live in Fairfax."

"I lived there the whole time I was growing up. Went back there every winter for a while." She held her hand up now to shade the sun from her eyes. He moved so she was back in his shadow.

"Every winter?"

"That's where my job was. But I work down here now. Live here permanent."

"That's good," he said, wanting to move on down the beach but worried about how to extricate himself from this conversation without being rude. She put the book down and stood up. She brushed the back of her shorts with both hands. "This isn't really much of a beach," she said. "Where you going?"

"I was just walking." He realized she was waiting for him to say more. He looked down the beach and saw the Ferris wheel way off in the distance.

"I came down here every summer to visit my brother, Cecil," she said. He thought she liked to say those two words: "my brother." She seemed to pause on them. He was wishing his daughter wore her hair like this. "He owns the Ferris wheel."

"So now you live with him?" he asked.

"Oh, no. I stay over to Mrs. McCutcheon's."

"Mrs. McCutcheon?"

"Agnes McCutcheon. She owns the big house over there four blocks off the boardwalk, at the top of the hill. You can see it from here." She pointed.

He nodded, only half listening. "Did you say your brother's name was Cecil?"

"Yeah, why?"

He didn't know what to tell her. "Is he a big fellow?"

"Why?"

"I was just wondering."

"You were just wondering what?"

"I've heard of him," Caldwell said, matter of factly. "That's all."

"He's not what everybody says he is."

"I'm glad to hear it."

She looked away. He thought it might be easier now to move away, but then she faced him again, smiling. "Where'd you live in Fairfax?"

"We lived on . . ." he paused. He could remember the street, but he didn't want to say it. "It was on Prairie Lane."

"I lived on Prairie Lane. I grew up there. My mother . . ." She looked at him now, studying his face.

"Prairie Lane was a long street," he said.

"My mother just sold her house there a few years ago." He said nothing. "It was on the corner at the end."

"Which corner?"

"At the end by the school."

"Oh. We were miles from there."

"Still. I feel like I've seen you before. Was your picture ever on a poster?"

"No." He smiled.

"You know, an election poster or a TV ad? I didn't mean a wanted poster."

"I know." He did not know how to continue his solitary walk along the beach without rudely turning from her and just moving away, taking his shadow with him.

"When you got elected sheriff, didn't you have posters and all?"

"Just a few signs with my name on them. No pictures."

"Maybe I just ran into you walking down Prairie Lane or something," Lindsey said.

"Possibly you did." She blinked slowly, like a cat. Then she looked directly at him and seemed to be waiting, too. "Well, it's been nice . . ." he said lamely.

"I come down here almost every day in the summer to read." She seemed to want to keep him there. He didn't say anything. "Reading is good for you, don't you think?"

"Yes. It is."

"Sometimes it helps me forget things I don't want to think about." She looked out to the water beyond him. He moved a bit, letting his shadow leave her face. "Cecil's not the trouble here," she said. Her voice was suddenly cheerless and it touched him.

"I promise I'll keep that in mind."

"They just don't like him, and he doesn't like them."

"Who?"

She waved her arm. "All of them."

"The whole town?"

"He isn't a criminal," she said more forcefully. "They don't know him like I do."

He didn't know what to say. She waited there for something, and his awareness of that made him feel vaguely embarrassed. "Well," he said, stepping back away from her.

"There's nothing down that way," she said. "It's just broken branches and swamp down there." She looked down, her hair blowing in the breezes next to her face, then she turned and stared out at the water. She put her hands up, pulling her hair back out of her face. She was having trouble now looking him in the eyes. "Would you do me a favor?" She was almost whispering.

"What?"

"Don't tell anybody Cecil's my brother."

"Why?"

"He insists. He won't be my brother if anybody in this town knows about me."

"Is he ashamed of you?"

She looked at him, her hair blowing in strands across her face. "He hates them," she said. "The folks of the town. He just hates them all." Her voice was soft again, sweet, and sad. He noticed a mark on her cheekbone, just under her right eye, a small imperfection in the skin—a little dark spot shaped like one of the long states, Tennessee or Kentucky. But somehow it added to her beauty, as if it were a signature, the artist's claim of credit for such fine work. And her face was fine work. Her lips were full and soft looking, and her eyes were alive and dark green.

"Why?"

"I really don't know." She drew herself up to him, but turned her gaze back to the water and a slight rising breeze. He was conscious of the way her hair moved; long strands curled by her ears, rising and falling like visual currents, the light gleaming in it. She was waiting for him.

"I won't tell anybody," he said.

Now she looked at him. "You really can't."

"I won't."

She held out her hand and he shook it. "I'm Lindsey."

"David Caldwell." Her face changed. She let go his hand and started to say something, but stopped. "What?" he said.

"There was a family in Fairfax . . ." her eyes seemed to freeze on him. "A long time ago. When I was a little girl." Now she studied his face. He said nothing. "I know who you are," she said.

"You do?"

"It was on the TV. Every day for a week. I was just a little girl, but I remember my mom talking about it with everybody. Right up our street she said. And I put your picture in an article I wrote for my journalism class."

"Really?"

"I always saved it. Got it folded in one of my books. I thought you looked familiar when I first saw you." He looked away. "That was . . ."

"It was my son," he said, and he hated himself for feeling it again, for letting the revulsion and grief stride right back into his heart while he was standing there in the sand looking out at the blue water. She stood there looking at him, and then he just started walking back toward the hotel. She gathered up her blanket and book to follow him. When he realized she was coming up behind him, he stopped and waited for her. The muttering river lapped against the sand and seemed to mark the seconds.

"I'm sorry," she said finally.

"Look. Now I have a secret, too."

"Oh."

He said nothing. After a pause, they both started walking again, slowly, awkwardly, in the sand. "Whatever happened to—to your son? The one that . . ."

"I don't want to talk about it, and I'd appreciate it if you wouldn't tell anyone."

"I won't."

"This has happened to me before. People tend to remember a thing like that, and sometimes in circumstances I can't help it gets remembered."

"I'm sorry if I . . ."

"It's not your fault."

They made their way to the edge of the boardwalk and he helped her step up out of the deep sand. She draped the blanket over her shoulders and cradled the book in her arm. He saw that it was a biography of John F. Kennedy. The air picked up a bit and the water grew louder against the sand. "What ever happened to your boy?" she asked.

Caldwell looked out at the warm mist rising off the water. "Didn't you hear all the stories?"

"They said he did it, but that it was an accident."

"That's what he claimed it was."

"Was it?"

"We don't know. That's just it."

"I'm sorry. I always wondered. I just wanted to know."

"So do I," he sighed. "The truth is, no one will ever know. Except Todd. He knows."

"Todd. I didn't remember the name."

"Well," he said.

"I always thought it would be terrible to be him."

"Well, yes. I guess it was terrible. It was worse for his little brother, though." She shook her head, slowly, but she said nothing. "I promise I won't tell anybody about your brother," Caldwell said. "I'd appreciate it if you didn't mention—," he stopped.

"Your secret is safe with me," she said.

viii

W hat are you doing here?" Clary asked. He had just finished cleaning the front windows in the lobby when McDole walked in. For the third day in a row the warm weather held, and Clary had decided to do work he normally left until spring. "What'd you do? Close the gas station early?"

"I'm going to press charges," said McDole. "I made up my mind."

Clary shook his head, then picked up a newspaper that was spread out on the registration counter. "Let's see, I don't think that section of the paper is here."

"What?"

"Maybe it's in the back office." Clary flipped the pages of the newspaper, shuffling through the various sections of it, looking for something. "Maybe it's here and I just don't see it."

"What are you looking for?"

"The obituaries. I want you to see one so you'll have some idea what yours is going to look like."

"Shit," McDole said. "If the North Vietnamese couldn't kill me, I ain't worried about Cecil Edwards."

Clary leaned on the counter. "You're going to press charges."

"I got to do something, goddamn it. And I keep driving by

that damned jail and I see lights in there. That sheriff is in there, right?"

"I guess you could say he spends some time there. He's working."

"Why?"

"I guess he's setting things up and all."

"Well he can just enforce the law a little bit. Ain't that what he's supposed to do? The son of a bitch owes me money." McDole's voice was loud. Clary moved toward the end of the counter. He was wearing a white, short-sleeved shirt, brown slacks, and bedroom slippers which scraped along the floor as he walked. "Come on," he said. "Let's have a drink and talk about it."

McDole went into the café and sat down at the oak table, while Clary went back into the kitchen and got a fresh bottle of Chivas. When he came out, he cradled it like an infant, in the crook of his arm. He stopped at the end of the counter and reached under it for two glasses. "I'm glad you came by," he said, when he got to the table.

"I'm gonna do it."

Clary sat down across from him and poured two drinks. "This is the best there is," he said. "Have a sip and sit back and lets think about what you're about to do."

McDole took his glass and held it up to his lips.

"Maybe this will calm you down a bit," Clary said.

"I don't need to be calmed down."

They drank for a while, watching the white sun beaming through the high front windows. Clary had been taking sips of scotch most of the day, but he could not feel any of it. He could not remember the last time he had been truly drunk, but it occurred to him, sitting at the table drinking with his friend, that he'd like to be drunk again—would like to feel invincible and free and young. Lately he had been remembering times with Judy—days when everything seemed to be in front of them instead of behind them. He had been married more than twenty years, and until the last year or so, he would have said he was happy.

"Let's get drunk," he said.

"You can't talk me out of it."

"Shit, I don't want to do that. I just want to tie one on."

"I don't feel like it."

"You might have to be drunk to file."

"I'm going to do it. This is America. I've got the law on my side. What's that sheriff for, anyway?"

"Well, he's been waiting pretty patiently for his son to show up."

"Really?"

"That's what he's been bugging us about. Me and Judy. He called the desk again this morning, and when he came in last night he asked if he'd had any calls."

McDole sipped his scotch, gazing out the window.

"I think he's getting pretty anxious about it."

"About what?" He looked at Clary now.

"His son. He was supposed to meet—,"

"I don't give a damn about that. What's he doing about Cecil?"

"Well, nothing, yet."

"I've got the law on my side, and he's the law now, right?"

"The law will sure be on your side when Cecil kills you," Clary said. "Or when he crushes your ribs or breaks some bone or other."

"Am I just supposed to take it?"

"I'd rather be alive, myself."

"This guy—the sheriff. He really said, 'You got a problem here?' Like that? Like he knew about Cecil?"

"That he did."

McDole grunted, finishing his drink. "Cecil never killed no-body." Clary held up the bottle. "No thanks," McDole said.

"I tell you what," Clary said. "He's trouble. Big trouble, if you cross him."

"I know. I know."

"Just about all of us got some kind of complaint. There's no point in you taking him on by yourself because the rest of us don't want to stand up to him."

"He don't owe you money."

"No, but what if we all decided to teach him a lesson?" Mc-Dole shrugged, pushed his glass toward the bottle, and Clary refilled it. They fell silent. Clary could hear McDole breathing and wondered if he might stick around now and get drunk. But then the door opened and David Caldwell came in. He was wearing jeans that were splotched with paint, a flannel shirt, hunting boots, and a Yankee baseball cap.

"Speak of the devil," McDole said, watching Caldwell cross the lobby. He finished his drink, pushing the glass across to Clary. Caldwell stopped momentarily, looked at them, then approached the table.

"This here's my new tenant," Clary said. "And our new sheriff."

"Eventually," Caldwell said, looking at McDole. "You run the station up by the highway, right?"

McDole got up out of the chair. "Yes, sir. Something I can do for you?" He extended his hand and Caldwell shook it. "McDole's the name."

Clary said, "He's the one having all the trouble."

"Trouble?" Caldwell said.

"With Cecil Edwards." McDole nodded.

"What kind of trouble?" Caldwell asked.

"It's money he owes me, and just the fact that he robbed my store."

Caldwell let go of his hand. "When?"

"Just a few days ago."

"Did you report it?"

"No, sir."

"Why not?"

"Well, it wasn't exactly a robbery," Clary said.

McDole looked at him. "What was it then?"

"You should have reported it the day it happened," Caldwell said. McDole didn't seem able to look him in the face. He shook his head and seemed to mumble something.

"What can he do now?" Clary asked Caldwell.

"He can file a complaint and get a lawyer to pursue it. But it doesn't look very good that he waited all this time to report it." They all said nothing for a while. McDole sat back down in the chair and reached for the bottle. Caldwell turned to Clary. "I don't wish to be disturbed this evening. I'm going to try and sleep."

"Fine," Clary said.

"But my son—," he stopped. Then he said, "If he comes here looking for me, it's okay, though. Send him up."

"I'll do 'er."

"Make sure it's my son and not one of the contractors working on the jail. I'd like to be left alone if it's possible." A long pause ensued, then Caldwell seemed to nod toward both of them. He walked across the lobby and went up the stairs.

"Unfriendly son of a bitch," said McDole.

"He's right, though. You should have reported it right away."

"I told him about it just now."

"I guess it's not the same thing."

"I don't know. He doesn't look like a sheriff in those clothes, does he?"

McDole went to the door, while Clary put the bottle and glasses back under the counter. "Think it over before you go getting lawyers involved," Clary said.

"You know what I might just do?"

"What?"

"I might just get my pistol and stroll over to Cecil's place and demand my money." He stopped by the door and nodded toward the elevators. "See what he can do about that."

"Cecil'd break you in two."

"Not if I got my pistol. I'll give old Cecil a taste of his own medicine. See how he likes it."

"I wouldn't do that."

"It's just what he'd do, isn't it?"

"I don't think he'd need a pistol."

"He held one on me the other day."

"If you ever want to really do something, let's talk."

McDole came back in a bit. "What do you mean?"

"We should get together and all do something."

"I don't need any help."

Clary smiled. "No, I guess you don't."

"Thanks for the drink." McDole waved his hand and went out the door. Clary sat by the window for a while and watched low, gray clouds, bruised and threatening, move behind the far trees, inland. Presently the phone rang. The sudden noise scared him, but when he picked up the receiver, he said very calmly, "Yes?"

"I need towels again," Caldwell said.

"Oh, sure. I'll have my wife bring them right up."

"Don't bother now."

"Oh, it's no bother."

"I don't want them now. Just put some in here tomorrow."

Caldwell hung up without saying anything else. Clary put the receiver back in the cradle and went back to the window, thinking *I should have charged the son of a bitch four hundred dollars a week.*

· · ·

Dear Laura,

Well, he's still not here. No sign of him. It's like I'm waiting for a ghost. Has he called you? I tried to get you last night until nine, but after that I gave up. I didn't want to wake you if you were home and sleeping. But tell me if he's called you or e-mailed you. What could have happened to him? I'm starting to worry. You told him I was going to be here on the 18th, right? Does he think I'll be here indefinitely? Did we give that impression? I hope he's not going to wait too much longer. It's already the 22nd. Soon it will be November.

Jeez I hate not knowing how to get in touch with him. I feel like I want to put up a big billboard outside of the town to tell him where I am. I've spoken to most of the folks who might run into him down here. Told them where to tell him to go. Maybe he already came here and saw that the old hotel is gone and didn't think to come here. It's really crap that I can't call him and just tell him where he can find me. I hate this.

I wish you'd call me more often. I wish this was not happening in just this way. I mean, you know what we both wish for, but if only he was just at home and in our lives and we didn't have this disastrous pull on everything. This downward pull. That's what it feels like. Like we're being pulled down by his not being here, by his not being anywhere we can know. I know. I'm complaining again.

I spent all day today with contractors, getting the walls painted in the sheriff's office. I thought it might make me forget some things if I was real busy, and I saved the county a good penny by pitching in myself. Contractors don't like that much. But I don't care. The place has two fairly large jail cells, good solid iron bars, but the locks for the doors are all screwed up, and nobody knows where the original keys are. I've got locksmiths coming down tomorrow or the next day to figure out how to re-match keys to the locks, or to put new locks on. I've replaced all the bedding and had a plumber in to get the toilets working properly. The cages over the lights needed replacing. The others were so rusted out I was afraid of a short every time I turned the lights on. The gun cabinet needs new locks, too.

I'm sorry. I didn't need to bore you with all the details. I'm keeping busy. I've driven up to the office twice in the middle of the afternoon, and both times I was tempted to drive all the way over to your office and just stop in to say hi. Maybe I will next time. Usually when I get back to the sheriff's office there's so much work to do, I just pack it all up and take it back down here with me. I could take an afternoon and make the drive up to see you.

I miss you honey. I hope you are not missing me too much. Not like I'm missing you, anyway. I have this kind of weak feeling around my heart when I think of you, I really do. I don't know how to describe it. Like a kind of mixture of grief and fear, you know? And maybe a little anticipation, too. I want so much to see you again. I'd come home this weekend. But then I know that's when Todd will come looking for me. I wish you'd just come down here. I still don't understand why he insisted on me alone. I know how awkward it would be if you were here and he did show up. I'm not asking for a change in what we agreed on. But this feels more and more like a kind of separation—like I'm getting further and further away from us. From us. You know what I mean?

Caldwell stopped typing and stared at the screen. His wrists were getting sore because of the small keyboard on which he was trying to write. He did not know if he would send this latest e-mail to Laura. He'd written others where he tried to tell her how he was feeling, and then he'd let them sit a while, read them over in the morning or later in the evening, and each time he'd see that he was beginning to sound like he was whining. He could almost see the look on her face, reading his complaints from so far away. He never withstood being away from her as easily or readily as she did from him. They joked about his need for her. Something in the sound of her voice soothed him as no song ever could. He would tell her that, and she would smile and kiss him, without really understanding how serious he was, without truly believing it was possible that one's voice could have that effect on another person. But his description of it was accurate. Her voice calmed him when he was worried, excited him when he was uninterested, settled him when he was angry, cheered him up when he was sad. And it worked both ways. The sound and tone of her voice frightened him when she was worried, robbed him of interest when she was bored, angered him if she was angry, and saddened him when she was melancholic; her voice engendered every emotion music can give a person, and he needed it like a person needs music.

In spite of their losses, in spite of the gradual coming back from death and the leveling out of everything passionate and intense in their lives, he still needed her as he always did, even though now he frequently felt like a beggar, like a person pleading for small treats in order to retrieve or recreate some little token of the past and temporarily escape the dull present and bleak future. Laura had said to him once, "I think you hold onto the past too much."

"No," he said. "I don't hold onto it. I cherish it. I remember it. It's all we have of him."

"It's all we have of *them*," she corrected him. "We've lost both of them."

"I know," he whispered.

They'd been in bed. They'd just made love quietly, almost perfunctorily. While it lasted, it was passionate enough, but afterwards they did not linger in the bed as they always had before. There was no embrace or loving chatter while their breathing returned to normal. She had gotten out of bed and gone into the bathroom to wash up, and he'd stepped into the shower. When he'd come back to bed, feeling alive and chatty, he talked about a fishing trip he'd taken with Todd and Bobby, and that's when she'd said he was holding onto the past.

"I think," she said, "we're never going to get our lives back until we let go of it."

"Let go of what?"

"The past."

"You don't mean that."

"I do."

"He's in the past. Bobby. You want to give him up?"

"I already have. I gave him up when he died."

"So you just forget about him? Like he didn't exist."

"Don't."

"Is that what you mean?"

"You know it's not."

"Well, what do you mean then?"

"I don't know. I just don't know. I'm tired of grieving."

"I can't let go of him. I won't let go of him."

"But you can let go of Todd."

"I didn't say that."

"You might not have intended to."

"I didn't," he said. "I for sure don't have to let go of Todd. When he's done down there, I intend to welcome him home."

She had said nothing. There was no moon, and the room was absolutely dark. Caldwell had felt almost blind from the effort of his wide-open eyes to discover any light. He'd lain a long time just out of her reach, listening to the night. He hadn't been able to tell if she was crying or just breathing slightly fast from their lovemaking. He had pictured Bobby's eyes, then had tried to get the whole face into memory, but he just couldn't do it. He could remember photographs. Not the living face. He could never get the living, changing, beautiful face in his memory. "I guess we have to find a balance," he had said finally, but he'd waited too long to say anything. He heard her even breathing and realized she was asleep.

NOW HE went back to his e-mail to her.

> I just wish I could make you laugh really hard, one time. Like I used to. That would be wonderful wouldn't it? The free laughter of a kind of sweet summer night. That's all I want now.
>
> I'll call you when Todd finally does get here. If he's not here by the week of Thanksgiving, I'm going to forget about it and just come home. Call me tomorrow if you can.
>
> Love,
> Dave
>
> P.S. Tell Terry I miss her and I love her.

This time he didn't let it sit. He read it over briefly, then sent it. He made up his mind that he would not call her on this night.

ix

E arly the next Saturday afternoon, Cecil was sitting on the top
step in the doorway to his trailer when Lindsey walked up the
long street from Mrs. McCutcheon's place. It had rained hard that
morning, straight down in dull gray light without wind or thun-
der. Now, in spite of an occasional early rogue November gust of
wind, the weather had cleared. Lindsey was wearing shorts and a
halter top. Draped over her shoulder was a purple and white
oversized towel. She looked like she was just returning from a
morning trip to the beach. Cecil wore baggy blue shorts and an
orange T-shirt that had a V-neck collar. His neatly combed hair
was damp from sweat, and she could see water dripping down the
side of his face and along his temples. He'd been having trouble
breathing so he was red faced and wet from the sweating, and
Lindsey offered him her towel.

"Where you goin'?" he gasped.

"To the beach. Where else?"

"It's a little cold for that, ain't it?"

"You're wearing shorts again." In truth, although the sun
burned coldly in the sky where it always did at this time of year, the
air had warmed considerably by noon, and the scattered puddles
of clear, cloud-reflecting water had already begun to dry up.

"Thought you were coming here this morning," Cecil said.
"I didn't say when."

He wiped his jaw and under his chin with the towel. She
stood next to him, her hand covering her navel. She seemed
oddly conscious of him looking at her stomach, which looked
soft and pouchy over the top of her shorts. He was aware that she
noticed him glance briefly, almost furtively, at the small blue halter top she wore. He wiped his face with the towel. "Are you all
right?" she asked.

He waved his hand. "Just the asthma."

"You look sick."

He took a deep breath, felt again the failure of it—the empty,
withering sense of drawing in nothing while his lungs suffocated
for lack of air. "It's just the asthma," he gasped. "Leave it."

"Have another cigarette," she said, pointing at the butts collected at the bottom of the steps. She often scolded him now,
without rancor. It was almost teasing, except that banter was not
something he ever readily responded to. He had gotten to where
he could accept her reproaches without threatening to send her
on her way, and it pleased her to know she was the only one who
could talk to him the way she sometimes did.

"Why don't you choke on another one," she said. "Go on. I
won't stop you."

He shook his head. Sweat still dripped down the side of his
face.

"I'm sorry," she said. "That was mean." She put her hand on
his shoulder. "Are you going to be all right?" He closed his eyes.
"I mean do you feel like . . ." His hands worked the towel, turn-
ing it and twisting it. He pressed the tip of it against his forehead.
He thought she probably felt exposed without the towel. "Should
I get some help?" she said.

He looked at her, then turned his face away and coughed. It
was deep and lingering, but when it subsided, he felt air almost
break through. His chest felt cold and full suddenly, and he knew
the attack was subsiding. "There," he said. "I can breathe." He was

still gasping, but now it seemed to be doing some good. It was like he was a low, weakened tire being pumped up again. He sat up more, rested his hands on his knees.

"That was a bad one, wasn't it?" Lindsey said. He handed her the towel and she threw it over her neck so that it draped down in front and covered her. "I never knew it could get so bad."

"You never noticed." When he looked at her he saw something in the way she regarded him that passed for a kind of concern for his condition, even distress and worry. "It's okay," he said. "It never goes on for long." She said nothing. "Anyway. It's not always that bad."

"I know."

It was quiet for a while. "The towel came in handy," he said. His hair was still wet at the top of his forehead, but he wasn't gasping for air so much anymore. "It's been tough today."

"Why don't you go to a doctor?"

"It's just asthma. Something I picked up in the Marines. I got out because of it."

She leaned against the trailer wall next to the steps. "It can't do you any good sitting out here in this air."

"I feel like I breathe better." The V-neck of his T-shirt dipped down far enough to show the thick black hair on his chest. She was watching the movement of his chest as he breathed. "This feels really good," he said.

"What does?"

"I'm taking in air. A whole lot of air. It feels really good." The sun glowed brightly just over the roof of the trailer. The metal plate on the door frame was warm and it felt good on his shoulder and arm as he leaned back against it.

"I got to tell you about the really weird thing that happened," she said. He looked at her. "The other day, when I went down to the beach, there was a man walking down there. Not somebody from the town. A stranger."

"Really?"

"He was walking all by himself."

"What's so weird about that?"

"I talked to him."

"So?"

"David Caldwell. He's a sheriff. The Dahlgren County sheriff."

Cecil almost laughed. "Just what we need. Local law."

"He said he was going to be staying here the whole year." She pulled on both ends of the towel, moving it back and forth over her shoulders as she talked.

"Why don't you put some clothes on," Cecil said. He did not want to look at her bare skin, the smooth area around her navel and down along the top edge of her shorts.

"I'm not staying long," she said. She seemed exasperated. "Would you just listen?"

Cecil coughed again, clearing his throat. Neither of them said anything for a while. She folded her arms in front of herself and stared at him. He wanted to light another cigarette, but realized he would not because of what she would say about it. This thought almost amused him. She was the only person in the world who could keep him from doing his will, and she could do it simply by her presence. She had no idea what sort of allowances he made for her all the time. "So you talked to him," he said. "Go on. Then what happened?"

"He was an older guy. Maybe a little older than you even."

"I ain't that old."

"I didn't say you were old. He wasn't young, that's all."

"You think you know, don't you?"

"What?"

"About men and women."

"What's that supposed to mean?"

"You just talk to anybody. Anybody at all."

She looked down at her feet. "No I don't." He said nothing. "Turns out, he's famous."

"Really?"

"I mean, in a way he's famous."

He looked at her. "I guess folks are bound to know who the sheriff is. They elected him, right?"

"No, I don't mean about that."

"Did he say he was here to get me?"

"You think he's here for that?"

"Did he say anything?"

"No."

"Well, why's he famous then?"

"You think he's here because of you? Really?"

He shook his head. "Maybe he didn't come for me. But he will."

"I wish you wouldn't talk like that. It's like you're wishing for it."

"It's not a wish. It's a prediction."

"I don't care. You don't have to get yourself into trouble if you don't want to."

"Yeah, well. Tell me why he's famous."

"I read about him—about his family—in the newspapers when I was still in middle school."

"You don't say."

"We lived in the same neighborhood, on the same street."

"It's a small world."

"It's a tragic story," she said, still pulling on the towel around her neck. She talked of how it happened, all she remembered of it. She told him that the older boy claimed it was an accident. "But they found the body in the backyard, buried in a plastic bag."

"Then it wasn't no accident," Cecil said.

"That's the thing. How does anybody know? Only the two boys were home. Nobody else knows what happened."

"Well, the one boy does."

"It's sad." Lindsey reached into Cecil's shirt pocket and retrieved the pack of cigarettes. She lit one, then handed him the pack. He took one out, looking at her frowning face, then lit his own. "I swear," she said. "Isn't it really weird that I'd actually meet him and talk to him?"

"I guess." He started to light the cigarette, then he caught her looking at him with real scorn. "You quit and I'll quit," he said.

"You mean that?"

"Yeah, I mean it."

"Okay," she said. "I'll put this out right now." She moved to snuff out her cigarette but he grabbed her arm.

"Well?" she said.

He let go of her. She looked into his eyes, pleadingly, but he shook his head. "I ain't never gonna quit, so leave it alone."

"Then why'd you say you would?"

He shrugged. "I was bluffing."

They were quiet again. Cecil folded his arms across his knees, the cigarette between the fingers on his left hand. They smoked without looking at each other. Finally Lindsey said, "I felt sorry for him." Cecil said nothing. "He wasn't bad looking."

"What kind of little girl were you? Reading the newspapers . . ."

"I saw it on TV first. My mom—I wanted to read about it. I was always wishing I had a big brother and then I hear this story about a big brother and all. It definitely stayed in my mind a while. I wrote about it later in journalism class. In ninth grade."

"And then you run into the son of a bitch on the beach."

"Not the big brother. The father." He nodded. "I really felt sorry for him."

"Well," Cecil said, "you got—you're free to hunt that species of animal, I expect."

"What do you mean?" She tried to look into his face, but he turned toward the great rotting Ferris wheel in the short distance across the yard.

"You said you like the name Hunter. You said you hunted me down. So I guess you're entitled to be hunting a husband. You're old en—"

"I'm not hunting for anything like that," she snapped. "The guy was old enough to be my father." He looked at her. "You don't need to put it on that kind of level," she said more calmly.

"Whatever." He rubbed the side of his face, then took the tip of the towel and pulled on it. She let go of it and he took the edge of the towel, leaving it draped around her neck, and wiped his brow with it, then dropped it and curled his fingers into fists and placed both hands against his temples—as though he were trying to cave in his own head right by each ear.

"You want this towel again?" Lindsey asked. He shook his head, breathing slowly and easily. He was suddenly feeling a kind of affection from her again—the intimation that what was lost between him and his mother all those years ago, what he'd never really known in his life since he was a little boy, was somehow there for him again. Or at least that she was there to guide him toward it; it was a tenderness he'd never really known and never would know if she wasn't there to show him. It was the way he often felt with the young children he would gently lift and place in the cars on the wheel. A longing—almost an impulse—to take a person into your arms, and by your embrace, shield them from the erratic and capricious storms of the world. He looked at her now. "What are you hunting for then? You found me. I ain't what you expected. You've seen all the pictures of my—you've seen the pictures of your mother. What else do you want?"

"I want to know who my father was. That's what I want."

"And you think hanging around here, you'll find out?"

"Don't you wonder?"

He looked hard at her. "What the hell do I care?"

"Well," she said, "I guess you really don't have a reason to care, unless you're curious about—unless you want to know about who your mother . . ."

"I'm not."

"I don't want to make you think of those things," she went on. He put his hands back up on his head. "I'm sorry I made you think of those things, I . . . ," she stopped talking. They were quiet for a long time, then she said, "You don't look too good."

"Just hot. And tired."

"What'd you do today?"

He shook his head. "I just been sitting here."

"Weren't you going to take the truck up to Dahlgren today? Monday's November first."

"I gotta take it to the dealer. But it's gonna cost me. It needs a new electronic ignition. I may wait til the fifteenth."

"You can't take it to McDole?"

"No, I took it to McDole. He said it was water in the tank."

"Oh."

"Then he gave me a bill for a hundred sixty-three bucks, and the thing still don't run." She was quiet, watching him. Sweat collected under the hair on his forehead and began running down into his eyes. His face felt as though it was absorbing the heat of the sun. "I told him I wasn't gonna pay him," he said. She flipped her cigarette butt into the sand under the stoop. He was still puffing on his. "I went over there a couple weeks ago and settled things with him, though." He smiled. "I had to hold a gun on the son of a bitch to get him around to my way of thinking." He looked at her now, still smiling slightly, as if he were remembering something they both shared with affection. "He won't be trying to get his money after that."

"I wish you wouldn't—," she stopped. He frowned at her. "I know," she said. "It's your business."

"I don't ask you what you're up to."

"You just asked me why I'm hanging around."

"That's not the same thing." He looked back toward the wheel.

"I don't suppose it matters how it makes me feel when you ask me that."

He considered what she said. He was aware of her eyes on him, and he was feeling as though he had to be careful. He had to be absolutely sure to say the right thing, and he had to be sure she could not read anything from the expression on his face. It was a feeling he was not used to, and it made him nervous. "I just didn't see how you could want to be here with me. You're young and life's waiting for you." She said nothing. "I didn't mean anything else by it. You can stay as long as you like."

"Thank you." She offered him the edge of the towel again but he shook his head.

"I don't know why anybody'd want to stay in a place like this. Full of assholes, mostly."

"Why do you hate all of them so much?" She had asked this question only once before, and he had told her to mind her own business.

This time he said, "I don't hate them."

"You don't?"

"If I did, they'd all be dead."

"Sometimes you scare me," she said.

He knew she meant it—a certainty that made his heart grow cold and reminded him of a truth he steadfastly refused to accept: that this was his sister, and often he didn't really care about her at all. In fact, there were times when he did not even like her, and whenever he realized this he would suddenly feel an oddly exquisite ache that brought almost the sensation of weeping, and he could not fathom or deal with it. He hated himself, her, and the whole world. It was as though he had created the world and put her in it and then caused her pain. He felt so sorry for her that he would try to compensate by striving to please her and make her happy. And he realized that what he was feeling must be some form of affection; that in reality, he was loving her, all the time.

"I just don't take any shit," Cecil said. "Not any. From anybody."

"It sure sounds like hate a lot of the time."

"I don't owe them people nothing."

"I didn't say you did."

"They never lifted a finger to help me or my mother—ever."

"People got to feel like you'll accept their help."

"You don't know," he said. He tried not to speak any louder; he did not want to frighten her, but his subdued vehemence seemed to transform what he said into something other than mere human speech. The way she looked at him, he felt like an idol, muttering the truth. "My mother died in there on that bed. I watched her go. Right there on that thin mattress. She just gave out, like an old motor." He pointed to it, his hand disappearing inside the door. Lindsey moved slightly and seemed ready to come around the steps and look in at his mother's deathbed. But then he said, "Not one of those bastards even gave a damn. I had to put her body in the back of the truck and take her over to Fredericksburg. I swear to god." She was not looking at him. "Shit." He spit on the ground in front of him. "You should have seen her body under the wind in the back of that truck. I drove the thing no faster than thirty miles an hour because I couldn't stand the sight in the rearview mirror. Her clothes blowing in that wind. I dressed her. I put shoes on her, make-up on her face . . ." His voice trailed off, losing its power.

All he had given Lindsey of his mother was a few photographs of this large-boned woman smiling at the camera as though she expected it to start issuing money, or jewelry, or some valuable thing she coveted; her mouth always seemed open in a red-lipped smile. Her almond-shaped bright eyes—covered in too much make-up—looked slightly used from years of smoking and booze. Lindsey did not have to remember her lying on the bed of the truck, senseless and cold, her white feet turned down and bouncing as it moved along.

"Not one of those bastards even sent a card," Cecil said. "She cooked for them, helped them fix up their cottages when they had them to rent. She even spent some time in that goddamned hotel." He sat up straight, straining to stretch his back. "They all found some way to break her heart. And when she died, they didn't even give a damn."

"I wish you had told me before." Lindsey wanted to soothe him now, even put her arms around him. In spite of his bulk, the tone of his voice and the expression on his face were her first intimations of vulnerability, even childlike helplessness. She moved slightly toward him, but he leaned back away from her, frowning. "I wish you had told me," she said again. Her expression wounded him, made him feel again that he had caused her suffering.

He said, "This is just my—I'm only bitching. I don't think about any of this shit. You know it."

"Well, it sounds like you've thought quite a lot about it."

He dragged the tip of the spent cigarette butt along the top of the step until the filter paper came off. He leaned over as he did this, studying the whole thing, watching his hand as if it were not a part of him. Small bits of unburned tobacco collected in the ruts on the step. He leaned further down and tried to blow them away, but he didn't have the air for it. He patted them with his hand, as if he might brush them off that way. He was not looking at her, but he knew she was aware of his eyes, and he felt as though she had seen him fail at something important. He threw the torn filter away.

"You want me to leave?" she asked.

"What?"

"I understand if you want me to leave."

"What's that got to do with what I was saying?" He was absolutely mystified sometimes by the things she said. It was as if she knew what he was thinking before he did, and it always made him feel self-conscious.

"Just that you want me to leave."

"Really? What was I talking about?"

"Just the folks in this town and why you hate them."

"I didn't hear nothing in there about wanting you to leave."

"Well, I don't feel welcome." She smiled.

"I told you. It ain't nothing I think about no more. You brought it up."

"I just don't understand it."

"Understand what?"

"How you can hold onto feelings like that so long."

"It ain't feelings. It's judgment. That's what I'm holding onto. Feelings got nothing to do with it."

"Okay," she said. "Don't get upset."

"I ain't upset." He took a deep breath, realizing he needed again to gasp for air. But once he filled his lungs the sensation subsided.

She stood up straight, smiling at him. There was a long pause, and when he didn't return the smile she said, "You got my towel all dirty." He looked at her now, and wanted very much to smile. "I won't stay at the beach long. I'll go back to Mrs. McCutcheon's and change," she said. "Then I'll come back and see if you want any dinner, how's that sound?"

"I'll be goddamned," Cecil said, looking beyond her. "Would you look at this shit?"

"What?"

"I'll be a son of a bitch." He straightened himself, placing his hands on his knees. She turned and saw McDole stumbling and weaving up the path to the trailer. His mouth was open, but he was not saying anything. He seemed to be watching his feet, taking each step as if he didn't trust the ground under him. He carried a gun in his left hand, as though he needed it for balance.

M cDole stood still, holding the gun down by his leg. He was dressed in blue coveralls with just a sleeveless T-shirt underneath, and his Atlanta Braves baseball cap. His undershirt was yellow and stained with sweat. "This is just insurance," he said, holding the gun up so they could see it. He stood at the end of the walk that led to the trailer, a distance of less than ten feet from the bottom step where Cecil waited for him. Behind McDole the blue street stretched down to the long row of buildings that lined the beach. Beyond the buildings, high above, white birds dipped over the roofs and down to the metallic gray water. The gun looked small and black. He held it loosely in his hand—as if the metal was too cold and he could not stand to have his bare skin on it.

Lindsey heard the distant hum of an airplane and noticed the labored breathing of her brother.

"What can I do for you?" Cecil said. His voice was tired and disinterested—as if he were a clerk in a busy store.

"I want somebody to admit that you owe me money," McDole said. He looked almost as if he was suppressing laughter, but he was not steady on his feet. He faltered a bit, seemed to lurch backwards, then leaned forward to get his balance. He was very drunk. Lindsey moved to the steps, putting her hand on Cecil's shoulder. He looked at her, his expression almost placid, as if he had just awakened from a long and peaceful nap. "Go on home," he said to her.

"No." She couldn't believe him. He looked at her with small sleepy eyes, and he was completely at ease. "I'm going to stay right here," she said.

"Go on, now. I don't feel like company."

"You listening fat man?" McDole said.

Cecil turned to him, "I'll be right with you."

"I'm not going anywhere," said Lindsey.

Cecil got up, stepped down to the dirt in front of the trailer. Lindsey looked for some sign of fear or anger in him. She was so afraid she could not move. She watched helplessly, her eyes moving first to Cecil, then to McDole, to the gun in his hand, then back to Cecil. She felt her heart shivering. Cecil stood straight up, pulled his pants up around his belly. "Go ahead," he whispered to Lindsey, not looking at her. "Get out of here now." Then to McDole he said, "Miss Hunter here was just leaving."

"She can stay or go, I don't care."

"I'm not going anywhere," Lindsey said. "This is just stupid."

Cecil said, "Suit yourself." Lindsey didn't answer him. It was quiet for what seemed like a long time.

"She going or not?" McDole said.

Cecil spit in the dirt at his feet. "I guess not."

McDole shook his head. He took a few tentative steps forward, moving as if he were standing at the edge of a great cliff. "I want somebody to admit that you owe me money." Now he had the gun tightly in his hand, pointing directly at Cecil.

Lindsey shouted, "You better stop this." Cecil started laughing. Lindsey realized it was the first time she had ever heard him actually laugh out loud like that. She had never heard more than a slight chuckle under his breath. She looked at him with wonder now, but he didn't seem to notice that she was still there.

"You been drinking?" he asked McDole.

"I fought in Vietnam, you fat bastard," McDole said. Cecil looked down at his feet, spreading them apart a bit further, then crossed his arms in front of him. He was not laughing anymore, but his expression was still almost playful. "I killed men—I shot people before," McDole said. "It's nothing to me."

"Go ahead and shoot me then." Cecil was smiling. Lindsey could not believe it. McDole seemed to raise the gun a little further, taking aim.

"I'm a witness to this!" Lindsey said, again very loud.

"Admit you owe me money," McDole said.

"Shoot me. Let's see you do that."

"You ain't fooling me," McDole said. "You're scared."

Cecil took a step toward him, and McDole seemed to waver a bit. He stood his ground, but something in his stance seemed to sink a little, as if he almost stepped back but thought better of it. Cecil took another step. "I'm coming to get that gun from you, so you better shoot."

"You want to die?"

Cecil opened his arms in a kind of welcome. "Somebody's gonna die here. Maybe it'll be you, old man."

"You owe me a hundred and sixty-three dollars." Something had happened to McDole's voice. In the middle of what he was saying he seemed to swallow. "You can make payments if you want. But you got to pay it." Lindsey took a step toward him herself now. She suddenly felt very calm and certain that McDole would not fire the gun. In fact, she was a little worried about what Cecil might do to him. "You better stay where you are," McDole said.

"No. I'm coming for the gun. I'm about to take it away from you." Cecil took another step.

"I'm pressing charges," McDole yelled, waving the gun now. "I'm taking you to court."

"I thought you were going to shoot me."

"You son of a bitch."

Now Cecil started walking slowly and steadily toward him, and the movement seemed to force McDole backward. "Don't move," he said. "I really will shoot you." But he continued to take short backward steps. He didn't seem to know what to do with himself.

"I got a question," Cecil said.

"What?" McDole stopped moving.

Cecil walked right up to him. He was close enough to reach out and take the gun. Lindsey was still a few feet in front of the steps of the trailer, and she could barely hear what Cecil was saying. His voice was soft, but certain and forceful—like a man giving instructions. What Cecil said was, "You got any idea at all what you're going to do tomorrow when you sober up and you know I'm coming?"

"You don't move," McDole almost yelled. He seemed short of breath, and he held the gun with both hands now, but he let his arms drop down so that it only dangled in front of him like something too heavy to lift.

Cecil was right in front of him, waiting there. "Well?" he said.

McDole took a quick look behind himself, then tucked the gun in his trousers, turned, and trotted up the street toward the huge Ferris wheel and beyond that, the boardwalk. He was muttering to himself as he went.

Cecil turned, a wry smile on his face and walked back to where Lindsey stood in front of the trailer. "What was that all about?" she asked him.

"I'm going to have some fun tomorrow." They walked back to the front stoop and Cecil sat down again on the top step.

"Weren't you scared?" Lindsey asked.

"No. Of course not. Were you?"

"Yes. At first I was."

He gave a short laugh.

"I can't believe you weren't."

"You don't have to be afraid of folks like that. They're all talk."

"What are you going to do?"

He shook his head. "I don't know. I'll think of something."

"Don't hurt him," she said. He reached for the towel around

her neck and wiped his forehead with it. "You won't hurt him, will you?"

"I won't hurt him bad."

"I don't want you to hurt him at all."

"You don't?"

"Can't you just leave him alone?"

"He said he's going to press charges."

"You think he will?"

"He might."

"Well, you won't improve things any if you hurt him."

He smiled. "Who said I'm trying to improve things." She said nothing. "I just want to win, that's all."

"So, it's a contest?"

He looked at her. She thought he might laugh, but then he said, "You can call it whatever you want."

"Well, what is it then?"

"I have no idea."

"Then why do it?"

"Hell, it ain't nothing but something to look forward to. How about that?" he said.

• • •

"You think he'll come here looking for you?" Clary asked.

"I don't care if he does," McDole answered. They were sitting in the abandoned café off the lobby of the hotel, sipping coffee. McDole had just told them what had happened the day before when he went to Cecil's place and confronted him. He even told them how he had backed away and decided against firing the pistol.

"You wouldn't of shot him, would you?" Mauldin said.

"I really think he wanted me to shoot him."

"Maybe he did." Clary's hands were wrapped around his cup and he turned it slowly, staring at it. He had something else on his mind. He studied his coffee cup as if he were trying to decipher some sort of intricate writing on the side of it.

Hamlin said, "You guys hear the one about the traveling salesman that knocked on this farmer's door and said, 'Can you put me up for the night,' and the farmer says, 'All I got's the one bed with my two young sons a sleeping there. You can share that if you want, but don't touch neither of my sons,' and the guy says, 'Oh, I must be in the wrong joke.'" No one laughed. "Guess you had to be there," Mauldin said.

"I thought it was funny," Hamlin said. He sat back and put his foot up on the edge of the table.

The day had dawned gray and cool. The water in the river looked dirty and oddly metallic, and the sun ran behind a thin, dark layer of shifting clouds. It was cold in the room and steam rose from their coffee.

"If I intended to shoot him, he would've gotten what he wanted. I think he tried to get me to do it," said McDole.

"I told you to leave him alone," Clary said.

"You told me not to press charges."

"Well, I never dreamed you'd go over there."

"I'm not afraid of him. And who are you to tell me to do anything?"

"I didn't mean it the way it sounded," Clary said disgustedly.

Mauldin leaned forward and tipped his cup toward his lips, then sat back. No one said anything for a time. No one wanted to look directly at McDole. He had just told them how, even though he had a pistol in his hand, Cecil had backed him out of his front yard. Also McDole's voice had trembled slightly when he wondered out loud how he could get the new sheriff to protect him once Cecil made up his mind to come for him. It was pretty clear to Clary at least that McDole was terribly afraid. He didn't see how the others could miss it either. Just as that thought passed through his mind, Mauldin said, "You seemed a damn sight scared of him just a minute ago."

This had the unexpected and unwanted effect of making Clary laugh, but he caught himself before he really got into it. "I just got that joke," he said.

McDole glared at Mauldin. "It's the way it seemed," Mauldin said. "I ain't saying that's how it was."

"I'd be scared," Clary said. "You bet your ass I'd be scared."

"You're scared of your own wife," McDole said.

"And you're not scared of Cecil. Right."

Hamlin said, "It don't do no good for us to start fighting."

"Fuck you," said Clary to McDole.

"Such language, and on a Sunday, too," Mauldin said.

They all sat there, staring at the coffee cups on the table. Finally McDole said, "I don't take it kindly."

Clary wouldn't look at him. He'd been hurt by what McDole said, but just then he was not thinking at all about Cecil or McDole or any of it. This morning he and Judy had had a terrible fight—he had screamed at her that she was letting herself go, that she was just sloppy and ugly to him, and it had made her cry. She did not fight back. She looked at him, her eyes brimming with tears, then she walked back into the apartment, away from him. She almost ran—as though she feared what he might say next. And he had not had the will to follow her. All morning he had been feeling sorry, and not just for the fight and what he had said, but for all the grand things that had not happened for his wife over the years, for all the ways he had failed her and continued to fail her. He didn't try to do whatever she wished all the time out of fear, as the others believed. It was profound and implacable guilt. She deserved so much more than he had given her, and he knew it. He feared every day that she would finally come to realize that, and then he would lose her. If he was afraid of anything, that was it. And how could he talk about what had happened this morning with these men? With anyone?

Mauldin said, "Whatever Cecil does, he can't continue to break the law."

"What if we all just stuck together in this?" Hamlin said.

"What do you mean?" asked McDole.

"We'll all four stand up to him." He looked at Clary. "Ain't that what you said to me the other day?"

Clary leaned back in his chair, holding onto the table, but he said nothing. He smiled at Hamlin.

"Ain't it?" Hamlin said.

"I been saying it all along. He's our problem. So we take care of it."

"How?" Mauldin said. Clary looked at him, momentarily silenced by the question. "I hope you don't take this the wrong way," Mauldin said. "But I don't have a problem with Cecil."

"I don't, either," Clary said. "He minds his own business where I'm concerned."

"Well, shit," McDole said.

"Really what's the problem here?" Mauldin pointed his cup toward McDole. "You started this thing up with him—or at least—"

"I started it?" McDole couldn't believe what he'd heard. "I started it?"

"Wait a minute," Clary said.

"I didn't mean you started it," Mauldin broke in. "But it is your problem. Why should I pick a fight with Cecil if he ain't done nothing to me?"

"Some friend you are," McDole said.

"He's not threatening me directly," Hamlin said. "If I leave him alone, he'll leave me alone."

"Shit."

"No, seriously," Hamlin said.

"One minute you say we all ought to stick together," McDole said. "And the next you're saying you got no problem with him."

"What'd you go over there for yesterday?" Hamlin asked.

"The son of a bitch owes me money."

"Just about everybody in here owes you money for one thing or another, but we don't—"

"I know you'll pay it," McDole interrupted. "I don't have you telling me you don't owe it."

"Why don't you just write it off as a bad debt?" Mauldin suggested.

Clary felt a slight sensation of dread cross through the back of his mind. The men were getting loud and he could see that McDole was moving toward one of those destructive outbursts that cancels longtime associations and ruins alliances. He was also a little shocked at this sudden show of disloyalty on the part of Hamlin and Mauldin. "I think . . . ," he said. "Wait a minute. I think we got to approach this thing as a problem we all have."

"I don't see it that way," Mauldin said. "It may be a problem, but I don't have it. Not right now, anyway."

"But," Clary said, raising his hand to forestall the objections of the others, "maybe you will have it some day, and when you do, you'll have to face it alone."

Mauldin shrugged. "I guess so."

"Why do that?" asked Clary. "Why on earth do that?"

"Hell," Hamlin said to McDole. "Why don't you just go on down to that new sheriff's office and tell that son of a bitch down there to quit eyeing the contractors and painting and hammering and such his own self, and do some sheriffing?"

"Yeah," Mauldin said. "I don't have trouble now. I don't want trouble now. That's how I feel." He picked up his mug and downed the rest of his coffee.

"Suit yourself," McDole said calmly. He didn't look anyone in the face, but Clary could tell he was seething.

"I'm sorry if you think that's a betrayal," Mauldin said. "I don't think you really got a problem as long as you stay away from him."

"Right," McDole said.

Hamlin remained silent, sipping his coffee, not meeting anyone's gaze. Clary felt a growing and odd sort of disillusionment—a sensation very much like having been proven wrong publicly. His attachment to these men was not so great as his desire to keep to this routine—he was worried that if things continued on their present course, the morning gatherings for coffee would be ruined somehow. And he loathed the idea of just being by himself with no one else to talk to in the mornings. He could not have put these feelings into words. He was watching everyone, almost apprehensively. Then he said, "I'll go up to McDole's place this morning. I don't mind." McDole looked at him.

Hamlin said, "Me, too. Hell, my place is right across the street."

WHEN THEY finished their coffee, Clary went up to the top floor and sought out Judy. She was sitting on the couch in front of the television with the sound off, just glancing at the screen occasionally and flipping through a magazine. It broke his heart to see that she had combed her hair and put on make-up. He had to take a deep breath to keep from breaking into tears. He went into the kitchen and stood in front of the sink for a minute, came back out to the entrance, and looked at her. With her head down, staring at the magazine, she was beautiful, and he loved her again with a kind of ache and fear of loss that always moved him.

"Would you mind watching the desk this morning?" he asked her. She looked at him. He was afraid she would not speak to him, or that she would insist on talking over their fight, but she put the magazine down and smiled at him. "What are you and the boys going to be doing?" She was not being sarcastic. She frequently emphasized "the boys" when referring to her husband and his friends.

"Some things up at McDole's place we want to see about."

"What?"

"Nothing important. He's got some new duck decoys and such he wants to show me." She said nothing. "Do you mind, hon?"

She got up and stretched. "No. Go and play with your little coffee klatch." This was sarcastic.

"I won't go if you don't want me to."

"No, go ahead," she said, leaning down and picking up the magazine again.

He went over to her and took her in his arms. "I'm sorry," he whispered. She put her head against his shoulder, but she said nothing. "Sometimes, I'm just an old fool." He stroked her soft hair, breathing in the fragrance of it.

"So," she said, leaning back. "You and the boys are going up to McDole's station then?" There were tears in her eyes.

He wanted to tell her how far from the truth everything he said was, how beautiful she was, and how often he just loved to look at her. But he knew she wouldn't believe it. She would never really believe him anymore. "You're so beautiful," he said.

She smiled up at him. "You and your friends are just a bunch of little boys, you know that, don't you?"

He kissed her on the cheek. "I'll be back in the early afternoon or so."

"Can you make it before noon? I might want to go to church this morning."

"Church?"

She looked away. "I haven't been in a while."

"Okay," he said. "But if I'm not here, just close the place. It won't hurt for an hour or so if you want to go . . ."

"Just by eleven," she said. "I can go to eleven thirty mass."

"Don't wait for me then. Just close the place."

"Okay."

He kissed her on the forehead. Then held himself back and tried to look into her eyes. "You're not still feeling bad about this morning, are you?"

"No." She would not look at him.

"Oh," he said as he was going out. "Don't forget towels for our guest today."

"I won't." She waved the magazine.

DOWNSTAIRS, McDOLE and Hamlin were waiting for him, still sitting at the table. Mauldin had gone on up the street to his place.

"You ask permission?" Hamlin said.

"She said she'd watch the front desk," Clary said.

So the three of them walked up the long street to the edge of town and McDole's gas station. It was close to nine in the morning. McDole went inside and lit the signs and turned the pumps on. Already cars had pulled off the highway and were waiting at the pumps. Hamlin took a seat in the garage next to the lift, and Clary strolled over to the desk next to the cash register. The place smelled of oil and grease and a sweet, unidentifiable odor that was probably the soap in the men's room. Everything was dirty, including the papers on the desk and the dull-colored service tickets that were tacked to the wall. McDole sat on a stool in front of the pay window and worked the cash register. For most of the morning the business was steady. There was no sign of Cecil Edwards. Near noon Hamlin said, "I'm getting bored."

"What's different about this?" Clary said. "You sit in almost an exactly similar chair in your office all day."

"It don't smell like this," he said. "And I can play around on my computer." He seemed indignant. "It's more pleasant than this place, I can tell you."

"Why don't we get some lunch or something?" McDole said.

"I could run down to the McDonald's at the next exit on the highway," Hamlin offered.

"That'd take too long," McDole said. "You got to go all the way back to the hotel and get your car and then drive down there."

"Well, what do *you* want to do?"

McDole turned to Clary. "Why don't you just call Judy and have her get something ready at the hotel."

"You know how she likes to make sandwiches and such," Hamlin said. He was smiling.

"No, she really doesn't." Clary didn't like Hamlin's smile, which looked slightly curved and disingenuous, but he wasn't sure if this was mockery or if Hamlin really believed what he was saying.

"We'll pay for the sandwiches," McDole said. "She won't mind that."

"All right," Clary said. "I'll go down and see if she's got some fresh bread and maybe some lunch meat." He got up and started down toward the hotel. He only walked a few feet before he noticed Cecil's truck in the parking lot. He turned back to the others. "Hey, you see that?"

"What?" McDole asked.

"He's at the hotel." They turned and looked. "Cecil's at the hotel," Clary repeated.

"I'll be goddamned," Hamlin said.

Clary started walking faster back down the street. He never took his eyes off the pickup, expecting it to move any second, expecting Cecil to drive it up to McDole's place. But as he approached the hotel, getting close enough to see inside the truck, he could see that Cecil wasn't there.

When he got to the front door of the lobby, he realized that McDole and Hamlin were not with him. He looked back. They had followed him a short distance, but then they had stopped, and now they were waiting at the end of the street, not far from McDole's gas station. They watched him. He turned and went around on the boardwalk to the front of the hotel. From that vantage point he could not see McDole and Hamlin anymore. He walked into the lobby and there was Judy sitting at the desk, still reading her magazine. The lobby was empty.

"Where's Cecil?" he said.

"Who?"

"Cecil. Cecil. Did he come in here?"

"No. He's in the café drinking coffee. What's the matter with you?" She sat up straight and closed the magazine on the counter in front of her.

"What's he doing here?"

"He just wanted a cup of coffee."

"What'd he say to you?"

"Nothing. What's wrong with you?"

Clary stood in the entrance, staring at her. In the light above the desk she looked lovely again, with her dark eyes and the red lipstick. He was glad that she had put on the make-up; he felt a slight remnant of his earlier guilt over the fact that his insults had prompted her to make herself presentable. They were okay again, though. He was sure of that. "Did he pay you for the coffee?"

"Not yet."

"He's in there by himself?"

"I've been sitting here reading my *Vanity Fair* and keeping an eye on the front desk," she said. "We did have a visitor, though."

"We did?"

"That fellow who's staying here. Caldwell? His son came in this morning just after you left."

"Caldwell mentioned he'd be coming."

"He didn't stay. All he wanted to know was if his father was here." Clary came to the desk and leaned on it. "When I said yes, he looked almost shocked," Judy said.

"Shocked."

"What's so important about Cecil coming here? He's been here before."

"McDole's expecting trouble."

Judy opened her magazine again. "I swear. I think McDole looks for trouble sometimes."

"Why'd you say Caldwell's son looked shocked?"

She flipped a page, almost snapping it, then she considered for a second, staring off behind him. "When I told him his father was here, he just got this look on his face. Like it scared him or something. Then he just walked out."

"Really?"

"Not a word, either. Just went to the door and disappeared. I don't think he expected he'd have to see his father right away like that."

"Well, what'd he come here for?"

"Who knows?"

"Did you get him his fresh towels today?"

"First thing," she said.

"Does he know his son was here?"

"Not yet. I haven't seen him."

"Where'd the boy go?"

"He's not a boy. He's a grown man."

"Where'd he go?"

"How should I know?" She looked at him. "Are you back for the day?"

"Well, no," he said. "I was wondering if—," he stopped. He watched her turn back to the magazine. "Did you go to church?"

"No." She studied the magazine for a while, then flipped another page. Presently she looked up again. "What?"

"I was going to make some sandwiches and take them back up there."

"You going to get paid for them?"

"Yeah. They said they wanted to order sandwiches. I didn't offer it or anything."

"You want me to make them?" Her smile was genuine and warm, and he felt very close to her again.

"Would you?"

. . .

Moments later, David Caldwell got off the elevator and headed across the lobby of the hotel. He was wearing a blue jacket and white slacks. His black leather shoes clacked on the brightly shined tile floor and echoed in the empty lobby. His dark hair was combed straight back, and he was wearing a loosely knotted red tie. Clary sat quietly at the desk and watched him approach.

"Do you have a morning paper?" Caldwell asked.

"Sure." Clary leaned down, retrieved a *Washington Post* from a shelf behind him, and threw it on the counter. As he did this he said, "Your boy was here."

Caldwell glanced down at the paper, then what Clary said seemed to register. "What did you say?"

"Your son was here. This morning."

"Why didn't you . . . ?"

"I wasn't here. My wife talked to him."

Caldwell seemed puzzled. He turned toward the double doors, then looked back from where he had come. He gave the impression of a man standing at a high place in the darkness, unsure of the next possible step. When his eyes met Clary's again, he focused on him—as if he had to watch everything the other man might do. "My son was here?"

"The wife told me he asked about you. Wanted to know if you were here."

Caldwell seemed to be watching Clary's mouth for other words that might fall from it. "When she told him you were here, he just turned around and walked out."

"How long ago was this?"

"Early this morning—around nine fifteen or so."

"Why wasn't I told?"

Clary shook his head. "You'll have to ask the wife."

Caldwell rested his hands on the counter. "Seems like you didn't want to be disturbed," Clary continued. "The other day when I . . ."

"Forget it," Caldwell interrupted. "Did he leave anything for me? A note or . . ."

"No, I don't think so." They stood there, appraising each other. Then Clary said, "The wife said he was kind of upset . . ."

"Upset?"

"No, not like that. Shocked. That's the word she used."

Caldwell shook his head.

"You know. Shocked that you were actually here, I guess. Then she said he backed away, turned, and walked out."

"Where is *the wife*?"

Clary did not miss his tone. "She just now went next door, to the café. You can go on over there and talk to her if you want."

"Next door?"

"Right through there." He pointed to a wide set of double doors across the lobby next to the exit that led to the boardwalk. Above the doors a sign announced it was the "Sunrise Café." Caldwell stared at the doors for a moment, then turned back to Clary. "It looks abandoned."

"It's closed, but I still use it every day to make coffee and sandwiches and such. It used to be owned by the hotel, then another fella bought it, and then it went out of business."

Caldwell walked across to the doors and studied them for a while, then he pulled the handle on one, and when that didn't work, he pulled on the other one and the door came open. Standing there in the opening, holding the door for him, was Cecil. He glanced briefly at Clary, then stepped aside and let Caldwell pass. Neither man spoke. Cecil let go of the door and let it close, gently, then tucking in his shirt and walking slowly, he approached the desk.

"Well," Clary said. "What're you doing here?" Cecil let his arms rest on the desk, leaning down to do so. He said nothing, but he looked at the newspaper on the counter. "That was for the sheriff," Clary said.

"The sheriff?"

"That fella that just passed you there on the way into the diner. He's the Dahlgren County sheriff."

"You don't say. He looked familiar."

"Familiar?"

"I think I've seen him before. Can't remember when, though. Seems like somebody I know."

"Maybe you saw a poster or something."

"Maybe."

"He asked for that paper, but then he didn't take it."

Cecil just stared at him.

"Can I—," Clary stopped. It was quiet for a few seconds. "What'd'ya need? It's too early for lunch, ain't it?"

"It's almost noon," Cecil said.

"Well, maybe it's not too early then."

"Y'all had your coffee, huh?" Cecil straightened himself and pulled on the waistband of his pants, still getting his shirt tucked in the way he liked it. He had not shaved, and the burned look of his lower jaw and chin made him look even more menacing. His eyes did not blink or look away from Clary's eyes.

"We had our coffee."

"Too late for me. I had to drink alone."

"Well, I wish you'd have come early," Clary said, feeling slightly less wary. "Judy's just gone in there to make some sandwiches. She'll brew a pot for sure, if you'd like another cup."

Cecil put both beefy hands on the counter and leaned slightly forward. "What do you and those others think you're doing?"

"What?"

"You heard me."

"I don't know what . . ."

Cecil reached out, almost gently took the front of Clary's shirt in his fist, and pulled him up close, so that Clary was stretched awkwardly across the counter. "Does he think he's safe gathering you guys around him?" Cecil whispered. His breath smelled of tobacco and damp, rotted wood. He was so close to Clary that his eyes looked magnified and glittery, like something whirling in planetary space. "Does he?"

Clary reached up and grabbed the other man's shirtsleeve, but he did not struggle too hard. He simply pulled steadily and directly on the fabric, as though he might rip it unless Cecil let go. "Please," he said. "Let go of me."

Cecil seemed to smile, then he gently let go, and Clary slid back down off the counter and to his feet. "You tell him for me he ain't safe," Cecil said. "Ain't none of you safe."

"Maybe you didn't hear me about the sheriff."

"I ain't worried about no sheriff."

"Maybe you should be."

"Sheeit," Cecil said. "He don't look like much."

"You can't just do whatever you want," Clary said. He hoped the door would open and Caldwell would come back in. He wanted to see what Cecil would do if Caldwell was standing right there, watching him.

"Just tell McDole I'm coming."

Clary stepped back a bit, but he rested the tips of his fingers on the counter and regarded Cecil with a kind of curious interest.

He was in this—dealing with it the best he could—and he realized he was not afraid. Cecil seemed to think Clary was going to say something, and when he didn't it momentarily stopped him. After a short pause he said, "Just tell him."

"Why don't you tell him?"

Cecil had no response. "Why don't you just leave all of us alone," Clary said. "How about that?" Cecil glared at him, but he was still silent. "Jesus Christ. Ain't all of this shit just a lot of work?"

"All of what?"

"All you got to do to keep this shit up."

"Keep what up?"

"You know what I'm talking about, Cecil."

"I know what you and that other three are up to," he said. "I can see it. I ain't blind."

"Doesn't it get to be like a job after a while? Keeping track of who you got to hurt or go after? You need a fucking accountant to keep it straight."

Cecil seemed to smile briefly, then he shook his head and started to laugh. He slapped the counter and leaned over it. Clary watched him. The laughter was a deep, gradually disappearing reverberation that surrendered to just the small, definite, whining sound of air being forced out of a very small opening, and then Cecil was coughing, gasping for breath. "Jesus," Clary said. "It ain't that funny." Cecil had both hands on the counter now, and his head was down, between his arms, as though he were drawing air up from the floor. The coughing subsided, but now he was still struggling to breathe. The sound he made was horrifying— a high-pitched whooping noise in the hollows of his throat. It made Clary remember an owl he once heard that got trapped in a small, damp sewer tunnel.

Judy came in with a miniature cooler and the sandwiches wrapped in wax paper and neatly stacked in a small cellophane bag. "What happened to him?"

"I don't know. He was laughing at something I said." They watched him gradually get the air he needed. When he could manage it, he took a small inhaler out of his pocket and sprayed it into his mouth. Judy said nothing. Clary said, "You okay?"

Cecil looked up, and Clary saw that his face was bright red and he had tears running out of his eyes. "An asthma attack," Clary said, matter of factly, though he was only guessing at what he had just seen. He did not know that Cecil had asthma.

"I'll get him some water," Judy said, putting the cooler and the sandwiches on the counter.

When she came back with the water, Cecil was breathing normally. He took the glass from her and drank it down carefully and slowly, but he did not stop until it was all gone. When he handed her the glass, she said, "More?" He nodded his head, gasping now because he held his breath to drink the water.

Just at that moment, Clary realized he felt good. He had helped Cecil—or at least his wife had helped him—in a kind of crisis, and maybe this was the way he could get to the place where he didn't have to fear what Cecil might be up to. Judy came back with another glass of water, and this time Cecil only sipped at it. The three of them stood there in the dimly lit lobby, Cecil with one hand on the counter, sipping his water, and Judy and Clary watching him. Gradually his face returned to a normal color and he wiped his mouth with the sleeve of his shirt. "That was a bad one," Clary said.

Cecil did not even nod his head. He took another slow sip of the water, then handed the half-empty glass back to Judy. "Thank you," he said.

Judy remained there, holding the glass in two hands, watching him. Something in the way her eyes seemed to shift down slightly, then glance back up in genuine concern at Cecil's face, made Clary profoundly anxious. Suddenly he did not feel very good at all. The look on his wife's face was something new to him, and he realized he would remember it; it would come back to him later, and it would only serve to amplify his fear of loss and make him even more conscious of what time had stolen from him—a sense of intimacy and power no other woman had ever been able to give him. There was a kind of joy in longing for her, for everything he could have of her. Now, looking at her eyes as she gazed at Cecil, he knew exactly how he would feel if she told him she was leaving him. At the same time he realized he could have her again only if he could somehow get her to look at him the same way she now looked at Cecil. In her eyes, a kind of melancholy light shone, but there was excitement and mystery, too. It was as if she was both drawn to him and repelled by him at the same time. Clary believed such tensions were what attracted most intelligent women—not looks, or physique, or even charm. It was this paradoxical pull toward violence and passion, sexuality and power—the apprehension of intense experience—that made some men irresistible to women. At least some women. Women who, like his wife, smirked at conventional wisdom and went at life with a kind of assertive and wistful, undefeated will; women who never seemed happy, and who saw accident and fate as the natural order of things.

"Are you going to be all right now?" Judy asked Cecil.

"He'll be okay," Clary said. "Just a minute ago he had me by the neck and he was threatening me."

Cecil looked hard across the counter at Clary, but then he smiled again. He turned to Judy. "I was threatening your old man. Forgive me." He seemed to tip his hat toward her, then he moved to the door and went out.

"What the hell's he doing here this morning?" Clary asked.

"I have no idea."

"He's supposed to be coming after McDole, not bothering us."

"He's going after McDole?"

Clary nodded, still watching the door. "Sometimes," Judy said, "I feel like I'm trapped in a big, underachieving high school."

"What's that supposed to mean?"

"He's 'going after' McDole. Good lord. Why don't you guys grow up?"

"What are you yelling at me for? I'm not involved in any of it."

"I'm not yelling at you." She came around the counter and stood next to him. He looked at her, but he didn't move. "Well?" she said.

"Well, what?"

"You staying here, or are you going to take the sandwiches up to McDole's place?"

He wanted to say something else to her, but he stood there in front of her eyes, feeling small. She would not look away. He placed the stool between them and said, "Have a seat."

She smiled, but it was more to herself than at him. She took her place on the stool, her eyes cast down now, but still smiling. He picked up the bag of sandwiches, placed it carefully in the cooler, and headed for the front door. He did not want to be where she could see and appraise him. He felt suddenly embarrassed and self-conscious—as if he were a teenager and in her presence for the first time.

xi

Just as Clary came out of the hotel, he saw Cecil's big black four-wheeler with giant, wide Michelin tires easing its way up the street. The bright black finish still gleamed just as it did when Cecil bought it brand-new, four years ago. He always kept it spotless. Even the white lettering on the sides of the tires seemed to increase in the sunlight. Cecil drove up the street very slowly, as if he were looking for McDole and the others in the windows and shops that lined the street. As he approached McDole's service station, he saw the two men sitting in chairs just outside the entrance to the gas station office. Both looked patient and comfortable, even though it was not yet forty degrees and the slight breezes off the water made it seem much colder. McDole had leaned his chair back against the wall, and Hamlin was bent forward with his elbows on his knees. From where they were sitting, they could see the long road down to the town and, a few hundred feet to the left of the road and running parallel to it, the boardwalk, and beyond that, the white, unimposing beach that ran almost deferentially next to the river. From that distance, the river didn't look like moving water. It looked as if a small portion of the gray and cloudy sky had fallen down into the sand just at the horizon.

As Cecil approached the station, he could see one car at the first island of pumps and a heavyset gray-haired man leaning over the back end of it, pumping his own gas. The breezes blew his hair straight up. He wore a checkered shirt and seemed to be impatiently explaining something—either to a person in the car, or perhaps he was talking to McDole and Hamlin. Cecil could see the two men making an effort not to notice that he was coming, but when he slowed his truck to a stop and waited there just across the street, Hamlin sat up straighter and McDole let his chair down from against the wall and sat forward a little himself.

Cecil thought to just sit there and watch the reaction. The gray-haired man finished gassing up, paid, and drove off. Another car pulled in. Then another. Cecil watched it all, his engine still running. Hamlin remained seated, studying him now, watching as warily as a deer near a stream before it steals a drink of water. McDole went inside and worked at the register, taking credit cards and cash from customers. Finally Hamlin got up and went inside as well. Cecil remained where he was until the last car pulled off and the station was momentarily empty, then he drove up on the right side, by the first island.

In front of him was a neon sign on the ground that said Exxon, and under that, the gas prices in block letters: Reg. 119.99. Prem. 139.99. Under the prices were several pictures of cigarette packs and prices above those in smaller letters. Cecil drove up to the sign, inched forward until the huge front bumper of his truck was against the frame that held the sign, and then he gunned the engine a little and flattened it. His truck rose up over the broken glass and the twisted aluminum frame, crushing it completely. He made a hard left and knocked over a display full of oilcans. The ones he crushed squirted oil in great explosive jets along the pavement, and the others rolled crazily across the entire width of the station. He turned the truck again and swung through by one of the islands, pulling up to a big Coke machine next to the garage door in front of the mechanic's bay and slowly pushing it over. He laughed out loud at the sound it made when it hit. Coke leaked out of the side of the machine like a kind of blood. It ran down the slight incline of the station and mingled in puddles with the oil that was smeared everywhere and running more slowly toward the level ground.

While he was doing all of this, Cecil heard McDole hollering his name, cursing him. He saw both McDole and Hamlin standing in the doorframe, and he waved at them as he passed one last time. He didn't look back. He opened the window and let his arm rest on the door as he pulled out of the station and drove on up the road. The cold air on his face felt wonderful, and he drew in great deep breaths of air as he drove along. There was nothing at all on his mind.

WHEN HE got back to his trailer, Lindsey was waiting there for him. "Where'd you go so early?" she said.

"Early? It's after noon."

"I just wondered where you were."

"I went to church."

"You did not."

"I went . . ." he looked at her. "Nowhere." He got down out of the truck and walked around to inspect the front bumper. He leaned down and looked closely at the tires, then he went on up the broken walk to the front door of the trailer. Lindsey was shivering when she came up next to him.

"How long you been waiting here?" he asked.

"I just got here."

"You walked?"

"No. Mrs. McCutcheon gave me a ride. She was going up to Warsaw today."

"What's the matter with your Cavalier?"

"Nothing."

He opened the door of the trailer and they both went in. It was warm and close inside the trailer, and the air smelled of newsprint and mildew. "Where'd you go this morning?" Lindsey asked again. She had her arms folded in front of her, but she had stopped shivering. He didn't answer her, but he forced a smile. "I want to know," she insisted.

"I drove down to the hotel and then up to McDole's gas station."

"What happened?"

"Nothing happened."

"I heard it. There was a lot of noise down that way. And I heard McDole hollering."

"I didn't hurt him."

"What'd you do?"

He moved to the couch and sat down heavily. She closed the door and stood there for a moment, then she sat in the chair by the small TV tray. He did not have to fight for air, and the fact that he was breathing normally made him feel strong and young.

"What'd you do?" she said again.

"I expect you'll hear about it." She didn't seem to know what to say to him. For an awkward moment, he continued to stare at her and then he looked away. He didn't want her to know that he was aware of her discomfort. "You had breakfast?"

"I don't want anything," she said.

"What's wrong with you?"

"I had a dream last night."

"Really?"

"You were in it."

"I hope I wasn't bad."

"I thought I could stop you today," she said. "I really believed I could come up here and stop you."

"That was a dream all right."

"No, not in the dream. When I woke up this morning I thought I could stop you."

"You didn't get up early enough."

"It's not early."

"I went down there this morning," he said. "Where were you?"

"I couldn't sleep. I had a bad night. It's why I didn't want to drive this morning."

"The dream?"

"I guess."

"You dreamed about me? I guess it must have been a nightmare."

"No, that's not it. That's not why it was a nightmare."

"Well, you should have got out of bed earlier."

She had no answer for that. She'd worn her thick red jacket, dark Levi's, and a blue turtleneck sweater. The wool of the sweater started to get to her. She reached up and scratched around her neck. She removed her jacket and draped it over the back of the chair. "I didn't think I'd ever get warm," she said.

"Why not?"

"Tell me what you did."

"You really want to know?"

She sighed.

"Well, I didn't do much." He told her everything. He could not keep from laughing when he got to the part about the oilcans. "You should have seen how they rolled and scattered. You'd have been proud."

"No, I wouldn't."

"Well. It was a sight to see."

"So what do you think McDole will do now?"

"I don't care what he does." He reached up and rubbed his eyes with both hands, leaning forward with his elbows on his knees.

"It's just childish," Lindsey said.

"Look. I'm a carny. You know what a carny is?"

"No."

"And you read all those books?"

"What's a carny?"

"A person who lives and works in a carnival." She said nothing. "Carnies don't behave like other folks, and they don't have the same rules."

"Really."

"They fight their own fights and take care of their own. It's just the way they are."

"So . . ."

"So I'm not being childish. I'm being who I am."

She shook her head. Now he looked at her again. Her hair was mussed by the wind, and water lined her eyes as though she'd been crying. "You okay?" he said.

"I'm fine."

"I'm pretty tired."

"Already?"

"I been up since five."

There was a long silence. Presently he said, "Well, I need an afternoon nap."

"And you don't think you'll see McDole again with a pistol?"

"I hope I do," he said, leaning back in the cushions. "That would be just fine."

"Really?"

"It's too cold to go down to the beach and read. So why don't you hang around here and later we'll have dinner or something."

"Is that what you want me to do?"

"What's the matter with you, anyway? You look like you been crying." She shrugged. "You been crying?"

"No."

"Well, you don't have to hang around here. Do what you want. How would that be?"

"What are you going to do?"

"I told you already. Jesus Christ." Then in a calmer voice he said, "I'm gonna take a nap. I had quite a day so far."

"Sometimes," she sighed, "I wonder why I bother."

"Really?"

"Yes."

"Bother about what?" She didn't answer. "I'm gonna be straight with you," he said. "I promised you I'd always shoot straight with you."

"I don't remember that." He looked down, letting his head sink toward the floor, but he said nothing. "Yeah?" she said. "You're gonna be straight?"

"No, I mean it. I told you I'd be straight with you and I'm going to tell you that I feel that . . . I feel like I'm angry with the tone of what you're saying to me right now."

"You do?"

"Yeah. That tone right there. I don't much like it." He did not raise his voice and he was still breathing evenly.

"What did you expect? You go down into the town and cause all this trouble, and I'm supposed to—"

"I do not like to be talked to like you're talking to me right now."

"I don't know what you mean. I'm being very calm. I am not aware of any particular tone."

"That, right there," he said. "That. Any particular tone. Any particular tone—like that."

She put her hand up to her chin, seemed to pull on it, then pushed her hair back and sighed. "Really, Cecil. Sometimes you're just too much."

"Why don't we just forget it?"

"I'm sorry if you don't like what I say to you."

"Leave it," he said. "Can you do that?"

• • •

Caldwell checked for Todd on the beach first. He saw no one. He walked a long way up toward the end of the sand where the trees hung low over the edge of the river. He knew he was not going to find Todd out on the beach, but he looked a long time anyway, thinking it would be good to find him there. When Todd was a boy he had loved to stand by the shore and watch the water as it lapped steadily at the sand. Caldwell understood that he was both hoping to find his son here and avoiding the moment when he would look him in the face. Finally he went back to the boardwalk and walked up to the end by the Ferris wheel. He saw Lindsey coming from Cecil's trailer. She leaned over and opened the gate that led to the Ferris wheel and came down the slight incline toward him. He stepped down off the boardwalk and into the sand and walked up to meet her. Lindsey kept her hands in her pockets and her shoulders hunched in the slight breeze off the river.

"Hey," he said. "Where you going?"

"I'm just walking."

"Kind of chilly for that."

"You coming to arrest Cecil?"

"Arrest him?"

"What are you doing up this way?"

"I'm looking for . . . ," he didn't finish the sentence. He was aware of her waiting there for him to finish, but he was looking beyond her toward the old Ferris wheel. Standing under the wheel, gazing up at it as if he were waiting for it to move, was a young man—tall, dark haired, lean, but strong looking. "Who's that?" Caldwell said, but he knew. It was Todd.

"I don't know," Lindsey said. "He just knocked on the door and asked me if he could look at the Ferris wheel for a while. I told him it was okay. Cecil's trying to nap, so I—"

"Mind if I talk to him?"

"Go ahead," she said. "I'm going down to the hotel to see if they got any milk."

He nodded, but he didn't really hear what she said. He walked as steadily as he could make himself, through the small red gate at the entrance, past the red ticket booth, and up to where Todd stood in the dirty sand, staring up at the top of the wheel.

"Todd?" Caldwell said.

The young man turned and looked at him. His face was blank, almost pitiless. "Yeah?"

"It's me."

"I know it."

He looked into his son's eyes and tried to remember some hint of the long ago love he felt for him; he had dreamt of this moment many times, but now that it was here, nothing seemed to be working in his memory. The sight of his son didn't even stir a small sinew of affection. He saw nothing. The only thing he felt was an odd sort of detached fear—as if the wrong word or gesture might cause his son to take flight; he was afraid of hurt, of what he might say, or might not say. Todd's face was inscrutable, almost featureless. His light blue eyes reflected the gray light, and his mouth was straight under the sharp nose. His features seemed enlarged, more solid than Caldwell remembered. He was astonished to see the coarse stubble of a beard, deep-set eyes, and thick, wavy, light brown hair, and it struck him that no matter what might have happened in their past, this was a narrow-faced and indifferent stranger; this was, simply, another man. Then he realized there was a little of his own father in the way Todd tilted his head slightly back, in the way he looked down his nose at the world, not judging it, not looking superior, but, rather, looking as though he was curious about everything in his view. He was smoking a cigarette, letting it dangle from his lips.

"You made it all right?" Caldwell said, foolishly.

"Yeah." Todd looked down at his own hand as he offered it to his father. "I been here more than a week."

Caldwell reached out, awkwardly shaking his son's hand a little too rapidly. "Well, it's good to see you."

"Yeah."

"I'm at the hotel." He spoke fast, afraid of what might happen if he fell silent. Todd put his hands in his pockets and turned back toward the Ferris wheel. "I'm going to be here a while, so you can stay with me if you want. I mean—isn't that the plan? That you'll stay with—"

"Didn't we ride on this thing a lot?" Todd pointed at the wheel.

"A few times."

"I remember it as *the* ride down here. The one Bobby . . . the one we all liked." Caldwell said nothing. A stronger than usual breeze brushed the back of his neck and gave him a chill. Todd hiked his collar up. "It's getting colder, I think," he said. "Colder up here than down in Richmond."

"I guess it is."

Todd took a deep puff on the cigarette, looking down at his feet. He turned the cigarette in his mouth and stared at the wheel. Caldwell wanted to say something kind, something welcoming, but he could not get his mind to give him the words. Finally he said, "You look good, son."

"I been staying at the motel," Todd said.

"I hoped you'd get here sooner and—"

Todd interrupted him. "This place is so rundown. It's weird."

"Yes, it is."

"It's depressing."

"Yeah."

Todd flipped his cigarette into the sand. "Fucking cold, too."

They looked at each other. "Damn," Caldwell said. "It's good to see you, son. It really is." Todd almost smiled. Something in his countenance seemed to let go, and then he turned his gaze back to the Ferris wheel. "You think the thing still runs?"

"I don't know. I think it does. It looks like it could." They were quiet for a moment. Caldwell put his arm over his son's shoulder and grasped him tightly. Todd stared ahead, smiling now. For a brief moment, Caldwell felt the most profound sense of loss and sadness—for all the years he had missed of his older son's life—and then he remembered Bobby and something happened to his grip. He clapped Todd on the back and stepped back. He realized he was fighting tears. "This is not much of a place," he said.

"No, it isn't."

Caldwell cleared his throat, then got control of himself.

"Not much of a place at all," Todd said.

There was a long silence. Todd reached into his shirt and took out another cigarette. He offered one to Caldwell who shook his head no. When Todd had lit the cigarette, he held it in his lips and put both hands in his pockets. He was still staring at the wheel, squinting against the gray smoke.

"I don't know what I should say," Caldwell said. "I mean, I've been thinking about this for a long time ... and I ..."

184 · Robert Bausch

Todd looked at him, the cigarette still dangling from his mouth. "You're not in uniform."

"No. I'm doing things more and more without it. A sheriff can do that."

"Really?"

"It's not like being a state trooper, or . . ."

"Well, you don't look like a sheriff."

Caldwell didn't know what he should say to that. He stared at the wheel. "What are you doing at the motel?"

At the same time Todd asked, "So you've been planning this a long time?"

"What?"

"You said you've been planning this for a long time?"

"No."

"I thought you said—"

"I said I'd been thinking about it."

"Oh."

"I just don't know what I should say here."

"I didn't come down here to get you to say anything."

"Well, but why did you want to do this?"

Todd shook his head, reached up, and took the cigarette out of his mouth. "I don't mean it's not a good idea," Caldwell added. "But why didn't you just come home?"

"Home?"

"That's right."

Now Todd stared straight into Caldwell's eyes. Another silence ensued while they looked at each other. Then Todd turned his eyes back to the Ferris wheel and said, "You look much older than I remember."

"I am much older."

"You've put on weight, too."

"Yes, I have."

Todd took a long puff on the cigarette. "We've all changed," Caldwell said, and simultaneously Todd said, "Home was always the Juvenile Detention Center."

"What?"

Todd dragged on the cigarette still staring at the wheel.

"It didn't have to be," Caldwell said.

"Sure it did."

"I mean after. When you got out. I thought you'd come home then."

"Yeah, well."

"I mean, we were planning on it and everything. And when you didn't even want us to pick you up . . ."

"Well," Todd said. "I felt kind of funny about it."

"Funny?"

Todd nodded his head.

"I suppose I should have insisted," Caldwell said. Suddenly he felt the old anger—the terrible frustration of helplessness and loss. "I don't know what you expected."

"I couldn't believe the old hotel was gone when I got here."

"Yeah. Everything's changed."

Now his son looked him in the eye. "I feel like we just met."

"I just don't know what you want."

"Seems odd. What'd you think a guy like me might want— taken away and locked up all his life?"

"You weren't locked up all your life."

"The hell I wasn't."

"You were—"

"I was locked up, Dad. Okay? All my life. It's almost all I remember."

"Yeah well . . ." Caldwell didn't know what to say. Suddenly everything Todd said seemed aggressive and pointedly hostile, as though he had forgotten completely the magnitude of Caldwell's loss and the terrible truth about how it had come about. It was wrong to expect anything but a kind of distance between them, and it would not ever be set right unless one of them was willing to call attention to the thing that neither of them was saying: that the engine of Bobby's death was still a mystery between them, and that nothing Todd had said, or could say, would ever erase the possibility that what he had done to his little brother had been on purpose. Only Todd knew the truth, and only he was the one who *would* ever know it. "This is not fair," Caldwell said. "If you came here to exact some sort of retribution for—"

"It's just the truth. Fuck it. Don't let it bother you."

"And you know the truth," Caldwell said, trying to control the tone of his voice. Also, he realized he was trying not to say the unutterable truth that Todd had no right to complain about anything. Not as long as he was alive and breathing and little Bobby was buried in a box.

"I know the truth about what my life's been like," Todd said.

"Maybe you do. I don't know what difference it makes now."

"It makes a hell of a difference to me, I can tell you."

"And what do you know of my life since—," Caldwell stopped himself. His voice was loud, and he was afraid of what he might say.

"Let's not argue," Todd said. "I didn't come here for that."

"Well why did you come here?"

"You don't know?"

"No. I don't."

Todd shook his head, letting the cigarette drop to his feet, where he crushed it in the sand. "Hell. I don't really know, either. I just wanted to come down here and . . . ," he fell silent.

"Well, here we are," Caldwell said.

"Yeah. Here we are."

Neither of them spoke for a long time, then Caldwell said, "I'm in the hotel. You know where to find me." And he turned and started back down toward the boardwalk. He didn't look back.

• • •

Caldwell was in his room later that afternoon when Todd checked into the hotel. Clary put him in a room on the same floor—just a few doors down the hall. They made a bit of a commotion going past his room, and Caldwell, who had been checking his e-mail, got up and listened at the door. He wrote to Laura that Todd was there and he told her a little of their conversation. He did not know what to think of it, so he didn't say much. He lied about how it ended. It was a relief to him to go back to his computer and report that Todd was in the room down the hall, and that he would have more to say about things after they'd had dinner together.

As it turned out, though, they did not have dinner. They saw each other only briefly that night—in the hallway, both smiling and nodding as though they had been together the whole day. Caldwell said, "You going to eat something?" and Todd replied, "I'm too tired to eat. I'm just going to bed."

"Come on. I'm buying."

"No, I really don't want anything now."

They both hesitated a moment, then Caldwell said, "Well, have a good night then." Todd gave a slight farewell gesture with his hand and went into his room.

The next morning, Caldwell went to Todd's room and knocked on the door. He waited there in the hall, listening. Finally the door opened and Todd stood there in his underwear. "Did you knock?"

"Yeah."

"I'm sorry. I didn't hear you. I was brushing my teeth." He stepped back from the door.

"Want to go get some coffee?"

Todd scratched his arm, and yawned. "Sure. Why not?"

Caldwell watched him put on a pair of black trousers and pull a blue T-shirt over his head. His body was lean, muscular. He had a tattoo on each arm, a lot of hair on his legs and his chest and arms. It was so odd to see him—a full-grown man. They had not seen each other in almost three years, and his son had matured completely in that time. It was almost as if his boy had suddenly been inflated to this manly size—had suddenly grown all this hair and stubble, all the hard muscles, and the burned-looking jaw.

"So you got tattoos," Caldwell observed.

"Everybody has one of those in the . . . at the detention center."

"Really?"

Todd smiled. "You disapprove?" He sat on the bed, putting on a pair of loafers, still looking at Caldwell—as if he were expecting disapproval, almost encouraging it.

"Most of the cops I know and respect have tattoos," Caldwell said.

Todd stood up and held his hands out a little from his waist. "Ready?"

"Get your room key," Caldwell said.

They came down silently on the elevator and walked into the café. At the only big round table in the room, Clary sat with Hamlin, McDole, and Mauldin, sipping coffee. All the other tables had chairs stacked up on them.

"This really a restaurant?" Todd said under his breath as they approached the counter.

"It used to be," Caldwell whispered. "The owner serves coffee in here."

"That's it?" Todd settled on one of the stools.

"Sometimes you can get a sandwich."

No one was in sight behind the bar, so they waited, watching in the mirror behind stacked glasses, bottles of catsup, mustard, vinegar, and olive oil. Presently Clary got up and came around behind the bar. He was wearing a long-sleeved white shirt, open down the front, and a pair of sweatpants. He wore black tennis shoes, and a gold chain dangled around his neck.

"Good morning, Sheriff."

Caldwell looked at him.

McDole got up and walked to the seat next to him. "You are the sheriff, ain't you?" McDole's lean frame seemed bent from a great weight on his shoulders. He was wearing his Atlanta Braves baseball hat tilted a little too far back so that it looked like it might fall from his head if he moved too suddenly. He wore blue denim coveralls and a faded red T-shirt underneath. His hands seemed to crawl over the top of the bar.

"What's the problem?" Caldwell asked.

"You hear what happened here yesterday?" Clary said.

"Here?"

"Up the road, at my gas station," McDole said.

"I sure didn't."

"You supposed to be the law around here." McDole leaned on the stool next to Caldwell, but he didn't sit down. He had his elbow up on the bar.

"We'd like a cup of coffee," Caldwell said. "Then I'll get right down to business."

"I'd just like a Coke," Todd said.

"Well," Clary said. "So this here's your son."

"Yes," Caldwell said. He gestured toward Todd, but Clary said, "Did you know your boy was a hero?"

"What?"

Mauldin got up and came to the bar. "I want to shake your hand," he said to Todd.

"Yes, sir," Todd said.

"You don't know what happened the other day?" asked McDole.

Caldwell felt crowded, as though these men had planned to gang up on him when he came down. He looked at Todd, wondering if he, too, was feeling cornered, but the look on his son's face was impassive. He stared into the mirror and waited for his Coke. Clary said, "Me and young Todd here had quite a talk last night."

"You did?" Caldwell said.

Todd glanced at him, then gave a kind of shrug. "I came down here last night for a while. I couldn't sleep."

"And Mauldin here recognized him," said Clary.

"What happened the other day?" Caldwell asked.

"Your boy there is a hero," Clary said.

"You're a hero?" Caldwell asked turning to Todd.

"Oh, it was something," Mauldin said. He let go of Todd's hand. "This was that really warm night in October, right after you got here." Then he told the story of the fat man with the bungee, and how Todd had disarmed him. The whole time Todd did not meet his father's gaze. He seemed to be embarrassed by Mauldin's adoration. "I swear," Mauldin said, "I don't think I've ever seen anything like it."

"Thank you," Todd said.

Mauldin turned to Caldwell. "I mean, he did it in one quick, almost automatic motion. Walked up to the guy, hit him two good whacks with the tire iron, and put him on the ground. Then he whacked him again for good measure."

"I heard all about it," Caldwell said. "I didn't know it was you." He put his hand on Todd's shoulder. "The deputy up in Dahlgren thinks you're a hero, too."

"Really?" Todd said. He looked at Caldwell's hand. "I'm no hero."

"I couldn't believe how you took aim for that last blow," Mauldin said. Todd said nothing. Mauldin looked at Caldwell. "I swear, he just held the tire iron in both hands and leaned back like he was a batter waiting for a fastball, then he took a step, hauled off, and hit the guy square on the side of the head. I thought he'd knock his head right off."

"Goddamn," Clary said.

Caldwell did not know what to feel. If he'd had time to think, he might have expressed pride. He looked at Todd with a kind of wonder, squeezed his shoulder lightly, and took his hand away. He wished he could say something that would sound like praise, but he did not like what Todd had done. It was simply another kind of mayhem. Now he could not take his eyes off the tattoos on Todd's arms. Something like bad music, a discordant song, worked at the back of his mind. Here was his son, and lawlessness. Random violence. Bobby was dead, and here was the engine of his death, waiting at the bar for a Coke. Talk of heroism seemed exaggerated and foolish.

Clary went to the end of the bar and retrieved a tall glass, then put ice in it from a chest under the bar. He opened a Coke and poured the glass half full and placed it in front of Todd, who picked it up and took a long slow drink out of it.

"That's on the house," Clary said.

"I guess you were certainly in the right place at the right time," Caldwell said. "I wish I'd been there for it. Maybe I could have prevented it."

"What are you saying?" Todd said. He set the glass in front of him and wiped his mouth.

"Nothing. I guess I didn't know you'd been in town that long."

"Just a few days."

"Listen," McDole said. "I'm glad to hear about the hero and all, maybe I can get your boy to do something about Cecil."

"What?" Caldwell looked at him.

"About yesterday. You ready to listen about what happened and all?"

"Could I at least get my coffee?"

"I just want to know what you're going to do about it," McDole said.

"About what?"

McDole smirked.

Mauldin leaned over the bar next to Todd so he could see McDole. "You really going to swear out a complaint?"

Clary emerged from the back room with a cup in his left hand and a coffeepot in the other. Steam rose from the top of the pot. He put the cup in front of Caldwell and poured it full. "I'll get you some cream and sugar," he said.

"I'll drink it like this."

"I guess I want to swear out a complaint," McDole said.

Caldwell took a slow sip of the coffee. He stared at McDole the whole time. Now Hamlin got up and came over to the bar, too. He sat down a few stools away, leaned over, and held out his cup for Clary to refill it. Caldwell felt as though these men were about to force him to do something he didn't want to do. He didn't like the way they looked at him, waiting to see what he might say. He took another sip of his coffee, watching the look on Clary's face as he poured more coffee for the others. The lines by Clary's eyes made him look wiser than he probably was. His eyes had a way of smiling, though, of looking bright, on the verge of laughter, and last night Todd had confided in him. Todd had been here for more than a week. Caldwell wondered what else Clary knew. It was quiet for a while, but he was still conscious of McDole leaning over, staring at the side of his face, and he finally had to look at him again. "It's kind of hard to fill out a complaint when I don't have any of those forms with me."

"Forms?"

"It's a form you have to fill out. To make a formal complaint. I think the best thing would be for you to drive on up to Dahlgren and fill one out there. The police up that way will send somebody down here."

"Ain't you the county sheriff?"

"I am."

"Why can't you do it? I want somebody arrested."

"I can't just arrest somebody because that's what you want. You have to swear out a formal complaint, unless—"

"Unless what?" McDole interrupted him.

"What'd this person do?"

"He wrecked my gas station."

"Really?"

"I was there," Hamlin said. "I saw it. He flat-out drove his truck over signs and displays and knocked over a Coke machine and what-all . . ."

"Who did all this?"

"Cecil Edwards." McDole was impatient and it showed in the vehemence of his voice.

"The fellow owns the Ferris wheel," said Caldwell.

"You know it," Clary said. "You seen him in here."

"I saw him yesterday morning. I remember him. I arrested him once before. A long time ago."

This quieted all of them.

"He went quietly then. I expect if I have to arrest him again, he'll go quietly this time as well."

"Cecil Edwards?" McDole said. "I'd like to see that."

"Well," Caldwell said. "I'll need a complaint from you to arrest him."

"He held a gun to my head and stole money from me."

Now Caldwell was interested. He put his cup down and looked into McDole's eyes. "You say he robbed you?"

"That's right."

"At gunpoint."

McDole nodded.

"Well," Clary said, "that's not exactly what happened."

"Yes it is," McDole said.

Caldwell looked at Clary. "What do you mean?" He sensed Todd's eyes on him, and suddenly he wanted to be better than he was; he actually felt as though he was in some sort of competition and thriving under approving eyes as he had so many times dreamed while growing up with his distant father. He was always dreaming of doing great things while his father was watching him. In spite of the fact that he had never, as far as he knew, made his father proud, it was a thing he had always longed for. Now, with Todd's eyes on him, he felt that familiar impulse to do something exactly right; he felt as if he was again seeking the approval of a father he had never known, only this time it was Todd he sought to impress. "I want to know exactly what happened," he said.

"Well," Clary said, "he didn't just go into the station and hold a pistol on him and rob him, if that's what you're thinking."

McDole glared at Clary. "He may as well have."

"Tell me what he did," Caldwell said.

McDole told him. His voice was calm and steady as he talked, but something in the way he worked his hands defied his demeanor. It was as though he were a child telling on a playmate by the way he rubbed his fingers together and turned his hands, as though he was washing them under water. He looked at Caldwell's shirt and throat and anything but his eyes.

"He actually held a gun to your head?" asked Caldwell.

"Yes, he did."

"And when was this?"

"A couple of days before you got here," Clary said.

Caldwell did not look away from McDole. "Why'd you wait so long to report it?"

"I don't know."

"Well, you shouldn't have."

"I know."

"Tell him about when you went up there to Cecil's place and held a pistol on him," Mauldin said.

Caldwell turned to him. "What?"

Todd gave a short laugh. To cover it, he quickly took another long sip of his Coke.

McDole grudgingly said, "I went up there and did the same thing to him."

Caldwell stared into the mirror and shook his head. His eyes caught Todd's and for a moment he thought his son smiled at him, as though they were both sharing a secret understanding. He took a sip of his coffee. He didn't feel like this kind of trouble right now, and the realization that this feud was probably harmless and ongoing was almost a source of relief. He did not feel the need to do anything short of letting McDole know proper procedure. "You want to swear out a complaint, you'll have to go up to Dahlgren and swear out a complaint," Caldwell said. "I'm in the peacekeeping business, but I can't just arrest people because you want me to."

"I'll be goddamned," McDole muttered.

"Don't get me wrong," Caldwell told him. "I'll stop any trouble I see—and I'm sorry I didn't see what happened yesterday. But I don't have a jail here yet—at least not one that's ready, and there isn't a magistrate or a courtroom down this way, so anything that gets done is going to have to begin up in Dahlgren anyway. Even if I was going to do something about it I'd need the complaint."

Mauldin sat down on the stool next to Caldwell. "That's what I was telling him this morning."

Hamlin said, "I guess you're stuck" to McDole, who shook his head and went back to the table. He sat down there and hoisted his cup for the last bit of coffee. He stared at nothing, his legs splayed out under the table, his fingers wrapped tightly around the empty cup on the table in front of him. Mauldin held his cup out to Clary, but Clary said, "It's all gone. You want I should make some more?"

"Whatever," Mauldin said.

Caldwell still had half a cup and he sipped it, watching McDole in the mirror. Hamlin sat down, too, but he had his back to the bar and faced into the room. "I guess it's like this," he said: "A kid was eating candy in front of school, and a teacher seen him and says, 'You shouldn't eat candy, little boy. It's bad for you.' And the boy says, 'My granddaddy lived to be a hundred.' And the teacher says, 'Did your granddaddy eat candy?' And the little boy says, 'No. He minded his own fucking business.'" Only Clary and Todd laughed. "I guess," Hamlin went on, "We should do what the boy in the joke suggests and mind our own business."

"What do you mean by that?" Clary asked.

"Nothing. Just that it looks like the sheriff here just told us if we want to do something about old Cecil, we're going to have to do it ourselves." Caldwell put his cup down and looked at Hamlin. Mauldin said, "Fuck all this. I'm going on back to my place." He nodded to Clary and moved on past Caldwell and Hamlin. When he got to the exit he turned and looked at McDole. "Vince, you need help cleaning up, I'll be glad to oblige. I'm sorry about it. I really am." McDole said nothing.

Caldwell realized he felt as though he had denied help to someone in trouble and he didn't like it. Todd was watching him, and he had refused to do anything. He turned around and leaned against the bar. "I'll have a talk with Cecil if you want," he said. "I'm not going to let him just do whatever he wants."

"That's the trouble," Clary said. "He does just what he wants all the time."

"Well, we'll see," Caldwell said.

McDole still had nothing to say. He picked up his cup and made a motion as if he were going to sip out of it, then he looked into it and put it back down again. "Want more coffee?" Clary asked him. "I can make some." McDole got up and, dangling the cup from his forefinger, walked slowly to the bar and set it down. "Forget it," he said. Then he turned to Hamlin. "Let's go figure out what we're going to do."

"Wait a minute," Clary put in. "I'll go with you."

"You got to go ask Judy," McDole said.

"I'll be right there."

"We'll be up at the station," McDole said. "If you don't mind we won't wait for you." He placed the hat more firmly on his head, turned, and walked out, with Hamlin close behind him.

Caldwell said to Clary, "Before you go, I need to know what you're going to be charging my son here."

"He gets the same rate as you if he stays."

"That will be fine . . ."

"You know, those boys are going to do something about Cecil, don't you?"

"What?"

Clary buttoned his shirt and tucked it in as he spoke. "Cecil's been the problem with law enforcement you spoke of when you first got here. A real bona fide tyrant if you ask me." He gathered up the empty cups and took them to the kitchen. When he came back out he said, "They're going to figure out what to do about him."

"I said I'd talk to him."

"They don't want to wait for that, maybe."

Caldwell said nothing. Todd pushed his stool back and stood up. "You want to take a walk up to the Ferris wheel and see this Cecil fellow?" he asked his father.

"I don't need any help," replied Caldwell, and immediately regretted it. Something in Todd's demeanor seemed to weaken. He shrugged, placing his hands in the pockets of his jeans. Clary said, "You guys would make a good team." He seemed to notice Todd's reaction. "Hell, it'll take more than one man to deal with Cecil."

"We can go up there," Caldwell said to Todd. "If you want."

xii

A lone in her room at Mrs. McCutcheon's late that night, Lindsey did not know if she could express what she was afraid of—or what she was looking forward to. She found it hard to focus on anything for even a few seconds, and the stillness of her room seemed vaguely threatening. She felt a painful mixture of apprehension and excitement. She sat at a small table situated back in an alcove that contained the only window in her room and tried to think of what to write to her stepmother. She felt a need to write this day down and get it exactly right. She kept going over in her mind what had happened that afternoon when she and Todd Caldwell had gone down to the beach for a walk. She wrote frequently, and most of the time Alicia would either answer the letters or call her on the phone. But on this night Lindsey's heart was still beating with the heat of wonder and excitement, and she didn't want to write to her mother without making sure of what she was going to say. She and Todd had spent a breezy, cold afternoon walking along next to the water and talking, and then he had taken a small, tightly rolled joint out of his pocket and lit it. They sat down in the sand and he offered it to her. She could not believe she was doing this. She smoked it with him, feeling the gradual deceleration of time and a slow, warm increase of all her senses. The cold air caressed her and his voice took on a sweet kind of musical quality, like the bass string on a violin. She seemed to be watching herself with a kind of wonder and shock.

Earlier that day Todd had come with the sheriff to speak to Cecil. It was the first time Lindsey had seen Caldwell dressed in his sheriff's uniform, and at first she was frightened. His shoes were brightly polished, and a black revolver hung at his waist in a black leather holster that seemed too small for it. The handle of the gun looked immense to her. He wore brown slacks with a darker brown stripe down each leg and a state trooper's flat-brimmed hat with the chin strap wrapped around the back of his head and the brim of the hat tilted forward over his eyes. On his chest was a gold badge almost as big as his shirt pocket. The light brown shirt had pleats on the breast and down the sides. He came up the walk, stepping slowly through the tall weeds that grew out of the cracks in the sidewalk. There was no wind, but a slight breeze still found its way down the beach and filtered through the passages and alleys along the boardwalk. It was damp—cloudy and densely gray—and the air was cold. Todd walked behind his father, staring mostly at the ground as he approached. Lindsey was sitting on the steps of Cecil's trailer, watching them stride up the walk. She had been smoking a cigarette. Cecil had just flipped his cigarette into the yard and stepped back into the trailer. He did not see the sheriff coming.

When he was close enough that she could hear him, Caldwell carefully removed his hat and said, "Hello."

Lindsey smiled. "We meet again."

"I wonder if I might have a word with your . . ." Caldwell caught himself, looking directly into her eyes. "I wonder if I might speak to Mr. Edwards?" Lindsey was grateful to him for re-membering not to say "brother." She smiled, stood up, and with both hands, brushed the back of her jeans. She did not make a move to open the door. Todd looked at her.

"Hello," she said.

"This is Todd," Caldwell said.

"Yeah. I figured that out yesterday."

It was quiet for an awkward moment while the three of them stood there. Then Lindsey started to speak. "Are you—here for—," she stopped. The trailer door opened and Cecil stood in the doorway.

"What's going on?" he asked.

"Nothing," Lindsey said. "The sheriff here wanted to see you. That's all."

Cecil regarded Caldwell. "I'll be dogged," he said. "A real, live sheriff. Down here."

"Well this is part of the county," Caldwell smiled. "Can we talk a bit?"

"Go ahead."

"No. I mean some place private."

Cecil shook his head slowly, started to close the door, and then thought better of it. "We can take a walk down yonder," he said, pointing at the big Ferris wheel at the corner of the yard.

"That'd be fine," replied Caldwell. He put his hat back on and turned to Todd. "Stay here for a bit, will you?" Cecil stepped down to the ground. "You don't remember me, do you?" Caldwell said.

"No, sir, I don't."

"Years ago I came down here and arrested you for brandishing a firearm. Something about back taxes."

"You don't say."

"You were right, I think. But you remember that day? All that followed it?"

"I remember the tax office. I don't remember you."

"You remember all the time you spent waiting in court and all?"

Cecil said nothing.

"Walk with me a bit," Caldwell said. "Let's talk." They moved off toward the Ferris wheel.

Todd put his hands in his back pockets, but he was still looking at Lindsey. She did not understand why, but she liked his face.

Something in his eyes made her want to have him looking at her, made her want to look at him.

"You ever been high?" he said when Cecil and his father were well away from them.

"Sure. I don't like it much."

"Not even on a few beers?"

"I don't drink."

"Damn," he said.

"What?"

"Seems like you'd be pretty miserable in the morning if you knew that was about as good as you were going to feel the rest of the day."

Lindsey laughed. "That was supposed to be funny, right?" He said nothing. "You were in prison, weren't you?" she asked. This seemed to shock him. He looked out at his father then back at her, but he didn't answer her.

The sheriff and Cecil came back, and after a brief pause by the door of the trailer, Caldwell said, "Think about it then, sir. You'll do that?"

"Ain't no harm in thinking."

"It's a simple matter of avoiding a whole lot of trouble for everybody." Cecil said nothing. "You pay what you owe—as any responsible citizen should—and I promise there'll be an end to it."

"No charges against me?"

"That's right. You can go on about your business."

"I pay for damage and that's it?"

"Damage and what you owe Mr. McDole."

"I won't agree to that."

"What about half what you owe him? Would you agree to that?"

Lindsey looked at Cecil. "That sure is reasonable," she said.

"Remember how it feels to wait all day in the Dahlgren County courthouse," Caldwell said.

"I've done that before."

"Well you can avoid doing it again."

"I guess so."

"It's not fun. But I promise, you pay half of what you owe. No more, no less. I'll be there, and I'll make sure that's all you pay."

"It's a reasonable request." Cecil's eyes were almost smiling, but he looked at the sheriff with the same dead look he had for everybody.

"Don't see why we shouldn't avoid trouble if we can," Caldwell said.

"I don't want more trouble with the law."

"I'll set a meeting some time the middle of the week, say, Wednesday, if you think that's soon enough?"

"Whenever," Cecil said. He still wore a kind of half smile on his face, as if he had something else on his mind and was only pretending to listen.

"What's next Wednesday?" Lindsey asked.

"We're going to settle this dispute," Caldwell said. He leaned on one leg, almost proud. Lindsey started to say something, but her eyes caught Todd's and she realized he was gazing very intently at her. Caldwell turned to leave, but Todd hesitated. Cecil went back inside the trailer and looked back at Lindsey. "You coming?" he said.

"I think I'll take a walk down to the beach," she answered. Todd moved on down the walk behind his father, but she was sure he heard her. When she got to the beach, it was only a few minutes before Todd came down, too. She saw him come from between the boarded-up buildings next to the hotel. The air was even soggier down by the water, but she was not cold. She was excited. She felt exactly as she did that day when she had first gotten into her car and struck out on her own to find her real mother.

Todd walked right up to her, and it seemed as though he would have gone past her, but she turned and walked with him. They moved along the gray water. In the distance the clouds seemed to let in a bit of bright sunlight, but it broke up in weak columns as it approached the horizon, and by the time it touched earth, it diffused into a kind of dull whiteness that made the water look almost like moving ice.

They smoked the joint for a while in silence. Todd's face was flushed, and he seemed about to laugh, but he said nothing. The gray water rippled in front of them and curled around the edge of a pile of rocks. The sand was almost warm.

"Were you really in prison?" Lindsey asked.

"It wasn't a prison." He leaned back on his hands and stared off in the distance.

She took a drag off the joint, aware of his eyes on her. She blew out the smoke and handed it to him. "I guess you don't want to talk about it."

"My father tell you about me?"

"Sort of."

He looked at her.

"When he first got here he was walking down the beach, and I was down here reading a book, and we talked." Todd was quiet. "I recognized him, really."

"'Cause he's the sheriff?"

"No. I remember. Back when it happened. I lived in Fairfax."

His eyes widened. She was amazed at how dark they seemed in this light. They were deep set and looked like polished glass, but there was something that seemed to spin in them, too, a motion of the light or the color as she gazed at him. She was afraid of what the dope would do to her. She thought something was happening to her heart, and that everything was too much like an interrupted, ongoing dream of wakefulness. "I really feel strange," she said.

"You never been really high?"

"Every boyfriend I ever had was stoned most of the time. It never really worked on me."

"You might start laughing in a minute," he said.

"Where'd you get this stuff?"

A slight look of wonder crossed his face. "Every kitchen in Richmond's got a regular supply of it."

"Really?"

"You ever been a waitress or worked in a kitchen?"

"No."

"How'd you miss doing that?"

"I just never wanted to do it."

He drew on the joint and held it in, looking at the river with a painful expression on his face. "Those rocks out there?" He pointed to dark heaps jutting out of the water near where the beach turned to tall dune grass.

She nodded. "Just where the river bends—a pile of rocks some construction crew dropped there."

"How do you know it was a construction crew?"

"They're mostly big blocks of cement."

"The water looks deep there."

"It is."

He handed her the joint and she puffed on it again. "Hold it in longer," he said. "It's great weed." She let herself feel it filling her lungs, drawing deeply on it. She held her breath as long as she could, but it made her want to cough. "First time I smoked was in prison," he said.

"I thought you said it wasn't a prison."

"Well," he smiled, "you may as well call it that. I was locked up."

She was quiet. He held up the joint and looked at it. And then briefly he was laughing. But his eyes were so sad it seemed almost like a kind of weeping. He tried to be quiet and control it. He put his hands across his stomach and leaned over, then sat straight up again and caught his breath. At that moment she felt the most exquisite affection for him. But she did not laugh. She only felt oddly tired and enthralled by time—as if she'd gone into time and moved with it, riding down the hands of a clock. It was not a vision, but a feeling—as if time were now in her head. "This is really weird," she said.

He laughed again, briefly. "Your first real high can be pretty scary sometimes."

"I'll get this back, won't I?" she said, pointing to her head.

"Get what back?"

"This." She tapped her fingers on her head. Suddenly the word "this" was the most hilarious noise in English. She began laughing at it, at the odd way the "iss" sound seemed to let the air out of "th." She thought of punctured rubber balls. While she was laughing, the idea that she was worried about getting her mind back, and that she had reduced her entire consciousness—her way of perceiving and understanding earth, all her memory, and desire—to the simple word, "this," struck her as the funniest thing she had ever heard. This made her go even deeper into it, until she found it hard to get her breath. She could not stop laughing. He laughed, too, and it seemed to go on for a long time. Then it got quiet. They both just sat there. He finished the joint and flipped the small bit of what was left into the river. The quiet water lapped at the sand near their feet, and a few inquisitive white birds lifted overhead and swept down into the shadows around them. Presently Todd said, "What were we laughing about?"

Again they were shattered with laughter, holding onto each other now. When they calmed down again, they were still holding on, and she realized she was wishing very much that he would kiss her. But he looked out over the water and didn't say anything for a long time. Then he smiled down at her and said, "I killed my little brother."

She pulled herself away slightly and sat up straight. "I know."

"I didn't mean to."

"I know." She looked into his eyes and she saw such longing there, she almost started crying.

"We were wrestling. Roughhousing, as my mother called it. We were not allowed to roughhouse, and both of us knew it. But no one else was home. Terry was with one of her girlfriends..."

"Terry?"

"My sister." He sniffed, put his hands in his jacket pockets, and scrunched up a bit.

"Go on," she said.

"Mom had stopped at the store, and Dad wasn't home. It was

just us. For a little while. It was okay—my parents trusted me."
His voice broke. She was afraid he would not go on, but he only
paused for a moment. He seemed in a hurry to tell her.

"My dad had to work late that day. He was a Fairfax County
cop. We were just home by ourselves, but it wasn't like it happened that often. Dad was our little league coach. We were a close
family . . ." He looked down at the sand between his feet. "A really
close family. Dad coached us in basketball and soccer. Bobby was
pretty good at soccer. Anyway, we were home by ourselves, and
Bobby jumped me. He came at me from behind and just leaped
up on me. He'd do that sometimes." Todd laughed briefly. His
eyes were watering. Lindsey wanted to put her arms around him,
but she just watched his eyes and listened.

"We had just gotten home from school and Bobby threw his
backpack on the floor and took off his shoes. I knew what that
meant, so I backed away, then turned to run, but he jumped me.
I said, 'Not in here,' and he was laughing. We were in the living
room, on my mother's white carpet. When he jumped on me we
both went down. I was laughing so hard, but I knew we should
stop it. I kept saying, 'Not in here, Bobby.' We rolled around on
the floor, both of us laughing. I kept saying, 'Stop it. Stop it,'
laughing, like that. And he wouldn't stop. Sometimes—sometimes he just knew he didn't have to listen to me. We were having so much fun, wrestling like we always did."

"Your parents let you be home alone like that?"

"Not a lot. But I was eleven. I was old enough. I was proud
of the fact that—," he stopped, reached down, and picked up a
handful of sand, letting it run through his fingers. "They thought
I could take care of him." His voice broke. "Just for a little while."

"I'm sorry," Lindsey said.

"I thought I'd get him to stop if I threw him on the couch
and started tickling him. He hated that." He looked out at the
water, his eyes still watering. It was quiet for a while, then he said,
"I wish I had another joint with me." Lindsey remained silent.

After a while, he went on. "Anyway, I was going to throw him on the couch. I'd done that to him so many times. But this time, when I picked him up—I was moving toward the couch, leaning toward it—and my—my movement—the momentum of it . . ." He turned to her, and the look in his eyes was so full of sorrow, she reached up and touched the side of his face. He leaned back gently, not quite refusing her caress, but not accepting it, either. "I was still carrying him in my arms and I tried to lunge toward the couch and I fell into the coffee table. Bobby—," he stopped again and seemed to gasp for air. "Bobby hit the back of his head on the corner of it. All of my weight was on him."

Lindsey realized she was crying. She wiped the cold tears from her cheeks under her eyes, waiting for him to go on. It seemed like hours passed while he sat there picking sand up and letting it run through his fingers, studying the steady movement of it. She could not believe what the dope did to her sense of time or to the intensity of her feelings.

"Bobby didn't make a sound. I told him I was sorry and tried to get up. I said, 'You okay?' and he just dropped to the floor. He was limp. I called his name. I saw a little bit of blood—kind of bubbles of it coming out of his ears . . ."

Up by the boardwalk, somebody hollered a name. He looked back over his shoulder, and she saw tears streaming down his face. He turned back toward the water, wiping the sleeve of his jacket over his face. "Anyway," he said. "That's what happened."

"What'd you do?"

"I knew when I saw the blood."

"It was an accident."

"I sat him up on the couch and tried to look into his face, but his head dropped down. I knew it was—I knew he was—but I held him there for a long time. Hoping he'd wake up. I kept saying his name, begging him to wake up. I don't think I could believe it yet—I mean, I was so sure I could wake him up and bring him back. But he didn't move. He didn't move ever again." He sat back and let his legs splay out in front of him. "Shit," he said. His face was suddenly passive, and the tears were gone. A slight breeze lifted the hair over his ears. He would not look at her.

"It was a terrible accident," Lindsey said, feeling helpless.

"I was going to call for help, but when I got to the phone, I looked back across the room and saw Bobby's eyes . . ." He started choking back tears again. "I don't know why I'm telling you all this."

"You don't have to."

"I know."

She was silent, watching his face. He only glanced at her momentarily, then back out at the water. "When I saw his eyes," he went on, "staring blankly at the ceiling, I knew for sure. And then I remembered my mother and father, my sister—the family. I mean—I couldn't—I didn't want this to happen. You know?"

"Yes."

"I didn't want it to happen to us."

"I know."

"No, you don't know. Not really. I didn't—I couldn't tell them about it. I couldn't let them see it. I thought it would be better if they thought Bobby had . . ." She waited. "If they thought . . ." He studied her face now. "I killed him. That's what I had to tell them. You see?"

"Yes."

"I couldn't think of any other thing but this terrible thing that would happen to them."

"It had already happened."

"No. You don't understand." He got control of himself again. "It hadn't happened to them. Not yet. So I just sort of went around the house like a robot, doing things automatically. I put him in a bag—in a plastic trash bag. I put his backpack in there, shoes, his cap, everything . . ." Now he broke into sobs. He had his face in his hands, and Lindsey rubbed his shoulders, the back of his neck, crying silently herself. The dope was wearing off, and she was only feeling deeply sad and wishing to get away from this pain. She was afraid he would hate her once he'd told her all of it, and yet she wanted him to finish it.

"I put him in a bag. A trash bag. Then I carried him out to the backyard—back to a place where my father had buried our dog—we had a dog named Buster and—that's where I buried Bobby. I dug that hole so fast—I kept throwing the dirt out of it. I was angry a little, I think. I couldn't believe what the whole world had turned into, you know? I still remember that day as the whole world. The whole fucking world. I kept saying, 'I'm sorry little buddy. I'm so sorry.' And I was crying and saying 'Fuck,' too. 'Fuck, fuck, fuck.' And when I pushed the bag into the hole, I tamped the dirt down on it and just laid down on top of it, crying. I hated the smell of that dirt. To this day—to this day I hate the smell of pine needles and earth. I started praying, too, I think. I was saying the Our Father. But I think I was praying for myelf by then. I was so afraid. So afraid they'd find out. I didn't want them to know what happened."

"What did you think they'd—I mean, how were you going to explain . . . ?" Lindsey started.

"I had to make myself as calm as possible. I had to make myself wonder, along with everyone else, what had happened to him. Where he was."

"What were you thinking?"

"You know, a lot of people have asked me that."

She averted her eyes. "I'm sorry. I don't want to be like everyone else."

"No, it's okay. I don't blame you," he said. He took a handkerchief out of his pocket and wiped the tears from his eyes. He handed it to her and she did the same. "Look at us," he said. She handed back the handkerchief but she said nothing.

"I wish I could tell you what I was thinking," he went on. "But you know what? I don't know what I was thinking. I only know what I was feeling. Maybe I believed I could get to a place—we could all get to a place—some wide-open tomorrow where it would be okay, and it would all go away somehow. As long as no one knew where he was, Bobby might still be alive. Isn't that better than knowing? Maybe I thought it wouldn't be true if I didn't admit it. I don't know. I was only eleven, remember."

"That's a terrible time to learn about permanence," Lindsey said.

This touched him. His eyes softened and he almost smiled at her. Then he said, "I shouldn't have told you all that."

"Why not?"

"What's it to you, am I right?"

She shrugged. "It could mean a lot to me, if . . ."

"If what?"

"Well, just now I feel close to you. Like I know you better than anyone."

"A little dope and a sob story, and here we are, best friends."

"You shouldn't denigrate it like that." She wrapped her arms around her knees, leaned forward, and rested her chin on her forearms. He was quiet for a long time, and she did not know what to say. She felt almost as if he'd tricked her somehow. Finally she looked at him and said, "That was a cheap thing to say."

"I'm sorry." His voice was soft. "I didn't mean it like that. I just felt like I shouldn't have been telling you my whole life story. Maybe you didn't want to hear it."

"It was very moving," she said, feeling her voice lose a little of its force. "I feel for you, sincerely."

"I'm sorry," he said. She didn't answer him. Presently he said, "Do you believe me?"

"About what?"

"Everything. About what happened."

"Of course I do."

He looked away and seemed to withdraw from her mentally as well as physically. He leaned back on his hands again. "I wish my old man would believe me."

"I think he does."

He smiled at her. "No. It's sweet of you to say it. But he doesn't. He really doesn't know what to believe." She said nothing. "I guess I can't blame him." They were quiet for a long time, then he said, "But you know what? If he did believe me, I might not of—," he stopped.

"What?" she said. He shook his head. "What?"

"Just, you know," he said quietly, his voice almost breaking. "I never had a damn childhood." He picked up a handful of sand again, but this time he threw it into the water. She wished she could place her hand gently on the side of his face once more and look into his eyes, but he had gotten impersonal now, and distant.

NOTHING HAPPENED at the beach. That is what she told herself when they finally got up and walked back up to the boardwalk. They stopped in front of the hotel and he said, "You all right?"

"Sure."

"I mean, you can make it home okay? You're not too stoned, are you?"

"No. I mean yeah, I can make it home, and no, I'm not too—," she stopped. She wanted to laugh again. It had been the best laughter of her life, and she sought to produce the same kind of closeness to him as when they had both been helpless in it. But he was very serious now.

"See you," he said.

"Okay." She wished she had said something else, or that he had had more to say. But she turned and walked back up toward Cecil's place.

NOW IT seemed as if time were constricting her. Tomorrow loomed. She wondered how it was possible that one could feel such odd excitement and intense anticipation of tomorrow while at the same time fearing it absolutely. A part of her wanted to deny it, was intent on forestalling it somehow. She must find a way to stop it. Most of all she wanted to stop herself from thinking what she was thinking. If somebody had asked her the day before what she wanted more than anything else in the world, she would have said, to look in the eyes of her biological father, to know at least one of the people responsible for bringing her into life. But now, today, what she wanted was almost frighteningly stupid. She knew it. All she wanted was to be back on the beach again with Todd, smoking his weed and laughing so freely the world could not have slightly troubled her. Every minute seemed to save the day. That's how it felt. But it was past, and nothing had happened, and she did not want to be this person waking up with hope that Todd or any man would call her, or that she might run into him somehow, or that he would be there on Mrs. Mc-Cutcheon's front porch asking for her. She did not want to get herself ready for work the next day, thinking about how attractive she looked; wondering how she might see him. Now she hated the slight bulge of her belly. In one day she grew this hatred for it, and when she looked in the mirror, that's all she saw. This was just romantic nonsense and foolishness again. And she did not want to stand for it. She could feel her heartbeat no matter what position she sat in, no matter what she was doing.

So she tried to calm herself by writing to her stepmother. She preferred writing letters because lately, during their many phone calls, Alicia always got around to asking things like, "When are you going to get on with your life?" Or, "Have you thought about school?" Or, "Have you met anyone yet?" These questions always felt aggressive and discourteous, but Lindsey resisted the temptation to argue about it.

No, Lindsey wouldn't call her mother. Not on this particular night. But she was too excited and worried to write to Alicia with smalltalk and busy chatter about the rumors and measures in her life. She did not want to ask about Alicia's cooking classes or her disdain for men or her new life in Cleveland. Lindsey wanted to give her mother a little of herself, of her doubts and fears. She wanted to say it just right and for it to matter in some kind of grand way—like the memory of a treasured time with a loved one. She wanted to expiate her growing anticipation and fear of tomorrow by putting it on a page.

She opened with, "Dear Mother," instead of "Alicia." Then

she wrote, "I think I'm going to stay in Columbia Beach at least another year before I begin to think about school. I know I'm wasting my time with my 'brother'—" She stopped momentarily, staring at the word "brother" and the curious fact that she had put quotations around it. Of course Cecil was not her brother in any real familial sense. She had come to understand this even if she'd never mentioned it to anyone. Cecil was a kind of experience, though. She was breaking through to him in a way, pushing back the hard exterior, the silent, spiteful brooding, and up to now the effort had kept her so enthralled she could think of almost nothing else. Even her reading had become secondary, an obligation. She had to force herself to concentrate on each word because her mind kept wandering back to Cecil and the oddly complex nature of his unaffectedness. Cecil was the first real man she had ever known. And he was without attachments of any kind. She was certain that before she arrived, he had had no relationships at all. Perhaps that was it. Being near him, watching him, talking to him, challenging him, working to get him to relax a little bit, getting him to talk, even to laugh a little, felt like the most exquisite triumph, as if she had gotten an ape to speak. That's what it felt like. And now the whole experience seemed almost comical to her. Suddenly it didn't seem so important or meaningful. She was beginning to see that she had been doing just what Alicia had been implying: wasting her time. She continued writing:

> I know that Cecil will never really be like a true brother to me—even though we really are related by blood. Even so, I thought I needed to know him better. I thought I could get him to talk about his mother. I thought maybe if I got him to do that, and maybe if I got to know some of the folks around here, I could discover who my father was. Or who he is. I don't know how to write that. I wanted to know everything I could about Cecil, because he might tell me about my mother, and maybe he'd know something about my father. Anyway, that was what I saw

as a kind of quest. And Cecil can be nice to me, and when he is, it always surprises and pleases me. And the way people around here treat me because I'm with him is amazing. It's like I'm a celebrity. Not a queen or anything, but a rock star, maybe, or an actress. I can hear them whispering about me when I walk by. All because they don't know what I'm doing here with Cecil. I think some of them believe I'm his girlfriend. Mrs. McCutcheon asked me the other day if I was his daughter. I couldn't answer her because then the guessing game begins and there are only a few guesses before the truth comes out. So I just smirked at her and went up to my room. I know she spent hours on the phone to folks telling them what she thinks she discovered.

She stopped and read over what she had written. She realized she really did want to know her father; she understood it as a part of her imagined future, like a wishful outcome in the story of her life. She was surprised and glad to see that she had written a full page and she had not yet mentioned Todd. But as soon as she realized that, she felt something leap up slightly in her heart. She went on:

Today I met a guy. A young guy named Todd. You don't know him. But you know of him. He's famous in a way. I don't want to go into it now, and I don't want you to worry. But he is different. Not like the others. I felt close to him today. I'll tell you about him when we talk. We smoked a joint and for the first time it worked. I got really high. Don't panic. It's not a hard drug, and I don't intend to make a habit of it. But it was fun. Maybe the most fun I've ever had. Nothing happened. He didn't even kiss me. So don't go thinking anything is going to happen. But I like him. In a way, he's looking for his father, too. Maybe even his mother. He's such an orphan, really. I keep thinking about him and I don't like that. It feels a little romantic again. Like being a teenager, really—nothing so rational as adult feelings or anything, don't worry. But Todd's story is so sad. I was feeling so close to him today. Trust me, I don't want another hairy adolescent screwing with my heart. Sorry for the language. I know my desire to look into my father's eyes, and this quest to get Cecil to actually demonstrate affection for something or someone—I know these things are not rational. But that is what should be most important to me now, since that is why I'm here. Why is it that sometimes you can make yourself think whatever you want, and other times your mind just seems to have its way with you? I hate that.

Maybe I won't stay down here so long after all. Things are about as far as they can go with Cecil, really, and I know where my real family is. I know I've had a family because of you. I've learned to love because of you. I've also learned patience and understanding. I think I'll be a good mother. I think I'll insist that my children be independent, as you always did with me. What I've learned from you will be with me always. No school or degree or even life experience can change the unalterable fact that what I learned in your house, being your daughter, was how to be human.

I am grateful for that.

I hope you know how much it means to me.

I love you . . .

Your daughter, Lindsey.

After she had folded the letter, placed it in an envelope, and addressed it, she put it on a small table by the front door so she wouldn't forget it in the morning. She undressed and took a long, hot bath, then put on her flannel pajamas and climbed into bed. She would have to work late tomorrow, so she planned to get up early, mail the letter, and then get over to Cecil's trailer to see what he was up to. She would not think about Todd at all. She would wake Cecil if she had to. Perhaps Todd would be standing in the yard, looking at the Ferris wheel again. This idea, she was sorry to realize, thrilled her; it made her aware of her nerves. The only thing that soothed her was the thought that she was the kind of woman who faced the world boldly.

She drifted easily into sleep, and after a long and peaceful interval, things began happening swiftly. She felt herself jerk a little and then seemed to relax and fall, softly and insouciantly, as though she were descending from a great height to an easy landing in clouds, and gradually she came to see that she was dreaming. She let events unfold, wondering at the fact that even in her sleep she could sense the odor of seaweed and sand and saltwater. She knew she would never understand this dream while it was happening, and she actually had a waking sensation of wanting to, of hoping she would. She felt insubstantial suddenly—as if her skin was the outer layer of a hollow, boneless, inflatable thing that held only a thin, weightless gas. She did not like the feeling but mused over it anyway. "I'm a balloon," she tried to say. "I know this is a dream." She began to realize that she had become fear. That's what she was. The weightlessness, the feeling of being inflated and of floating was just what fear felt like to her. She could not say what she was afraid of. She knew she would never be able to say it. She wanted to be able to fly, to rise up over the blue river and the trees and look down at the water, at the reflected lights of the glittering sky, but instead she only moved around the room, up against the walls. It was like the wind blew her, but she was in a room and she told herself wind could not be there. She struggled to wake herself. She thought she said, "I don't have to answer any questions."

"Yes, I'm afraid you do," Cecil said.

What are you doing here? she thought. It was a face. It floated, as she did.

"I'm not afraid," she said. And then she was laughing, as she had that afternoon. She looked for Todd.

"I can't see you clearly. Todd?"

"You're not looking."

God, this is a funny dream

She tried again to wake up, and the face was suddenly Mc-Dole's, leaning toward her, breathing very close to her cheek. "Come on," he whispered. "What do you stay here for?"

"My father," Lindsey said. Then Cecil was there, sitting in water. The room was full of water, and it seemed to be getting deeper. It was high enough that it spilled out the window, and the table where she had been writing only a few minutes ago floated past her.

Cecil? She tried to scream. *I'm dreaming about you again.* She looked at Cecil, fought fiercely now for any language, any vocal sound. Only her mouth moved, and Cecil stared at her as if he needed words to keep from drowning in the deepening water.

"You don't have a father."

I know it

She'd said the word "father," and in the dream she realized she had never used the word in her life, ever. She had never written it. She felt quite certain she had never heard the word until that very moment. That was the logic of the dream, that the word "father" was totally new to her. Then she looked at Cecil, and the water reached to his chin. He struggled to keep his mouth and nose above the water. He was looking at her, pleading, helpless.

"Cecil!" she screamed, and the sound of it woke her. Her voice still echoed in the room. She was covered with sweat and lay there for a moment, shivering under the covers. When she sat up and put her foot down on the dry floor, she had such a feeling of relief and escape from harm that she almost started crying.

She went into the bathroom and drank a cold glass of water, staring at her eyes in the mirror. Even as she remembered the dream, as she considered it, she could sense details of it dropping out of her memory, disappearing like water into a sponge. She was not quite ready to go back to bed and tempt sleep again, but she felt her stammering heart returning to normal, and by degrees she came to see that her bad dream revealed nothing of any importance. It didn't mean anything. She always knew it was important to her that she someday know her father. Still, she could not wait to tell Todd about it. She went back to bed trying to get the entire dream back, thinking already about how she would describe it to him. She wished she had asked him what his dreams were like. Certainly they could talk about that.

In the dark, with her eyes closed, all her imaginary conversations were effortless, and she did not see her heavy thighs or her slightly bulging stomach—she was only young and beautiful and free. She went back to sleep feeling almost high again, almost as if the drug had reemerged in her blood and lulled her into languid time once more, and she felt herself stretch in the memory of it, briefly capturing happiness.

xiii

During that week, real November weather rolled in like a sea squall. A steady wind blew in off the river and sent water crashing against the rocks and an icy mist careening through the alleyways and against the boards and windows of the town. Clary got out of bed early Wednesday morning and stood at his window watching the gray, smoky mists swirling against the tops of the trees.

"Where you going so early?" Judy asked. She was curled up in the bed, the covers up against her chin. She was not looking at him.

"Today's the big day," he said.

"Really."

"Sheriff Caldwell wants all of us to gather at McDole's place."

"Aren't you making coffee for the boys?"

"No."

"You think Cecil will show up?"

"Don't you?"

"It doesn't sound like him."

"Caldwell said he actually promised to pay McDole half of what he owes him."

"And McDole agreed to that?"

220 • Robert Bausch

"Well, it's at least half. It's better than nothing. And Cecil's paying all the damages for what he did at the station."

"Don't you think it's a mistake for all of you to be there?"

He turned and looked at her. "Caldwell insisted on it."

"It seems like it might humiliate Cecil to have everybody watching him do what he refused to do for so long."

"I don't believe he'll do it," Clary said. "But this guy, Caldwell—I guess he's trained for this sort of thing. He said he wanted us all there for—," he stopped.

"For what?"

"I'm trying to remember it. He used one of those terms they use these days." Judy sat up against the headboard and arranged the blankets around herself. "Conflict something or other," Clary said. Judy gave a short laugh. "What?" he asked.

"Nothing."

"What's so funny?"

"I don't know. You guys are still in high school, for god's sake."

He went to the door and opened it. Her judgment angered him again. She pronounced things about him with such clarity and without any doubt—as if they were somehow the observed truth. In the face of her certainty he was frequently speechless. What he was involved in felt like the kind of trouble adults were often, and more often than not, perplexed by. There was nothing adolescent or childish about it. Wars had been cheerily begun on less grounds and with less provocation.

"I'd appreciate it," he said, "if you would put clean towels and linens in the two rooms we're renting. If it's not asking too much."

She scrunched herself down under the covers again. "What's wrong with you?"

"Not a thing."

"It doesn't sound like it."

"I'm not in high school. That's all."

"Go on to your big meeting," she said, turning over.

"Resolution. That's what it was. Conflict resolution."

"Sounds like a peace conference."

"Well, that's sort of what it is."

He walked out and purposely left the door open. Downstairs he went to his office and took a brief sip of scotch, then he put on his coat and went to leave, but as he stood at the double doors of the entrance to the hotel, he suddenly felt bad. He knew leaving the door wide open bothered Judy, that she'd get out of bed to close it and it would disturb her sleep. So he went back up the stairs and tiptoed to their room, but he could see that she had already closed the door herself. He almost went back in to apologize, but he heard her singing and moving around, so he crept back down the stairs and then strode through the double doors out into the cold morning. He thought of waiting for Sheriff Caldwell to come down but then decided against it.

In the misty air he could see the steam from his mouth as he walked. Behind thick, gray clouds that covered the sky, a pale, lusterless sun inched its way over the eastern horizon like a sullied moon. He wore a heavy jacket, but he was still shivering in the icy air, and he did not like having to be out so early without coffee. His shoes crunched on the gravel under him, and as he made his way up the deserted street, he noticed that McDole had not yet turned on the lights at his station. The building was dark and appeared empty. He saw Cecil's big truck pull slowly into the station, and park next to the restrooms. He picked up his pace, and when he got to Cecil's truck, the big man got out and slammed the door. "Morning," Clary said.

"That it is," Cecil said. Big puffs of steam came from his mouth.

Neither man spoke for a while. Clary wondered if the inside of Cecil's truck was warm. "Cold out here," he said.

"Where's your sheriff this morning?"

"My sheriff?"

"McDole, too. Ain't he supposed to open this place soon?"

"Normally he'd come down to my place for coffee first. I don't think he ever opens until eight or so."

"Well, where is he?"

"I don't know."

The two of them stood there by the truck, and Clary realized that no matter how high the sun rose, this was all the light they were going to get. Everything took on a gray pallor, as if a black and white film had swallowed them. A car came down from the highway, cruising slowly by the station, then went on back up to the entrance ramp. A long time seemed to pass, then the door to Hamlin's office opened across the street, and he emerged, wearing a long white coat and a black slouch hat. He leaned forward in the drenching breezes and walked to where Clary and Cecil were standing.

"Where's McDole?"

"Don't know," Clary said. Cecil turned around and got back in his truck. "Where you going?" Clary asked.

"Just getting warm," he replied. He turned on the engine, then slammed the door. Clary went around to the passenger side and tried to get in, but it was locked. Cecil did not look at him. He pulled on the handle again, made a clatter with it. "Let me in, Cecil." The big man leaned over and unlocked the door. Clary signaled to Hamlin and he came around the back of the truck and both of them scurried onto the seat beside Cecil. It was crowded because of Cecil's big frame, and the cab of the truck was really only a bench seat designed for two people. Hamlin sat with his legs straddling the floor shift, the collar of his coat jutting up in his face and his hands trapped under the shift lever. "Little tight in here," he said, and when he saw Cecil scowling at him he added, "But cozy warm." Cecil said nothing. The windows began to fog. Clary tried to scoot against the door on the far side and give Hamlin some room. Cecil had the heat on high, and the fan blew dry, hot hair from under the dash. A few more minutes passed. Cecil kept looking in the rearview mirror. After a while he said, "I don't think your friend is coming."

"He'll be here," Hamlin said. "He wouldn't miss this for the world." Clary elbowed him to shut him up. "What?" Hamlin said, squirming. "What are you poking me for?" Clary glared at him, wanting somehow to tell him not to be gloating about this.

Cecil said, "Wouldn't miss what?"

"Nothing," Hamlin said. He tried to turn himself so he could look Cecil in the face. "Just peacemaking, you know."

"Peacemaking?" Cecil said.

"Smoke the peace pipe," Hamlin said, lamely. Clary shook his head. It was quiet for a while. Then Hamlin said, "You hear about the golfer who went to Japan to play in a tournament? And the night before the tournament he goes to this geisha house and gets this hot girl."

"They ain't prostitutes," Cecil corrected him.

"What?"

"Geishas ain't really prostitutes."

"Oh. Well," Hamlin said, "it's just a joke." After another brief silence, Hamlin went on. "Anyway, while he's banging this Japanese girl, she's hollering, 'FujiMama! FujiMama!' over and over, and he's thinking, 'Man, I'm really doing great with this chick.' The next day, he's at the tournament and he hits his tee shot on a par three, and the ball rolls up onto the green and into the cup. A hole in one. He wants to impress the Japanese businessmen he's playing with—you know, show them that he speaks their language—so he hollers, 'FujiMama!' and one of the businessmen says something in Japanese that he doesn't understand. So he turns to his partner and whispers, 'What'd he say?' and his partner says, 'Oh, he said, "No, you got it in the right hole."'"

Clary didn't get it at first, but then he started laughing. Cecil did not even smile. He glanced in the mirror and said, "Here comes Mauldin."

Clary was still laughing. He liked Hamlin's jokes sometimes, and this one had taken a turn he hadn't expected. He watched Mauldin as he approached the truck.

"There ain't no room for him in here," Hamlin said. "I hope McDole and the sheriff get here soon."

"We'll wait outside for a while," Cecil said, and with that, he turned off the truck and got out. Hamlin and Clary piled out too.

"You guys all ride up here together?" Mauldin asked.

"No," said Clary. "Just keeping warm."

"How precious."

Cecil glared at him, but he said nothing. He stood a short distance away from all of them. Mauldin signaled Clary to come closer. When he was next to him, Mauldin whispered, "You seen what's been going on with his girl?"

"Who's girl?"

"His," he gestured toward Cecil, "for chrissake."

"No, what's going on?"

"I think she and Sheriff Caldwell's son got something going."

Clary whispered, "I've seen them together. But I didn't think . . ."

"Mrs. McCutcheon told me he's been over there every day this week. In the afternoons, when she gets off work."

Hamlin asked, "What are you two whispering about?" Cecil watched them.

"Nothing," said Clary. "Shut the fuck up."

"You shut up."

Mauldin said, "That boy's got more nerve than a polar bear."

"Who's got nerve?" Cecil asked.

"Oh, nobody," Mauldin answered. "Just something we were . . . Just making conversation. How you been, Cecil?"

"I ain't waiting here much longer," Cecil said.

"It is right cold," said Mauldin. He reached into his jacket, retrieved a cigarette, and lit it. The smoke looked dense in the cold air.

Clary started shivering. He turned to Cecil. "Mind if I just sit for a spell in the truck while we wait?" Cecil just looked at him. Down the street, Caldwell emerged from the hotel and began strolling up the street. He wore his uniform and a black leather jacket with the badge on the outside. He walked confidently, his hands in the coat pockets, not really looking at anything but the street in front of him.

"Well, now," Cecil said. "We only got to wait for McDole."

THEY WAITED until nearly nine in the morning. McDole came down the road from the highway in his own red Chevy pickup. He parked in the space in front of the mechanic's bay, and the others watched him wrap a scarf around his neck, adjust his baseball cap, then slowly, almost painfully get out of the cab of the truck. He shut the door carefully and strolled to where Cecil was standing. The others gathered around.

"We should have had this meeting in the hotel," said Clary.

"I wanted it here," Caldwell said. Cecil did not take his eyes off McDole. "Okay," Caldwell continued, "let's get it said—what we've agreed to here."

"Where's your son?" Mauldin said.

Caldwell didn't answer him. He looked at McDole. "You've agreed to forgive half the debt on the truck that you couldn't fix, right?"

"I did what I thought was good diagnostics. I ain't admitting it wasn't good mechanical work or nothing."

"You never fixed the damned thing," Cecil said.

McDole started to say something, but Caldwell said, very loud, "Now we're not going to get into that here and now, fellows. You understand?" They were both quiet. "Nobody has to admit anything. Just answer my question," Caldwell said to McDole. "You only want $81.50 for the work you did on Cecil's truck?" McDole, still staring at Cecil, nodded his head. Cecil's expression was totally inscrutable, his eyes almost glittering on the edge of mirth or menace. It was hard to tell. He seemed to be thinking of something else while glaring at McDole, and whatever it was, it amused him or threatened to provoke him into a rage. "And," Caldwell went on, "Cecil will pay you for the damage to the Coke machine, a new sign, seven Cokes, and eighteen cans of oil?"

"That's right."

"Did you figure out what that came to?"

"Well, the machine only needed new Plexiglas on the front of it. I got an estimate over the phone of $31. The oil, the Cokes that broke, and the sign came to $26, so that would be—"

"Twenty-six dollars my ass," Cecil interrupted. "You call Shell and they'll replace the sign for nothing."

"That's what it was," said McDole, seeming to raise himself— as if he were trying to make himself taller—as he leaned toward Cecil. "And Shell ain't paying for it. You're paying for it."

"I ain't paid for it yet," Cecil said. He hadn't shaved, and the way he scowled when he said those words seemed to cause Mc-Dole to shrink down a bit. He didn't step back, but he paused, then looked at Caldwell.

"So, do you have a total?" Caldwell asked impatiently.

"It all comes to $138.50," Clary said.

"Yeah," McDole said, "$138.50. And that still ain't the total amount he actually owes me." Cecil reached in his back pocket and pulled out a checkbook. "No, no," McDole said. "No checks." Caldwell sighed.

"I don't have cash on me," Cecil said. "You don't want a check, then I guess you don't get paid today."

"I knew it," McDole said, shaking his head.

"Oh for chrissake, take a check," Mauldin said.

Cecil took out a pen and walked over to his truck. He leaned over on the back of the gate and wrote out a check. The others milled around a little in the cold. Clary watched Caldwell, amazed at how powerful he looked in his black jacket, boots, and uniform, with the big gun resting on his hip. Cecil finished and carefully ripped the check out of his book. He was smiling now. He'd said almost nothing since McDole had pulled up in his truck, but now he turned and ceremoniously carried the check to him, handing it over as if it were a plaque of some kind. He almost bowed as he backed away from McDole. "Your check, sir," he said.

McDole folded it and put it in his shirt pocket.

Caldwell said, "Okay, now I'm not expecting you to shake hands or anything, but I want all of you to agree that this foolishness between you will stop."

Clary put his hands in his pockets and looked at the ground. Hamlin said, "We don't have—I don't have a problem with Cecil."

"I don't either," Mauldin said.

"I want this foolishness to stop," Caldwell repeated. "I don't want any more disputes leading to this sort of thing." Cecil turned and started for his truck. Caldwell did not stop him, but he said, loud enough for all of them to hear, "Do I have your assurances that the trouble down here will stop?" Except for Cecil, they all seemed to mumble their approval of the idea. "Cecil?" Caldwell said.

He stopped and turned slightly around. His face was incredulous, as if the suggestion that he might be a source of trouble was not only laughable but impertinent. "I don't ever want any trouble," he said.

xiv

C aldwell and Todd went home together for Thanksgiving dinner. Caldwell drove, hoping the long drive would allow them
to have the serious conversation he'd been expecting since Todd
had arrived at Columbia Beach. The road that led away from the
town was newly tarred and wound its way through deep shaded
forest for a long time, then it came out along broad open fields
and rolling hills strewn with black wooden fences and stone bar-
ricades. White farmhouses, gray barns, old tractors, abandoned
cars on blocks, bright red cultivators, and black plows adorned
the countryside. Cows stood along the fences like bored specta-
tors, and horses walked regally in the fields, nodding their heads
in the cold air. Caldwell sat back and held the wheel with one
hand, driving just a few miles over the speed limit, enjoying the
smooth ride. Although the weather had cleared and great white
clouds drifted above the trees, it was still cold and windy.

During the first part of the drive neither one of them spoke.
The sun warmed the car through the glass, and it was peaceful
watching everything pass by on the road. Caldwell was thinking
about the problem between McDole and Cecil. He'd heard the
other men talking and laughing at the idea that the check Cecil
had written would probably bounce.

They had been in the café early in the morning following the meeting. As Clary got some coffee brewing, the men sat around waiting for it while they discussed the previous day's turn of events and what it might mean in the ongoing feud between Cecil and McDole. Caldwell had come down for a newspaper, and when he saw them all sitting around the table in the café, he decided to drop in. As he approached the bar, he heard Hamlin say that McDole probably didn't believe for a single second that Cecil would show up. "Hell," he said, "I didn't believe it, neither."

"Cecil pretty much does what he says he'll do," Clary said.

"Yeah, but he's stubborn," said Hamlin. "McDole just probably didn't want the embarrassment of waiting for who knows how long, falling for what he probably expected was just another one of Cecil's maneuvers. It'd just be one more humiliation, wouldn't it? That's why he was late, I'll bet."

"Well," Mauldin said, "I never would have believed Cecil would pay him like he did."

"Me neither," Hamlin said. He looked at Caldwell. "I got to hand it to you, sir. I got to hand it to you."

The coffeepot started boiling and bubbling behind the bar. They all watched it for a minute, waiting for the pot to fill.

"I guess if Cecil's got a badge to look at, he don't behave so badly," Mauldin said.

Now, on the long drive back toward home, Caldwell looked over at Todd, who was staring out the window, turning almost completely toward the door.

"You sleeping?" Caldwell asked.

"No." He did not turn around.

"You nervous about going home?" Todd said nothing. "Todd?" Now he turned and looked at Caldwell. "I said, you nervous about going home?"

"I guess I don't feel like I'm going home," he said.

"You don't?"

"It's not really home for me, is it."

"What do you mean?"

"I haven't been there in, what—how many years?"

"A long time."

"Seems like never. I mean, I never have seen the house you're in now."

Caldwell realized this was true. It got quiet again. He wanted to say something, to get some sort of conversation going that would steer them away from the awful past. But the silence seemed to have force—as if the ability to speak was unfamiliar to both of them. There was so much he wanted to say—but he couldn't find words that made it possible. He wasn't even sure he could put it into words. He wondered why Todd had insisted on this time together—that was one thing. The business with Lindsey seemed to cancel out all Todd's plans and intentions. He'd spent the last few days hanging around the hotel—showing Clary how to cook certain things in the kitchen or reading in his room. The only time he had spent with Caldwell was at breakfast, and even then he had nothing much to say. He'd read part of the newspaper until they were finished eating, then he'd get up and go back to his room. "See you later," he'd say. Or, "I'm going up to read."

In the afternoons when Lindsey got off work, he'd go directly from the hotel to Mrs. McCutcheon's. He'd return late at night and go right back to his room. Caldwell had heard him some nights going by and was tempted to open the door and try to talk to him, but he never did. He would sit and stare at his laptop screen, trying to think of something to say to Laura about what they were up to and how things were going. He had written her only once. He'd told her, "We'll be home for Thanksgiving. We'll talk about it then. Things are fine."

Now Todd shifted a little in the seat and said, "I don't remember much about the other—about home."

"You mean the house in Fairfax?"

"Well . . ."

"Well, what?"

"That was your home."

"What's that supposed to mean?"

"It seems like it was never really home to me. I mean, when it was home was a long, long time ago. I grew up somewhere else. That's all."

Caldwell had no response. He realized his son was right—his whole life had been spent in some other place.

"My home was . . ." Todd didn't finish the sentence.

"I guess I'm sorry," Caldwell said.

"You guess?"

"No, I *am* sorry. I didn't mean that the way it sounded."

Todd turned away again. They drove in silence for a little while longer. They reached the end of the newly paved road and suddenly they were negotiating potholes and black repair patches that rattled and shook the car as they drove along. Caldwell slowed down. "You been getting along pretty well with that young girl," he said. "What's her name?"

"You know her name, Dad." Caldwell watched the road, steering the car with both hands now. "Lindsey," said Todd.

"Yeah, Lindsey." Caldwell did know her name. But he wanted to talk about the relationship, and he didn't know how to broach the subject any other way. "You two have been pretty much of an item in the last week or so."

"Really?"

"I mean, you're definitely seeing more of her than anybody else down here."

"She's Cecil's girlfriend. I hope he doesn't think we're an item."

"She's not his girlfriend. Who told you that?"

"Clary."

"Well, I know for certain she's not."

"She's not?"

"Trust me. I'm surprised she didn't tell you."

"Tell me what?"

"Just that . . ." he thought about it for a second. "Just that she's his sister, not his girlfriend."

"You're kidding."

"Nope." A silence ensued. Caldwell had to concentrate on what he was doing to negotiate the bad road. Finally he said, "You do spend a lot of time with Lindsey."

"I guess so."

"I can't get you to sit still for a simple meal."

"You complaining?"

"No. I just meant you're an item. That's all." It was quiet again for what seemed like a long time. Then Caldwell said, "Walking on the beach and all."

"She's just a good friend, Dad."

"You know she—she knows—," Caldwell stopped.

"What?"

"Have you told her where you spent your childhood?"

Todd looked at him, a slight pained expression on his face. "She knows all about it."

"Well, I knew she was aware of it. She said she remembered me from the newspapers. I just wondered if you told her anything about . . . ," he didn't finish. They fell silent again, and both of them listened to the whir of the wind outside and watched the front of the car gulp the road. The miles rolled away. Finally Caldwell took a deep breath.

"What?" Todd said.

"What was . . ." Caldwell started. He couldn't finish the sentence. He felt Todd's eyes on him again, but he gazed at the road, steering gently around the biggest potholes.

"What was what?" Todd asked.

"What was the reason for this?"

"For what?"

"Why'd you want to meet me down here?"

"You don't know?"

"Did you tell me?" Todd shook his head slowly, staring straight ahead now. "What, son?"

"I don't want to talk about it."

"You don't want to tell me the reason?"

"I shouldn't have to."

"Am I supposed to guess?"

"You ought to know." Todd settled himself again, his head turned toward the window, leaning back in the seat.

"Come on, son," Caldwell said. "That's a woman's trick. Don't play that sort of trick on me."

"There's no trick. I never noticed that women play any sort of trick," Todd said.

"It's not fair to insist I should know, when it's clear that I don't."

"It's not a trick. I really do think you should know."

"Well, I don't know."

Todd almost laughed. It was a sound in the back of his throat that could have been suppressed laughter, but he gazed out the window and said nothing.

"Why don't you just come out and say it?" Caldwell asked. He felt something turn in his stomach and he realized he was nervous. He had been working at this thing—at discovering what Todd was up to for more than a month, and he was determined to get it out in the open now, on this trip. What would he say to Laura when they got home? She would want to know what it was about, why Todd had arranged this solo meeting in their old vacation haunt, and there would be nothing to say about it because he still had no idea.

Todd looked at him again. "Really, Dad. Let's just leave it for now."

"Your mother is going to want to know what we've accomplished here."

"What we've accomplished?"

"You know what I mean."

"No, I don't."

"You set this whole thing up. You must have had a reason."

Todd shook his head. "I swear, Dad. Sometimes . . ."

"Sometimes what?"

"Let me ask you something."

"All right."

"Do you think you know me?"

Caldwell stammered. "W-what do you mean?"

"What part don't you understand?"

"Of course I know you."

Todd began laughing. It was a kind of derision that struck Caldwell in the heart. His immediate thought was, How dare you? He said, "You must think I'm pretty much of a fool."

This seemed to shock Todd. "No, I don't."

"You have no right," Caldwell said, not masking his vehemence very well. He gripped the steering wheel, and without intending it, the car's speed increased.

"I don't want to argue, Dad."

Caldwell said nothing. In his helpless memory he found Bobby—he heard the boy's distant, lost voice in the center of his consciousness. Todd sat next to him, with his tattoos and his inexpressible demands, breathing. That was the thing. Todd was breathing and taking his days like something that cuts through ice—chipping away for himself a kind of daily amusement, and forgetfulness, and silence. "You have no right," Caldwell said again.

"What?" Todd looked at him. "No right to live?"

"I didn't say that."

"No, you didn't."

"You have no right to sit there and laugh at me. You have no idea what I've been—," he stopped himself. "You have no idea what this family has been through."

"No," he said, thoughtfully. "I don't. That's because since the day it happened, I have not been a part of this family. But you don't know what I've been through, either."

These words seemed to spark something that gave off heat in Caldwell's brain. But he did not want to say it. He did not want to say, again, what seemed to burn slowly in his skull—that Todd had murdered Bobby, and now he was complaining of the consequences. "Since it happened," Caldwell said very slowly, measuring his voice, "this family has not really existed. You . . . ," he paused. "You see, it's not just that you're not a part of it. No one is. It doesn't exist anymore."

Again, he felt Todd shaking his head. Then his son let his hands fall to his lap in a kind of exhausted motion—as if he'd just finished holding his arms up for hours. "I give up, Dad."

"What do you mean?"

"I just wanted to get to know you," he said. "I thought if we spent this time together, we'd . . ."

"What time together? You're off with Lindsey every day."

"I'm sorry," he said. "I didn't intend . . ."

"You have a strange way of getting to know a person."

"You've been pretty busy getting the jail ready."

This was true, in a way. But it was not fair—Caldwell's work at the jail was what he had come there for, it was his job, and he never went to work there thinking he was leaving anything un-done with Todd. He went there when Todd was in his room, ap-parently insisting on being by himself, reading. "So, is it your contention that we'd have spent more time together if I hadn't been busy at the jail?"

"I don't want to fight, Dad. Okay?"

"I was just wondering."

As they rounded a sharp turn they came up behind a Volks-wagen bus, the exhaust of which sent out great white clouds of smoke. Caldwell slowed down, letting the distance between the two cars increase, but he was looking for a place to pass. They drove that way for what seemed like miles, both of them think-ing. Finally Caldwell said, "Lot of smoke."

"I just want something to happen, maybe," Todd said.

"What do you mean?"

"I'm going to school. Did you know?"

"Yes. Well, no. I guess I didn't."

"I'm thinking of studying history, but maybe political sci-ence." Caldwell had nothing to say. "I'm the kind of person who's interested in current events."

"Really?"

"I'm not a politically conservative person. I'm more interested in change than the status quo."

"I guess I wouldn't say I was conservative either," Caldwell said. "I don't think we need to change just for the sake of change, though. Sometimes people just want to stir things up and . . ."

"I'm going to make something of myself, Dad."

This seemed to cause something in Caldwell's throat to rise. He felt it come from someplace in his heart, and only later would he comprehend with a kind of loathing and sadness that it was pity. "I hope you do," he said, trying to keep the strength in his voice.

"I'm going to make a difference in the world, someday. I don't know how or in what field—not yet anyway—but that's very much in my plan."

Now Caldwell felt as though he were talking to a complete stranger—as if Todd's marred and blackened soul had somehow withdrawn from the world and now this person sitting next to him was a hitchhiker discussing his future; the change was so complete and so swift, it momentarily stunned him. "We were a family once," Caldwell said, hopelessly. "A family. Do you realize what that is? What it means to someone like me? What it means in the world? I'd like us to be a family again. That's my plan." He felt Todd move on the seat—as if something had stricken him. He made a sound that Caldwell could not hear. "What?"

Todd's eyes filled with tears. "It's just a family. That's all . . ." He waved his hand, and turned again to stare out the window. "Not everybody has a family. Lindsey doesn't."

"Well," Caldwell said, but he couldn't find any other words. He suddenly felt humiliated and embarrassed for his lack of words and for what he had already said. How could he take back the words that now seemed to cause Todd to suffer profoundly? The young man looked out the window as they drove, tears running down his face. Caldwell wanted to pull the car over and put his arms around his son—a thing he had not done in a long time—but he couldn't bring himself to do it. He felt vaguely manipulated—as if this show of emotion carried with it the emotional freight of intentions. Also, he felt a kind of vindication. This was something he'd wished for when it had happened all those years ago: some sign of emotion from Todd, some suggestion of regret or grief—anything. All the boy had done was maintain a blank expression—almost a sullen mask—refusing to speak of it, refusing to defend himself or make any claim except to say it had been an accident. He had seemed stunned that anybody would think anything else, and he had looked around himself like a mute child sinking slowly in quicksand, trying to find a long, sturdy stick. He had stared at Caldwell during the police proceedings, the hearing, the brief trial before the judge. He had said, "Yes, sir" and "No, sir," when spoken to, and he had not shed a tear.

Now these tears seemed inadequate to the task. Caldwell was torn between wanting to show his affection and wanting to register his scorn. He could not have put into words how he felt. "I'll tell your mother that's what you wanted," he said, almost whispering, choking back his own tears. "To be a family again." Todd said nothing. "It will make her happy."

"That is what I wanted, Dad."

"Really?"

"I wanted a family again." Todd's voice broke, and he lay his head back on the seat and stared out the window.

"Well," Caldwell said lamely. "Yes, of course. That's what we all want."

. . .

On Thanksgiving morning, Caldwell took the whole family to church. Laura sat next to him on his left, her perfume smelling sweet and like Sunday morning long ago. Todd was on his right, and beyond him sat Terry, her purple hair brushed almost straight up off her head, but she looked happy and almost pretty to Caldwell on this morning. He had decided to tolerate her extremes, just so he could be the head of this family for one quiet but festive day. It would feel normal to him. That's what mattered most.

When they had arrived home the day before, Laura greeted them at the door with bright, dry eyes. She was determined not to cry, but when she saw Todd, when she saw how much of a man he'd become, she broke down. "My lord," she kept saying. "Look at you."

Todd held her in his arms. He was much taller than she was. Terry came down the stairs laughing. "You're a man. A full-grown man," she said. "You look like a rock star."

"Good god," he said. "What'd you do to your hair?" This silenced everyone. They were all standing in the foyer, the door open behind Caldwell and Todd, and the bright, freezing afternoon sun cast their shadows into the room. Terry stopped smiling. She put her head down, looking at first to the floor, then at Laura. When she met Caldwell's gaze, she shook her head slightly and turned to leave the room.

"I didn't say anything to him," Caldwell said.

"What?" She faced them.

"What'd you do to your hair?" Todd asked. "You look like a cigar store Indian."

"Fuck you," Terry said.

"Hey!" Caldwell shouted.

For an awkward moment, they all stood there in the doorway. Then Caldwell said, "Let's just settle down a bit, okay? No need to . . ."

Laura reached up and put her arms around Todd's neck. "Welcome home, son," she said, fighting her tears now.

"It's a nice house," he said, and it struck Caldwell again that his son had never seen their new home. It almost hurt him to realize it.

"We moved here three years after . . ." Laura started. She wiped her eyes with the back of her hand. "I've got a room ready for you."

Todd smiled at Terry. "Hey kid." She, too, seemed suddenly to be fighting tears, and for the first time in a long time, Caldwell saw something besides bitter resistance in her. It was actually a kind of femininity; Terry was, he realized, a woman. "Welcome home," she said. Todd held out his arm and she came under it. He smiled down at her. "I'm glad to be here."

"Let's all get in and shut the door," Caldwell said. "We're heating up the neighborhood."

So they began the holiday together in the house. A little later in that first day, Todd and Terry went to her room and listened to loud music. If they talked, neither Caldwell nor Laura could hear it. Once, they both went to the room and knocked. The music instantly lowered, and they heard whispering. Then Terry opened the door.

"You guys—you interested in some lunch or something?" Laura asked.

"You both had to come up here to ask that?" The expression on Terry's face was almost a scowl, but when she heard Todd's laugh behind her, she smiled.

"We just wanted to get in on the fun," Caldwell said.

"Listening to this music?"

Todd waved his hand. "Let them in."

But once they were in the room and the music had been turned up loud again, there was nowhere to sit comfortably. Laura sat on the bed for a while, and Caldwell stood by the door, leaning against it with his hands on the knob. The music was very loud—a sort of howl too indiscriminate to make any sense, with somebody banging very hard on all the strings of an electric guitar, playing essentially two chords over and over, Caldwell realized. It was not even a small attempt at music, really—or at anything one might describe as pleasant. It was simply noise, very loud noise, but it had a kind of energy. He could understand why the young were attracted to such brute simplicity; the music made no demands on the ear whatsoever except for a capable tolerance of extreme racket at high decibels. You could easily listen to it and feel nothing, think nothing. Conversation was, as it always was with any sort of rock music, very nearly impossible. Caldwell had spent many a night in his own youth at loud clubs, screaming over blaring guitars in an effort to be heard. It was not new to him. Just different. The music was less melody and more pounding force, less lyrical lament and more angry sullenness—almost a call to war, and social war, at that.

So Caldwell tried not to judge it, tried not to show how he was reacting to it. Terry watched him the whole time he stood there, waiting for his reaction. He felt as though he had stumbled into a kind of trap, and she was going to spring it on him if he let the slightest disapproval show on his face. He tried to keep smiling while the noise insulted him, and eventually Terry began reading the notes on the backs of the CDs, flipping them over in her hand while she chewed her gum and mouthed the lyrics of the songs.

Laura seemed oblivious to the noise. She sat next to Todd, who sprawled across the bed on his stomach, holding his chin in his hands. Caldwell suddenly found himself trying to picture this scene if Bobby had lived, if he was here too, on a family holiday, grown to manhood—or almost grown. He'd be sixteen. Also now, he had to admit, as he watched Todd bouncing slightly to the music, his fingers tapping his jaw, it was just as pleasant to imagine a life for Todd that did not include those long years in the detention center, or the two years after, living alone in Richmond, less than a hundred miles from home. How did that happen? He could not believe he had let a thing like that happen to his family. He studied Todd's face, the light in his eyes, the way his hair shown in the sunlight that leaked in at the window, and he suddenly hated himself for letting so many years go by. At some level he must have wanted Todd to suffer, and this knowledge hit him hard: a cold, pitiless feeling swelled in the chambers of his heart. It felt like something hot and icy at the same time—

like a sudden realization of his own death—and without wanting to, standing there by the door, he began to weep.

No one saw him. He wanted to go to Todd, lift him up, and just hold him, but he couldn't make himself move. He was trying too hard to mask the tears that brimmed in his eyes and ran down his cheeks. He wiped his face with a handkerchief and quietly opened the door and went out.

He spent the rest of that afternoon thinking of Bobby, of the life and time he missed—the years of little league and hunting and fishing, the long bike rides in the country, the movies, and yes—the music. What would he be like now, and what music would he be listening to? Would he be like Terry? Would he seem to want a kind of distance that made his parents strangers and all other members of the family servants? Caldwell longed for the small troubles of a happy family. He hoped to feel like this was his life on this one day, Thanksgiving Day.

So the day began with church, where they could all privately thank God for whatever fortune they could account for in their lives. During the mass, while the priest bent over the host, Caldwell looked over at Todd. He was kneeling as everyone was, but he looked down at his clasped hands as though he was hoping to find something there. Caldwell reached over and very lightly touched his shoulder, and Todd turned to him, his sad eyes reflecting the sunlight through the stained glass windows of the church. Caldwell tapped him, smiling, as if to say, I'm glad you're here, and Todd seemed to recognize something between them. He nodded and turned back to studying his hands.

It would be just as awkward to talk about being thankful, even on this day, as it was to be thankful on any day since Bobby's death. He should say nothing about their losses, but how to be thankful? Perhaps he could say he was pleased that Todd had finally come home. He could say that. As he sat in the church and heard the mass, he made up his mind he would say something about it at the dinner table, before carving the bird.

But when the opportunity came, after they had come home from church and the long day of cooking, watching football and listening to more music was under way he lost track of what he was planning to say. He just enjoyed himself, feeling for the first time in a long time as if this was an escape from memory and death; as if he had wandered into a warm, relaxing, and almost quiet existence in the arms of something too lovely to consider consciously. He did not want to think about it. All afternoon the sun lit the room in panels of soft light, and a fire hissed and sputtered and flickered in the fireplace. Terry moved around in the kitchen with her mother—basting the bird and making rolls, sweet potatoes, stewed cranberries. He heard both of them talking and laughing for what seemed like the first time in years. Once, he got up and went in there, took Terry in his arms, and kissed her. She smiled up at him, and he was momentarily embarrassed for her—because of how bad her purple hair looked, and because she wore too much dark makeup. But he only kissed her again, lightly on the forehead, feeling as though he might start crying. He told her he loved her. "I love you too, Dad," she said. Her smile was beautiful, and he realized this was just his little girl, asserting herself, becoming herself.

Todd sat in Caldwell's recliner, one leg dangling over the arm of the chair, reading the newspaper. Later on he stretched out on the couch and slept. The young man was home. Home. For almost the first time in his life. And he was so comfortable in it, so normal, it didn't seem possible that he could have spent so many years in another place. Caldwell's awareness of this made him happier, he realized, than he had been in a very long time. It was a kind of perfect contentment, brimming with joy, and it astonished him. Something was in back of it that he knew could destroy it in an instant, but he went on reveling in it, forgetting, temporarily, the other side of his days.

Just before dinner, Todd volunteered to make the gravy, promising that he would do a masterful job; and when the time came, Caldwell watched him working over the stove, taking extra care with the task, and again tears came to his eyes. He realized, as he waited for dinner to start, that he had spent the whole day striving not to think of Bobby at all.

• • •

At Columbia Beach that morning, the sun burned brightly, but it was still breezy and cold. The erratic wind hurried over the water and then cut through the streets and alleyways that ran off the boardwalk and onto Main Street. Lindsey drove to Cecil's trailer in her yellow Cavalier. On the back seat was an eleven-pound stuffed turkey already in a roasting pan, properly tied and ready for the oven. She prayed it would fit in Cecil's small stove, and when she parked the car just outside the gate that led into the yard and up to his trailer, she felt as though she were bringing food to someone who was destitute and near death. Even under the cold sun, the trailer loomed darkly at the end of the yard, but there was light in the windows under the awning, and it looked almost warm as she approached the door. This was a kind of charity, she realized. Cecil had said the night before he didn't care if she came or not. "You know I don't celebrate those kinds of things." She told him then, "Well, we'll celebrate it tomorrow." She had already told Alicia that she was not coming home this year. It was a telephone conversation she had dreaded for days, but when, a few weeks before, she finally broached the subject, Alicia seemed resigned to it. "I expected you'd be staying down there this year."

"You did?"

"It just seemed like the next step."

"The next step in what?"

"It's nothing, honey. I wasn't expecting you this year. I know you're still on a mission of sorts, so . . ."

"Will you have dinner alone?"

"No. Actually I'm going home. To my mother and father."

"Really?"

"Yes. It's been years, and they're getting so old." Lindsey said nothing. "They live so near to me here, it would be wrong not to spend the day with them. They'll miss you, though. They were so looking forward to . . ." She didn't finish the sentence.

"I'm sorry, Mom."

"Don't worry about it. You have a nice time cooking for your brother."

"I will."

When Lindsey hung up the phone, she felt released from something—almost as if she had been given a kind of reprieve. And she realized that she loved Alicia with all her heart, even though, at times, she had heard the words, "Aunt Alicia" echo in her mind like a thing she had always said and thought. Alicia was her mother. She understood and accepted this completely, but she kept hearing her own voice saying, "Aunt Alicia," as if that was what she had lived, as if that was reality. She hated the tricks of her mind and often wondered if anyone else had the same kind of problem: words would intrude on her, breaking into her thinking, and phrases would echo in her head—her own voice, saying unwanted things to her. It was worse than hearing an unwanted song, over and over.

Now she carried the roasting pan with the turkey in it up to Cecil's trailer door. She set the edge of the pan down on the top step and knocked on the metal door. Cecil opened it and stepped back. "What you got there?"

"Dinner," she said as she lifted the pan and came up the steps.

He watched her put the bird down on the counter. She reached over and turned the gas on in the oven, and after a brief hissing sound, the flames burst around the heating element. "Every time you light that thing I think we're going to blow up," he said. She took a shelf out of the oven and placed it next to the stove, then leaned down and was relieved to see that the pan fit nicely when she put the bird in. She closed the door and set the temperature to 375 degrees.

"Shouldn't you cover that thing with aluminum foil or something?" Cecil asked.

"I don't know. I've never cooked a turkey before. I never cover a chicken."

"You never saw your mother do it?"

"Once a year. I don't remember much about it. She basted every ten minutes."

"Put some foil over it." He opened the cabinet under the sink and retrieved some foil. He pulled out a long wide strip and then placed it neatly over the top of the roasting pan, crimping it along the edges so it would stay put. "Like that. See? This way it won't dry out while it cooks. And you don't have to baste it as much." Lindsey noticed how carefully he worked his fingers around the pan as he crimped the foil, and she suddenly felt true affection for him. Affection, and a tinge of sadness for what his life had turned out to be. She wondered what his youthful ambitions were. What he hoped for. He never talked about things like that, but he must have had some sort of dream for himself when he was a young man, and the whole, long arc of his life stretched out before him.

While the turkey slowly cooked, Lindsey peeled and cut up potatoes and set them on to boil. Then she sat down with a bowl in her lap and snapped green beans, while Cecil stretched as best he could on the small couch and watched football on his old black-and-white television. Neither of them spoke much. If she had said anything to him, he would not have paid much attention because he seemed intensely interested in the game on TV. She had never seen him pay so much attention to it, though. On ordinary Sundays he ignored the TV and didn't seem interested in any sports except an occasional car race. So she worried that he was trying to avoid conversation with her. She found herself thinking of Todd, wondering how his day was going, if he was happy. Maybe he was feeling at home, although he had told her before he left that he was dreading his weekend with the whole family. "I feel like I'm going back to prison," he had said.

Cecil seemed content, if not talkative. Finally during half-time, and after she'd snapped the beans and washed them, she said, "So. What do you want to do?" He shrugged, still watching the TV. "Don't you think we should have something special to drink?"

He looked at her. "Did you bring cigarettes?"

"Yes, I have cigarettes." She went to her purse and got them for him. He lit one, then leaned over, unlatched the door, and swung it open. It banged against the outside of the trailer. He pulled his legs up and sat against the side of the couch so he could flick his ash out the door. She got up, went over by the door and, leaning against the frame, lit a cigarette for herself. The TV still blared with sports voices.

"Used to go down to the Howard Johnson's in Romney for Thanksgiving," Cecil said.

"Who?"

"Mother and me. Even when my father was alive we went down there."

"What was your father like?"

"Like nothing." He puffed on the cigarette, not looking at her.

"What do you mean?"

"What was your father like?"

"I never had one."

"Neither did I," he said, almost smiling now.

"You mean you didn't know him?"

"Hell, he didn't know anyone," Cecil said. "He yelled at me a few times. Looked at me funny if I came near him when he was eating or drinking. I really can't remember a thing he ever said to me."

"He must have been awful."

"It wasn't so bad," he said, exhaling a cloud of smoke. He got up and went to the refrigerator and got himself a glass of milk. With the cigarette tucked in the corner of his mouth, he drank the milk as if he was in a hurry to get rid of it. Then he put the glass down and looked at her. "Goddamn my mouth is dry."

"I'm sorry your father was so . . ." She didn't know how to finish.

"He didn't have some part of his brain. Got shot off in the war. The front part of his brain."

"Really?"

"He may as well have been a robot."

"I wish I at least knew who my father was."

"Why?"

"I need to know. What if you didn't know, wouldn't it bother you?"

He shook his head.

"It wouldn't bother you at all?"

"I don't know."

"I just think it's something a person ought to know, that's all."

They finished smoking then closed the door. It had gotten very cold inside the trailer, so Lindsey moved over and opened the oven for a brief time to let heat into the room. "It'll just take longer to cook," Cecil said.

LATER, AFTER they had eaten and Cecil was again seated on the couch smoking a cigarette—this time flicking his ashes into an ashtray and blowing smoke out of a crack in the window behind him—Lindsey lay her head back on the top of her soft chair and let her eyes close slowly against the weak lamplight. It was late in the day, and the sun had weakened considerably. The light in the windows was white and tinged with gray. It would be dark soon.

Cecil said, "That was good." She said nothing. "I want to thank you for making it," he added.

She raised her head and looked at him. This was a triumph— or it should have been. This morning, if she thought at all about what she expected that day, she would have been happy to believe he might actually thank her. But now it didn't seem like such a great thing. She believed he was sincere, but she found herself as-tonished at how unimportant it seemed now. He had eaten slowly and with a kind of patient understanding of a task before him. He did not seem to relish the food or the company; he did not seem grateful or even aware of what it cost her to put the dinner together and have it ready for him. And now she was thinking of Alicia and her grandparents, feeling as though she had given up something important in her life, something she might have experienced that she would find herself thankful for and that she would always cherish. Something better than this. Presently she asked, "Have you thought about how things will be now that the war with McDole is over?"

He shook his head. "You just won't give up, will you?"

"Give up what?" He didn't respond. "Why can't you just answer the question? Haven't you wondered yourself?"

"No. I haven't."

"Why?"

"I don't care."

"But now you've put an end to all this . . . all this . . ."

"What?"

"Bickering."

"It's not bickering. And it won't put an end to it."

"Why not?"

"They called that sheriff in. They sent him up here. You don't wonder about that?"

"No."

"Well."

"I don't. What's there to wonder about?"

"I'm going to take it out on them," he said.

"What?" She couldn't believe what she was hearing.

"They sent that sheriff up here. They caused this. It will be on them." His voice was quiet, calm, and dripping with malice. She felt something cold deep under her skin—something desolate and sad that seemed to gulp outward from the center of her body. Then Cecil said, "And you got something going with that kid, don't you?"

"What kid?"

"The sheriff's kid. What's his name?"

"Todd. And I don't have anything going with him."

"You sure spend enough time with him."

She didn't want to look at him. She sat up a bit in the chair and tried to calm the feeling of ice slouching toward her heart. She thought she might be sick, but it was not nausea, it was the most powerful and implacable feeling of regret. It was the sort of feeling that empties out the bottom of one's soul. And yet she knew it was silly for her to feel this way. Alicia was probably having the time of her life. Nothing fatal had happened to anyone she loved. This was just one day.

Cecil snuffed his cigarette out and coughed. It wasn't an asthma attack, but it startled her anyway. "You all right?" she said.

"What's the matter with you?"

"Nothing."

"You look very sad, did you know that?"

"I do?"

"If I hurt your feelings I'm sorry."

"You didn't hurt my feelings."

He reached behind himself and shut the window. "It's getting really cold out there." Lindsey stared at the television and felt herself calming down.

"So what do you and the sheriff's kid do, anyway?"

She looked at him.

"I don't mean to pry."

"We don't do much of anything. He likes to get high."

He leaned forward, a look of gradual awareness taking hold on his face. "Get high how?"

"You know."

"No, I don't."

"He smokes dope. I've smoked it a few times myself." He shook his head. "It's not what you think," she added.

"What do I think?"

"It relaxes him. I don't mind it, either. In fact, when it makes me laugh I think it's great."

"So the sheriff's son is a pothead?"

"He's not a pothead." She wished now she hadn't mentioned it.

"I'll be damned."

"Didn't you get stoned when you were in the Marines?"

"All the time," he said.

"Well. There you go."

"There I go what?"

"It's not such a big deal."

"When the sheriff who's threatening me with jail has a son who's doing illegal drugs, it's a very big deal."

"Oh, Cecil," she said. It was almost a moan. "Please don't get me in trouble over this."

"How am I going to get you in trouble?"

"I wish I hadn't told you."

"You won't be in any trouble."

"You know what I mean." She lit another cigarette. "If Todd's father finds out . . ."

"You really do like him, don't you?"

"No. Yes. I mean . . ." He waited. "I think he's sad."

Cecil smiled, then turned and lifted the window again. He handed her the ashtray. "Want me to make the coffee?"

"I'll make it," she said.

"Finish your cigarette."

"Please don't tell anyone about the pot."

"I won't."

"I mean it."

"I said I won't. It's just nice to know, is all."

"I think Todd is—I think he's got enough on his plate," she said wistfully.

"If the sheriff gets himself a bit too involved in things down here, he's got to expect . . ."

"What?"

"I won't say anything about his son and the illegal drugs unless I have to."

"You said you wouldn't say anything at all."

"Unless I have to."

"Thanks, Cecil. Thanks one whole hell of a lot."

"Now don't get yourself all riled up. I probably won't have to say anything." She wouldn't look at him. After a long silence, he said, "In any case, I'll leave you out of it."

XV

The Monday after Thanksgiving, in his room again at the Clary Hotel, Caldwell awakened suddenly and turned over in his bed. His eyes burned, but he had slept through most of the night. He lay there facing the wall and tried to come fully awake before turning to the window to see what kind of day it was. He did not hear any wind or noise in the hall, and he wondered if Todd was still asleep. He glanced out through the fully open window shades and saw it was bright and clear outside. He got out of bed and went to the window, thinking he might open it just to get a whiff of the air outside, but he couldn't break the seal countless layers of paint had made between the sill and the sash. In the distance he could see Maryland, and black trees across the water.

Yesterday he'd driven back with Todd; it had been a long, quiet drive in which neither of them had spoken much. They'd stopped at a Burger King on the way and, with the engine off, they had enjoyed a hamburger in the car, with everything so quiet Caldwell could hear Todd chewing. The silence was not tense— it was almost relaxed and pleasant, except Caldwell had wondered what was next. Would Todd remain with him in Columbia Beach, or would he eventually drive his own car back home? When would he begin looking into schools? What was he thinking now about Bobby and all that had happened? What was he thinking about all that had not happened? Did he have plans concerning Lindsey? All of these questions had worked in Caldwell's mind, but he had not been able to get himself to ask a single one of them. He hadn't known how to start. When they'd looked at each other, he said, "That was a nice Thanksgiving," and Todd gave a slight smile, then turned back to his burger. Something had not been said, but neither of them had seemed willing to press for it. In a way, Caldwell had liked the silence—in spite of the definite sensation that nothing very much was resolved, and there was so much more they would have to finally talk about. He knew there was more, but his holiday had been so fine—he'd actually enjoyed four full days with his family, which was at least partially the result of Todd's return, and he did not want to sully the feeling of pride and comfort he was still savoring even after the holiday had ended.

He took a shower and then put on dungarees and a sweatshirt. He would be putting the finishing touches on the jail today. The locksmith was coming to install new locks on the cell doors. Then it would be ready. He'd already installed a security gun rack and two computer stations. The phone company had installed new phone lines and a direct service line for the computers. He had a radio dispatch system ready to go. He'd gotten the bathrooms refinished and he bought a new safe.

When he was ready to go, he went to Todd's room and stood outside the door, listening. It was quiet so he didn't knock. He waited for a while, feeling tentative and anxious. Then he went downstairs to the café. As he was passing through the lobby, he saw Clary's wife behind the counter. "Where's your husband?" he asked.

"Why?" She looked at him. He thought her eyes registered a kind of gloom, as if she was aware of some awful news she would be forced to reveal, and she only waited for his words to provoke willing despair.

"What's the matter?" he asked.

"Nothing." She looked away. He realized his perceptions were probably distorted by his own intimations of what it must be like to work in this small, slow place, with no companions to speak of, and only the petulant battles of this town to talk about. "Is Jack in the café?"

"Where else?" Again she regarded him. This time she seemed about to say something to him and changed her mind.

Caldwell approached the counter. "You all right?"

"What do you think?"

"I'm sorry," he said. "I didn't mean to . . ." He felt sorry for her, watching her through all the days, working like a maid in her own hotel. Yet there was something beautiful about her—she seemed capable and ready for kindness in spite of the constant demands of a town basically full of men. But he did not really know her at all—had never even had so much as a conversation with her—so he could not simply engage her in familiar talk, and he was embarrassed that he'd asked her if she was all right. He wished he had his uniform on.

"Do you know if my son is here?" he asked.

"I don't know. I haven't seen him. I've been here since before dawn." A silence ensued in which they stood there looking at each other. She averted her eyes, finally, fidgeting with the hem of her skirt.

"Well, I guess I'll go to the café," he said.

"You really want to know what's wrong?" She averted her eyes again momentarily, then looked directly at him.

"Is something wrong?"

She sighed. "I'm just utterly bored."

Her frankness surprised him. He found himself smiling as if to reassure her, and then he said, "Aren't we all?"

"Are you on duty?" she asked suddenly.

"Well, yes. I guess I am."

"I've never seen you in a uniform." He said nothing. "Could I ask you something?" she said.

"Sure."

"What are you doing here?"

"What?"

"Why'd you come to Columbia Beach?" Her eyes still gazed directly into his.

"Mrs. Clary," he said. "I didn't have one reason. There were many, and I don't really have time to go into it now." She shook her head slowly.

Clary came out of the café and stopped when he saw them talking. He was a short distance away, but it seemed to embarrass him to see them together. "Hey," he said. Then, before Caldwell could speak, he disappeared back through the doors of the café.

"It seems strange that you should just suddenly be here," she said.

"Are you sorry I came here?"

"It just seems like more trouble's been brewing since you got here."

His heart sank. It struck him that she would think of this as the certain truth now—and nothing he did or said could change it. In her mind, and perhaps in the minds of the others, whatever happened in the town from now on would be placed at his feet.

"Well," he said, "maybe that's what you need. Trouble isn't ever boring, is it?"

"Oh, of course it is. It's probably the most boring thing on earth."

He didn't know what to say, so he smiled and nodded her way, then he walked across the room and into the café. Jack Clary had set out coffee, and he, Mauldin, and Hamlin were gathered at the counter. Clary was on the other side, with a white apron on, wiping the top of the counter as if he were a bartender. "Your boy coming down?" he asked when he saw Caldwell come in.

"I don't know," Caldwell responded.

"Have a nice holiday?"

"It was fine," Caldwell said. "How about you?"

"Oh, the wife and I just went on down to the Howard Johnson's and had turkey dinner."

Caldwell looked around the room. "Where's McDole?"

"He didn't show up this morning."

"Really."

"Seems odd, doesn't it?" Clary said.

Caldwell looked at him. "What do you mean?"

"Well, it's Monday. He's never missed the Monday after Thanksgiving before, that I can remember."

Hamlin seemed to nod his head, but when Caldwell looked directly at him he said, "I'm not too sure that's exactly true."

Clary poured steaming coffee into a white porcelain cup he'd retrieved from under the bar and offered it to Caldwell, who took hold of the saucer and moved it toward himself on the counter. He held up his hand to signal no cream when he saw Clary reaching for it, and then he carefully lifted the cup with two hands, still looking at Hamlin.

"I don't remember, really," Hamlin said. "I think he's closed it before."

Mauldin said, "You never know what McDole's up to half the time. I think he's missed a lot of Mondays myself."

"My shop is right across the street," Hamlin said. "I think I'd know if he was open or not."

"You might not remember it accurately, though," Clary said.

"I'm telling you he's missed Mondays before."

"And my memory is that he's always been right here, for coffee," Clary insisted.

The coffee was hot and tasted very fresh. "Coffee's good," Caldwell said.

"Thank you kindly." Clary went back into the office and returned with a stool that he pulled up to the counter. When he was seated, he poured more coffee into his own cup. "This is a special blend I get. Judy buys it, actually."

"You think something fishy's going on?" Hamlin asked. Mauldin shrugged and almost seemed to suppress a laugh. Caldwell sipped more of the coffee, but he said nothing.

Clary looked at Caldwell. "Looks like you're going to be working some more in the old jail."

"That I am. I plan on finishing up today or tomorrow."

"Then what?"

"Then you'll have a working jail."

"Who's going to man it?"

"I think I just might. For a while, anyway." Caldwell sipped his coffee. "It's a nice building. I might move my office down here permanently." This is what he planned, but he didn't want to confirm it for anybody yet.

"What do you think happened to McDole?" Clary asked him.

"Who says anything's happened?"

"Aren't you a little suspicious?"

He looked at Clary. "I guess I'm not as suspicious as you are."

"I think something's happened."

"You're more sure than these other fellows," Caldwell said. "Seems like he's missed other Mondays."

"Well they don't know."

"And you do?" Hamlin said. Clary lowered his head. He seemed resigned, but then he shook his head and leaned forward on the bar as though he were disgusted with everything he could see. Caldwell held his coffee up so he could feel the steam and savor the aroma, then he took another sip. "Was McDole here for Thanksgiving?" he said. Clary gave a halfhearted smile. No one said anything for a moment. Then Clary shook his head.

Caldwell was thinking maybe later in the day he would take the time to come back to the hotel and pick up Todd for lunch or something. He felt very thankful for his son now, and once again he was astonished to realize that in spite of the constant sorrow over Bobby, he was beginning to enjoy having Todd so near to him. He never would have dreamed such a thing was possible, even a few weeks ago. He had always believed that Bobby's death had robbed him of two sons—and now? Now he didn't know. This was all so new to him. It was hard for him to concentrate on much of anything but the next time he would have the opportunity to actually talk to Todd about these things. As he stood in front of the bar and sipped his coffee, it gradually came to him that he'd awakened this morning with a feeling of longing in his heart. It was almost as if he had consciously believed that on the long ride back to Columbia Beach, they would come to each other as men, and he would say all he had to say and Todd would do the same. Something fixed and permanent between them would be healed. Nothing like that had happened, so this morning it looked like a lost opportunity; like a letter from someone you love had burned before you could read it. He made up his mind that he would know what to say the next time. He had the whole morning of working in silence at the jail to think about it. He did not want to be intruded upon by these men who were standing around him now, watching him drink his coffee. He was not interested in their suspicions.

"What do you think, Sheriff?" Hamlin asked.

"About what?"

"You think there's been foul play?"

Caldwell shook his head. Hamlin was so sincere and earnest, he did not want to do or say anything that might hurt his feelings. Still, he hated it when people talked to him and tried to use the language they learned watching cop shows on television. "Well, sir," he said, "I really don't know what to think."

"I know he wouldn't leave that station closed today," Clary said.

"Maybe he wouldn't," Mauldin continued. "But hell, McDole's never been a body you could predict—not about some things, anyway." Mauldin was as much a friend to McDole as anyone else in Columbia Beach, and he had known him longer. They had hunted and fished together, and they had been through some things the others could scarcely guess at. And maybe it was true that you couldn't always count on him being where he said he would be, but McDole had been there when Mauldin's wife had died—had seen to it that the stricken man did not empty himself into a bottle, or otherwise give himself over to his grief. He had been there when no one else had the nerve for it—it is, after all, very difficult to be very long with a person who is in the hot anguish of such a terrible loss. McDole had had the courage for that, had insisted on being there and making the time busy with things.

"He shows up to the meeting and he wins. Right?" Hamlin said. "That's what he thinks, that's what we all think. And Cecil just doesn't let anybody . . ."

"Well, I wouldn't put it like that," said Caldwell. "It was a compromise. They both agreed to it."

"He got what he wanted," Mauldin said.

"Most of it," Caldwell said.

"And now, he's gone," said Clary.

Caldwell sipped more coffee. Hamlin said, "The holiday and all. I mean, there was a holiday coming up."

"And now he's not up there. So where is he?" Clary addressed all of them. He looked around the room as if he had just finished making a speech.

"Anybody go over to his house?" asked Caldwell.

"Nobody there," said Hamlin. "I went over there this morning."

"What'd you go over there for if you didn't think something was wrong?" Clary asked.

"I just wanted to see if he was home."

Mauldin stretched, then pushed his empty cup and saucer across the counter. "I've had enough," he said, and it was clear he wasn't just talking about the coffee.

"I'm just saying," Clary went on, "it's just too coincidental for him to be missing. And I think he is missing."

"Here," Hamlin said, moving the coffeepot over next to Clary's cup. "Have some more of your fine coffee." Mauldin threw a dollar on the counter and strode toward the door. "See you," Hamlin said.

"Yeah. Tomorrow."

"What about this afternoon?" Clary said. Mauldin nodded, but he said nothing. It was as if he had agreed to something clandestine, and when Caldwell saw this, Clary smiled sheepishly. "We're playing poker this afternoon. Just a friendly game."

"Whatever you want," Caldwell said. "I'm not going to raid a private game of poker between friends."

"No, sure," Hamlin said.

A brief silence ensued. Caldwell stared at a bank of photographs on the wall behind the bar. "I think you should do something about McDole," Clary said. He rubbed the bushy gray hair on top of his head, then took off his thick glasses and wiped them with a napkin. He was trying not to look at Caldwell.

"I don't know what I can do," Caldwell said. "You could file a missing person report."

"Where? All the way up in Dahlgren?"

"It's only forty miles."

"That's a pretty long way to go for curiosity," Hamlin said.

"It will take a lot more than curiosity to get somebody to pay attention to a missing person report. You're going to have to have specific things to go on."

"Like what?" Clary asked.

"You know his social security number? His age? His full name? The names of other members of his family?" Caldwell stopped and looked at Hamlin. He did not want to do too much to discourage anyone. "You can do what you want, though. I understand your concern."

"I just wonder where he is, that's all," Clary said.

"Well, like I said, why not let that be enough for a few days, and then we'll see."

"Sure," Clary said. "Why not?" He raised his cup, almost smiling.

• • •

"Want to get stoned again?" Todd asked.

"Is that all you do?" said Lindsey.

He was standing by her Cavalier, leaning against the front of it, his feet crossed. He had left the hotel early—just before Caldwell had stood before his door listening for him. He went down the stairs, out the back door of the hotel, and up the hill to Mrs. McCutcheon's place. He wore a black jacket, zipped up to the chin. His dark hair glistened in the sunlight, and he kept his head tilted downward, shielding his eyes from the sun. In spite of the bright sun and the breezeless day, it was very cold. She could see the steam coming from his mouth, and when he drew on his cigarette the smoke he let out was thick and white. She had seen him coming from her small window cove, and she had run down the stairs and out the door to meet him. But when she saw his eyes, she pretended she was on her way somewhere and started toward her car. Todd beat her to it.

"Where you going?" he asked her.

"Cecil's."

"Why?"

"I go there in the mornings sometimes before work. Make him breakfast and all."

"Doesn't he work?"

"Sometimes."

"What does he do, anyway?"

"He's a kind of handyman."

"Really?"

"Well. Not around here. He goes up to Dahlgren and Warsaw when folks need work done. Mostly he just makes do with what he makes in the summer off the wheel."

"Can't be much."

"What are you trying to find out?" She went to the door of the car and opened it. He didn't move.

"I'm not trying to find out anything."

"You sound like your dad."

"I do?"

"You know. A sheriff."

"Why do you say that?"

"You got nothing but questions."

"I got some dope, too." She said nothing. "Let's get high."

This had been what he always wanted to do with her. It never led to anything but the laughter that she loved so much the first time. But now it seemed lusterless and mean, like something he did to take advantage of her weakness for it. She was, for the first time, suspicious of him, or at least of his motives. She realized it wasn't really suspicion so much as dissatisfaction. She wanted more from him. When they were high, the whole experience seemed to whirl in a haze, so she could not get a real sense of it later, when she wanted to think about what was happening to her. She often felt alone now—something not totally new to her, and at the same time, she could not stand the way her stomach seemed to clench whenever she saw him—the way tension seemed to grip her, as though she were looking down from a great height. She actually felt the strength go out of her knees and legs. Someone told her a long time ago that when you look down from a high place and suddenly realize that your legs have weakened and your heart is racing, it's because a secret, vestigial remnant of your primordial self wants to leap out into the air and test the theory of flight, and your body is reacting to the possibility that you might do just that. She hated the way it made her feel to be under the gaze of his eyes; and she loved it, too. She loved the fact that it was exciting, and felt almost dangerous.

"Come on," he said again. "I got some good stuff here."

"I don't want to now."

"Why not?"

She started to get in the car, and he came around the door and put his hand on her arm. When she looked into his eyes she felt something small drop in her heart. "Don't," she said.

"Why don't we take a ride up toward Warsaw," he said. "We can go to a movie up there. Or maybe we could go to Fredericksburg."

"That would take the whole day."

"We'll come back early. I've missed you. We have fun together."

"Getting high," she said.

"Okay. We don't have to get high if you don't want to."

She looked at his hand, which still rested on her arm. He moved it slightly and seemed to decide something, then he reached up and touched the side of her face.

"I really did miss you," he said.

She felt her breath stutter and give way. She smiled, but she felt like crying. She hated it when a man got to her like this. It was such a familiar experience to her, she almost screamed at him, almost pulled away from him and slammed the door to the car. How could she forestall it? How could she let him know that she did not want another adolescent pulling at her heart until she failed him in some perfect way. A slight breeze lifted the hair next to her face. She was cold and frightened.

"Get in the car," she said. It was an order, and for a moment it seemed to take him back—but then he dropped his hand and went around to the other side and got in the car. When she was seated herself, she looked at him, as if the sight of him was a source of true wonder. "Goddamn," she said. He leaned over and kissed her on the mouth. He did not put his arms around her, and it was not a long kiss. When he leaned back and looked at her, she felt her face flush, and she tried to turn away so he couldn't see her reaction. But he reached up now and put his hand lightly on her cheek again. "I just know I'm going to regret this," she said.

"Regret what?"

"Where do you want to go?"

"Just drive," he said.

· · ·

When Todd lit a joint while riding in the car next to her, she turned to him and said, "I wish you wouldn't do that."

"Why?"

"I just don't want you to, that's all."

He took a few more long puffs on the joint, then pinched it out gently with his fingers.

"Doesn't that hurt?" She was very happy that he was doing what she'd asked.

"It burns a little," he said. "But it doesn't waste it."

"How much does that cost?"

"I don't buy much of it. People are always ready to give you a little dope when you work in a kitchen."

"Really?"

"I bet every chef in the world's got a little dope stashed somewhere." He put what was left of the joint in his shirt pocket and sat back in the seat. Lindsey drove all the way to Fredericksburg, then up Route 95 to Fairfax, where she used to live. She drove to the very street. The whole time, Todd remained silent in the seat next to her, listening to the music on the radio or searching for the music he wanted to hear. When he found a song he liked, he'd listen to that station for a while until a commercial came on, then he'd start searching again. He seemed totally relaxed, as if he knew what she was going to do, but when she pulled the car onto Prescott Lane and drove on down toward the street—the street where Todd and his father and mother and sister and little Bobby last lived together happily—he sat forward and looked at her.

"What are you doing?" he said.

"Nothing."

"What are you doing here?" The way he said this reminded her of Cecil when he first saw her standing on the bottom step of his trailer. Todd had the same tone in his voice as Cecil: a sort of command with nothing behind it, almost an expression of weakness in the face of her will. It made her sad for both of them.

"Don't you want to see it?" she asked.

"No." He started to say something else, but then he fell silent as she drove down the narrow streets. He watched out the window, a look of complete wonder on his face. She pulled up to a house and stopped.

"That's where I lived," she said. "Me and my mother, right up until I moved down to Columbia Beach." Todd stared at the house, slowly shaking his head. It was a small, two-story frame house with a single gable in the center over the front door and a modest front porch. She reached over and turned the radio way down. She didn't want to miss anything he might say, but he remained silent, his head turned away from her. She put the car in gear and continued down the street, heading for the end of the road—where it curved right and led to a cul-de-sac. She turned the corner on the street and slowed to a stop in the shade of a shedding sycamore tree. "Is this it?" she asked.

"No, I don't think so. I think it's the next house. But don't go over there."

"Why not?" She knew this was where Todd's parents used to live. She pulled up in front of the house and stopped the car. "That's the house, isn't it?" she said.

"Jesus," he murmured. "It looks so different. The trees are so much bigger." He stared at the house as if he expected it to lift off the ground and fly over the horizon. His eyes gleamed in the late afternoon sun. She thought she saw tears forming. "Jesus," he whispered again.

"This is what I wanted to see," she said. "I wanted to sit right here and look at it."

"Why?"

"I lived right back there. I grew up only a few blocks from this very spot."

"So?"

"I could ride my bike down here in less than ten minutes. It's only about two miles." He said nothing. She stared at him, waiting for him to look at her, but he did not take his eyes off the house—the blue shuttered house and the two sycamore trees in the front yard that clung to the last curling leaves and seemed to dangle them in the breezes like small flags. She could not tell what he might be feeling, but she wanted to let him know it was all right. This was a way, she thought, of confirming a kind of truth between them, of making his attention to her more than simply a retreat from memory and grief. She wanted him to know she believed him, too.

"Looks kind of forlorn, doesn't it?" she said. The white trim on the eaves, the shutters, and along the windows was peeling and cracked. The blue siding looked dull and mildewed in the twisted, crisscrossed shadows of the tree branches. Now he looked at her. "What'd you bring me here for?"

"I told you."

"No. Why did you want to do this?"

"I guess I wanted to see my old house, and then I thought of you—of where you used to live. I didn't get the idea until we started getting into Fairfax." He glared at her. "Are you angry?"

"I don't know why you wanted to do this."

"Didn't you want to see it?"

"I never thought about it."

"Well, I . . ."

"I mean I never thought about it on the drive up here. I thought about this house and nothing else for years and years," he said. "For fucking years and years."

She thought he was fighting tears and anger at the same time. "I'm sorry," she said. "I just wanted you to see it now. It's changed. It's not the house you've been thinking about. It's some other house." He said nothing. "It's over. See? I thought it might help if . . . ," she trailed off. The look on his face had stopped her. He wore an expression of impatient disdain—as if she had asked him for money, and this was some sort of illicit business transaction. "I'm sorry," she said again.

He looked back at the house, and for a long time neither of them spoke. Then he turned to her with a softer expression on his face. "We didn't live very far apart, did we?"

"No."

He gazed at the house again, this time with a look of wonder on his face. He shook his head slightly. "Seems like the day before yesterday," he said. She felt new tenderness toward him, wishing she could take him in her arms and keep him safe. "Everything since that day," he whispered. "Everything . . ." He didn't finish.

"What?"

"Nothing."

"No. What?"

He looked at her again, and now she did see tears in his eyes. "Everything since that day is just a kind of long, loud, unbelievable shout. You know? A howl. In my head."

"I'm sorry. I think I know how you feel . . ."

"No. You don't. Nobody does." She was quiet, watching him. He shook his head again, sat back in the seat. "Well look at it. Just look at it."

"I bet it looks great in the summer with those trees . . ."

"It needs a paint job. My father would never let it get to looking like that."

"I still bet it looks nice in the summer. And cozy in the snow, too."

"Another family lives there now." He turned his head lazily toward the house again. A strong breeze hissed through the remaining leaves of the sycamore tree. "See that window on the right corner of the house?"

"Yeah."

"That was our room. Bobby and me. I wonder what it looks like now."

"Want to knock on the door and see if anyone's home?"

"No." He sat up again.

"Come on. Maybe they'll let you look at it again."

"I don't want to."

She shrugged. "I don't know why not. I'll ask them, you don't have to do a thing."

He pointed to a white board fence that led into the back yard. "We never had the fence," he said.

"Come on," she insisted. "Let's knock on the door."

"No!" he said. He was loud. She didn't say anything for a long time. He put his hand up to his mouth, as if to shush her, or himself, then he brushed her hand and sat back. "I'm sorry, I didn't mean to shout."

"It's okay," she said.

"You know, my parents didn't move far from here."

She put her hand on his arm. "I'm sorry if this was a bad idea. I just wanted to—I wanted to let you know . . ."

"What?"

"I felt close to you because you told me about it. I feel like it is something we both remember . . ."

"You own no part of it," he said coldly.

"I didn't mean it like that. It's just—I believe you, and I feel terrible for what happened."

He looked at his hands. "I wish we hadn't come here."

"I'm sorry." She felt as if she had bilked him in some way, and she was cursing herself for what she now knew was a terrible mistake. In her attempt to get to some level of depth with him, some place beyond where she had been with all the men she had known, she had only alienated him. She didn't yet know the difference between true empathy for another person and simple pity. She did not want to pity him, but she did feel deeply sorry for what he had been through, for what had happened to him by accident. She did not understand until too late that she did not know him well enough for anything but pity. She moved closer to him, put her hand on the side of his face, and gently kissed him. He did not put his arms around her, but he let the kiss linger, and when she pulled away, she gazed directly into his eyes. She thought she could see the small refracted image of the car window and the trees beyond in the bright cornea of each eye. "Please forgive me," she said. Now he kissed her, tenderly, without any suggestion of passion, although he embraced her. It was, she realized, a kiss that meant something more than pleasure or lust. When he pulled away, she said, "I love you," and immediately regretted it. Her words felt pathetic and adolescent and insincere. "I mean that," she said, lamely. Then she put her arms around his neck and pulled him toward her. He let his head fall on her shoulder. She held him there, listening to his breathing, hoping against all hope and with all her heart that he felt the same thing she was feeling. She did not want to ever let him go.

xvi

Later in the afternoon on that Monday, Clary, Hamlin and Mauldin sat in plastic lawn chairs under the low lights of a pool table in the center of Mauldin's shooting gallery and talked quietly about what was going on in the town. The table was covered with a large flat piece of plywood. They had been half-heartedly playing cards, but mostly the talk turned to Cecil's various crimes, the mystery of what had happened to McDole, and the scary future of Columbia Beach. It had been a long, slow afternoon, as the sun began its gradual retreat behind blue, distant clouds. Just before dark, Hamlin noticed Caldwell emerge from the new county jail. He saw him stand in the street with his hands on his hips, proudly admiring it.

"Wonder what that's all about?" he said. All of them got up and went to the small glass windows in the garage doors that looked out on Main Street and up toward the jail.

"I guess he's proud of his handiwork," Mauldin said.

"Wonder if he's talked to Cecil about McDole," Clary said.

The three men stood for a while longer, watching as the sheriff locked the door and then got in his car and drove out toward the highway. Clary opened the side door to Mauldin's place and strode to the end of the boardwalk, gazing at Caldwell's car as it started up past McDole's gas station. To the west of the town, where the river bent around again and headed toward the bay, the sun still lolled near the horizon, weakly lighting the bottom of a cluster of rolling black and blue clouds and sending shimmering light across the surface of the river. It was not cold anymore, and the street was windless and bare. Clary hated this time of year— the end of fall, and nothing but early darkness and damp, cold drizzle in his soul. He put his hands in his pockets and started back toward Mauldin's place. He felt vaguely weak in the stomach—almost sick—and the waning light beyond the edge of the river seemed to increase the feeling. He had a sudden sensation of being quite hollow, a husk of himself, ready to fall to ash. He had been brooding most of the day over how it made him feel to see the look on Judy's face as she talked to Caldwell that morning. He was certain she had been telling him something private, but later in the day when he asked her, she looked at him as though he was crazy. "He asked me where you were, and I told him," she said.

"You were talking longer than that." He leaned on the counter across from her. "It looked like you were asking him for something."

"What would I be asking him for?" He shook his head. "Are you jealous?" she asked.

"No."

"I think you are."

"You just seem different to me these days. Maybe I'm extra sensitive."

"May be," she said, the two words separated like that. "May be," and she looked away from him.

Now, in the waning sun at the shooting gallery, he gathered himself and pulled the door open. The others were seated again at the table. He stood there in the opening for a moment regarding them, then he pulled the glass doors closed as if fending off something behind him and walked back into the room.

"Where'd you go?" Mauldin asked.

"I just walked out to the end there, see what he's up to."

"What'd you find out?" said Hamlin.

"I don't know where he's going," Clary replied. "Maybe he's looking for McDole."

He made his way back to the makeshift table. Mauldin dealt another hand. "Ante up."

"What's the point?" Clary said. "You need four to play poker."

Hamlin opened another beer. "Might as well go home," he said, leaning back in his chair, but he made no move to leave.

Mauldin gently placed the remaining cards in the middle of the table. "We could double the ante. Make it more interesting. Or we could play blackjack."

"Let's double the ante and go around a few more times," Hamlin suggested. "I'm out a few bucks here."

So they continued to play, until the light in the window was almost completely gone. Mauldin got up to turn on the outside lights, and as he did so, Sheriff Caldwell knocked on the glass. It momentarily startled all of them, but when Mauldin saw who it was he scurried to the door and opened it.

"Sheriff," he said quietly as Caldwell stepped inside. He had gone back to the hotel and changed into his uniform. The black leather belt and boots, the revolver, and the flat trooper's hat engendered quiet respect, and no one spoke at first. The table was covered with cards, money, and beer bottles. Cigarette and cigar smoke clouded around the overhanging light of the pool table.

Caldwell smiled. "I'm not here to break up the game or anything." The men neither laughed nor acknowledged what he had said.

"Join us," Hamlin said, squinting his eyes in the smoke of a cigar stub that drooped from his mouth. He was picking up the cards and getting ready to shuffle them. "It ain't no fun playing with only three."

"You should probably use chips instead of cash," Caldwell said. "That way I couldn't break the game up even if I wanted to."

Hamlin folded his arms across his chest. "McDole show up at his place yet?" he asked Caldwell.

"I guess not. I went up there a little while ago and the place is still closed." Caldwell pulled up a chair and sat down. He took a deep breath and looked at them. "I've got to go back up to Warsaw. Official business. I just wanted to be sure you fellows hadn't heard from McDole."

"No, sir," Clary said.

"Official business, huh?" Hamlin said. Caldwell nodded.

"So you're thinking what we're thinking," Clary said.

"I have no idea what you're thinking."

"About McDole."

"The jail is finished. I've got some things to do up there, that's all."

Mauldin still stood by the edge of the table. He had a beer in his hand. "Is it what I think it is?"

Ignoring Mauldin's question, Caldwell said, "Mr. Clary, I was wondering if you'd seen my son."

"No sir. I haven't seen him today at all. He wasn't in his room when Judy went to clean it."

Caldwell looked around the room.

"Is it about McDole?" Clary asked.

"Is what about McDole?"

"The official business."

"Look," Caldwell said. "It's Monday. If McDole doesn't show up by Wednesday, when I get back, then I'll file a missing person report myself."

"Goddamn," Clary said. He dropped his hands to the table, almost angrily. "I told you guys . . ." He looked at Caldwell. "*You* think something's happened to him too, don't you?"

"What'd I just say?"

"It is kind of odd that he didn't come back today," Mauldin put in. "It's not like him to just disappear."

"Are you fellows always so ready to panic?"

"I know the man," Clary said. "He'd open that station today if he was able to." Caldwell said nothing.

"You didn't happen to check and see if Cecil was home, did you?" Mauldin wondered.

"I didn't go knock on his door or anything. But I drove by the trailer. He's still there."

"How do you know?" asked Clary.

"He won't run," said Hamlin.

"No, I guess he won't," Mauldin said.

They were quiet for a moment, then Hamlin said, "You're going to have to go get him. You know that, don't you?"

Caldwell didn't look any of them in the eye. After another brief silence, he said, "If I have to. That's my job."

"What do you want us to do?" Mauldin asked.

"There's nothing to do. I just wanted to see if you'd heard from McDole. And I wanted to see if Mr. Clary here knew where my son was."

"You know he's been messing around with Cecil's girl," Clary said. "You knew that, didn't you?"

"She's not Cecil's girl," Caldwell said. "She's—," he stopped himself.

"If Cecil gets wind of it, Todd better watch out."

"That boy just might be a match for Cecil," Mauldin said flatly.

"I wouldn't bet on that," Hamlin said.

"Trust me," said Mauldin. "I've seen the kid in action."

Caldwell rose from his chair. He was smiling. "Well, when you see Todd, tell him I had to go back up north for a while. I'll be at the house if he needs anything."

"I'll tell him," Clary took a long drink from his beer. When he put the bottle down on the table, he said, "Before you go, Sheriff—" Caldwell waited. "I bet I know what happened to Mc-Dole." Clary realized he was nervous—almost as if he were about to recite lines in a play. This was the beginning of trouble, and it would bring untold changes, and it was always change—even the small possibility of change—that enthralled him. He realized that change was something he both feared and coveted. He did not want his routine to change, only how he felt about it. He wanted Judy to once again express her happiness to him. "I'm just thinking out loud here," he said.

Caldwell took off his hat, set it on the table, and then rubbed his hands over his eyes and face. "Yeah, go ahead," he sighed. "Let's hear it."

The others were staring at him. Clary suddenly got this image of McDole laid out on a slab, his skin pale and wet, his hair stiff and pasted back on his skull. "McDole was my friend," he said. And he had a brief intimation of himself as a man who must act, a man whose reaction to a vanished friend would be important to the world, and the world only waited to see what he would do. What if Cecil had finally gone too far? "I think Cecil went up to McDole's place and something happened. Maybe it was an accident. But if you drag the river up that way . . . It's real deep up there behind McDole's house."

Caldwell couldn't help himself. He let out a short laugh. Clary glared at him. "I'm sorry," Caldwell said. "It's not funny. But you've jumped to some pretty wild conclusions, don't you think?"

"It's just a theory. But it's easy enough to prove it or disprove it."

"Where's McDole's car?"

"It's deep enough for the car up there."

Caldwell shook his head. "You watch too much television." Clary had nothing to say to that. "If McDole's not back by Wednesday," Caldwell went on, "maybe we'll see about getting the Maryland State Police to search the river over there."

"Why can't *we* search it?"

"Anything in that water is under Maryland jurisdiction. They own the river. If something is there—well, it's better if Maryland finds it."

"You want a beer, Sheriff?" Mauldin offered.

"No. Thank you kindly." No one said anything for a long,

awkward moment. Then Caldwell said, "You gentlemen wait until Wednesday. I'm sure McDole will be back by then." He turned to leave. At the door he said to Clary, "If you see my son . . . ," but he didn't finish the sentence. He looked tired and beaten—as if he'd suffered from a long climb up a steep sandy hill—but he smiled when he mentioned his son. That seemed to be the only thing he looked forward to as he put his hat back on and made his way out of Mauldin's place and up the boardwalk toward the hotel.

It was quiet for a long time. Then Clary said, "I guess I should get back and see if Judy needs any help."

"I guess it's fair enough we wait until Wednesday," Mauldin said.

"You know what I'd like to do?" Clary said. They both looked at him. "If McDole's not back in his station tomorrow morning, I'd like to take a walk over to Cecil and ask him a few questions."

"Shit," Mauldin said.

"You know he won't lie about it. If he did something, he'll tell us. He thinks nothing can get to him."

"He wouldn't admit to . . ." Mauldin didn't finish the sentence.

"Let's just face him," Clary said. "Haven't you had enough of this shit?" He realized that everything he'd been feeling on this day had turned to anger. It surprised him, but he was glad for it. He wanted to do something, once and for all. "Goddamn it," he said.

"I think we should do just what the sheriff says," Mauldin said.

"I'll go up there and have a talk with him if you want," Hamlin said. "I'm not afraid of him."

"If McDole opens the station tomorrow, we'll know it. And if he doesn't . . ."

"You guys are just looking for trouble," Mauldin said.

"We won't do anything," Clary said. "I'd just like to see what he says if we just ask him point-blank."

"I'm not going up there without something to defend myself with," Hamlin said.

Mauldin shook his head in disgust. "You guys."

• • •

Caldwell waited in his room until almost eight o'clock, and when Todd still had not returned, he got in his car and drove out to the Burger King on the highway. He ate a cheeseburger in silence, staring at his reflection in the black glass. He was trying not to think about Todd and where he might be. It seemed as though the day had begun a long time ago—a lifetime ago. And still he had not seen him or talked to him. He hated ending his day like this, eating alone, with nothing to divert him except what was on his mind. People stole furtive glances at his uniform and tended to avoid him. He hated thinking about Clary's theory and he wished the idea had not been planted in his mind. What if something *had* happened to McDole? Caldwell had investigated homicides committed by husbands, wives, and total strangers. He had been among the first officers on the scene in most of the homicides in Fairfax county, even in his own backyard, right after they pulled up the plastic bag that contained little Bobby.

He did not want to think about that now. He realized he was chewing very slowly and his throat was beginning to close on him. Murder was never the way it was always portrayed in movies or on TV. It amused him sometimes when the television hero or movie cop, the "veteran" homicide investigator, came upon a crime scene and began coldly and unaffectedly gathering evidence. As if you could get so used to horror that you don't notice it. No human being ever really gets used to it, any more than you could get used to being puked on every day. How could a person? It would never get to where you didn't notice it, to where it didn't bother you. So he tried not to think about anything in the immediate future. He was certain that Cecil would not be stupid enough to do anything to McDole.

When he was finished eating, he sat for a while longer sipping his Coke, then decided to start the long drive back home. When he got to the door, he saw Todd and Lindsey get out of her Cavalier and walk towards the entrance. They walked arm in arm, looking at each other, so neither one of them saw him at first. When they noticed him standing in the open doorway as if he'd beckoned them, Lindsey seemed to flag a bit, and Todd withdrew his arm from hers. "Dad."

"Well," Caldwell said. "I guess I didn't need to wonder where you were."

"Hello," Lindsey said.

"We're keeping this place in business," Todd said. Caldwell nodded, trying to think of something to say. There was an awkward pause while the three of them stood there staring at each other. "You're in your uniform," Todd said, finally.

"I'm on the way home."

"Really? Already?"

"The jail's done. I have things to do in the office, and I don't want to drive up there in the morning. Besides, I get to see your mother again." Todd's eyes were dark in the light under the Burger King sign. Caldwell said. "I'll be back Wednesday."

"Fine," Todd said. Caldwell realized he was still smiling, still holding the door. "Can we get by?" Todd said.

"Certainly." He stepped back feeling helpless and slightly humiliated, and Todd went by him, dragging Lindsey by the hand.

"Say hello to Mom and Terry for me," Todd said.

"Have a nice meal," Caldwell said to no one. He did not know what he should do, what was expected of him. They had not asked him to join them. He felt like he often did when he had to talk to someone as a police officer and they'd seem friendly enough until the conversation was over, then they'd ignore him just as surely and completely as they would if he were an object of furniture. He really did not know what to do. Todd ordered for both himself and Lindsey—two cheeseburgers, two fries, two

Cokes—and she took hold of his arm again. They leaned against the counter talking rather loudly about long drives and the early dark. They did not look at him, and he felt it would be an intrusion to simply walk over and join them. He stood there, foolishly holding the door open, then he went back to his car feeling discarded and truly temporary. He opened the door and got in, then looked back through the brightly lit glass to see if they had noticed he was gone. But it was almost as if he had not been there at all.

He drove out to the highway, thinking it was not fair to judge what had just happened. He had not made any plans with Todd for dinner, and he was glad that things seemed to be going so well with Lindsey. On some level, he understood this feeling of having been abandoned was normal. He had not yet lived through the unfortunate but necessary inevitability of his children leaving him in this way. Yes, he told himself. It was normal. Still, he suffered the reluctant, almost forlorn wish that he had not told Todd that Lindsey was not Cecil's girlfriend, and once again he had the imagined image of McDole's pickled body covering his tired mind like something hot and wet.

· · ·

Later that night, when he was home again, sitting in his family room with Laura, he told her about Todd and Lindsey and what had happened with Todd in the Burger King, and she almost laughed. "I'm glad he's with someone," she said. She sat on the couch next to him, sipping a glass of wine. He had his arm up over the back of the couch, and she leaned in under it. She was close to him, her hair pulled back into one braid down the back. She wore a white sweater and black slacks. "I think it's a good sign."

"Me, too, absolutely," Caldwell said.

"He wasn't rude to you, was he?"

"No. He told me to say hello to you and Terry." She smiled at him. "You know what?" he said.

"What?"

"I think he was happy."

This seemed to touch something deep in Laura's heart. Her eyes filled with tears, and she placed her hand on his chest. Caldwell felt the heat of her tears, but he said nothing. He just held her for a while. Presently she leaned back and wiped her eyes. "I hope he is happy."

"What a time we've had," Caldwell said. She said nothing. "I was just beginning to feel like I might be his father again, or . . . you know."

"Don't."

"No," he said. "I'm not complaining. But look at it. I'm trying to figure out how this is going to work, and it's already changing into something else."

She pulled away from him. "I swear, honey. You really do think too much."

"I'm sorry," he said. "I don't know what else I'm supposed to do."

"Can't you just be happy for him?"

"I *said* I was." He realized he'd raised his voice. In a lower voice, he said, "For chrissake, honey."

Later that night, as they sipped a glass of wine after supper, he told her about McDole's apparent disappearance and Clary's suspicions. She was quiet for a while, then she said, "You know I hate it when you talk about *that* aspect of your work."

"I'm sorry. I'm pretty sure it's going to be nothing, though."

"Why are you worried about it?"

He told her about Cecil.

"You think Cecil had something to do with it?"

"Well, whenever there's been trouble down there, Cecil's been in the middle of it."

"But it's just one day. Right? It's not like anybody is really missing."

"His friends are all suspicious. He's been gone since before Thanksgiving. They claim he wouldn't just go off like that."

"Be careful, dear."

"If I have to arrest Cecil, maybe I can get a posse together," he said, only half meaning it. She had never expressed any fears about his work, and it had never been a source of tension between them, but this time her silence seemed to betoken something; when she lowered her head and seemed to study the wine in her glass, he remembered their losses, and how this kind of thing might affect her now, so he quickly added, "I won't take any chances with him."

"Please don't," she said.

He understood what was in back of her fear—the knowledge that life had already shackled her with the most horrible and irretrievable loss. She could not take another.

The front door swung open and Terry came in, her face flushed, her hair blown by the breezes. "What are you doing home?" Caldwell asked.

"Sup?" she said. One word, like that. Then, "I might ask you the same thing." Laura put her glass on the coffee table and sat back away from Caldwell a little. Terry closed the door and took off her coat and very carefully hung it in the hall closet. When she came back around the corner, she said, "Is Todd with you?"

"No."

She started to head for the stairs, but Caldwell said, "Wait a minute, honey. Come sit down for a minute."

His desire to talk to Terry seemed to energize Laura, almost as if it were a consummation she had wished for, hoped for: that he would ask for time with his daughter without prompting. She put her hand on Caldwell's leg and scooted close to him again. "Come on, honey," she said.

Terry came into the room and sat in a broad chair across from them. Caldwell tried to be as relaxed and cheerful as he could be. "How are you?" he said.

"I'm fine, dude." She was talking to him as she would to any of her friends, so it momentarily encouraged him.

He said, "You staying for dinner?"

"No. I already ate."

"I just wanted to chat a bit."

"How come you guys are eating so late?"

"I got in late."

She seemed bored but cheerful enough. He had to concentrate on averting his eyes from the purple, swirling mass that adorned the top of her head. In spite of the black lipstick and dark black eyeliner, it was easier to look into her face, since she resembled her mother so much. None of her attempts to defile her face were equal to the task.

"I just want to say...," his mind went blank. She waited while the silence in the room began to gather force. She did not look away from him though, and the smile on her face was, he believed, genuine. "I thought this last holiday was wonderful," he said finally.

"Me, too."

"It was good watching you and Todd..." He didn't finish.

"Watching me and Todd what?"

"Seeing you together again. The way you talked and laughed and..." He struggled for words. "You seemed to be buddies again."

"I don't remember ever really doing very much with Todd when he was little," she said. "I mean, we weren't really ever together that much."

"Well, you don't remember."

"I guess not."

There was a long silence. Then Terry said, "What's the matter?"

"Nothing," Caldwell said.

"Did I interrupt something?"

Caldwell laughed. "We were just sitting here sipping some wine and talking."

Terry cast her eyes down. "What's wrong, hon?" Laura said.

"Why do you always think something's wrong?"

"You just look so sad, just now," Caldwell said.

"I'm not unhappy. It's just . . ."

"What?"

"Nothing."

"Tell me, hon. We have to start talking to each other if we're going to be a family again."

"Well, that's what's bothering me."

"What?"

"One of the things Todd said when he was here was that we'll never be a family again. Not ever." She almost whispered this, and he realized it cost her something to reveal it.

"He said that?"

"He told me not to say anything to you."

"Why?"

"He's just weird. That's all. Totally weird."

"What do you mean?"

"He said we stopped being a family when Bobby died. At the end of the trial."

"The trial?"

"Yeah."

"Why then, particularly?"

"I don't know."

"Why not the moment it happened?"

"Dad," she said, impatient. "I really don't know. He said something about you, though."

"What?"

"I mean, he said you let him know it at the trial, at the end of it."

"I let him know what?"

"That we'd never be a family again."

"I never said anything like that. To him or anyone else." He looked at Laura. "I didn't."

"I'm just telling you what he said." Terry got up and stood in front of them. "Can I go?"

"It doesn't make any sense," Caldwell said.

"I told you he's weird."

"We just don't know him yet. That's all," Laura said.

"I love him, but he's totally weird," said Terry.

"Did he say anything else?" Caldwell asked.

"I have tons of homework," she said. "Can I go?"

"I'm sorry to keep you," Caldwell said.

"I didn't mean it that way," she said. "I'm sorry." Her voice softened. He realized this was who she was for now, and all he would be able to have of her until things changed. But things would change. He was counting on it. He loved her so. He got up and put his arms around her. She wore too much perfume and it almost choked him, but he held onto her, then kissed her on the cheek and stepped back. "It was nice talking to you," he said. "I mean that."

"Don't tell Todd what I said, okay?"

"I won't." He was about to tell her he loved her, but she turned and ran up the stairs to her room.

THAT NIGHT he couldn't sleep. He lay on his back, staring at shadows on the ceiling, thinking about the trial—the very brief hour and half they had all spent in front of Judge Bass. He could still see the bright sun cutting through the venetian blinds behind the judge's wide, dark-paneled wooden fortress, the American and Virginia state flags draped on either side of it. That's all he could remember. He tried to picture faces, the sound of voices, what people said. He could not even remember the words of Judge Bass's sentence. Even now, lying in bed trying to recall some portion of those days, the only thing he could recall was the one, unalterable fact of Bobby's death. But he must have said something about the family. *Todd remembers it.* He could not believe anything as complex and subtle as the idea of a family could have entered his mind at that moment. He was certain he did not understand a word Judge Bass had said. He vaguely remembered their lawyer explaining what would happen to Todd now that he was convicted. *Convicted.* That word stuck. He remembered that. But he was so numb, so totally outside himself and inside himself at the same time—as if his whole body had been turned inside out. He was only a pair of dripping eyes, moving from one place to the other. Terry said it was *at the end of the trial.* What could he have said? It wasn't him speaking or standing there, or breathing. It wasn't him.

xvii

Early Tuesday morning, Clary and Hamlin strolled over to Mauldin's Billiard Room and Shooting Gallery. Both were wearing down vests with high fur collars, and hunting boots. Clary wore jeans, and Hamlin had put on a pair of canvas fatigues from his days in the army. Mauldin saw them coming and lifted the broad double garage door that opened onto the gallery. He only raised the door high enough so both men could duck under it to get in. He had a small kerosene heater that sat against the wall in the back of the pool hall, and that is where he had placed his chair this morning so he could look out through the glass doors on the other side of the room. The pool table they'd been playing cards on was still covered with beer bottles and packed ashtrays. In spite of the sliding glass doors that opened out to the board-walk and the river, it was almost dark in the room. The sun, shimmering just above the dark river, barren and cold, would soon light the room through the glass doors, and its light would magnify in the glass and provide enough heat for the entire building. Now, even with the garage doors closed, Mauldin could feel cold air leaking into the room. When Clary and Hamlin had gotten inside he told them to pull the door down hard. "The goddamned thing leaks wind in here," he said. He got two folding chairs and placed them next to his own. "Take a seat."

Clary sat down, but Hamlin seemed nervous. He stood behind his chair, leaning with his hands on the back of it.

"Well?" Mauldin said.

"We can't do much of anything without you," Clary said.

Hamlin let out a kind of sigh. "It's hot in here by that heater."

Mauldin got up and went to the glass door and cracked it open. Beyond the door, where the boardwalk ended and the beach began, cold air seemed to skim the top of the sand and send slight wisps of it into the rising sun. It wasn't windy, but the air seemed to rush through the open door anyway.

"Stand over here," Mauldin said.

"Now it's cold," Clary said. Mauldin laughed slightly.

"That'll do," Hamlin said. "Just leave it like that." Clary seemed to adjust himself in the seat, then he looked at both of them.

"Ain't you got a joke this morning?" Mauldin said to Hamlin.

"No." He didn't meet the other man's gaze.

"Well, what's up?"

"You know what we're here for," Clary said.

"I told you how I feel about it last night. I don't want any part of it."

"McDole didn't show up again this morning," Hamlin said.

Mauldin spoke patiently, trying to be as reasonable as he could. "Look, you guys. We go up there and start up with Cecil, and then we're all in some kind of war . . ."

"Are you afraid?" Hamlin asked.

"I'm not afraid of anything. I like peace."

"You seemed to like McDole, too," Clary said. "What about that?"

Mauldin nodded. "Yeah. So?"

"So what do *you* think happened to him?"

"Maybe he went up to his brother's place."

Hamlin scoffed at the idea. "He never said a thing about

going up there. Not to me or anyone else. Don't you think he'd of mentioned it?"

"I don't know that he would." This was not completely true. McDole was unpredictable, but he was also among the most reliable men Mauldin had ever known. You could count on him to keep his appointments. If he said he'd meet you at the hotel or anywhere else in town, he'd be there. Everybody knew this about him. He was frequently late—he was on time for fishing and hunting but almost nothing else—but he would always be there. He almost never missed his morning coffee at Clary's hotel, either.

"I think we owe it to him," Clary said now. "Don't you?"

"Owe what to him?"

"Owe it to him to find out what happened?"

Mauldin shook his head. "What is it you guys want to do again?"

"We just want to go up there. That's all. Have a talk with Cecil," Clary said. "You know if he's done something he'll be proud of it. He'll tell us."

"And you think it will take the three of us?"

"I think we won't get anywhere with him unless we stick together," Clary said. He reached up and unzipped his jacket, then sat back and folded his arms. "I think whatever it is you wanted the sheriff to do this morning, we can do ourselves."

"I didn't want the sheriff to do anything this morning."

"Well. I did."

"Yes. I saw that."

"Jesus Christ," Hamlin said. "McDole's still not back. Where do you think he could've gone?"

"I think we should wait until the sheriff gets back, like he said. That's all."

"And does what? What do you think the son of a bitch can do?" Hamlin said. He stood upright, moving the chair a little further away from himself. He seemed to be huffing a bit, and Mauldin noticed his chest bulged under the jacket. He looked like a man trying to show off his physique, although it was buried in the thick pads of the jacket he wore. Then Mauldin began to wonder about the way Hamlin's chest bulged. "What you got under the jacket?" he asked.

"What?"

Mauldin stood up and strode over to where Hamlin leaned on the back of the chair. As he did this, Hamlin straightened up and backed away, until he was up against one of the pool tables. Mauldin came right up to him. "What's under your jacket?" he said, reaching up to open it.

Hamlin took hold of his wrists. "Don't do that," he said. He was strong, and he held onto Mauldin's wrists, even though the other stopped trying to unzip his jacket. "Just fucking don't do that."

"What's that under your jacket?" Mauldin said.

Hamlin put the other's hands down, then reached up and opened his coat. Under it he had a leather shoulder strap with a revolver in a holster that dangled down over the right side of his chest.

"Shit," Mauldin said.

Clary stood up and raised the jacket he was wearing, to reveal that he had a short-barreled shotgun tucked in the side of his pants and down his pants leg. "We're ready," he said.

"Where the hell'd you get that?" Mauldin couldn't believe it.

"My father-in-law made it. From a twelve-gauge."

"Judy know you're carrying that thing around?"

"Oh for chrissake," Hamlin said. "Are you with us or not?"

"You don't need me."

"McDole was your friend," Clary said.

"You got him in the past tense already," Mauldin said. "What the fuck."

"You know he'd never leave that station closed this long," Clary said. "And we know it. Something's happened to him. And we're just going to go up there and find out what."

"Why don't you boys just quit playing cops and robbers and go home?"

"Some friend you are," Hamlin said. Mauldin shook his head.

"I thought last night you said you'd be with us," Clary said.

"I never said that."

"You did," said Hamlin. "I know I thought you were with us."

"You thought wrong."

"We're just going up there and ask him a few questions," Clary said.

"And let him know we won't take no more shit from him," Hamlin said. "Don't forget that."

"I'm not getting involved in this foolishness, okay? That's all you need to know."

Hamlin closed his jacket again, shaking his head. "I guess we got to worry now about what you'll do once we've gone." Both Clary and Mauldin looked at Hamlin. He carefully zipped the jacket all the way up, then raised the collar. When he had pulled on his gloves, he regarded Mauldin. "You going to run to the sheriff now?"

"What sheriff? He won't be back until tomorrow."

Clary said, "Just walk up there with us. Will you do that?"

Mauldin turned and faced him. "Not as long as you're carrying the artillery."

"*He* wouldn't go if we had the guns or didn't," Hamlin said. "Don't let him sucker you."

Clary said, "Would you go if we left the guns here?"

"I'm not leaving *my* gun," Hamlin said, and at the same time, Mauldin said, "I'd consider it . . ."

"You know," Clary said. "We're your friends too. You know that." Mauldin had no response. "We need your help," Clary said. "That's all. We're asking for your help."

Now all three of them seemed frozen in the blanched air— the sharp angle of the sun and shadow crossing in front of them like a flat, dark surface. Hamlin rubbed under his nose with a gloved hand, then went to the aluminum garage door at the back of the hall. He did not wait for anything. He lifted the door halfway up, leaned over, and went out. He didn't make any effort to close the door again. Clary looked at Mauldin, a kind of apology in his eyes, but he went out, too. Mauldin started to close the door, but then he cursed under his breath, went to a coat tree in the corner, retrieved his navy pea coat, blue stocking cap, and a pair of black gloves. On the other side of the door, he stood for a moment, watching up the street. Then he leaned over and locked the door, put the keys in his jacket pocket, and walked on up the hill where the others waited.

• • •

Cecil got out of bed early that morning. He was hoping Lindsey would show up and make him breakfast, but when he walked out to get his newspaper, he realized that she was probably not coming. If she came in the morning at all, it was always before the sun had risen fully above the water, and he could see it between the Shooting Gallery and the hotel gleaming across the water. He couldn't remember what she'd said about it on Thanksgiving Day. But if she didn't have to work, she would have been there by now, so he gave up the idea. He went back in the trailer and made himself a pot of coffee.

When he'd poured himself a cup, he settled down on the small couch and began leafing through the newspaper. He studied the legal notices very carefully, but only glanced at the comics. He used to like Larson's Far Side cartoons, but they were long gone. Nothing in the paper made him laugh anymore, but he liked looking at the drawings anyway. It was something he always wished he could do: make pictures with a pencil. He would have loved making cartoons for children. He loved the sound of children laughing—a thing he grew up listening to on the Ferris wheel. It would have been such a good life, he believed, if he could have been the kind of person who could make children laugh by pictures he drew or words and music he wrote. His mother used to say to him, "You can be creative if you want." But it wasn't true. He could never think of anything new in the world. Everything in his experience came to him from outside his mind and acted on it, a kind of stimulus and response existence that often exhausted him and always excluded even the possibility of his own design on things. Even his thoughts were often wordless. This was just something he accepted—a kind of willing deficiency that he was occasionally sorry for. In truth, it only bothered him when Lindsey came to visit and they'd sit here in his small living room while her chatter would gradually subside and he realized he had nothing to say. His mother always told him he was her "solid boy, the strong, quiet type."

Now he put the newspaper down and went to get more coffee. As he was pouring another cup, he looked out the window and saw them coming. They approached slowly, moving toward the gate and his broken sidewalk, as if they were afraid of waking someone. He watched them, the cup of steaming coffee in his hand. The sun shone brightly across the river, and the three men coming toward his trailer cast long shadows before them. They stopped at the gate and seemed to decide without words who would bend down to open it. Clary slid the gate back in the sand, letting it rest crookedly against a small tuft of dune grass. Hamlin stepped through, then Mauldin, and Clary followed.

• • •

When Todd and Lindsey left the Burger King Monday night, they drove to Mrs. McCutcheon's house. Although the front of the house was lit up, it was very dark in the back, and Lindsey went up to her room, opened the attic door on the back of the house, and led him up the back stairs and into her room, without being seen or heard. They spent the night together, giddy and excited, enjoying the secretiveness of his being there; enjoying the furtive, lovely, almost painful laughter. She felt like a child again, a little girl reckless and disobedient, late at night in her small, dimly lit room. For a long time they held each other in the bed.

He wanted to read the letter she'd been writing to Alicia, and when she handed it to him, smiling in a way she hoped would be inviting, he took it over to the table by the nook in front of the window, turned on the lamp, sat in the chair, and began reading. She was nervous about what he'd say, but when he was finished he said, "You call your mother Alicia?"

"Sure. Why not?"

"Seems odd."

"She's not really my mother. I'm adopted." She'd told him this, so he looked at her quizzically. "I called her mom when I was growing up. But now that I'm grown . . ."

"You tell her a lot in this letter."

"What do you mean?"

"You told her about smoking dope?"

"Yeah."

"You don't tell her about me, though."

"I told her about you in the last letter I wrote. Anyway, I'm not finished with that one." She lay on her stomach across the bed with her chin resting in the palms of both hands.

"This is all about Thanksgiving with Cecil," he said.

"Yeah. I wanted to tell her about it."

"My Thanksgiving was nothing to write home about," he said. Then he gave a short laugh. "I guess I *was* home."

"You didn't have a good time?"

"Dull. I sat around and watched football with my dad. He didn't say five words to me. He just sat there looking at me every now and then with this happy sort of smile on his face. I pretended to be asleep."

"That's sad."

"I read the newspaper for a while and stared at the screen during the game."

"Cecil and I had a quiet time. It wasn't all that great, either."

"My dad built a fire and it was so hot in that room, I thought I'd suffocate." He put the letter down on the desk. "But the dinner was okay."

"Yeah, ours too."

"If my sister hadn't been there, I think I would have gone nuts."

Lindsey lifted her lower legs in the air behind her, moving them back and forth like a pendulum. "You know, I don't even have a father." He said nothing. "I never called anybody 'Dad.'"

"Does that make you unhappy?"

"No. I'd like to know who he was, though."

"Why?"

"I don't know. I guess just . . . it's just curiosity. It's not like I'm interested in genetics or anything."

"It really seemed like the first Thanksgiving dinner I ever had with my family," he said pensively. "But I know it wasn't. The others were so long ago and . . ."

"You didn't have Thanksgiving dinner in the . . . at the . . . ?"

"Jail. Just say jail. That's what it was." She was quiet, watching his face. "They had turkey in jail. It wasn't Thanksgiving dinner."

"Oh."

It was quiet for a while, then he picked up the letter and brought it back to where she was lying on the bed, and she turned to her side, looking up at him. "It's nice that you take the time to do that," he said. He sat down next to her and handed her the letter.

"I like it. Writing's fun. I love to *get* letters from people, too."

"My mother used to write me when I was in jail. Two or three times, maybe—each month. Nothing ever as straight shooting as *that*," he pointed to the pages in her hand. "My mother never said anything in her letters that you could classify as personal. You know what I mean?"

"Yeah."

"They were nice letters, though. Full of news and such. I was always glad to get them."

"Your dad didn't write?"

"Never. Not one."

"Really?"

"He's not a letter writer," Todd sighed. He thought a minute, then he said, "Every now and then my mother would write, 'Your father says to say hello,' or, 'Dad says to keep your spirits up,' but hell, I never knew if he actually said those things."

"I'd write to you every day if you were . . ."

"You mean if I go back?" he laughed.

"If you had to go away."

"Don't worry, I'm not going back."

"I meant like school or something."

His eyes seemed heavy lidded now, and almost sinister. But then he smiled. "I *am* going to school," he said. "But I'm never going so far away from you that you'd have to write me every day."

This made her heart seem to breathe. She raised her arm up and beckoned for him to lie next to her. He lay down, taking her in his arms. They were quiet for a long time, enjoying the sound of their own breathing. Then he kissed her, long and slow and softly. He looked into her eyes.

"I'm so glad I came down here," he whispered.

"Me, too."

"I was going to straighten some things out with my father." He leaned back on his hand, staring down at her face. "I really thought it might make my life a little better—just a little better— if I could just deal with him over what happened. But then I met you, and now my life is so much easier, I don't care."

"You don't care about your father?"

"I care about him. Of course. But I don't care if I ever say what I wanted to say to him."

"What did you want to say to him?"

"I don't care if I ever convince him that I didn't mean it. That it was an accident." His voice broke, and he put his other hand up to push his hair back. She saw him decide not to go on.

"It still bothers you, doesn't it?"

He rolled over on his back, staring at the ceiling.

"Doesn't it?"

"It will be with me until the day I die."

"No, I mean about your father."

"That, too. Until the day I die. Not when he dies. When I do."

"And you'll never be the same with him?"

"The same as what? I can't even remember now."

She studied the side of his face, loving him.

"You have no idea what it's like to have somebody that big in your life—a father—look at you and behind his eyes there's a murder going on. You know he doesn't trust it . . . he doesn't credit his will *not* to believe it."

"I have no idea what it's like to have a father look at me at all."

He turned to her again. "I know," he whispered, touching her cheek.

"You don't have to feel sorry for me," she said.

"I don't feel sorry for you. I envy you."

She smiled.

"I'm serious. It's fucking rotten having God walking around looking at you, believing you just *might* be a murderer."

"How do you know that's what he's thinking?"

"I don't know it. But that's how it feels when he looks at me sometimes. Like he's wondering . . ."

"But you don't *know* he is."

"Freud says there are no such things as accidents." He sat up, looking at her now with eyes that frightened her. "You know what I mean?" he said.

"No, I don't know."

He shrugged. "What if at some level . . . how can I know I didn't intend it somehow?"

"Do you think you might have?"

His eyes softened. "No. I know what happened. I was there. But sometimes . . ."

"Don't worry about it all the time," she said.

"I don't worry about it, Lindsey. You got me talking about it."

"I did?" She reached for him, but he pulled back, still looking at her. Then he got up and went back to the chair by the window.

"I'm sorry," she said. "Don't be mad at me."

"You want to know what I worry about?" he said, almost to himself.

"What?"

"I worry that I'll never have a single day when this craziness isn't soaking my mind in blood."

"Don't."

"I'm not feeling sorry for myself," he said, but he didn't seem convinced. "I take these days one at a time, and I always remember what my mother and father have had to get used to. I always remember what might be going through their unwilling minds. I'm not totally—"

"Stop this now," Lindsey said. "You're taking yourself down into such dark places . . . You don't have to anymore."

He made a sound, almost a whimper, then he said, "I lost my balance, for chrissake. I just fell down with him." She thought he was weeping, silently, his fist in front of his mouth. She got up and went to him, and when she tried to put her arms around him, standing next to him as he sat in the chair, he gently took her hands and placed them at her side, and she saw no emotion in his face at all. She waited there watching him, but then he turned himself and stared out the window, his back to her, and gradually she came to see that whatever he was fighting in himself had subsided; he'd gotten control of it. "Whew," he said, taking a deep breath. "It's been a long time since I felt like *that*."

"Like what?"

He said nothing.

"Like what?"

Reluctantly, he said, "Like I'd rather be dead."

"I'm so sorry," she said. "I didn't mean to get you thinking about it."

He reached for her, wrapped his arm around her waist. She put her hands across his shoulder, looking down at him. "Forget it," he said. "You got so many things I don't know in your mind . . . Don't ever be afraid to say them."

"I won't."

"Maybe I can learn as much from you as I do in school, and it will change things."

"I'm going to college, too. Maybe we can go together. We can start out in Dewey, at the community college there."

"I've got all kinds of money saved," he said, smiling again. She loved the flash in his eyes, the way his smile seemed to brighten all the colors of her memory. And as he spoke to her about the future, she realized none of it would ever be really possible. She knew they would not go to school together, and that eventually he would have to go his own way, and she would go hers—but in the meantime, she wanted every single minute of this time with him. She wanted to watch him and be with him and love him until the last second, when the earth and change, reality, and need would separate them. She could pretend things were forever; she could have the joy of this planned future, even if it was, as she knew it must be, a lie. Maybe, just maybe, when the time came around to it, they could maintain some of their loving and their friendship and their need for each other. It was entirely possible—not probable, but possible—that he would be the kind of man who once he loves a woman, continues to love her, right down to the end of the earth. She would not hope for this, but she would live her life as if it were true as long as time would allow. She told herself that this love would be memorable, not just because he was so different from the others and therefore the first, but because they were both so intensely alive while it was going on. In this state of mind, even her suffering seemed exquisite, and she did whatever she had to do to please him. If this was not love, it would be like love. Very much like it. She put her head against his chest and whispered, "I don't want this minute to ever end."

"I know," he said.

She felt warm, and almost permanent. There was nothing in the world but her body and his, embracing in a cathedral of tenderness. They made love quietly, almost desperately, holding onto each other in this new sweetness, and then she fell into a deep and satisfying, dreamless sleep. She woke against him, warm and lazy, feeling safe. She loved the way his body smelled, the sound of his

298 · Robert Bausch

even breathing. Outside the world seemed bathed in dull white light, and she knew it must be a cold damp morning. She did not know a person could feel so completely content; it was as though the warmth of his body against hers provided a kind of invincibility. Nothing could hurt her at that moment, and she did not want the clock to move. She stirred closer to him, nuzzling against the back of his neck, and he turned to her and put his arms around her. He held her there, in silence, his eyes closed. Her head rested just under his chin, and she played with the hair on his chest, drifting in and out of light sleep.

"Hey," he said, startling her. "I'm sorry, did I scare you?"

"I was falling back asleep."

"I'm hungry," he said.

"Okay." She smiled at him. "Where do you want to go?"

"Don't you have to work today?"

"Not till noon."

"It's pretty early."

"Let's walk down to Cecil's," she said.

"What for?"

"I don't know. I usually go down there on my mornings off. He's probably wondering where I am."

"I thought he was your boyfriend when I first came down here."

"That's what everybody thinks."

"Yeah. I'm glad he's not."

She snuggled closer to him. "Me too."

• • •

Cecil opened the trailer door before anyone knocked on it, and stepped down to the ground. The three of them stood there watching him. No one said anything for what seemed like a long time. "Well," Cecil said, finally. "If it isn't the Clary Hotel coffee klatch."

In spite of the cold air, Cecil wore only a sleeveless undershirt and a pair of dungarees with suspenders that dangled down both sides of his body. He did not feel the cold at all. He was aware of the way his stomach bulged over the front of his pants, but he did not seem bothered by it. In spite of his girth, he was still built like a weightlifter around his chest and shoulders. He was not afraid, but he was interested, almost excited. "What do we have here?" he said.

"We come up here for a reason," Hamlin said. He stood with his legs apart, bracing himself.

Clary looked at the other men, then said to Cecil, "We'd like to know if you have any idea what happened to McDole."

"Nope. I have no idea," Cecil said. Then he showed his teeth in a wide smile.

"We think you do know," said Hamlin.

Cecil waited calmly for what might happen. He was concerned about the look on Hamlin's face—the fierceness in his eyes and the way he seemed ready for this thing they must have planned. He thought he might have to deal with Hamlin first. Mauldin stood next to Clary, without making eye contact. He would not be a problem, and Clary wouldn't be, either. Already Cecil knew what he would probably have to do if they tried to begin anything, and he was fairly certain about the order in which he would have to go at them. He would have to take Hamlin first, then either Mauldin or Clary, he wasn't sure.

"You haven't seen Vince McDole, have you?" Clary asked.

"What do you three think you're going to do?" Cecil said. He had not really paid much attention to what Clary was saying. He was focused on Hamlin's movements.

"Just answer the question," Clary said. Mauldin stood up more now and looked directly into Cecil's eyes.

Cecil took a step toward them and Clary stepped back. Hamlin moved too, but more to the side, and to the left. Mauldin moved to the other side, just slightly to Cecil's right. They got far enough away from each other that Cecil knew he had to make a definite choice as to which one of them he wanted to go for first. It would be Hamlin then, so when he took another step toward the three of them, he went more to his left. Now he was off the broken sidewalk that led from his trailer to the road. He was in deep sand, and when he realized that, he stopped momentarily. The sand would make it difficult for him to move very quickly, so he needed to be closer before he made his move.

"What's it going to be?" Cecil said, buying time. He moved steadily through the deep sand toward Hamlin, but the other backed up, maintaining his distance. Cecil stopped moving. "Well?" he said. "Who's going first?"

"Don't act like you're in a fucking movie or something," Hamlin said. "We're not in a damn cowboy movie here." Cecil turned slightly, back toward the walk, but he kept his eyes on Hamlin.

"Did you do something to McDole?" Clary said. "That's what we want to know."

Now he looked at Clary. "What do you think I might have done?"

"Do you know where he is?" Mauldin asked.

"I don't know and I don't care."

"We're going to find out what happened," Clary said, getting exasperated.

"Really?"

"*Did* you do something to McDole?"

"I'm about to do something to *you.*"

"We're not afraid of you," Hamlin said. He reached under his jacket and brought out the pistol. When Cecil saw him move, he started toward him, but again Hamlin backed away, this time holding the pistol up and pointing it at him. This had no effect on Cecil. In fact he realized that at some level he expected it. He was right in supposing he would have to go after Hamlin first, but he didn't want them to know that that was what he was going to do, so he looked around at all of them. "Which one of you wants to get hurt first?"

"Just tell us what happened to McDole. Do you know anything about it?" Clary said. Cecil took a step toward him, and when Clary began backing up, Cecil kept coming toward him. He almost expected to hear the report of Hamlin's pistol, but nothing happened. So he lunged through the sand toward Clary, who was almost back to the gate that still leaned open in the sand.

"You better not," Clary said.

"Stop right there," Hamlin said, pointing the gun.

Cecil turned to face Hamlin. The brief exertion in the sand had him breathing hard now, but he could still get air. He took deep breaths, sweat beginning to form on his forehead and running down the sides of his face. He almost laughed, then he gasped, "Shoot me. I dare you."

Mauldin said, "Cecil, just tell us if you've seen McDole. That's all they want. Do you know anything about where he might be?"

"He knows," Hamlin said.

"Come on," Cecil said. He moved steadily toward Clary again, hoping Hamlin would move in close enough so that he could get at him. Clary suddenly opened his jacket and retrieved the shotgun. When he had it pointed at Cecil, he stopped backing up. "Now just hold everything a goddamned minute Cecil."

Cecil laughed. "Where'd you get that thing?"

"You're going to tell us what we want, or . . . ," he didn't finish.

"Or what?" Cecil said. He was still not too worried, but he did not like the shotgun. Clary had it pointed right at his belly. He looked to see if Mauldin had a weapon, too. He realized his heart was beating very fast, but he was ready. This was not fear. It was intense excitement. He never felt so powerful or strong. "Or what?" he said again. He realized his voice was getting louder, so he stopped talking and just stared at Clary, then at Hamlin. He began to think he would have to grab the shotgun out of Clary's hands first. Hamlin would have to wait. Then Mauldin moved toward him—circling him on the right.

"Where you going?" he gasped. And he lifted his heavy legs and moved across the walk toward him, thinking now he'd back him up, too. He'd face all three of them one at a time and not think about the order. Whoever let him get close enough, that's the one he would grab, and after he got his hands on somebody, he'd see what happened next. Mauldin did not take out a weapon, but he had no trouble keeping his distance, either. He moved back toward the base of the Ferris wheel, keeping his eyes on Cecil, who kept coming, working his way through the yielding sand, his arms waving to keep his balance. Cecil heard Hamlin say something behind him, and when he stopped and turned, he saw that both Hamlin and Clary had crossed the walk and were circling toward him.

No one moved for what seemed like a long time. "Well?" Cecil said.

Mauldin's voice softened a little. "This is not getting us anywhere," he said. He started to move toward Clary. "I knew this is just what would happen."

"Ain't nothing happened yet," Hamlin said.

"This is just stupid," Mauldin said. "What do you think you're going to get out of him? A confession?"

"Confession?" Cecil said. Again he trudged toward Clary, who backed away quickly enough so that Cecil could not get close and grab for the shotgun. Hamlin had closed in from his left now, and he was even nearer, so Cecil turned and started for him, but he too got back out of the way. Now Cecil was moving back and forth between them, backing each of them up, laboring in the deep sand to keep his feet. They had surrounded him, in a way. One of them was always behind him no matter which way he turned, and when he moved to get closer to one of them, the others would move too, keeping their distance, but somehow closing the circle, too. At least it felt that way. "Which one wants it first," he said again, gasping for air.

Hamlin laughed. "Look at him," he said.

"Look at me?" Cecil tried to run at him, but he lost his footing and fell down.

"Not such a big tough guy now, are you?" Hamlin said, jeering at him. Cecil got to his feet, lunged at him, and fell down again. Hamlin laughed even louder. "Look at him. He's like a helpless animal."

Mauldin looked over at Clary and said, "Put the goddamned gun away." Then they all were stunned to hear a woman's voice behind them. It was Lindsey. "What are you doing?"

Todd stood next to her, his arms at his sides.

Mauldin stepped back. "It's between them," he said. Clary took several quick steps toward Cecil. He leaned down and it seemed as though he wanted to help him get up, but Cecil got to his feet quickly and tried to grab the gun right out of Clary's hand. Mauldin shouted, "Look out!" and Clary pulled his shotgun back and up so that Cecil couldn't reach it. Then he held it upright and fired it into the air. The blast seemed to shock the trees and all the earth into silence. All of them stood there staring at Clary, who was looking now at the smoking gun.

"You see?" Mauldin yelled. "You see? You might have killed somebody with that thing."

Todd walked over to Clary and jerked the gun from his hands. He leaned toward him as though he might hit him with it, but then, without taking his eyes from Clary, he hurled the shotgun high over the fence toward the Ferris wheel. It almost buried itself in the sand when it landed.

"Jesus H. Christ," Todd said.

"Stay out of this," said Hamlin.

"Do you people have any sense?" Todd said. Lindsey moved next to him, glaring at Hamlin, who still held the pistol. Cecil had stopped, but now he seemed to grow larger, his chest heaving. "You sons a bitches," he said, panting. Then he was wheezing, struggling for air.

"Did you shoot him?" Hamlin said. He held his pistol in two hands and, pointing it at Cecil, moved around behind him. Cecil was bent over now, gasping and coughing. He reached out his hand and staggered toward Clary.

Lindsey started screaming, "Stop this! Stop this! Stop this!" Hamlin pulled the hammer back on his pistol.

"Did you shoot him?" Hamlin said again. "What's wrong with him?" Clary turned, still watching Cecil closely, and walked to the side, as if he were dodging a weakened but still dangerous bull.

Todd shouted, "Put that gun away, mister." He was frozen in place, watching Hamlin—then Cecil.

"Where's he hit?" Hamlin said.

"I didn't shoot him!" Clary shouted. "Jesus! I fired the god-damned gun in the air."

"You hit him," Mauldin said.

"It went up in the air," Clary said. "For chrissake."

Cecil was bent over, his eyes bulging, staring at the sand, and he saw blood begin to drip into his shadow. He tried to look up to see the men encircling him, but he didn't have the strength in his neck. He felt blood in his mouth, tasted the saltiness of it.

"For chrissake," Clary said, "he's bleeding."

"What?" Hamlin moved around so he could see.

"Cecil!" Lindsey cried. She ran to him. He saw her shadow spilling over the sand near him, knew it was her. He went down on all fours.

"It's running out of his mouth," Clary said. "Jesus god!"

"Did you shoot him?"

Cecil wanted to say nobody shot him, but he couldn't get out any words. All three men stood there watching him as Lindsey and Todd tried to help him up. They each took hold of an arm and tried to lift him, but he pulled away from them. He was still kneeling on all fours, his head down between his extended arms. He worked with all his strength to draw in air. He was embarrassed at the sound his throat was making, and then he started coughing, and his eyes watered to the point that everything around him was a blur. He only wanted to get ahold of one of them. He believed he would be able to breathe again if he just got one of them in his hands and could squeeze the small life out of him. That's what he wanted to do. But then his mind seemed to list toward darkness and sleep. He looked down at the blood dripping into his darkened shadow. The top of his head reeled, and suddenly he thought of summers long ago, when he lifted children up and placed them carefully in the seats on the Ferris wheel; he remembered how it felt to be so completely trusted, knowing his strength and using it to turn the wheel, hearing the children laugh as if it were something he'd created, something he'd given them from his imagination.

Then he felt a heavy, deep, utterly crushing pain in the center of his chest, and before he could place his hand there, all his coughing and gasping for air suddenly ceased, and he dropped to the ground, feeling nothing at all, his face buried in the blood-soaked sand.

xviii

W ell," Judy said. "I guess you and your *friends* were wrong about Cecil."

"My *friends*? Why'd you say it like that?"

"Like what?"

"I don't know. It was—you said it with such contempt."

"No I didn't."

"That's how it sounded."

"I just meant that Cecil wasn't as indestructible as you all thought he was."

"No, he sure wasn't," Clary said.

He'd just come up from the lobby. Judy was already in bed with the television on. She was sitting up with a small bowl of popcorn in her lap. She wore a silvery pair of pajamas and curlers in her hair. The TV was turned down low, but she seemed intently interested in the action on the screen when he came in. That morning, she had heard the wail of the ambulance, had seen it come down off the highway and pull in up by the Ferris wheel. When he told her about it he had hoped she would agree that no one was really responsible for what happened. But she only looked at him, and then turned her glittering eyes away.

"Are you crying?" he said.

"No, of course not."

"It wasn't anything any of us intended."

"But you went up there with guns."

He felt something cold fall in his stomach. It sounded like something he was afraid he would have to answer to, and soon. He was astonished at the fear stuttering in his heart. They were standing in the living room of their apartment, just after it happened. Judy had just gotten dressed and was getting ready to clean the rooms of their two guests when she heard him come in. He was apologetic at first. He wanted to make what happened sound better than it was.

"You went up there with guns," Judy said again.

"Because you never know what Cecil will . . . ," but her look stopped him.

"And you *certainly* tried to help him," she said. Now he saw tears welling in her eyes.

"You *are* crying."

"Whatever."

"Was there something going on between you and Cecil?"

The look on her face revealed unutterable pain—as if he had somehow wrenched everything in her that was vulnerable and gentle. "What?" she whispered. It was almost a sigh. She could not believe what he said.

"Was something going on?"

"How could there be?" she said. "Tell me how?"

"I'm sorry. I just don't know why the sudden tears."

"Aren't you just a little bit upset?"

"Of course."

"I can't believe it," she said.

"It was nothing anyone intended."

She faced him, determined. "And what has become of my kind, fair man?"

"What?"

"Where was my fair and gentle man?" Her voice was weak, and he realized she was crying for him; she was grieving over what she must have felt was lost in him, and not for Cecil at all.

"Everybody just panicked," he said. "I wish it hadn't happened."

"And you all ran. What if he could have been saved?"

"Honey, he was dead when he hit the sand. I'm not kidding."

"And if the three of you hadn't gone up there, carrying guns—if you'd left him sitting in his trailer, do you think he'd be dead now?" She lowered her eyes. He noticed the fine hair in the crown of her head, and he wanted to pull her against him and kiss her there, but she turned and walked away from him. "God knows what you're going to tell the sheriff."

"I'll tell him the truth. I have nothing to hide."

She went into the kitchen, and he waited there for a moment, then he hollered after her, "It was just a terrible accident . . ."

She poked her head out of the kitchen and said, with disgust, "But what caused it?"

"Yes," he said. "I know it can be looked at in that way. But you saw him in here the other day. He was having trouble with the asthma anyway."

"Yes, he was." Her eyes met his and seemed to freeze them in place.

"I'm sorry," he said. "You know I'd never intentionally do harm to anyone."

She put her hand up and gently wiped tears from under her eyes, still looking at him. Then she said, "No. I know you wouldn't do that."

Now, he crawled into bed next to her. She steadied the bowl as he got himself comfortable. "What are you watching?"

"Some western movie. John Wayne."

He smiled. "Can I have some?"

She handed him the bowl. "Take the rest. It's almost all gone, anyway."

"Didn't you want a Coke or something?"

"No."

They watched the screen for a while. He wanted to know what she was thinking, and he hated the judgment going on in her eyes whenever she looked at him. After a long silence in which both of them stared at the action on the screen—a lot of men on horses chasing a lot of other men on horses—he said, "I love the way these movies show horses running for hours on end. They never get tired. Just run and run. A real horse is dead tired after about five minutes of running—just like any animal, including human beings. But they have regular twenty minute chases in movies like this." She didn't say anything. "It's so silly," he said. She only glanced at him, her eyes looking sad. Finally he said, "I'll talk to the sheriff."

"You will?"

"Yeah. Soon as he gets back."

"He probably knows about it by now."

"I guess."

"Poor Cecil. I wonder if he knew he was that sick."

"I never thought I'd ever hear anybody say 'poor Cecil.'"

"I bet he didn't do anything to McDole, either."

"How do you know?"

"I just know it. That's all. I'm not suspicious and paranoid like . . ." She didn't finish. She took a deep breath but said nothing.

"I wonder why McDole hasn't come back then?" he said.

"Who knows?" They fell silent again, briefly. When people on the television started talking, she used the remote control to mute the sound. "You can keep watching," he said.

"I'm not that interested."

He reached for the remote, but she held it away from him. He ate popcorn for a while, then he put the bowl down on the small table next to the bed and got up. "I'm going to get a Coke. You want one?"

She shook her head, still staring at the screen. He had the feeling this day was the beginning of the end of something, the very start of a sea change between them, and he was helpless against it. He remembered how Mauldin had talked about what happened when he and his wife knew that she was dying, how their lives went on for a long time in this new routine of ending things, of final passages together; there was never a single moment of farewell or goodbye, but an expectation of it, of that precise moment, every hour, until the time came and she was gone, and he'd never said anything to her about it at all because she did not want to dwell on it. "I swear," Mauldin had said, "It was like she intended to deny it until the last second and only then accept it. She never saw the last second coming and neither did I, but hell, most of all the seconds between us were last seconds. The change was god awful."

And that was how Clary felt: as though he and Judy had entered that final passage without knowing it. Cecil's death loomed in their future as though it was not accomplished yet. When he came back to the bed, she had picked up the bowl of popcorn and finished it. He had a glass of ice in one hand and a can of Coke in the other. "You sure you don't want one?" he said.

"No."

"Want to sip mine?" She looked at him but she said nothing. He opened the can and poured the Coke over the ice. "I love that sound," he said, as the Coke fizzed over the cubes and filled the glass too quickly. Immediately he realized how foolish and small he sounded—how utterly silly it was to express any small pleasure in the face of this culpable life he would now have to lead. He sipped at the foam before it spilled over the edge of the glass. Then he sat back and looked at Judy. "You look lovely tonight," he said, hopelessly.

"Don't."

"Don't what?"

"You don't have to do that."

"Do what?"

"I know how I look. I just got out of the shower. I don't have any makeup on."

"I'm just saying . . ."

"Are you going to tell me what you're going to say to the sheriff?" He looked hard at her, not sure what she meant. "You have to tell him the truth."

"As much as there is to tell; I'll tell him everything that's in the report we gave to the state police when it happened."

"I can't believe they didn't arrest you on the spot."

This shocked him, and his immediate response was anger. She was assuming so many things about him: that he was worried about what might happen; that he should be sent to jail for standing in Cecil's yard and eluding his grasp to avoid bodily harm; that he had fired a shotgun into the air; that he was trying to manipulate her into looking at it the way he did, so he was being insincere and only wanted to flatter her for selfish reasons. He didn't know what to say, so he sipped his Coke and stared at the television, seething with her words echoing in his soul. He felt betrayed. Finally, when he had calmed himself some, he said, "What would they arrest me for?"

She smirked. "I haven't done anything." Again she fell silent. She stared at the television as if the flickering light there bore the answer to all the mysteries of life. When she had been weeping this morning, weeping for him, he had felt so completely loved, even his recent worry and discontent about her seemed a distant memory of a bad dream, not quite real, not quite true. Now he couldn't remember what it felt like to feel tenderness toward her. After a long silence he said, "What do you think I've done?"

"I think you and those other hooligans went up there and *caused* Cecil's death. That's what I think."

"You do?"

"And that's what you think, too, or you wouldn't get so angry at me for suggesting it."

"Shit," he almost sneered. He felt his lip curl and when she looked at him, he realized he was ugly to her.

"Why are you so intent on defending yourself?" she said.

"Okay," he said. "Forget about it."

"You'd like that, wouldn't you?"

"Goddamn," he said. "You're just what I need right now. Some-body to make me feel worse than I already feel." At the last, his voice broke, and he realized he was crying. All he wanted was to go back in time and start that day over—begin again, this time with-out malice in his heart. That was what really bothered him. He could not remember any other time in his life when he had so sin-cerely wanted to hurt someone. And when he saw the blood drip-ping from Cecil's shocked mouth; when he saw the look of surprise, even wonder, on Cecil's face, and this powerful almost mythical force of a man suddenly grabbed the center of his chest as though something inside him was clamoring and scratching to get out, and dropped to the ground like a fallen idol; Clary knew this was something totally evil. Everything in his life ran behind his eyes now, all the grief and sadness, the loss and pain—and he did not know how he could ever come back from it. "Judy," he said, still fighting tears. "What have I done?"

She reached up and touched his face. "Honey," she said. Then she let her hand fall to her lap, leaned further back, and stared at the television. He heard her sigh, letting the breath out slowly.

"I'm so sorry it happened," he said. "I wish it hadn't happened."

"So do I," she whispered.

After a long silence, he said, "Forgive me."

"I forgive you." She reached for his Coke and held the glass to her lips, thinking. She seemed to take a long, slow sip, but she did not actually drink any of it. Then as she returned the glass to him, she said, "Look. I've been worried for a long time that we were losing something important between us. I've wanted our lives to change somehow."

"I knew you were unhappy."

"I wasn't so unhappy. I was a little bored maybe. Lonely."

"Lonely?"

"Yes. And I worried that you were unhappy, too. That we were both falling into a kind of . . . I don't know, it's hard to ex-plain." He said nothing. "The word stagnant comes to mind."

This hurt him, made him remember their first wonderful years in this place—how excited she had been when she first saw this very room, the huge suite on the top floor of a great hotel that would be their home. "I thought we had it made in the beginning," he said. "For a while there, anyway."

"It was never what you thought it was," she said.

"I'm in trouble here, Judy," he said, fighting tears. "I'm in a bit of trouble here."

"Don't," she said. She leaned herself against him, buried her face against his shoulder.

"I'm frightened, honey," he went on, getting control of himself. "Not about what I've done. But about us—about that life we were getting so—so used to—the life we thought—I thought—was turning into something—I'm absolutely terrified it's going to be taken from us."

"Maybe it's already happened," she said.

He put the rest of his Coke on the nightstand and shifted himself so he could put both arms around her. She rested her head against his chest. "You are a wonderful woman, Judy," he said. "And I love you." He waited, listening to her breathing, but she said nothing. He realized she was weeping silently. "If it comes down to it, I won't disappoint you," he whispered. This seemed to make her cry harder. "I'll be the man you want me to be."

She held onto him, as if she was afraid that any second the bed would suddenly fall from a great height, spinning and tumbling through space.

xix

On Wednesday night, Caldwell pulled into Columbia Beach well after dark. Early that morning he'd gone to Calvert Hospital to check on the remains of a body that had been found in the water near Dewey Beach. It wasn't McDole, and he didn't think it would be, but he was relieved none the less. It was the body of a drunken young man who had thrown himself into the river up near Wellington Beach, on the Maryland side. According to his friends, he had jumped from a speeding boat, laughing hysterically—giving a "good old rebel yell," one of his friends said—and apparently when he hit the water it broke his neck. Most people who have limited experience on the water don't know that it is only a little less dangerous to jump from a speeding boat than it is to jump from a speeding car. The fellow never surfaced, and the Maryland Department of Natural Resources had been looking for the body in the waters around Wellington and Sizemore beaches for more than two weeks.

Caldwell had been surprised at how happy it made him when he knew the body wasn't McDole's and he didn't have to look at it. Instead of driving back down to Columbia Beach, he turned off Highway 301 when he got back to Virginia and drove to Dahlgren to his office. He worked there until early afternoon, assigning officers for subpoena runs and arranging leave schedules for Christmas. Just after noon, deputy Lewis came in. "Can I bother you for a minute, sir?" he said.

"Sure, what is it?"

"I got a complaint here—it was filed before the Thanksgiving holiday, and somehow it never made it down to you."

"Let me see it."

Lewis handed it to him, kind of sheepishly. He was a big, swarthy man, with an impeccably pressed uniform and shined shoes. His badge gleamed in the overhead light. "What's the matter?" Caldwell said.

"Well, sir. Part of the complaint there—it's against you. Not the warrant or nothing, but in the complaint it states some things . . ."

"Let me guess," Caldwell said. "Was it sworn out by a man named McDole?"

"I believe it was."

Caldwell opened the envelope and read the complaint. McDole filled it out the day before Thanksgiving and it accused Cecil Edwards of assault with a deadly weapon, extortion, and illegal use of firearms. It also stipulated that the Dahlgren County Sheriff was "not capable" of providing even "moderate protection under the law." Caldwell let out a short laugh. "Well," he said. "I guess this fellow won't vote for me in the next election."

"No, sir." Lewis seemed embarrassed.

"I wonder if he realizes that this form is a petition to me, that it has to come to me?" Lewis shrugged. "That he's asking *me* to do him a favor, 'under the law,' as he might put it."

"I guess not."

Caldwell could not contain his amusement. "It's like he's saying here, 'Could you do me a favor, you stupid incompetent swine?'" Lewis didn't say anything, but it was clear he thought it was funny, too. "You know," Caldwell said, "when you serve the public, you really *serve* the public."

"Yes, sir."

"And most of them have no idea."

316 · Robert Bausch

Lewis said, "I don't know that any of them do."

"I'll take care of it," Caldwell said. "I'm going back down there tonight."

When he was certain there was nothing more that demanded his time, he left the office and drove home. He intended to go out to dinner with Terry and Laura, but when he got there only Laura was home.

"Terry's running with her friends," Laura told him.

"Well, let's you and me go get a bite."

"Why didn't you call?"

"I didn't know I was going to stop back here until I was leaving work. I'm sorry."

At dinner she wanted only to talk again about how he thought Thanksgiving had gone. She, too, thought it was a turning point in their lives, as if you could get to the end of grief—the official end of it—and have the life you always had, busy with joy and work and without even a hint of remembered sorrow. As if you could be someone other than a man and woman who have lost a child.

Still, he let her feel good. He realized there was something in his soul that augured hope and he did not want to sully it, or her happiness, by thinking about it too much, and when they were headed back to the house, he almost decided to spend the night. She tried to talk him into it, but he had this sworn complaint in his briefcase. He had to take care of that because it was official business. He hoped he could get McDole to withdraw it, but if the old man wouldn't do that, he'd have to serve the papers on Cecil. He was worried over the trouble that might cause. Also, in the back of his mind he had this notion that he was returning to round up Todd. He was thinking of getting Todd to help him look for a house down there—a place where the whole family could live. It would be a way of temporarily bringing Todd home so he could pick a school and begin his new life as a student.

As he was leaving, he kissed Laura, and she held onto him a little too long. He said, "I really think we're going to be all right."

"Me, too," she said, tears in her eyes. She kissed him again, and he held onto her for a while, waiting for her to let go. Finally she stepped back and looked into his eyes.

"You know," he said. "I think I could actually forgive him. I mean . . ."

"I thought you already had . . ."

"You know what I mean. It was so nice having him home."

"Well, but he's grown. He'll be gone, anyway. He can't just come back here and have a childhood." She let her eyes fall. "I don't want that. I just would like to have a relationship with him."

"Aren't you a little afraid of what we will miss?"

"What do you mean?"

He put his hand up and patted the back of her head. "Just that if we come to have him . . . if we love him again, as we should, that we'll come to miss those years he was away. We'll feel an even greater loss."

"I don't understand that logic," she said. "It's past. We have him now. Or we *can* have him. We can't change anything in the past."

"I know."

"Sometimes," she said gently, "I think you really do look too deeply into things . . ."

"You've said that before."

She kissed him on the cheek. "Sure you won't stay just a little while?"

"You trying to seduce me?"

"It does feel like a kind of date."

This amused him, and once again he realized how much he liked to look into her eyes. "What do you think?" he said. "Should we?"

She averted her eyes, looking shyly past him, but she was serious. "I don't know when Terry will come waltzing in here . . ."

He held her again, briefly. "I'll be home soon," he said. She was still standing on the front porch when he got in the car and started it. He watched her in the side view mirror as he pulled away, saw her waving to him. He honked his horn as he turned on the street and headed to the highway. He had only the sensation of beginnings in his mind as he drove back down the road late that night.

When he pulled into the parking lot behind the hotel, he was surprised to see the place was dark. He didn't realize how late it was. He parked his car and walked up on the boardwalk and into the lobby. Clary sat at the desk next to a small reading lamp that he'd placed on the counter. He was staring into space, although there was a book unfolded in front of him. Caldwell walked over to the counter and stood there a minute, watching the other man, who suddenly looked at him, seemed to notice him for the first time. He sat straight up. "Sheriff," he said.

"The place looks abandoned from the parking lot. I'm glad you were up."

Clary shook his head, running his hand over his face as if he were trying to pull the skin down from his nose to his chin.

"Sorry to keep you up waiting," Caldwell said. "If that's what you were doing."

"No," Clary said. "I'm half asleep here. I'm not really completely awake."

"You were sleeping?"

"Daydreaming got out of hand." He sniffed loudly, then rubbed his nose again.

"I don't suppose you know if my son is here?"

"He's upstairs. I saw him come in."

Caldwell started to turn away, but Clary took hold of his arm. "Ah," he started.

"What?"

"About yesterday."

"You'll be glad to know McDole was up in Dahlgren the day before Thanksgiving."

"He was?" Clary seemed to sink down—as though something in his bones turned soft. Then he said, "But we still don't know what happened to him."

"No, I guess we don't. I know he swore out a complaint against Cecil. And there's a phone number on the complaint with a 410 area code, so he was going to be staying somewhere in Maryland." Clary looked down at the book in front of him. He started to turn the page, but his hand was shaking. "What time did my son . . . ?"

"Did you hear about Cecil?"

"No. What'd he do now?"

"Didn't somebody call you about it?" Clary asked.

"How could anybody call me? I haven't been here. I've been . . ."

"No, Mauldin said he called your office up in Dahlgren today. They said they'd get word to you."

"I left the office early this afternoon. What did Cecil do?"

"He's dead," Clary said, looking down now at the book in front of him. The word "dead" gave Caldwell a cold shock in the center of his heart. He said nothing. "Your boy was there. He can tell you what happened."

Caldwell could not believe what he was hearing. "Todd was there?"

"Your boy. Yeah. It wasn't—Todd couldn't stop it. It just happened."

The whole room seemed to close in on Caldwell, and the shadows took on depth and substance, as if everything breathed and moved. He did not want what was spinning in the back of his mind to fully form. An instant suspicion made him sick right down to the marrow of his bones. He could not have said what propelled him to the elevator and up to the fifth floor. He did not remember how he found himself in front of Todd's door in the dark hallway. He heard Clary calling after him as he rushed from the front desk, that it really was an accident, that it couldn't be helped, but he did not want to hear those words. They sliced through him like a hard blade.

He knocked a little too loudly on Todd's door. He was breathing deeply, trying to remain calm. Todd opened the door and stepped back into the room. He was wearing a T-shirt, and the tattoos on his arms seemed to sneer at Caldwell. "Hey," Todd said. "You're back."

Caldwell stood by the door, feeling like a policeman. "Sit down," he said.

"Just wanted to say good night?"

"I've got things to ask you," Caldwell said.

"Really?"

"Sit down."

"No. I don't really want to. It's late. And I'm going out." Caldwell turned and closed the door. Todd watched him now, his eyes dark and serious. It was almost as if he were expecting to be rebuked in some way. "What is it?" Todd said.

"Just wanted to say, ah . . ." He didn't know how to begin. "I thought maybe we could just talk."

"I'm kind of in a hurry."

"You had quite a day yesterday."

"You heard about it?"

"Tell me what happened."

"You don't know?"

"I want to hear it from you, first."

This seemed to draw Todd up a bit. "What are you so hyper about?" He straightened himself, then sat down on the bed. "What do you want to hear?"

Caldwell sighed. "I want to hear it from you first, son."

"Hear what?"

"The truth."

"Why would I tell you anything else?"

"What'd you do?" Caldwell said. "Tell me that."

"Nothing," Todd said. "That's the problem."

"What do you mean?"

"I did nothing. But I should have stopped it."

Caldwell strode to the chair by the desk, pulled it out, turned it around, and straddled it directly in front of where Todd sat on the bed. "All right," he said, taking a deep breath. "I'm asking you directly. What can you tell me about Cecil's death?"

Todd's expression changed. It was as if the question wounded him, causing him terrific pain behind his eyes. He stared blankly at the space between them, and Caldwell, realizing how his question might be taken, was stunned into silence. He could not think of a word to say that would not make it worse. Todd got up and went to the door, as if he was in a hurry to get out.

"Where are you going?"

He turned and almost sneered, "Good night, Sheriff."

"Come back here. I didn't mean anything by that."

Todd opened the door. "Are you finished with me?"

"Todd," he said. "I'm not . . . please don't . . ."

"Is the investigation over, Sheriff?"

"That's not fair."

He hesitated a moment, then he said, "Can I go?"

"I don't know what you think I meant by that. You were with his sister all day. You might have talked to Cecil . . ."

"I'm going, Dad. Okay? I'm supposed to meet Lindsey." Todd stood at the open door, his hand on the doorknob, leaning against the frame.

"Look," Caldwell heard himself say. It was almost a whisper. "You must believe I didn't mean that the way it sounded."

"I know," Todd said. "You staying in here?"

Caldwell was still sitting on the chair, staring at the floor. Todd said, "Well, I've got a key. Let yourself out when you're ready." With that, he quietly stepped out and closed the door behind him.

· · ·

He got the story that night from Clary: "Poor old Cecil just died. In front of his place. It might have been a heart attack or a hemorrhage in his lungs. There was a lot of blood."

"And Todd found him?"

"Well—no, he didn't find him. He was there. We all were."

"What was Todd doing up there?"

"He was walking by the place with Cecil's girlfriend."

"When was this?"

"Yesterday morning. Early yesterday morning. Me and Mauldin and Hamlin went up there to talk to him—to Cecil—and . . ." Clary stopped when he saw the expression on Caldwell's face.

"I thought I told you not to go up there," Caldwell said.

"We just wanted to talk to him."

" 'We?' Todd was with you?"

"No, not at first."

"What did Todd do?"

"He didn't do anything."

Caldwell took a deep breath and leaned on the counter. It hit him that Todd had still been in on this somehow; that there he was, once more, in the company of death. What must have gone through his son's mind? This was not anything Caldwell could recognize or apprehend in words, but it was there, like a remembered photograph.

"Maybe old Cecil couldn't take seeing all of us together," Clary said. "He just fell down in the front yard by the Ferris wheel. His girlfriend called the rescue squad up in Dewey and they came a-running. But it was too late. Your boy said Cecil was already dead when he hit the sand."

Clary smelled of whiskey, and Caldwell had gotten used to the half-truths and fantasies of drunks. He was accustomed to people working a lie on him or leaving out facts, and over the years he had developed a keen ability to sense deceit. It was not an unerring skill, and he did not trust it as much as others believed he should, but he was always aware of it. Just now he did not believe Clary was telling him the truth, or rather, he did not feel that Clary was telling the whole truth.

"The paramedics said he might have died from asthma. Can you believe it?"

"Really?"

"Or maybe it was the heart. They weren't sure."

"You talked to them?"

"No."

"Who . . . ?"

"Your son told me what they said. He was there all the way." Clary placed his hands on both leaves of the book and stared at him. "It's a hell of a thing. I don't know what will happen to that property up there."

"What property?"

"The wheel and all. I mean, that's prime property up that end of the boardwalk. I wonder who will take care of . . . who will own it now?"

It was a cold and pitiless question to ask on the day after Cecil had died, but Caldwell at first didn't say anything about it. He looked at the older man briefly, as if he wanted to be sure he'd heard him right, then he said, "It belongs to the girl."

Clary's eyes widened a bit, and his mouth dropped slightly open. It was quiet for a moment, then he said, "You think old Cecil left a will?"

"Why do you call him 'old Cecil'? He wasn't much older than you are."

"You wouldn't *know* if he left a will."

"He didn't have to. It belongs to Lindsey."

"Not legally."

"Legally. She was his sister. If he doesn't have any other relatives, it's hers." Oddly, telling Clary the truth about Lindsey gave Caldwell a terrific feeling of satisfaction. He was not aware that years before, Clary had expressed an interest in the property. But even without that knowledge, the man's attitude suggested he wanted to take advantage of this sudden change in circumstances somehow, and Caldwell did not like it. Not at such a time as this. "So," he said. "You needn't worry about it." Clary's face changed, but he was quiet. "The only way it isn't hers is if he left a will giving it to somebody else."

"I'll be goddamned," Clary said. "His sister. We thought . . ."

"I know what you all thought," Caldwell said. A long pause ensued. When Caldwell was certain he was not going to get any more of the story unless he asked for it, he said, "Anything more?"

"That's all there is to tell," Clary said. He swallowed. Then he said, "My shotgun went off, but I didn't hit nobody."

Caldwell wished he was wearing his uniform. "You had a shotgun up there?"

"And Hamlin had his pistol. Just in case. You know. For protection. You've never seen anything like Cecil."

"I swear to Christ. How'd the gun go off?"

He let his eyes fall. "Well, Cecil grabbed for it and then I pulled the trigger. You know, fired it in the air. Just to scare him. Nobody was hurt."

"Cecil's dead," Caldwell said. "Don't tell me nobody was hurt." Clary said nothing. "Where'd they take Cecil?"

"I don't know. I guess up to Dahlgren, or maybe Warsaw."

"Did anybody call a doctor?"

"It was a medical team that came to get him."

Caldwell shook his head. "It's a damn shame," he said.

"Yes it is," Clary said. "I never had any use for old Cecil, but I think it's a damn terrible thing, too."

"If you see McDole, tell him what he can do with his complaint." Clary blinked, but he had no response. Caldwell left him there, in the single weak beam of the lamp on the counter. From the bank of elevators in the darkened lobby, he looked like a much older man, lonely and sad, sitting quietly in his pale circle of light, waiting for a loved one to come home.

. . .

The next morning, Caldwell had just raised his hand to knock on his son's door when it suddenly opened, and Todd, who was apparently in a hurry, almost ran right into him. He looked up at the last second and stopped, almost falling back in astonishment.

"Jesus," Todd said. "You scared me." He was fully dressed, wearing a pea coat with the collar hiked up behind his neck.

"Where you heading?" Caldwell asked.

"What's up?"

"I wanted to talk to you."

"What now?" Todd unbuttoned his coat, but he didn't take it off. Caldwell came into the room. Todd said, "Did you find out all about Cecil?"

"Yes."

"Where the hell were you, anyway?"

"I was in the office up in Dahlgren. Then I took your mother out to eat."

They were still standing in front of the open door to Todd's room. The hallway was dimly lit, and the high collar of Todd's coat shadowed his face, making him look almost sinister. "So you know what happened," Todd said.

"Clary told me all about it."

"It was something."

"Are you all right, son?" Caldwell said.

"Lindsey and I are going to have breakfast. I think I should be with her."

"How is she?"

"She is going to work. I guess she's okay."

"It must have been a terrible shock."

"She was upset. But she didn't cry much. I thought she'd cry a lot more than she has."

"Jesus, son."

"She's going to the funeral home this afternoon to arrange a service for Cecil."

"I see."

"Her mom is coming down from Cleveland."

It was quiet for a moment, and Caldwell realized that his son was fighting to control his emotions. He wanted to put his hands on the young man's shoulders and stop him for a moment, but

Todd moved past him out into the hall. He followed him out, then reached back and closed the door. Todd moved past him, down the hall.

"Wait," Caldwell said. "Wait a minute." He followed him for a few steps. Todd stopped and turned back to him. He would not look at Caldwell now, but his face betrayed him. Caldwell could see he was fighting some tension in himself, his eyes mere shadows in the dimly lit hallway. The overhead light made eerie shapes in the gloom and both of them stood there searching for something to say. Finally Caldwell said, "I know it must have brought some things back." Todd remained mute. "I understand," Caldwell said.

Todd shook his head slowly, but he said nothing.

"I know how it must have made you feel—being—going—through all that again."

"Going through all what again?"

"You know."

"No," Todd said. "I *don't* know." He started to leave, but stopped suddenly. "You know what I wish?"

"What?"

"I wish I could have seen Cecil get ahold of one of them."

"I'd like to see that myself."

"I should have stopped it," Todd said.

"That's not your job, son. It's mine."

"Yeah," he smiled briefly, then seemed to want to avert his eyes.

"I think I understand how you feel, though," Caldwell said. They both began moving slowly down the hall as they talked.

"You know where I went the other day?" Todd asked.

"No, where?"

"Lindsey took me back to the old house. Up in Fairfax."

They stopped, looking directly at each other. Caldwell tried to concentrate on his son's countenance, tried to keep his own eyes steady. He didn't know what he was supposed to say. He wanted to say something kind—something that would take everything between them that was difficult or painful away. He hoped he could present a face that did not remember all that had gone on in that house or at least did not reveal that he remembered it. He almost said, "What house?" but he knew Todd would see through that. So finally he said, "So?"

"We sat there in the car and I just looked at it. I could see the fence in the backyard where you and I had so much trouble getting Buster . . . Remember when we found Buster dead and we couldn't get him over the fence so you could bury him?"

"Yes. I remember it."

"I sat there and wondered at how short that fence looks now. It's even bent down a little in the middle between the posts—like a swaybacked horse or something."

"Maybe we did that hauling the dog over it."

"No, all of them were like that. The trees were so much bigger. Even without their leaves they were thick enough to make the whole place seem almost shady."

"Why'd you go back there?"

"Lindsey took me back. She just wanted to go to her old place, and then she took me to mine." Caldwell looked into his son's eyes and waited. "I mean ours."

"What's it look like now?"

"It's painted white. The shutters are blue instead of green. And the trees in front are huge." Todd lowered his head but there was a slight smile on his face—as though he were remembering something pleasant. Then he said, "You should go back there. It gave me something to look at it."

"Gave you something?"

"Yes."

"What do you mean?"

Todd shrugged. "It's hard to explain."

Again they began moving down the hallway as they talked, and now they were in front of Caldwell's room. "Here's my room," Caldwell said.

Todd looked at the door, then stopped briefly, leaning against the wall. He stammered a bit, looking down at his feet, then said, "I've got to go. Lindsey is expecting me."

328 • Robert Bausch

"Tell me, son." Caldwell put his hand up and rested it on his son's shoulder. "Tell me."

"Tell you what?"

"You said looking at the old house gave you something."

"Yeah."

Caldwell shook his head. "We've been dancing around down here for weeks. Why did you ask for this—this time down here? With me?"

"It's no use," Todd said. "What would be the point?"

"How can I know that? *You* made the request, so the point was *yours,* wasn't it?"

"Maybe it was." Todd pulled back. He wiped his mouth with the sleeve of his jacket, which was almost a defiant gesture, then he said, "Things change."

"What do you mean, 'What would be the point?'"

Todd shrugged.

"You're not telling me something, son. And I don't think it's fair."

"It's fair." This was stated ruefully, and it angered Caldwell.

"I was just trying my best to . . ." Caldwell paused. He was feeling exactly the same way he felt on that first day under Cecil's Ferris wheel when Todd had seemed to accuse him of something. Only this time he did not want to give in to his anger. He was not thinking of Bobby at all now, or of what had happened all those years ago. Now he was thinking only of this young man in front of him—his son. That's what he wanted to remember, what he wanted to save now. "I know you don't credit it, but I was just worried about you and trying to be there for you in a . . ."

"Be there for me?" Todd almost shouted. Caldwell blinked. "Be there for me?" Todd said again, just as loudly.

"Yes." Caldwell said. Todd turned and started down the hall, but Caldwell grabbed him by the high collar of his jacket, and pushed him up against the wall. "You aren't going anywhere."

"Yes I am."

Caldwell was strong, much stronger than his son. He held

him there until he stopped trying to break away, but it really wasn't a struggle. Anyone watching them would have thought it was an affectionate exchange between rowdy friends. Both of them breathed a little heavier now, staring at each other. Caldwell turned his son and moved him back down the hall. When they were in front of Caldwell's room again, he opened the door and gently but firmly pushed Todd into it. "Sit down," he said.

"I've got to go," Todd said. "Really." He made as if to break away, but Caldwell took his shoulders and moved him back further into the room. Todd let himself be moved to the double bed where Caldwell forced him to sit down. As he was pushing Todd down on the edge of the bed, Caldwell heard a small, high-pitched sound, and for a second he thought his son was resisting laughter, as if this were a playful tussle between father and son. He stood back and looked at him. Some part of him longed for that; some part of him remembered with terrific sadness what it felt like to hold Todd in his arms. Just having his hands on the boy's shoulders gave him a powerful intimation of all he had lost over the years, and he thought something in his heart might dissolve at any second. But then he saw tears in Todd's eyes, and he realized this was one of those seconds in life that would haunt him all the rest of his days: a little, helpless reverberation in the back of Todd's throat that was nothing but the most elemental human response to pain, and he had mistaken it for suppressed laughter; had almost laughed himself. His heart ached, and he realized he was fighting tears, too. He went to the door and closed it, then he turned around and stood there, facing his lost boy. "We're going to have that talk," he said. "Okay, son?"

"What talk?"

"The talk about why you wanted this."

"I already told you."

"No. You said something on the way home for Thanksgiving about having the family back. You could have had the family back if you had just come home."

"I could."

"You had it at Thanksgiving."

"Yeah."

"Didn't you?"

"Lindsey's waiting for me," he said. "Is this going to take long?"

Caldwell sat down in a chair by the bed and took a deep breath. He was exhausted, he realized, and he had gotten himself into something now, something dangerous. Maybe this was not what he wanted, not what he intended at all. "I don't want to argue, son."

"Neither do I. So that's settled." Todd rose from the bed, but when he saw the look on Caldwell's face, he sat back down. It was quiet in the room.

Caldwell wanted to take his time, think about what he would say. He sat with his hands up, the tips of his fingers against his brow, staring at the floor. In a slow, calm, steady voice, he said, "You told your sister that we'd never be a family again, and that you knew it at the end of the trial. What did you mean by that?"

"Nothing, Dad."

"*Why* did you react that way when I said I wanted to be there for you?"

"What way?"

"You shouted it at me. As if I was . . . as if it was totally unreasonable to . . ."

"Where *were* you when they arrested me and hauled me off to jail?"

"What?"

"When they took me to court and charged me. When the whole goddamned court system came crashing down on me. Where were you then?" Todd's voice broke.

"I was right there . . ."

"Yeah. Right there watching me, judging me. You didn't believe a word I said. You didn't believe me any more than the juvenile court believed me."

"I did, son."

"Don't lie about it now," Todd said. "Jesus Christ."

"Son, I'm not lying."

"It's not the truth!" Todd shouted. "Isn't that a lie?"

"It *is* the truth."

"Maybe you think it is. But it isn't."

"What makes you think *you* have the truth?" Caldwell realized he was getting loud. "Really. Where do you get off . . . ?"

"We're not going to get anywhere if you don't just shut up and listen," Todd said. He was apparently making a tremendous effort to remain calm. He clasped his hands between his knees and spoke in an even, almost prayerful voice. "You have to just listen to me for once."

"I'm listening," Caldwell said, trying also now to remain calm.

"Maybe you think you were there for me, but you weren't."

"I was . . . I tried, son."

"Did you?"

"Yes."

Todd shook his head, clearly amazed. "You really believe that, don't you?"

"What did you expect?"

"Consciousness of guilt," Todd said with contempt. "You remember that phrase?"

Caldwell could not remember anything. His mind was turning on itself, striving to control the hurt he was always harboring, the loss that was always at the back of every perfect day. He would not let it into this hour, this minute with his son. This would be about them, only them. Nothing else. He wanted, more than all things possible, to be with his son again. To be Todd's father. "What are you talking about?"

"You really don't remember it?"

"Son, I don't remember much of anything from those days. I don't *want* to remember it. I laid in bed all night the other night trying to remember one detail of it. One sentence, one facial expression, even one . . ."

"Consciousness of guilt." Caldwell did not say anything. "That's what you said to the judge. I was there. You were worried about my consciousness of guilt."

"I was?"

"That's what you said. You don't remember it?" Todd was nearly crying now, but his voice was softer. "We were all in the courtroom and the judge asked you . . . he wanted to know if you, if *you* believed me."

"I told him I did."

"I know you *said* you did, but you really didn't and he could see it."

Caldwell couldn't think of anything to say. This was beyond him—so far beyond him that Todd might as well have been accusing him of calculating and exacting punishments in his dreams or on some distant planet. "I don't know how you can base anything on what you *think* Judge Bass could see in me."

"You knew him. The judge."

"Yes. I knew a lot of them. It was my job . . ."

"They all knew you. Even the cops."

"Yes. I worked there, son."

Todd smiled now, remembering something. Then he shook his head slightly, letting his eyes fall to the floor. "You told Judge Bass you believed me, but then you said you didn't understand my actions." At the time, he was so numb he could not have remembered how to tell time. So he could not recall any of it now and he had to accept, on faith, Todd's memory of these events. He tried to say as much, but Todd stopped him. "You said you'd listen."

"Okay, I'm listening."

"You told Judge Bass you believed me." Caldwell started to say he did believe him, but Todd looked sharply at him so he said nothing. "Judge Bass nodded at you. He almost smiled at you." Todd paused, remembering. Then, he went on, his voice strong now, assured. "You said, 'I worry about consciousness of guilt,

Your Honor.' Like that. And he said, 'I worry about that, too.' You were looking at each other as though this was something you agreed to. Then he found me guilty of manslaughter."

"Ah, son," Caldwell said. "It wasn't what you think."

"Shit," Todd said, and when Caldwell got out of the chair and reached for him he recoiled from it. "You think I wouldn't remember a day like that?"

Caldwell did not know what to say. He stood there, staring into the eyes of what now seemed more like hate than any expression he'd ever seen, even from felons and criminals he had arrested. Neither of them spoke for a long time and the silence began to feel lethal. "If you'll excuse me," Todd said finally. "I've got to get going now. I don't want Lindsey to have to wait for me."

"I didn't know that's what would happen," Caldwell said. "I didn't know Judge Bass would do that."

"The judge almost winked at you."

"Why do you think we fought so hard to keep it from a jury trial? We wanted him to decide because we thought he would be more lenient. You must believe me."

Todd got up and went to the door. The light in the room cast their shadows up the wall. "It doesn't matter anymore," Todd said.

"I wish that were true, son. But clearly it still bothers you."

"You asked. So I told you." Todd opened the door. "It really doesn't matter."

"So," Caldwell said. Todd stopped, turning back to him. "That's why you wanted to meet me down here? So you could tell me . . . what?"

Todd stood in the open door and tears filled his eyes. "I wanted to ask you why you didn't believe me, Dad. That's all. I wondered why you didn't believe me."

"I believe you now, son," Caldwell heard himself say, but he didn't really know how he felt about it. He had been working too hard all these days not to think about it at all. Now fighting tears again, Todd merely nodded at him, then, embarrassed and in a hurry, he went out into the hall. Still holding the door open he said, "I guess I don't really care if you believe me anymore."

"But I care, son. I care." They fell silent. Both of them remained very still. When it was clear neither had any more to say, Caldwell got up and offered his hand. "Let's just start over," he said.

"Yeah," Todd said, but he had no intention of coming back in the room or of taking his father's hand.

"I really want to," Caldwell said.

"Yeah, sure," Todd said. He nodded vaguely and started to close the door, but when he noticed Caldwell move a little, as if to forestall it, he stopped. There was a long, awkward pause. The silence in the room was terrible.

Finally Todd said, "Well. I'll see you."

"Sure," Caldwell said. "Absolutely."

Todd turned to go, but stopped again, still holding the door open. "By the way," he said, with more strength in his voice, as though he were offering solace, intending some sort of normal conversation to get them beyond pain and memory and grief. "Lindsey and I were there when Cecil died. Clary fired his shotgun when Cecil grabbed for it. It might have been an accident. No one touched Cecil. He just dropped dead."

"Clary told me about the shotgun."

Todd smiled. "I threw the son of a bitch a country mile."

"So you disarmed Clary?"

"Yeah," said Todd, and a smile crossed his face.

"You did good, son," Caldwell said, wanting to demonstrate pride; wanting to praise his son as fathers are supposed to, all their lives. He spoke now as though something had been settled. He felt the heat of his sadness still in the back of his throat, but he was speaking to this man, now, this new young man, as if he understood him very well and trusted his judgment. They had spoken truthfully to each other and now the minutes and hours would have to take them past what was said, would have to bear them to some vast future that offered uncertainty and possibility.

That's how this moment felt to him, and he hoped it registered with Todd. For all the grieving years after Bobby's death, he had worried that he would never be able to find a way to forgive Todd; he had despaired of ever having forgiveness in his heart or the skill at pretending such a thing was possible in his son's presence. For all the years, he had fretted over how he could feign love for this living child who had robbed him of so much joy and wonder—and now the most important thing he wanted was to look into Todd's eyes and see clemency there. More than anything, he wished he could bring himself to ask Todd to forgive him.

"Well," Todd said. "I thought you should know."

"Tell Lindsey I'm very sorry about Cecil."

"I will."

They stared at each other for a moment, then, without saying anything else, and giving a slight nod of his head, Todd gently closed the door.

xx

Lindsey insisted on having a funeral service for Cecil, a small one, outside by the Ferris wheel. Alicia, who had flown into Richmond and then rented a car and driven up the day before, sat next to her and held her hand, and Lindsey simply stared straight ahead, her face expressionless, as the minister—a Presbyterian with long, graying hair that covered his neck and collar—read his prayers. She wore a light blue dress with a white collar, and black pumps. It was the first time anyone except Alicia could remember seeing her in a dress. It was a clear, icy day— the sky deeply blue with thin wisps of high, lacey clouds curving across the bright blue depths far beyond the sun. Sharply cold breezes swept in off the river and steam chuffed into the air as everyone breathed. Lindsey's hair glistened gold in the bright sun, and the breezes seemed to caress it, lifting it by her ears and around her dark eyes. Cecil had wanted to be cremated and so that's what was done. The minister brought a small folding table upon which he rested the urn with the ashes, and Todd had placed seven wooden lawn chairs in front of the table. He had collected the chairs, with Mrs. McCutcheon's permission, from her boardwalk overlook. Lindsey did not want the urn with the ashes in it. When the minister offered it to her, she only bowed her head and whispered, "No." Then she turned to her mother and said she wanted something done with it. "I can't just leave it with them," she said, indicating the funeral director and the minister. She asked Todd to spread the ashes in the sand around the Ferris wheel, and he would do so, one afternoon shortly after the service.

The service was short, awkward, and sad. Aside from the prayers, it was also wordless. Alicia was kind to come all the way from Ohio to be there for her, but it had not been necessary. Lindsey had gone to work the day Cecil died, and she didn't miss a day of work until the afternoon of the service. She was happy to discover that the trailer, the Ferris wheel, and the property it was on belonged to her—news both confirmed by Caldwell and by the crude will that Cecil had written on loose-leaf paper sometime during the months before he died. He must have known something wasn't right because the will made reference to his death as if it were something in the near future. He wrote that he wanted to be cremated but left no specific instructions about what to do with his ashes. He talked in the will about what he hoped Lindsey would do in the coming summer, made a list of the things the wheel needed, and provided phone numbers of mechanics and electricians and other people who would have to service it before it was started up again. He made a list of the normal hours of operation, but she knew what they were; she had helped him run it for two whole summers. In the last part of the will, he wrote:

> *I am sound in my mind and do here wish that Lindsey Hunter inherit all I own even what I forgot to mention in this here Will and please keep the Ferris wheel running, Lindsey. I was glad you came to be my sister. I was glad you came to find me when you did and if you had no regrets about that I am very glad. I am also hoping you had no regrets. I think if you did you would have told me because you always told the truth about things. You were a good woman*

*my mother would say she was proud of. So would I. If I die
before I say that to you or if any other I want you to know
it now. Of sound mind, making this my last will and testa-
mony so help me God.*

Cecil Edwards

Lindsey, Alicia, Todd, Caldwell, and Jack and Judy Clary attended. The Hamlins sent flowers but didn't take the short walk
from their small home behind his office up to the Ferris wheel.
There was, of course, nothing from McDole or Mauldin. The
minister came from a church in Dahlgren, and since he didn't
know Cecil, he could only recite the prayers he spoke at every funeral service about departed souls. When he was finished, he
asked if anyone wanted to say anything. Lindsey stirred slightly,
but she remained silent.

All through the days leading up to the service and afterward,
Lindsey was quiet and kept to herself, even with Todd there to
console her. Although she had always been aware of the sorrows
and disasters each day might present, she was shocked into an en-
during kind of insensibility. If she had been that rare sort of person who is incapable of dreaming ruin, who refuses to see
anything but goodness in all events, she could not have been more
shocked by Cecil's death. Even in his worst battles for air, even
when the asthma seemed to shrink him, he had always seemed so
strong and indestructible. She did not yet know how she felt about
all that had happened. Something enormous had changed in her
life, but she could not imagine what it meant; and she could not
bring herself to pretend to feel any different than she felt, which
was—since she first realized that Cecil was gone—nothing. A
mere, numb, bewildered acceptance of things and no more.

A few days before Christmas, she packed up her belongings
and moved from Mrs. McCutcheon's place down to the trailer.
With Todd's help she carried all of Cecil's clothing to a Goodwill

store in Dewey. She kept most of the magazines and the cook-ware. She cleaned every surface in the trailer, pulled the carpet off the floor, and had it replaced.

Then one very early morning as she was going through the cabinets and drawers, she found the small blue spiral notebooks she'd asked him about so long ago. He had said it was just "ac-counts and such." There were nineteen of them, each numbered with a big numeral—one through eighteen—scratched heavily and repeatedly with a ballpoint pen. One of them was not marked with a number. Instead, Cecil had penned the letter *L* on the cover. Inside this book were pages of notes Cecil had recorded about Lindsey. The first page read, "Sister came today, June 1997. I don't know her. Didn't think I ever would know her at all. Sister so now what?" When she read these sentences, something dropped in her heart.

She went to the couch and sat down. Her hair was tied up be-hind her head and she wore a bandana that kept it out of her eyes. She was tired and feeling alone, so the notebook was like hearing from Cecil—as if he could speak to her from the dark.

The second entry, which was dated weeks later, said,

Told her about mother today. I plan good things. She looks like mother looked sometimes and talks way too much but she is fun to have here. I'll never tell her part of fun is goad-ing her and teasing her saying things that shock her and she acts like mother sometimes. She's cute. Not just a substitute sister. Would like to have know her when she was a little girl.

Some pages had only one word: "steak" or "laugh." All of the pages were dated. On October 5th of 1998, he wrote,

Linssy moved to Columbia Beach. I am happy about that. Now I have a family here with me in this place. Crazy fun.

Next Sunday she says she'll cook a dinner for me that I will not forget soon. Looking forward to it.

A week after that entry, he wrote:

Forgot to say about dinner. It was homemade spagetti with very good meats. Sausage and pork spare ribs and beef tips. She was proud of it and I liked it a lot but I didn't say anything to her about it. Remember tomorrow.

Some pages had only the single sentence, "breathed good today all day," or "good breathing today." Other entries made no sense—references to newspaper articles, plans for the Ferris wheel, and accounts to be settled. "Pay for axle grease and *p.*" A lot of things were abbreviated and she could not figure out what they meant. On one page he wrote diagonally across from the left corner down to the right corner, "today do *r* and make S&B directly." On another, he wrote in bold black lettering, "**tell linnsy about *m*. Turn off *J!!!*"** Near the back of the book, in smaller letters than the other entries, he had written, "tell linnsy about her father. Let McDole know how to behave if she goes to see him. Tell her what a prick he is warn her about him." A few pages after that, there was this entry:

She saw McDole today with his gun. He was drunk and stupid. She didn't like him and when I backed him down I was very proud of her for staying there even though he was waiving the gun around. Sucha ass. He doesn't even know. He never knew. If I tell her, he will know and I hate it because mother never wanted him to know. I think it will be bad to tell her about him. What will she think of mother. What will she think

In the last entry, which was written very small—as if to leave room for more on the last page—he wrote, "never give any one a chance to see this is what I want for her."

She closed the little book and held it against her breast. She realized that while she had been reading through it, the words on each page—even the ones she could not make out or that made no sense—produced the same tensions, the same feelings of anxious hope and fearful apprehension she'd always felt in Cecil's presence. It was almost as if he was in the room. And when she realized who her father was, she felt nothing. It was as if she had discovered a lost shoe after she had already thrown away the mate to it. McDole: in some ways, everything that had happened to Cecil was his fault. Cecil bore a responsibility, too—she knew he was not innocent. Still, she could not think of McDole without a sort of revulsion and loathing. She knew she would never tell him who she was. She would never tell anybody.

Just then Alicia came to the door and opened it. "You up and working already?" she said. Lindsey only tried to smile. "What's the matter, honey?"

She realized she was crying when she handed her mother the notebook.

"It's all right, honey," Alicia said. "It's all a part of grief."

Alicia stayed to help as long as she could, and Todd helped too, although when the work was done each day, he returned to his room at the hotel. Lindsey introduced Todd to Alicia as "her friend," so that's how he came to see himself. All during the service and while helping get things straightened out at Mrs. McCutcheon's—including the task of returning all seven lawn chairs, freshly rinsed of sand—and helping Lindsey move into the trailer, he never demonstrated anything but a willing friendliness. He did not lay a hand on her. He was especially courteous in Alicia's presence. When his father came up to the trailer right before the service, he introduced Lindsey to him as his friend.

"We've met, son," Caldwell said.

"Oh, of course," Todd said. He and his father still seemed to have difficulty looking at each other and did not speak more than a few words the entire day.

When Alicia finally got in her rental car to drive back to

Richmond to catch a flight back home, Lindsey stood with Todd at the foot of the yard in front of the Ferris wheel and waved as her mother pulled away. Then she turned to Todd and said, "I want you to move in here with me." He only looked at her. "Alicia wondered why you were still at the hotel, and I guess now, so do I."

"Alicia wondered?"

"I told her how I feel about you."

He averted his eyes, but she could see he was suddenly deep in thought—as if she had touched a subject that had occupied him much more completely than she or anyone had realized.

"Don't you want to move in?" she asked tentatively, afraid of his answer.

"We'll talk about it." He started to move away. Then he said, "I think it's wonderful she came all the way down here to be with you."

"She's my mother."

"I know."

"Why wouldn't she?"

He shrugged. "I just think you're very lucky."

She wanted to say something kind to him—something that would cancel all he had been through. But the only thing she could think to say was, "You don't have any experience of it . . ."

"What do you mean?"

"It's just that—," she stopped. Then she put her arms around him for the first time since they had witnessed Cecil's death. "I think you're wonderful because in spite of where you spent most of your childhood, you know what's right and good."

"We'll talk about what we're going to do after the New Year," he said.

"I want you to move in with me. That's what I'm hoping for."

"Here? In Cecil's place?"

"Yes. Why not?"

"After the holidays," he said. "Give it some time."

• • •

McDole showed up the week after the service on a cold, rainy Sunday morning. It was the week before Christmas, and just before the sun found its way up behind the murky clouds on the distant shoreline of Maryland, while Lindsey was busy tearing up the carpet in the trailer, he walked into the café at the hotel and sat at the bar as if he'd never been away. He was wearing the Atlanta Braves baseball cap and blue overalls under a long yellow raincoat. He took off his cap and placed it on the counter, then draped the raincoat over one of the stools to let water drip off it onto the floor.

"Where the hell *you* been?" Clary asked.

"Let's have some coffee," he said.

"You wouldn't believe the trouble you caused around here."

"Me? What'd I do?"

"Where'd you go?"

"I went to my brother's place up in Baltimore," McDole said. "Then me and him went up to West Virginia."

"What's in West Virginia?"

"He's got a little house up there on eleven acres. We hunted deer for two weeks. It felt good up there. I felt like I'd won a victory over Cecil."

Clary poured the last of a pot of hot coffee into a mug and placed it in front of him. "You might have mentioned you were going to do that."

"What?"

"You might have told someone."

"Sorry."

"We all thought something happened to you."

McDole shook his head slowly. "Why?"

"You know what happened?" Clary said.

"I heard. Hamlin came over to the station late last night."

Clary sat down on the tall stool behind the counter and rested his chin in his hands. "It was a terrible thing," he said quietly. He felt again the now familiar rush of remorse and it took his breath away. He could not stand how smug the others seemed to be. Now everything on earth was suffused with the cold chill of culpability and potential ruin. It was as if the one act of leaving Cecil lying face down in the sand had permanently destroyed something essential and innocent in all his memory. They had come to this very room that morning seeking escape; they had looked at each other in horror and silence, unable to forget momentarily that this was death; he could not catch his breath, and then he noticed the hard-featured grimaces of the others, the ugliness of their attempts to go back to normal in the face of what they'd just seen; and suddenly he realized that he had discovered something not only about himself, but also about the whole world and all people, and it was gruesome and terrifying. "A terrible thing," he said again, now.

"Really?" McDole did not seem convinced. "I think it's good riddance."

"We been waiting around here for days, just waiting for what the sheriff is going to do."

"Does he know about it?"

"I told him the truth. We had to. His son was right there and saw the whole thing. So was Lindsey."

"That's too bad."

"The sheriff's just been hanging around here, looking at us suspiciously since it happened. I think he's just waiting, trying to bait all of us. He never takes a day now that he doesn't wear that uniform."

"Well, fuck him."

"Judy says we didn't do anything wrong, really."

"No."

"She didn't like it that we went up there in the first place." At this, McDole laughed. "It wasn't funny."

"He deserved it. Whatever happened to him, he deserved every bit of it."

"I felt sorry for him," Clary said.

"I'm sorry if I caused you any problem, but I just couldn't stand giving in to that fat bastard," he said. "I wanted every penny of what he owed me. Not just half of it. So I piled some things into my Astro and drove up to Dahlgren to swear out a warrant on him."

"Without telling anyone?"

"I told *you* I was going to do it."

"No you didn't."

"I did too."

"That was a long time before the meeting with Cecil got arranged . . . I thought—," Clary stopped. Then he said, "I thought the meeting solved all of that."

"Nope."

"Well, I still feel sorry for him."

"You didn't have him hold a goddamned gun to the back of your head."

"No, I guess I didn't."

"He was a worthless bastard and I'm glad he's gone. He got just what he deserved."

Clary shook his head slowly, still staring at him. "You didn't see him die. It was awful."

"Hamlin said it was funny."

"Hamlin's an asshole."

A LITTLE LATER Mauldin and Hamlin came in, and while they slapped McDole on the shoulder and talked about where he'd been and what had happened in the town, Clary brewed more coffee and then poured each of them a cup. "It's not deer season this late in the year up in West Virginia, is it?" Mauldin asked.

"My brother owns the property," said McDole. "We can hunt whatever we want, and whenever we want."

"You get anything?"

"Nothing to brag about. A doe. Heavy son of a bitch, though. I thought I'd have a heart attack dragging it up that mountain to the truck so I could have enough light to clean it."

All three men moved to the table next to the counter and sat down. "Cold out there," Mauldin said. He took off his jacket and draped it over the chair he sat in. Hamlin wore a down vest, black dungarees, and combat boots. He had a little silver flask under his vest, and when he was seated he opened it and took a drink out of it, tilting his head back and pouring it down his throat. When he was finished, he wiped his mouth with his sleeve then held the flask out, offering it to anyone who wanted it. "A little early for that, isn't it?" Mauldin said.

"It's cold out there," said Hamlin, smiling. "This'll warm you up." No one reached for it, so he took another swig then put it back in his pocket.

"If you'd just *told* somebody where you were going," Clary said to McDole. "You might have saved us a lot of grief."

"Grief?" Hamlin said. "What grief?"

"Hell," McDole said. "It was right late at night when I made up my mind to go ahead and swear out a warrant. And I took off before the sun came up. Who would I tell?"

"You sure as hell had us wondering," Hamlin said.

"We thought Cecil'd done something to you," said Hamlin. McDole laughed slightly. "He'd a liked to try."

"Just about everybody thought you were dead."

"I'll be damned," McDole laughed. "Hamlin said you guys wanted to have it out with Cecil. I guess you guys scared him to death, literally."

"He had a heart attack," Mauldin said. "Maybe his asthma kicked it off. Right up there in front of the damned Ferris wheel."

McDole shook his head, sipping the cup of coffee. He looked as if he was trying to remember something. "Now I'll never get my goddamned money."

"No, I guess you won't."

"Unless I sue the estate."

"It wouldn't be worth it," Clary said.

"No, I guess it wouldn't."

• • •

A little before nine on the day of McDole's return, Sheriff Caldwell finished getting dressed and walked out into the hall. He wore his uniform, with the big revolver resting on his hip, the handle of which looked three times larger than the rest of it that was buried in the small black holster. His brightly shined leather shoes creaked as he walked. He stood in front of Todd's door, trying to decide if he should knock on it.

For the past few days they had barely spoken, but there was no apparent tension between them anymore. It was something else—a kind of embarrassing awkwardness that made it difficult for either of them to look too closely at the other. Some mornings Caldwell would hear Todd coming out of his room, and he'd get up and wait quietly by the door, listening for him, hoping to hear him knock and fearing it, too. It really was fear—fear that he would not know anymore how to talk to his son. And that very fear made it extremely ungainly whenever they did run into each other.

Todd went about his business as though he was just another tenant in the building and they were not actually related. He was always polite and he always answered when Caldwell said something to him, but he did not spend any time talking about anything. They would say, "Hey," or "How's it going?" to each other. This was a distance more intractable than the one that had been created by Bobby's death. It was almost as if Todd had made some sort of conscious decision, and part of it had to do with going on with his life bereft of familial ties of any kind. He did not even seem very attached anymore to Lindsey. Caldwell had watched him during the service, and although he was there helping out and observing the proper silence and decorum and respect, he never really came very close even to her. When it was over, he helped carry the wooden lawn chairs down the hill and up the street to Mrs. McCutcheon's place, then he went back to his room at the hotel.

Now Caldwell listened by the door. Softly, tentatively, he

knocked on the dull wood. He heard Todd say something, so he waited a while and when the door didn't open, he knocked a little louder. "Just a minute," Todd said. He waited, staring down the hall at the shadows and the stained windows. Todd opened the door, and when he saw Caldwell standing there in his uniform he averted his eyes—almost as if something on the uniform was too bright to look at.

"You busy?" Caldwell said.

"No." Todd was wearing a T-shirt and blue jeans. His hair was combed and he'd put on light blue sneakers.

"You going somewhere?"

"What's with the uniform?"

"It's my job, son."

"You been wearing that thing around here a lot lately."

"You going somewhere?"

"No. Not right away." Todd stepped back and made as if to welcome him into the room.

"I'm going down to have a talk with the coffee klatch, you want to join me?"

Todd got a puzzled look on his face. "Why?"

"I think it's about time I talked to them about what happened."

"Really, I thought you would have done it by now."

"I wanted to be sure of the cause of death."

"Oh." It was quiet for a moment while they simply looked at each other. Then Todd said, "What was the cause of death?"

"It was his heart—a hemorrhage in his lungs. They filled with blood and his heart stopped."

Todd nodded his head. "I thought so. He was blue, for god's sake. And there was a lot of blood."

"Well now, I just want to ask those fellows a few questions."

"Why do you need me?"

He shrugged, disappointed and saddened by the question. "I don't. I just thought . . ."

"I'm not into police work," Todd said.

"You were there," he said. "That's all. So I just thought . . ."

They looked at each other. Clearly feeling as though he was being made to do something he did not want to do, Todd said, "Well, let me put a shirt on. I'll go with you if you want."

"Don't do me any favors," Caldwell said.

"What do you mean by that?"

"You don't have to go if you don't want to."

"No. I said I'll go."

THEY WALKED into the café slowly, as if they were looking for somebody in particular. The men were seated at the one big table that had chairs around it, and when they saw Caldwell and Todd they stopped talking. Caldwell stepped up to the counter and asked for a cup of coffee. Clary got up and hurried behind the counter to get the coffeepot. His hands were shaking as he poured him a cup. He looked at Todd. "You?"

"Coke," Todd said. The other men were silently staring straight ahead.

Caldwell looked at McDole. "Well," he said, "you're back." McDole said nothing. Clary gave a short, nervous laugh: "Yeah, the prodigal son returns." He finished pouring Todd's Coke, then stepped back around from behind the counter and sat down at the table with Hamlin and Mauldin. Caldwell turned himself and leaned back against the counter. No one looked at him or said anything. "Anybody want to tell me what you guys were doing the other day up at Cecil's place?"

Mauldin moved himself so that he could look directly at Caldwell. "What we were doing?" he said.

"That's right. At Cecil's place." He turned to Clary and Hamlin. "I want to know what you were doing up there," Caldwell said, and just as he said it, he heard the elevator doors open. He stood there sipping his coffee and Judy wandered in, her hair freshly washed and still wet but neatly combed. She wore a blue cotton bathrobe and brown slippers.

"You going to church this morning?" Clary said.

"No. I got up too late. I'm just looking for my magazine."

Clary looked impatiently at her, waiting for her to say something else. It did not please him that she was standing there in her robe and slippers with her hair still wet. She went behind the counter and disappeared in the room back there. When she came back out Clary said, "Did you look behind the registration desk?"

"That's the first place I looked." She stopped and seemed to notice for the first time the tension in the room. "What's going on?" she asked.

"Nothing," Clary said hurriedly. But at the same time McDole said, "The sheriff here is investigating."

"Oh?"

"You men went up there with firearms, and now a man is dead," Caldwell said. Something changed on Clary's face. He seemed to sink down into himself, and then he looked at Judy. She did not move.

Mauldin said to Todd, "You were there. Didn't you tell him? Nobody touched Cecil until he fell. And then it was only you and Lindsey that laid a hand on him."

"If you produce a person's death by intimidation, you've still committed manslaughter," Caldwell said. In the corner of his eye he saw Todd turn toward him. Mauldin and Hamlin looked at each other, then at Clary. "What happened?" Caldwell asked again. "Did the gun scare him so bad that he had a heart attack?" Clary looked at his wife, and Caldwell noticed Judy's sad eyes watching her husband now with what seemed very much like pride.

"It wasn't an accident that the gun went off," Clary said. "I fired it in the air. But it didn't scare Cecil. Nothing scared Cecil." Mauldin and Hamlin still did not move or speak. They stared at each other while Clary told what happened. "We were just going to try and find out about McDole here," Clary said. "We didn't mean . . ." He didn't finish. He looked at his wife then let his gaze fall to the floor.

"Go on," Caldwell said.

OUT OF SEASON · 351

"We didn't mean for it to happen." He shook his head, and then Judy went over to where he was seated in the chair and stood behind him, her hands on his shoulders. He reached up and took her fingers in his own hands, not taking his eyes off Caldwell. It was quiet for a while. Judy was crying and no one moved, even to sip their coffee. Caldwell regarded Todd, who was staring intently at Judy and her husband.

"It was just a coincidence," Mauldin said. "He might have died whether or not we were there."

"Absolutely," Hamlin said.

"Well," Caldwell said, "you know how this might be viewed under the law?"

"It was an accident," Mauldin said. "We don't need any bullshit from you about it."

Caldwell moved from the bar and stood over Mauldin. "It was a death caused by reckless, armed behavior, sir," he said. He kept his voice as steady as he could, but he saw a look of fear cross Mauldin's face. "You know what involuntary manslaughter is?" Mauldin said nothing. Neither he nor Hamlin moved. "Involuntary manslaughter, sir," Caldwell went on. "I could charge you— and each of your friends—," he stopped. Across the room he saw Todd glaring at him, and it hit him with tremendous force that he was using the very words the law used to describe Todd's crime. He wished he had died before he'd ever uttered those words in Todd's presence.

Todd did not look away. He put his Coke down on the bar and walked over to the table and faced his father. "Well," Caldwell said lamely. "It just so happens that you're right about what killed Cecil. The medical examiner said it could have happened any time. Just walking down the street." Todd shook his head. He was just standing there, trying to find a place to put his hands. He might have been looking for something in his pockets. "What is it, son?" Caldwell asked.

Todd didn't seem able to look him in the face. It was quiet

again for what seemed like a long time. Judy put her hand on the back of her husband's neck and began caressing him there. Caldwell did not know what to say. He started to turn back to Mauldin, but then Todd said something under his breath. "What?" Caldwell said gently.

Todd whispered, "There was no consciousness of guilt."

"What?"

"It was an accident. That's all it was. They didn't run or try to hide anything."

"I know that, son."

"It was just an accident," he said quietly, trying to speak only to Caldwell, and then he gave a short sound in the back of his throat and spoke in a normal voice, so everyone could hear him. "Sorry. I should mind my own business. But you see they didn't *intend* anything." He seemed surprised at himself. He looked around the room at all the faces now staring at him, and he was clearly embarrassed. It was quiet in the room. Now he tried to force a smile. He didn't seem to know what to do with himself or where to let his eyes fall. He moved awkwardly back to the counter, picked up his Coke again, and sat down.

"Your son has good sense," Mauldin said.

"It really was an accident," Hamlin said. "Just what the young man said it was."

Caldwell kept his eyes on Todd, waiting for him to look back at him, but he only sat with his back to the room and continued to take small sips from his Coke.

"Sheriff?" Judy said.

He looked at her. She wiped her eyes and tried to smile. "You think maybe this time—," she paused. "Maybe this time you could . . ."

"I think I know where this is headed," Caldwell interrupted her. "And I'd like it if it was my idea." Judy nodded, understanding him. Clary sat up more in the seat, seemingly ready to take whatever Caldwell might say. Tears ran down his face. "I'm just going to leave this where it is," Caldwell said. He paused for a second, looking around the room. "That seems the right thing to do here." No one said anything. "But you all know what happened," he started. "You all know—" he stopped. Todd still had his back to him as he leaned over his drink on the bar. Caldwell turned and saw Clary take a Kleenex from his wife and run it over his eyes. "Well," Caldwell said, "I guess you all know what you've done. There's no reason to ruin your lives over an accident." But it didn't seem that anyone heard him. He felt useless and empty. It was quiet for a long time and everyone seemed intent on studying their hands or their coffee cup, or simply the spaces between them. No one looked directly at him. Caldwell shook his head, then turned and walked over to where Todd was seated at the counter.

"I'm done here," he said. Todd gulped down the last of his Coke and set it on the counter, and the two of them walked out into the bright sunlight together.

xxi

On Christmas Day Todd came to the trailer early and he and Lindsey had a quiet morning together opening a few small gifts. She gave Todd a collection of poems by Yeats and a new wristwatch, and he gave her a book of short stories by Guy De-Maupassant and a silver cigarette lighter. "I should probably just quit smoking," she said, admiring the lighter. It was quiet for a long time. Todd paged through his book of poems, not looking at her. She waited a while, watching his face, then she got up and cleaned up the wrapping paper. "Want something to eat?" she asked.

"No." He still paged slowly through the book.

"How about some coffee?"

"Okay."

She brewed a pot of coffee. While she waited for the water to boil, she smoked two cigarettes and paged through her book. She still did not know what to say or how to act, so she stayed away from the table where Todd was reading. She stood by the sink, then in front of the small stove. She remembered when Cecil opened the oven and covered the turkey with aluminum foil, and it made her sad momentarily. She wondered if this was all she would feel. When the coffee was done, she came back to the table with two cups and sat down across from Todd. "You just going to read that whole book now?" she asked.

"No." He closed it, then turned it so that he could read what was written on the back cover. Neither of them spoke for a long time. Then Todd reached across the table and lifted up the book of stories. "I read this collection when I was in the youth center. Guy DeMaupassant." He pronounced the first name so that it rhymed with pie.

Lindsey laughed slightly. "It's pronounced Gee, not Guy"— and suddenly she had tears in her eyes. He took a sip of his coffee, watching her. She said, "Cecil liked to do this."

"What?"

"Drink coffee at this table early in the morning."

Todd held his cup in front of his mouth and smelled the steam that rose into the bright air. He was not looking at her, but when she sat down he heard her sigh, and when he met her gaze, he saw her wiping the tears. "Are you okay?" he asked.

"Yes. Did your father get you anything for Christmas?"

"He gave me a certificate that he made up himself. It promises to pay my way through college."

"Really?"

He smiled. "I guess he's trying."

"Did you get him anything?"

"A few books. A couple of tapes."

"You know what I wish?" she said.

"What?"

"I wish I hadn't been so miserable at Thanksgiving." Todd was quiet, just looking into her eyes. "I wish I didn't begrudge Cecil that day."

"What do you mean?"

"I never thought he'd just *be* gone," she whispered, and then she was crying. He got up, went around to her side of the table, and sat down. He reached up to put his arm around her and when he did this, she put her head in the crook of his shoulder and wept. He wrapped his arms around her and held her there, not saying anything. Presently she got control of herself and sat back away from him. "I didn't really love him," she said. "You know?" He nodded. "I wish I'd known I was so important to him."

"You didn't know that?"

"He was keeping a journal. He actually wrote that he was happy when I moved down here."

"He was happy. That's what matters, right?"

"If he'd just showed it once in a while." Todd moved closer to her, offering her a napkin from the table. She took it and wiped her eyes. "I feel so sorry for him now. I can't get that image of him out of my mind. Down on all fours like that. I felt so sorry for him."

"I know."

"But I hardly knew him." Todd moved her hair back so he could see into her eyes, then he reached down to where her hands rested in her lap and took hold of them. "I mean, this is silly. I don't know why I'm crying," she said.

"He was your brother. It's understandable."

She looked at him. "I'm just so sad that I sat right in that chair at Thanksgiving," she nodded toward the other side of the table, "and I hated him for not being talkative and somebody other than who he was."

"There's no use—," Todd started, but she interrupted him.

"I was missing Thanksgiving with my mother—a really important holiday to me and her and her parents, and everything. And you, too. I was missing you. And he was just being himself. That's all he ever was. I wanted it to be more—more festive. And when it was just like any other day with him, I hated him."

"You didn't know he was going to die," he said.

"Yes I did. We're *all* going to die, and we *all* know it."

"Most people work real hard to forget it."

A long silence ensued. They both seemed to study the way his fingers were intertwined with hers. "I didn't hate him. I hated being here."

"Did you say anything to him?"

She shook her head, sniffed, and wiped her eyes again. "Cecil wasn't that perceptive."

"Then why do you feel so bad?"

"I don't really know. I said this was silly." She smiled. "Maybe a part of me feels like he deserves a few tears. From somebody."

Todd said, "He's not feeling anything now."

"And I didn't even love him," she said.

"Maybe that's what this is," Todd said.

"What?"

"How you feel right now. Maybe you're discovering that you *did* love him." She only stared into his eyes. "I mean, why would you care about that one day. It's in the past. Nothing can change it. Haven't you said those very words to me?"

"I wish I could have made it a really unforgettable day for him," she said, losing her voice, tears coming to her eyes again.

"You've made a few for me," Todd said, holding her close again. After a long, quiet time in which he held her against himself, she sat back and looked out the window. He moved away slightly and took another sip of his coffee. "This shit is cold," he said.

Without looking at him she said, "Have you thought about . . . ? Did you decide anything about . . . ?"

"What?"

"About moving in here with me or not?"

"I can. If you want me to," he said.

"You don't sound . . ." She didn't finish.

He let a long time go by, then he said, "I don't sound what?"

"Like it's something you want very much to do."

"No, I do," he said. "I really do." She looked at him, her eyes still rimmed with tears. "I promise I will. It's just . . ."

"What?"

"Nothing."

"What?"

"Lindsey, I love you." She blinked. "You know that, right?"

"Yes."

"I'm not going to stop loving you." She waited, feeling her heart stuttering. "I just want to—my family. I just got out of jail, really. I been living free just a little over two years." She turned toward the window, lifted her cup to her lips, and took a shaky sip of her coffee as if she knew what he was going to say. "My parents are folks I don't even barely know."

"It's okay," she whispered.

"No, listen. I'm going to move in," he said. He reached up and caressed the back of her neck. "But I'm bringing a lot of baggage with me. Are you sure you want that?"

She faced him, tears still brimming in her eyes. "What do you think?"

"I've been alone for so long," he said. "I don't know if I can be any other way."

"We can try," she said. "Can't we? We can try."

. . .

Winter seemed endless, full of rain, high winds, and snow. In the spring the river surged high over its banks, and for more than a week, brownish waves overran the beach and spilled up onto the boardwalk, submerging it under more than a foot of swiftly moving sand and water. Those residents whose shops and stores opened onto the boardwalk piled sandbags in front of the doors in case the river continued to rise, but by the end of April it had receded again and revealed stained, mud-slicked, sandy boards darkened by mildew and saltwater. It would take several days of baking in the warm sun just to render the boardwalk manageable for any sort of cleanup.

Outside the Clary Hotel, the river bottom sand had piled high even over the bags, so it was impossible to get the doors open. Anyone trying to get their morning coffee in the café had to go through the street entrance to the hotel and then all the way across the front lobby to the back. The fine, sliding glass doors of Mauldin's shooting gallery, which looked out over the river, had black mud streaks from top to bottom, and the muddy sand piled against the bottom of the glass made it look as though the doors had survived some sort of blaze. The boards outside the gallery were damp and slick, with long splinters of the older boards flaked off the edges and jutting into the air like white fishbones. It was dangerous to walk on them. As shop owners on the boardwalk, Clary and Mauldin had to share in the cost of the clean-up—which would be considerable.

"Looks like a hurricane went through here," Mauldin said. "It's almost enough to make me finally throw in the towel and sell the place."

"Yeah, but who'd buy it?" Clary said. He kicked a little at the black, wet sand that, when disturbed, revealed almost pure white sand underneath. "Maybe this is our Y2K disaster."

Mauldin gave a short laugh. "What a lot of bullshit that was."

"This is it," Clary said. "This is going to cost us a fortune."

The jail and the new sheriff's office was open for business and had been since late January. Caldwell hadn't yet moved his offices down to Columbia Beach, although he was still planning on doing that. He and Laura were taking their time, looking for a house near the beach, and in the meantime the new office remained only partially in operation. There were no inmates, and there promised not to be until the summer months perhaps, so when he needed to be working at the office in Dahlgren, Caldwell simply locked the place up and left it empty. He spent most of his time at home in Dahlgren. But when he could, he'd drive back to the new office for a day or so, and if he stayed overnight he'd sleep in one of the cells in the new jail.

Todd stayed in Columbia Beach. He was living with Lindsey in Cecil's old trailer and going to school with her at the community college in Dewey. They had registered for classes on the same days so their schedules matched. She was taking mostly English and art classes and Todd was studying political science and history.

Both Caldwell and Todd moved out of the Clary Hotel the second week of January. On the day they checked out of the hotel, they rode the elevator down to the lobby in silence. Caldwell tried to pay for Todd's room, but Clary told him it was already paid for. "Hell," he said. "Your boy came down here right at sunrise and paid for his own room."

Caldwell looked at Todd. "You didn't have to do that."

"Yes I did." He slung a bag over his shoulder and started for the door. "You coming?" he asked.

Caldwell paid his own bill and then carried his bags out to his car. He was driving back home that day, so Todd stopped with him to say goodbye. "Drive safely," he said.

"You bet," Caldwell said. They found it hard to look at each other. When he was in the car and pulling out of the parking lot, he saw Todd standing in the road with the bag over his shoulder, watching him. He rolled the window down and said, "I hope you stick to your plan."

"School?" Todd said.

"Right."

"You know I will."

"Come up and see us sometime."

"Sure."

Then, with just the briefest glance and a slight wave of his hand, Caldwell turned the car out of the parking lot and headed up to the highway. He didn't look back. He believed the future would be mostly the same as the recent past. He would live his life without both sons—the one who had died and the one who was responsible for it. But during the winter months, he'd get a call every now and then from Todd, and they'd talk about how school was going. Laura wrote many more letters and called frequently. They invited him to bring Lindsey up for dinner once—in late February. He and Lindsey had planned to come, but there was a long, deeply paralyzing snowstorm—what the locals call a nor'easter—and it tore through Columbia Beach and all up the eastern seaboard. Everything had to be cancelled, so Todd and Lindsey stayed home and the dinner plans never came about.

One weekend in the middle of March, Terry went down and stayed the weekend with her brother. She came back convinced that Todd and Lindsey were just "made for each other," but she also announced that she thought Lindsey was a snob.

"Why do you think so?" Caldwell asked.

"She's read all these books and she's always talking about them."

"Well, they're college students," Laura put in.

"So?"

"That's the best time to be enthralled by books," said Caldwell.

"I like books," Terry said with a tone that suggested she'd been wrongfully accused of something. "When I graduate I'm going to college, too."

"I hope you will," said Caldwell.

"And I won't be a snob, either."

Caldwell looked at her. She was still an affront to his eyes on first glance—with her hair dyed pink now, and a series of silver bands piercing her right eyebrow—but it was becoming easier to remember and recognize the young woman she was becoming. He could also discern a change in the way she approached him. She was less bitter and more ready to listen to him. He believed this change was probably a result of time and maturity, although sometimes he wondered if it wasn't the subtle effect of having Todd back in their lives. Yet whenever he entertained this thought, it immediately gave him a discernibly empty feeling in his heart because, of course, Todd was not really back in their lives at all. He was as far away as he'd ever been—and the distance was not simply a matter of miles and highways.

What troubled him, and what lay in back of any conversation he had with his son, was how he could take back an act he was not aware of until Todd told him about it. And how could he undo nine years of simple neglect; even unintended and unconscious neglect is still neglect, and it was in the past, and nothing he or Todd could ever do would change it or make it less painful to remember. That fact always loomed over them, no matter what they eventually found to talk about. Often they could not find anything to say to each other, and then the silences became almost threatening—offering the dark possibility that the years of empty neglect might come to the fore again and create even more distance between them.

Caldwell wondered sometimes if those years of estrangement *were* unintended. For a long time his grief had been so bound up with anger—with unutterable rage—and part of that had to be directed at something other than mere fate; Todd had been roughhousing with Bobby, and Bobby had been killed. It did not have to be anything more or worse than an accident for the rage to be any more or less intense. He was a victim of such powerful emotion, all memory and desire was erased for a time. Questions of love or affection—indeed, of responsibility or fidelity or duty—seemed completely unreal, even hostile. How could he be considering anyone's welfare at a time like that? And how could he be held accountable for something he had wondered aloud about to a judge when he was in such a numb state of being? Sometimes in the long drives back down to Columbia Beach, this thought would occur to him, and it angered him all over again. How could Todd hold this against him?

Then he would think of the years—day after day of collecting hours—in which he had struggled not to think about his losses. He should have visited Todd more often. He would remember with sadness all the gradually gathering days when he managed to forget the pain and go on with his life, and Todd did not even exist—nine years in which the boy was mostly out of his sight, growing, learning, sighing through the days, fatherless. And the shame would be so great he could not listen to a single note of music for fear it would cause him to break into great floods of grief. He did not know that Todd would come back into his life and remember all the ways he had been shunned; he did not know Todd would eventually let him know how much he needed a father, and how completely Caldwell had let him down.

Early in June, on one of his visits to the new office, Caldwell stopped by the trailer on his way home. It had been a bright, cool day, with small white puffs of clouds high overhead. He had worked much later than usual, still not used to the long days—it was nearly nightfall when he realized he'd worked through dinner.

Todd was sitting on the steps of the trailer sipping a Coke. Caldwell walked up to the wheel, opened the little gate, and approached the trailer. The bright lights of the wheel illuminated the steps and the whole yard in front of the trailer, and with the full moon overhead, it was almost as bright as early morning. "Hey," Todd said. "I thought you'd be on the way home by now."

"That's where I'm heading."

Todd moved over and made room as Caldwell approached, but he did not sit down. He stood in the yard, a few feet away. "Where's Lindsey?"

"Inside. She said she was going to read but I think she fell asleep."

"I thought I'd stop by." A slight, cool breeze swept across the yard. In the darkness beyond the wheel, tree frogs and crickets sang. This was just the kind of spring night that Caldwell always loved. He could stand outside in his shirtsleeves and walk along the water without shoes on. Todd sipped from his Coke and waited for him to say something. "Beautiful day today," Caldwell said lamely. Todd looked away. The bright lights of the wheel reflected in his eyes. "School going okay?"

"Yeah. So far. The summer semester's just started."

"You going to summer school, huh?"

"Sure."

"Ambitious." Caldwell wanted to say more but nothing presented itself. He could not put into words how he was feeling. He was only breathing this terrible, long-ago loss, and he was determined not to compound it further. What he wanted to do was save Todd's life. He realized with sudden clarity that he could not do that now; he'd had his chance and he ignored it all through the years. In the town below, the early revelers were arriving.

"You guys ever going to get this thing going again?" Caldwell asked, pointing at the wheel.

"We're planning on it. It's what Cecil wanted."

It was quiet again for a slight beat, then Caldwell heard himself say, "I'm sorry, son."

"What?"

He stood up straight and tried to say what he wanted to say without emotion—but he choked on the words. "I know now . . . ," he started.

"What's the matter, Dad?" Todd put his Coke down and started to get up. "Are you all right?"

Caldwell moved to the steps and sat down. He could feel Todd staring at him, but he did not want to face him. He gazed off toward the town—down the long street to the Clary Hotel and beyond that, to the drifting water glistening in the moonlight.

"It's okay," Todd said. "We're past all that now."

"No," Caldwell said. "It's not about that." Todd was quiet. "At least it's not *just* about that." Caldwell put his hands together between his knees and stared at them. "You see . . . ," he paused, wanting to say exactly what was in his heart. Todd sat completely still, watching him. "I know," Caldwell began again, his voice weakening, "I've always known . . ."

"Known what?"

"I've always known you didn't intend . . ."

"Dad," Todd said, looking away. He almost got up, but then he put one foot up on the second higher step and leaned over on his knee, staring at the bright wheel.

"I've always known that," Caldwell said, feeling disbelieved. "I'm telling you." Todd reached up and scratched under the thin whiskers on his chin. Then he looked into the can of Coke in his hand, put it to his mouth, threw his head back, and took the last gulp. He did not look at Caldwell. "You didn't intend it," Caldwell added, "But I did."

Now Todd looked at him. "*You* did?"

"Yes."

"What do you mean?"

"I intended this hurt . . . this distance between us. At some level I must have wanted it." Todd got up and stood facing the wheel, his back to his father. He said nothing, but he was listening. "It's my fault, son. I see now. I really do see now." Caldwell stood up, too, but he didn't approach Todd. They were only a few feet apart and he thought he heard the boy say something. "What?"

"I didn't say anything," Todd said.

"I could not face you—would not face you, all those years. I think I didn't care how much it hurt you. I might have cared if I'd thought of it. But I didn't." He lost his voice momentarily. Then he said, "I didn't think of you at all, son."

Todd flipped the Coke can into a rubbish bin that sat next to the steps. "Well," he said. "It's over now."

"I wish I could get those years back, but I . . ."

Todd faced him. "Sit down for a minute longer," he said.

Caldwell did as he was asked, and then Todd sat down next to him. "You remember that time you took me hunting?" he asked.

"What?"

"For deer. Remember? It was snowing and we were waiting under a tree at the top of a ridge?"

"Yeah." Caldwell wiped his eyes, tried to see his son's face through the tears that had formed there.

"We sat in the freezing cold all that morning."

"Yeah. I never saw snow like that."

"I was so cold," Todd said. Caldwell laughed a little, feeling even more sorrowful that this was one of the few memories his son would have to tell of his childhood. It was such a sweet gesture, talking of old times, of good times, but this was all there was—these few days in his earliest youth, when he had a father and mother and brother and sister and all of life in front of him, a life where he would be cherished and loved as any child should be. "You remember," Todd went on, "what got us laughing so hard?"

"Yes. You wanted to know when we were going to go hunting." He laughed ruefully now, remembering it—the innocence of that time seemed so completely foreign, so far away and distant, as if it had happened in some other life.

"Remember how hard we laughed?" Todd said, and his voice was full of remembering and affection, but he was not smiling.

Caldwell looked at him. "We'd *been* hunting all damn morning and I never made it clear that was what we were doing."

"Well," Todd said, "maybe it's like that with us now."

"I don't understand."

"Being father and son again."

"What?"

"Maybe that's what we've been doing all along."

Caldwell thought his heart would break. He put his arm around Todd's shoulders and kissed him on the cheek. This profoundly embarrassed both of them so he withdrew his arm and sat up straight. Todd said, "Maybe that's what we're doing right now and we just don't know it."

"Maybe we are, son," said Caldwell. "I guess."

The door opened behind them and Lindsey stood in the light that flooded the steps. "Oh, boys," she said, "I'm in here all by myself."

They both turned and looked at her. "You woke up," Todd said.

"Is this a private meeting?"

"No," he said, looking at Caldwell.

"We're just out here talking," Caldwell said, breathing back his grief.

"Well why don't you come inside? The bugs are murderous out here."

"I haven't seen a one," Todd said.

"Come on," she said. "I don't have anybody to talk to."

Caldwell stood up, wiping his eyes with both hands. Lindsey and Todd watched him in silence. He looked at them finally and said, "Well, I've got to be going."

"Stay," Todd said. He got up, too, facing him. "We'd like you to visit for a while."

"Please do," Lindsey said. "I don't know if I've been in the same room with you two for more than a few minutes yet."

"You'll have plenty of time in the same room with us," Todd said, looking at Caldwell. "Won't she, Dad?"

"I hope so, son," Caldwell said. "I sure do hope so."

THE END